What does it take to become a saint? Daisy Ridel is finding out. The communion of saints is replete with many shining examples who are remarkable for their youth. Not having yet earned a place among the powers of this world, young people like Daisy walk through the ordinary days of their life dealing with the people that God has placed in their path, trying to do what St. Teresa of Calcutta calls "doing ordinary things with extraordinary love."

Many are the personalities in Daisy's life. The Watsons, the Smiths, Jonah, Col, Peter and Paul. "Every life has a story", and Daisy tries to meet each person where they are, with their joys and sorrows, their ups and downs. A woman of prayer herself, she is committed to a life of prayer: daily Mass, the rosary, the examples of saints. Daisy exudes an acceptance of all whom she meets, trying to mirror the love and acceptance that God has for each one. She is the quintessential "volunteer", who steps in to offer her time, talents and treasure for any in need, without counting the cost. She follows the goal of at least one Church movement, Cursillo: to evangelize your environment.

Jesus tells us that what we do to the least of our brothers and sisters, we do to Him. Daisy is trying to live that teaching in every day, on every page.

Archbishop Gerard Pettipas, C.Ss.R.
Archdiocese of Grouard-McLennan, Alberta

Daisy: Walk Like Jesus is a stunning portrayal of a young woman whose heart is filled with the Love of God that overflows in thought, word and action to each person that she encounters. The characters that Daisy loves & serves are raw & authentic, faced with heartbreaking suffering, and I found myself wanting to keep reading to listen to more of their stories. Deanna Jones has written a book that gives us a glimpse into the mystery of woman, a true expression of what St. Pope John Paul II called 'The Feminine Genius'. Daisy shines as a bright light in a world of darkness revealing in us the truth that it only takes one person walking in the love of Jesus to liberate prisoners and set captives free.

Mr. Constantine Kolitsos
Alberta, Canada

Everyone, and especially every Christian whether Catholic or not, should read DAISY *to develop a deeper understanding of what it means to be a committed disciple of Jesus in the real world. This book can change people who are lukewarm for Jesus into people who are red-hot for Him*

Fr. Joseph R. Jacobson,
Catholic priest and former Lutheran bishop

Makes you stop in your tracks and say—I've been here. Keeps you turning pages to see if Daisy will do better, or if you can rely on her Humanness to build a bridge to God for you. It reminds me to pray, enduring the darkness until God shines his eternal flame

Leanna Flooren
Deanna's twin

Daisy is an inspiring and striking example of living the little way of love in a broken world. Giving hope to the idea that it is possible to be in the world but not of it. A beacon of light for all those who suffer, teaching them that it is redemptive and not cause for despair. This book has pierced my heart, and challenged me to love deeply, never counting the cost.

Elise Stang
Student at St. Therese Institute of Faith and Mission

Through the courageous vulnerability of living her faith, young "Daisy" brings Jesus' love and hope to an often despairing community. The dynamics are real, the struggles genuine and with every overcoming, we delight in the goodness of God.

Theresa Levasseur
Mother of 6, Educational Assistant

In this book Daisy displays over and over again the beauty of living in Christ's presence in every circumstance, letting His love in her heart dictate her response to people to whom it comes as a shock. Read this book to see what can happen when the love of Jesus possesses a committed teenager so completely that even the most damaged people cannot ignore Him.

Roberta Ann Siegel
Wife of the late Robert Siegel
Awarding-winning Christian novelist and poet

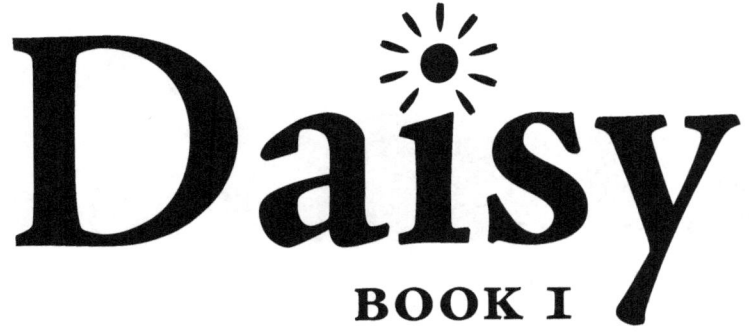

Daisy

BOOK I

WALK
LIKE
JESUS

Deanna Jones

DAISY
Walk Like Jesus

Copyright © Deanna Jones, 2023

Published by Deanna Jones, Ft. Vermillion, Canada

ISBN:
Paperback   978-1-77354-481-6
ebook   978-1-77354-482-3

Publication assistance by

PUBLISHING
PageMaster.ca

Dedication

All glory to God

Contents

————⇒❦⇐————

Tutor Time

"Christianity is love. Christianity is Christ."

Pope Francis

D aisy! DAISY!"

"Oh my!" I jump in startled bewilderment as my teacher slams his palm against my desk. My pen goes flying out of my fingertips as I straighten in my seat. I wince when it makes a sharp cracking noise on the cement floor. Some of my classmates laugh but others look upset at the way Mr. Nelson is treating me.

"What are you doing, Daisy?" My teacher, who for some odd reason doesn't like me, asks in a low, threatening voice. I plaster a genuine smile onto my face, looking at him earnestly.

"I'm so so sorry Mr. Nelson!" I smile at him with a huff as I finally manage to scrape the dried glob of gum off the bottom of the desk. Who does such a nasty thing? It's not hard to wrap old gum into the wrapper or walk ten steps to the garbage can. Maybe they were injured at the time, and couldn't move too much. Who knows? It's not my place to judge. I don't tell Mr. Nelson what I'm doing because he'd only think I was making an excuse, maybe I was. I hadn't paid attention to the last five minutes of class because I was too busy focusing on scraping the dried gum off the bottom of the desk I am using.

"Can you answer my question?" Mr. Nelson sternly asks with his arms crossed over his chest. I drop the gum on the floor, mentally reminding myself to pick it up once the bell rings and the teacher dismisses us.

"I'm sorry Mr. Nelson, I can't." I wince again as I clasp my hands together and look at the smart board at the front of the room. It isn't hard seeing it as I was in the first seat, middle row. It's usually my spot since people don't like sitting here and I don't want to argue with people over simple seating arrangements.

"Is the sentence on the board grammatically correct?" Mr. Nelson forcefully asks, slapping my desk once again before pointing to the front of the classroom. I frown at his growing anger before reading and rereading the sentence a few times. My teacher seems to stew in silence like a pot of water waiting to boil over.

"Um, it's fractured, sir?" I take a wild guess when I can't seem to figure out if there should be a comma or not. My fingers make their way to the miraculous medal on my chest and holding it gives me a sense of peace and the courage to continue my answer. "Maybe a semicolon is needed, there seem to be two sentences but they could be brought together with the proper... grammatical tool..." I trail off at the end, wondering if I was right.

"Thank you, Miss Ridel," the teacher nods in confirmation. I smile in relief, happy that I was right even if I hadn't been paying attention. The bell rings sharply, signaling the end of class. I place my papers neatly in my binder and zip them shut before bending down and picking the big blue piece of gum up. I'm not in a hurry since I'd scheduled a tutoring session for some jocks in the library. With their slipping grades, their coach had had a sit down with them. If they didn't raise their mark by the end of the quad they'd be cut from the team. Overhearing the conversation, I'd offered my help. All four of them had jumped on the offer while complaining it wasn't necessary.

"See you at the library," the sweet-natured jock shoots me a smile before catching up with his friends. He's an extremely nice guy, having such great natural athletic abilities but studying is not his forte. Also, he's already nineteen in grade eleven from having to drop out for three years due to his mother passing away. He hadn't wanted child protective services to take his little siblings away while their dad was at work overseas a lot of the time. This was his first year back in school since his youngest sibling, whose mother had died giving birth to her, had just started pre-school.

"Right on!" I give him a thumbs up with one hand as I throw the glob of gum into the garbage can. A soccer team girl rolls her eyes at me when it misses. I half-shrug with a sheepish smile as I pick it up and place it in the garbage. March Laughridge's grades weren't too bad but he wanted top-notch grades for higher-class universities. Col Chrysanthemum is another guy I'm tutoring soon. I enter lots of rodeos with him and often go quadding, mud bogging, racing, or sledding with him. He's a fun guy, a chill guy, just not really interested in studying. He hasn't been in sports before this year and they only wanted him when they found out what a good quarterback he makes. Then it would be two of the triplets, Harry and Landon Smith. They're a little rough around the edges and make me slightly nervous with their cocky, loud-mouthed ways. I can tell they are poor and they carry pent-up anger which they use forcefully in the field but I'm not afraid of them. I see the hurt hidden under the rippling anger, I know they need patience and love. It doesn't help I have more pity for them with the stories I've heard about them, living in the numero uno crack house of the town.

Reaching my locker, I take all my binders out to study. English was my last class but I hadn't been paying attention so it won't hurt to read up on it tonight. Math gives me trouble so I have to practice before the ritualistic ways of working a problem are lost in my mind. I'm in biology too right now which I enjoy because it's mostly a lot of memory. I like having reasoning known for the science-ee facts of my faith as a Catholic girl. There are scuff marks on the floor by my locker so I try to wipe them away with the toes of my white bottom shoes. It doesn't work so I mentally remind myself to make a gift basket for the janitors, for all the hard work they do that goes unmentioned.

With my backpack full and my locker empty, I walk my way to the library, the hallways emptied out. Kids are in a rush once they know they don't have to be in this brick building for another second. I don't mind, having my moped to ride to and from school and work so I was never in a hurry. Rounding a corner, I see Tyler Smith, the third triplet, on the floor, shaking. I shrug my backpack off and crouch down beside him, worried.

"Hey Tyler," I frown as I grab ahold of his hand and don't let go. I know he has a drug problem so he might be having a relapse. "You okay?"

"Sugar," he mutters his smelly clothing covering his bony body. A stained, fuzz-filled hood covers buzz-cut hair.

"Okay," I smile and sit across from him. Then I dig in my backpack for a chocolate bar. This isn't the first time this has happened and it won't be the last so I make sure to keep a stash in my locker and a couple in my bag. I pull out a coffee crisp and open it for him before he takes it out of my hand and shovels it in his face. His mom is a nice lady, reminds me of a mouse with how quiet she is, but she doesn't work and their dad spends all their welfare money on drugs or alcohol. While he's chewing on the chocolate bar, I pull out an orange and start peeling it for him. Tyler doesn't fight me on this anymore since he knows I can be as stubborn as a mule. With the chocolate bar downed I give him my water bottle to drink out of before leaving him on the floor with the orange and a little bag of chips. He never thanks me and I never remind him to. Thanks don't need to be verbally given. I know he's thankful without needing confirmation.

"Hey guys," I smile at the four boys crowding a table in the library. Col's friend, Danae Faidley, is sitting on a beanbag chair, reading. Col is her ride. It's an unusual friendship but who am I to judge? He keeps the bullies away from her and she brings calm into his life. People have warned him to stay away since he's eighteen and she's only fourteen but they are friends, that is all.

"Hi Daisy," Landon, the player of the four, grins cockily at me as his eyes roam over my body. I ignore it as I set my backpack on the table with a thump. They all look at it in shock when I pull out my bio notes and textbook for March to review, my English notes with the novel for Col to re-write, and math book problems for Landon and Harry to work on with me.

"I'll work with Col first since he has to leave the soonest, if you guys don't mind," I begin, shuffling papers for them to see from their spots. I feel ridges on the table and feel sad when I see people have carved their names into public property. "That will be quick because he only has to copy my notes since he didn't do it in class."

"Mr. Nelson writes way too fast!" Col interjects as he slides my notes his way. At the two pages filled front and back he groans and flops back in his chair.

"You did zone out for the last five minutes," March laughs when I blush, caught red-handed in my lecture. All three other boys laugh at me.

"Sorry Col," I wince in regret. "I don't have all of the class notes for today but I'll have them by tomorrow."

"It's cool, Daisy," Col waves my concern off. He doesn't care too much about school but at least he's here and not giving me a hard time tracking him down. The football team also really wants his grades raised, apparently, he's that good of an asset. Universities are looking at him even though this is his first year playing the sport. Jokes on them, Col is going pro rodeo once he graduates. That was the deal he made with his mom. She wants all her kids to graduate because she didn't have that opportunity.

"Okay March," I sigh heavily as I slide my bio papers his way. "Do you have a laptop?"

"Nah," he shakes his head but lifts up a chrome book. "Mrs. Lamberts said I could take this home for the night though."

"Okay, review my notes, then write the vocab down on Quizlet and make your own Quizlet test. When that's done you can test which ones you have memorized. It's slow and tedious but that helps." I fold some of my crazy brown curls behind my ear. It's useless because they pop right back out. Fifteen-year-old me blushes when seventeen years old Landon is hooked on the gesture. The library doors clang open and we all snap our heads that way in unison. Tyler walks in, his headphones on and his head pointed down. This time he has one of the school's bands instruments with him, a guitar. Without looking at us, he sits on the stairs and starts playing a soulful melody. I half-shrug and jut my thumb to him. "If you guys don't mind, I don't."

"I have nine younger siblings," March deadpans. "That's nothing."

"Noise don't bother me," Col shrugs when Harry and Landon glare at him. They're very protective of their brother. I sit across from Harry, sort of in the middle so I can help all of them without having to move too much.

"Whoa, no," I shake my head at Landon, who had pulled out a calculator. "Didn't you hear Mr. Jackson this morning? We have to practice without calculators because this portion of the testing is without any type of calculator."

"You're two grades below me, how do you know what he said?" Landon states gruffly, glaring at me. I'm pretty sure Harry kicks him under the table. Harry doesn't talk as much as his brother but when he does, he speaks more respectfully.

"I asked for a little help this morning because I was tutoring you," I answer honestly with a shrug. Good work takes effort, and that goes for tutoring and learning. "For my learners, I want to be as prepared as possible to help you to the best of my abilities."

"Doesn't that create extra work for you?" Harry asks, his voice gravelly from years of secondhand smoke. At least he hasn't picked up the habit yet himself.

"Not really," I shrug, slightly embarrassed. "I'm in AP courses." I don't like bragging about myself.

"My kinda girl," Landon winks at me and slides over the table to sit by me. I deadpan stare at him as he wraps an arm over my shoulder.

"Flirting and flattery will not get you out of this," I dryly comment, shrugging his arm off. He leaves it hanging on the back of my chair. I don't mind since I'm leaning forward anyways.

"My looks will," Landon shrugs arrogantly. I burst out laughing in shock. Harry laughs with me, annoying his brother. Landon kicks him under the table while scowling at him. He must not be used to rejection. If he continues being tutored by me, he'll get used to it. I'm not looking for a relationship or a "friend".

"I'm doing this for your future," I grab Landon's forearm and shove it back into his personal space. He needs a harder hint to stop the flirting. "Please respect my boundaries."

"You know we can't pay you, right?" Landon asks, anger in his eyes as he admits that. Pride is one of his downfalls but besides sports and his looks, he doesn't have much going for him thanks to his alcoholic, drug-dealing father. Well, until he accepts Jesus into his life, but I still have to figure out how I am going to do that.

"I didn't ask for anything," I shrug, opening his math textbook to the page Harry is on. It's true. I never volunteer for money. It's not true volunteering that way. Maybe Landon will follow my example, do an act of kindness for someone, and make a chain of acts of kindness. We could get the whole school to do it, teachers and students, to make it fun and easy. Picking up a pencil for a classmate, throwing away a gum wrapper someone drops, giving a friend a snack when they are hungry, speaking nicely to the teachers when in trouble instead of yelling and cursing. I'm getting sidetracked so I blow out a breath and tap Landon's blank loose leaf paper to start his work.

"Party on Friday, I'll bring your booze if you wanna join." Landon casually invites as he finally looks at the math work in front of him. He rubs his eyes at the numbers and letters mixed with dashes and lines. My eyebrows rise at his invitation. No one from school has ever invited me to their house, I'm not that close to anyone. They're friendly with me but I'm not the person they trust with their secrets.

"She's fifteen!" Harry definitely kicks Landon under the table this time. Landon laughs with Col, although Landon's laugh is cheeky while Col's laugh is more of a chuckle. My face flushes at his knowing chuckle. My dad is Col's step-dad's drinking buddy, sometimes he brings me drinking, and one time I accidentally drank too much.

"She's not a lightweight," Col speaks up. Now is really not the time to bring up drinking with his family. March has leaned back, looking on in interest at our interaction. Col smirks at all attention now on him and he smiles when he begins to tell the one story I'm embarrassed about.

"Let's go back to studying, guys." I firmly state, writing an equation down on lined paper for Landon to work through. It's no use as they all question Col's knowledge of me.

"How do you know?" Landon asks Col, obviously ignoring my statement. I deadpan stare at Col as I tap on the paper. It doesn't get his attention. At all. I feel a flicker of annoyance but breathe through it.

I can't be mad when people hear that I make mistakes, that I'm not as perfect or innocent as they think I am.

"She's my neighbour, parents are friends," Col smirks. I deadpan stare at him once again.

"I drank one time, Col! One time!" It's not a lie. I didn't get drunk but I've never drunk again. I'd made the decision to drink after finding out my dad had lied to me all these years, about the fact that my mother was not dead but had simply ditched me as a baby for her quest to get any kind of high. It makes sense now, why my father never took me to her grave. How did I not clue in that she wasn't dead if there was no place for her body to be laid to rest?

"Let's focus on studying," Col sassily retorts, knowing he had spiked the three other boys' attention and they would personally ask me now. I take a deep breath to follow through with his request but the other three boys have different ideas.

"What's your favourite type of alcohol?" Landon asks, leaning forward. Harry sighs loudly as he works on a math question. Harry likes to get things done as fast and as thoroughly as he can. A slight perfectionist, he must hate his struggling grades and not-so-good home life. March opens the chrome book to work on Quizlet, all ears as he pretends to work. With such a big family, he's learned how to pretend to be busy to avoid the many chores they have running a farm.

"We are focusing on schoolwork, Landon." I firmly state as I point from Col's face to his papers on the table. Col laughs but follows through, spinning his pencil between his fingers.

"I have a better idea of what to focus on." Landon breathes out, leans close, and once again wraps his arm around my shoulders, pulling me closer to him. I wrinkle my nose in disgust. What happened to chastity and purity in my generation?

"Do I need to get Mr. Jackson in here, flirty pants?" I elbow him away from me. Landon shoots me puppy dog eyes that are barely resistible. I simply smirk and tap his paperwork.

"This shit doesn't make sense though," he grumbles in frustration. Ah, his flirting was to distract himself from the math equations. I don't blame him for that, math is hard but we have to power through.

"That's why I'm here," I lean closer to look at his equation again. The numbers and letters make me rub my tired eyes. I might be pushing myself harder than I should lately with school, work, volunteering, daily mass, running, and my hours of solitude praying in nature and silence with God. "What can I help with?"

"Why a beautiful girl like you says no to a guy like me?" He smirks and I burst out laughing, even if I'm blushing. No one really flirts with me. I blame it on my wild hair and faith in God. My belief makes people wary to approach me unless they need help with something or clarification on a point in my religion.

"Just concentrate on schoolwork," Harry groans as his head hits the table. The thud is loud in the quiet of the empty library. Danae is lost in the book on her lap. She smiles sweetly at whatever is on the page and twirls some of her long, thin, brown hair between her thumb and fingers. Col's eyes linger on Danae and I spot the loving look in his eyes before he shakes it off and turns back to his paper. I laugh at the reaction Harry demonstrates because of his brother's flirting. The two boys are close, they usually wingman each other. "And stop embarrassing me."

"Oh, this is amusing," March laughs. Harry groans again, although it's muffled by the table. Landon shoots him a glare as he kicks him under the table. I barely hide my laughter behind my hand as Harry kicks Landon back.

"Landon Smith rejected by a nerd," Col teases both of us as he flips my paper over to write down the notes on the other side.

"I'm not a nerd!" I shout, then slap my mouth to make sure I hadn't upset the librarian. March laughs at me and my face burns when I realize that the librarian had left when school ended. That totally agreed with Col's declaration. Only nerds don't want to upset the librarian. Or, maybe, just nice people in general.

"She didn't reject me!" Landon declares, throwing his arm around my shoulders a third time. I'm not used to all this human contact, this connection of friendship within a group of friends, so it throws me off. It's second nature for friends to hug each other. Have they accepted me as a friend, or am I overthinking it?

"Yes, I did!" I shrug his arm off. I take a deep breath and exhale slowly, folding my wild hair out of my face. It doesn't stay back long. "Guys, let's just please study. I don't mind if we joke around but no more flirting and try to get some work done. Please."

"Ugh," Landon sighs and leans into my shoulder. I pop my shoulder up and down, laughing at his annoyed look. "I'll stop flirting I guess..."

"Thanks," I laugh and point to the equation on his paper. He lifts his head off my shoulder and focuses on the math work. True to his word, he doesn't flirt any longer. With the first question he needs a lot of help, someone hasn't been paying attention in class. I can't judge him though, I had zoned out for English class as March so blithely pointed out. Friends keep you honest if they are my friends. After years of friendless-ness, it's a welcome change.

"Got any plans tonight, Daisy?" Harry drawls as he shoves his paper at me. Friends hang out outside of school. Will I be invited along to something? I can't tonight, I'm busy volunteering. I check over Harry's work, nodding along.

"Looks good," I shoot him a smile and slide the paper back, shrugging in response to his question. "Prolly help at the soup kitchen since I don't work today."

"Damn, that's a thing?" Landon asks, sighing when I shake my head at him to indicate he got the equation wrong. He starts erasing. The sound sounds like scratching and it breaks Danae out of her book. Even though I'm the only one looking, she sticks her tongue out at him before returning to her book. I laugh at her vibrant personality packed into her introverted mindset. It'll take a lot of growth from her, but she'll be a wild extrovert when the time comes.

"I volunteer whenever I can, it's not too often." I'm too busy working or volunteering elsewhere to help at the soup kitchen, but the Watson family usually runs everything and anything to do with the soup kitchen and they're a pretty big family. Harry, Landon, and Tyler are Watsons from their mom's side but aren't usually associated with the God-fearing, hard-working, strong, and caring Watson side of their family because their dad controls their lives.

"Oh wait," Harry snaps his head at me with a smirk. "You the girl Pierre's always talkin' about?"

"I work with him sometimes, yeah," I shrug as March turns the screen of his chrome book to me. I like Pierre, he's quiet, keeps to himself, nice, sweet, and an insanely good cook at only seventeen years old. He wants to go to Paris for culinary school. He's also the triplet's cousin and used to be bullied for being overweight but Landon and Harry put a stop to that. I guess I can consider Pierre a volunteer slash workplace friend. We don't talk outside of the soup kitchen but can carry on decent conversations in the kitchen; we also goof off, sometimes making a mess but his dad and older brothers know we will clean up when the end of the shift is over. When Paul only had one kid, he used to stay late to help us as well but usually, Mr. Watson helps us close the building down for the night.

"You mixed up cerebrum and cerebellum," I point on the screen at the two words he mixed up.

"Ah, yes, I see that now," March sighs and quickly replaces the two words with the correct explanation. He's probably tired. From what I know about his family, April, who is two years younger than him, doesn't really help around the house even with their late mother and non-existent father. His two older brothers got caught up in gang business at a young age and now the older one is in prison and the younger one is dead. May is a year older than me and is always helping out, even if she can't join clubs or anything after school. She's decided that March had given up enough that he should be able to join sports clubs once he returned to school. She's probably watching Dekka, the baby of the family along with Nova here on the playground while June, who is in my class, caught the bus home with Toby, Ember, Gus, and Jay.

"Okay," Col stands up with a stretch. "I'm done for the day."

"We've only been here half an hour," I frown as Danae notices and starts packing her novel into her backpack.

"Your dad's coming over for some beers and roping practice," Col ruffles my hair with a smirk. I can't deny his argument. My dad is the best roper in the county, he's retired from rodeos but he helps Col and his siblings and our other neighbours out. The three of our families routinely hang out, the Ridel's, the Chrysanthemums, and the De Wilde's. Romain, my dad's friend, has a daughter Danae's age. They sort of get along. The other family to hang out with us, introduced to us by Danae, is the Laytons. That's another big family like Danae's and March's while Col's family and the De Wilde's have around four or five kids each. I'm the oddball out being an only child. "See ya later Daisy."

"Try to read the notes over at least one more time!" I call over his retreating back. He'd already wrapped an arm around Danae and was visiting with her. She's a really quiet girl, slightly shy with a very sarcastic wit. It's a great combination making for a very interesting introvert.

"We should go too," Harry speaks up before having a secret, telepathic twin conversation with his triplet. It's not so secret because March and I can guess what it is about. We've all heard the rumours, seen the bruises, and felt sympathetic to the anger and hurt the triplets carry.

"Don't want daddy dearest beating the shit out of us for studying again," Landon scoffs, cracking his knuckles. Their dad wants any excuse to control them and has kept them out of school countless times.

"He doesn't even need an excuse," Harry growls. He read my mind, I realize, as I look into Harry's ice blue eyes. The anger is clearly present in his eyes, the tension in his posture, the exhaustion in his mind. My heart goes out to him, to his brothers, especially to him and Tyler.

"Crash at mine any time," March and I say in unison. We both look at each other with wide eyes before smiling. Great minds think alike.

"We'll think about it," Landon states gruffly, kissing my forehead before walking out of the library. I stare after him in surprise, my hand touching my forehead. It's the first time a guy's lips have touched my skin.

"Didn't mean nothing," Harry laughs and repeats Landon's action. Did Harry kiss me so Landon's action wouldn't be so acknowledged? I shake my head in bewilderment at the two 'bad boys' of school. They're sweethearts underneath their hard exteriors.

"Yeah," March shakes his head. "I'm not doing that." We both laugh at his deadpanned words.

"Here," Tyler's soft, melodic voice whispers in my ear. I turn to him with a smile. He's always been my favourite out of the triplets, not a playboy like his brothers.

"Thanks," I say a little too chirpily as I grab my water bottle from his hands. Landon meanders back in, cooled off from thinking about his father. I also might have a little crush on Tyler and won't admit it.

"Wash that," Landon commands me when Tyler stumbles away, headphones in and soulful indie music playing. "Don't know what shit's been in his needles."

"Oh, okay," I mumble, blinking in surprise. That seemed a bit harsh but he could be saving me from some disease. I mentally remind myself to pray for the boys before bed tonight.

→ 2 ←

Soup Kitchen

———⟫•⟪———

"Hey Daisy, Daisy!" Jonah, a classmate of mine, another nice guy like March, waves at me as I walk to my moped parked in the student parking.

"What's up Jonah?" I stop in my tracks with a friendly smile directed at him. He's in his tracksuit, sweat dripping down his slightly long crew-cut blond hair. He's tall, like most of the guys that hang around me. I have to arch my neck to look at him and my eyes water from the glare of the bright sun.

"Sorry," Jonah laughs and stands beside me so I won't be staring into the sun. There's a crack in the asphalt that runs a meter or so long. I have to switch my foot to one side completely because it felt awkward on the bottom of my feet.

"Thanks," I half smile, stuffing my hair behind my ears to no avail. My thick curly hair refuses to be tamed. I'm half Brazilian, slightly on the shorter side, curvy with a dark skin tone. Teachers get me confused as Indigenous until they know what differences to spot.

"Can I catch a ride?" Jonah asks with a sheepish smile and scratches his neck. "Dad can't make it 'cause my baby sister started throwing up, Angie's visiting her boyfriend and the buses are all gone. Truck's in the shop," he adds as an afterthought. For his sixteenth birthday two years ago his parents bought him a deep red Dodge Ram Rebel 1500 4x4.

"Yeah," I wave my hands to my transportation. "For sure, I'll be waiting here."

"Awe, thanks! Means a lot!" He races back to the school building. I stuff my backpack into a saddle bag and jump on my moped. It won't hurt to be waiting at the doors for him. We train together sometimes, right now he's in the school's cross country running team but soon we'll be preparing for the half marathon race for cancer awareness. The football coach has also made it mandatory for his team to race that day. It looks like my competition will be Jonah, Col, March (who people call Art), Harry, Landon, their cousin BJ, Danae's older brothers Chris and Karl, Jonah's younger sisters, Betty and Esther, and the triplet's cousins Sadie and William, their younger brothers Cam and Jim and the rest of the football team. I appreciate any competition, the more runners, the more money raised.

It won't hurt to ask Jonah to volunteer at the soup kitchen with me. He's a chill guy, usually down to help people out but only if asked. He's shy when it comes to his good works so I try to pull him out of his shell by offering volunteer ideas his way. Jonah loves learning, it's something we also have in common; we take AP courses together. Well, he's in those classes in his last year of schooling. He's graduating this year with the triplets and Col. He plans on going to university to become a teacher or professor.

"Hey Daisy, Daisy," Jonah grins when he sees I had parked by the doors. "Thanks!"

"Not a problem," I laugh as he practically jumps on my moped. He loves the little bike but vows he will one day own a motorcycle. He wraps his arms around my stomach as I try to pull my crazy hair into a ponytail. It doesn't work too well but at least it won't be flying into my eyes.

"Where you going?" Jonah asks as I start the engine and push off. Unlike the first time, he now knows to balance on my moped. The first time his unbalanced weight caused the moped to topple and we gained a few scars but were breathless from laughter.

"Soup kitchen!" I raise my voice for him to hear as we pick up speed. I only hit thirty km an hour because we have to stop to exit the schoolyard. "Wanna come?"

"Sure," Jonah shrugs. I signal to the left at his answer. He lives on the west end of town but the soup kitchen is on the east side, closer to the poorer people of the town. "Ain't got nothin' better to do."

"Thanks!" I speed up and lean into the turn. Jonah follows my lead. Riding my moped always makes me happy, feeling the breeze hit my face. I never go over the speed limit because I always obey laws but I do have to admit, I break the helmet rule unless I plan on going over fifty kilometers an hour. The drive isn't too long and I pray a short rosary for the souls in purgatory along the way. Any free time I have, I try to pray. I try to follow Mother Mary's advice to *pray constantly.*

"Man," Jonah laughs when I park at the back of the soup kitchen building. "I need to get me one of these things."

"Pretty ingenious gift on my dad's part," I admit as I push the kickstand out. My little moped is a dark silver colour, pretty decent on gas, the motor has been reliable so far. "Gives me freedom but he's not too scared because it's not really meant for long distances or racing."

"You wanna go running one of these days?" Jonah asks as he holds the door open for me. I duck under his arm and pull my hair back into a non-existent ponytail again.

"Thanks," I shoot him a smile and nod. "Late evening works best for me. Usually working or volunteering." I gesture to the soup kitchen to get my point across.

"Sure," Jonah grins as we both wash our hands in the sink. "What you say 'bout tomorrow, eight pm?"

"I'm working until nine tomorrow and after closing and counting, I'd say I could start the run at nine-thirty." I hand him some paper towels to dry his hands off on and take some for myself. Jonah half-shrugs.

"Works for me, half marathon?" I wince but nod along. That will be a late night. I can run a mile in seven minutes but a half marathon is twenty-six miles so I'll have to decrease my speed which makes the whole run slightly more than an hour and a half.

"Hi, Daisy!" Mr. Watson, who owns and operates the soup kitchen, smiles at me and wiggles his eyebrows. I know him well enough now to know it's the question 'who'd you bring?'

"Afternoon Mr. Watson, I brought a classmate of mine today. His name is Jonah." They shake hands as I grab a stack of plates from the cupboard and place them on the trolley. Whenever I'm here, my job is the same. Dish duty. I make sure they have enough clean plates, bowls, and utensils out there and wash them once everyone is done eating.

"You were here a couple of weeks ago for that fundraiser dinner," Mr. Watson slaps Jonah's shoulder. "Annakin's oldest boy."

"Yes, sir," Jonah grins and leans his hip on the counter. "How can I help today?"

"If Pierre doesn't need help cutting vegetables you could make sure the bathrooms are decent," Mr. Watson states. "It's nice to have extra help but wherever you're needed just go, we're flexible here."

"Sounds good," Jonah makes his way over to Mr. Watson's youngest son. I finish putting the utensils on the trolley and push it out the doors. Some homeless people are already sitting at a table even if the food isn't done cooking. I laugh when I see Mr. Watson's two sons visiting with them. While that isn't exactly in the volunteer description it's a nice touch. People need to feel welcomed to feel comfortable. It takes a lot out of a person when they have to go to a soup kitchen for basic nutrients. I park the trolley by the edge of the long serving table and meander to the table of visitors. Shawn, Dickie's nephew, intercepts, twirling me around and taking my seat. I roll my eyes and find another open seat at the table.

"Hey guys," I sit between Paul, Dickie's middle son and a volunteer, and Pete, a homeless man with a scarred face from so many fights with sidewalks from his drunkenness. His words, not mine. Shawn smirks at me as he starts up a conversation with the two homeless men on either side of him.

"Howdy," Paul half hugs me and ruffles my hair. He's twenty-five, married with three kids, and owns a chain of hotels. A lot of his extra income he donates to charities. Dickie Watson is a God-fearing man and it rubbed off on his children, more so on his seven sons.

"It barely stays there when I want it to," I pout, fixing my thick hair into a barely contained ponytail once again. They treat me like their niece or a little sister, at least Paul and Peter do because they know about my dad and their sister's relationship. I think everyone does even though Aria and my dad don't confirm it.

"Hi," Percy, another of Dickie's sons and a volunteer smiles at me from across the table. Percy is thirty-one, has five kids, has been married for ten years and he's a firefighter or smoke jumper. He's Dickie's third-born child, second-born son and while he isn't as close to me or my dad, he's always there when my dad needs help, namely when he had dropped by to visit my dad when he was welding and started a fire. Percy had brought some veggies for our homeless friends to munch on before the meal. If Mr. Watson and Pierre are cooking, it's going to taste amazing.

"Hey Percy," I smile as more people walk in.

"I'll go usher," Percy slaps the table, his cousin Shawn following. They're the ones that leave because they don't leave me alone with the homeless guys. The Watson's aren't macho men but they're traditional, and protective. The homeless guys are harmless but better safe than sorry if you look at it from a cynical point of view.

Silence descends upon our table. Paul isn't as talkative as his brothers but it isn't an awkward silence. Two of the homeless guys on the other side of the table mumble to each other. Pete, the guy to my right, laughs quietly to himself.

"How's school going?" Paul asks, turning to face me. Our knees knock before he backs up in his seat. The seats are old and wooden, labeled with the initials BRCC, from the St. Bernadette's Roman Catholic Church in town here. Our church is poor but we split our five hundred extra seats and gave half to the soup kitchen when it was starting.

"I'm tutoring your cousins until their marks are high enough for their football coach." I offer, grabbing a carrot and munching on it. Even though the triplets are growing up in a bad environment, they're pretty smart. Tyler is a little slow from his drug use but Landon and Harry stay away from everything but alcohol.

"Huntley won't like that." Paul sighs and rubs his hands over his face. Mr. Watson and his siblings and some of their kids that have started their own families always help the triplets out any way they can. I love that about the Watson family. Family is everything to them. "We offer to let them stay with us but they refuse. Feel like they're letting us down."

"Yeah, I said they could stay with me and my dad too. Couple of other classmates offered too." I shrug. Unless they want the help, we can only keep offering it.

"At least it's their last year of school," Paul sighs. Paul and Peter are the only people that give the triplets jobs here in town. Every other employer hears the name Smith and runs the other way. When are people going to realize that just because their dad is a drug dealer and a bad guy it doesn't mean that they are? I would totally understand if the triplets left town and never came back, like their older brother Simon. "Hopefully they can get scholarships outta this town."

"That's why I'm tutoring them." Paul smiles at my remark. Plenty of people are proud of me but it's not like I set out to make them proud, I simply see where help is needed and gravitate there. I just hope one day people follow my lead.

"Thanks, kid," he ruffles my hair. About half my hair falls out of the low, loose ponytail.

"I better go help in the kitchen," I scowl and swat his hand away. Paul laughs as I try to tame my wild hair. "You did that on purpose."

"Did not!" He calls to my back before entertaining the homeless guys in conversation. He might not talk loudly or much but he can keep a conversation going when he has to. Paul is the most political out of his family, having to deal with plenty of people with managing his hotel business.

"I spot some dishes that need washing," I sing-song as I walk to the big sinks along the far wall. Everything is grey and gloomy in the kitchen, it's not a new building. This is the town's old community complex but with the growth of the population ten years back, they built a bigger community center. This building sat empty and decaying for a few years until Dickie retired from his full-time seasonal job, he was a truck driver and always saw homeless freezing on the street. This was his way of giving back to the community, treating others as the Lord commanded us to do. The soup kitchen here is the only one in the county privately run without grants but there is a jar by the front doors where people can donate money. Any extra little bit goes a long way. Mr. Watson has a part-time job, runs his farm, and keeps the soup kitchen going yet he never seems in a hurry or stressed out. God guides him, that's for sure.

"Thanks, Daisy," Mr. Watson smiles at me as he slices buns in half. It's a family tradition of theirs, bread and buns with peanut butter and jam or syrup after the meal but before dessert. Dickie uses his grand-mother's recipe, light, fluffy half whole wheat half white flour. No one rivals Mrs. Watson's bread recipe.

"I'll help," Jonah offers as he cleans off his cutting board into a serving dish. He'd been busy slicing peppers and celery for early comers to snack on.

"Appreciate it," I shoot him a half smile as I start running burning hot water into the big sinks. Pierre and his dad had made casseroles for supper tonight so all the preparation dishes are dirty. There are a lot of dishes already piled up. I snap on rubber gloves so I can bear the hot water better and organize the dishes to how I want to clean them. Utensils are dumped right in and pot lids first. I always clean the glass first, then utensils, then plates and cups, and lastly, the pots and pans.

"Hey Daisy, Daisy," Jonah drawls as he grabs a towel to dry dishes. It's threadbare, indicating very few donations in the past few months.

"Yeah?" I question, scrubbing hard on the rim of a pot lid. Grease had splashed into the little crevasse and hardened, now it does not want to come off. I don't mind the hard work, offering it up to God for people everywhere to believe in the good Lord.

"Some kids are interested in tutoring sessions with me." Jonah flips the towel over his shoulder and leans his hip against the edge of the sink. "And I was just wondering what the going rate is since I saw you tutoring today."

"Oh," I chuckle nervously. I don't like bragging about myself. What will he think when I tell him I tutored them for free? "I'm not the best person to ask."

"Why not?" Jonah frowns as I finally hand him the lid to rinse. Pierre chuckles, knowing my answer. He's a nice guy like me and March, who are good samaritans trying to make this world a better place and for people to feel more love.

"Well, I just don't, you know, charge the going rate," I finally stutter out. Jonah stares at me, a lightbulb going off in his head.

"You tutor for free," he assumes and shakes his head with a bitter-sweet smile. "Why didn't I think of that?"

"The world revolves around money," I venture an answer with a shrug of my shoulders. The next few pot lids are easier to wash, only used for steaming vegetables.

"Let's set up a system," Jonah suggests as he leans the lids up to air dry. Mr. Watson is a stickler for no fuzzies on his glassware. "Let's say, Mondays and Wednesdays after school we tutor from three-thirty to five for free for anyone in grades seven to twelve. Deal?"

"Yeah, man! I'm down for that. For the next few weeks, I'll be with Harry, Landon, Col, and March but after that, I'll be able to take on new learners. Even with them, I could try to rotate through other learners. Maybe then more students will be interested in learning! We could ignite the whole school on fire for the love of learning!" My voice had raised in excitement at Jonah's idea and I'd stopped washing dishes to look him in the eye. "We could do so much! Thanks for your amazing idea, Jonah! Let's do it!"

"Haha, no problem," Jonah chuckles nervously, stepping back from me. I spot the flush on his cheeks and realize I've made him uncomfortable so I quickly shrink into myself to avoid rambling on about how beneficial education is to teenagers.

"Sorry," I wince and turn back to washing dishes. "Didn't mean to seem so enthusiastic about it."

"Oh, no! That's great actually!" Jonah reassures me with a smile as he grabs a big pot from my hands to dry off. "That means you probably won't drop it."

"True, but I work Wednesdays so you'll have to carry the team that day," I say regretfully, scrubbing at a stainless steel pot so I won't have to look at him. I'm already bailing on half the plan. Dad didn't raise me to make promises I can't keep.

"Kinda works out because I have track practice on Mondays soon." Jonah laughs good natured-ly. It will be a good partnership if we both take a day, of free tutoring. I do like making money but I can make money at work, Peter and Paul always have odd jobs for me as well. If they can't think of anything they refer me to their uncle who recently retired from the army. He always putters around, looking for stuff to do. Peter and he are the ones that keep this place up to code for inspections and Paul offers appliances that his hotels don't use anymore. They have a pretty good system running, Paul pitches in appliances and furniture, and there is a little spot against the back wall with a pool table and couches, some bookshelves, and old books the library gave away. Peter and his uncle are the plumber, electrician, and carpenters that fix leaky toilets and fading walls. Dickie and Pierre cook and bake amazing, delicious meals, desserts, and snacks. The rest of the Watson family are usually the ones that donate money to buy the food, lights, cleaning supplies, and pay the utilities. It is privately owned but the property is sort of commercial because it is a soup kitchen and homeless shelter with four bedrooms near the bathrooms for homeless people in winter, so Dickie has to pay certain taxes. He has been audited for the past three years so he has to keep everything spic and span. Jonah leans closer to me to inspect the pot I've been scrubbing. "Pretty sure it's clean, Daisy, Daisy."

"Oh, yeah," I chuckle nervously as I drop the scrub brush and rinse the pot out. "I kinda zoned out there."

"Can you give me a ride home after this?" Jonah asks as he dries the well-cleaned pot. The burning hot water no longer tingles my skin; it has cooled off to a warmer temperature. It's a relief, I'm sure my face is red from the heat. I can already feel sweat building up on my body, the usual from using elbow grease to scrub hot pans.

"I wouldn't just abandon you," I laugh as I use my nail to scrub a hard piece of grease off a frying pan. It's one of the older pans, grease stains galore on it and chipped around the edges. Dickie, as Mr. Watson says we can call him, calls it 'character'.

"Just making sure," Jonah drawls, producing a pack of cards from his pockets. I stare in disbelief as he shuffles them, flipping cards and subconsciously playing tricks. He's a natural when it comes to cards but why is he playing with them right near a sink full of water?

"I'm pretty clumsy," I warn him, pointing at his brown-edged, soft-looking cards from plenty of use with my soapy hands.

"I'll take my chances," Jonah smirks with a shrug. My eyes widen when the dishrag slips from my fingers and plops into the water, soap suds and droplets of water spraying the surrounding surfaces. Jonah sighs when some land on his cards, but I did warn him. Then he shrugs it off. "Adds character." But he still wipes the soapy water off.

"Are you religious?" I question, washing some of the incoming dishes, plates, and utensils, from people who had finished eating. The question is abrupt so I understand and wait with patience when he doesn't answer immediately, mulling his answer over in his mind. I used to see him a couple of times a year at Easter and Christmastime but in the past five years or so his parents stopped bringing the family to church.

"Uh, well, I think my dad grew up non-denominational but my mom is a Catholic. We go to St. Bernadette's at Easter." My heart leaps in my chest, Jonah's answer giving me hope. I might be able to persuade him to come to church, to visit God! I absolutely love converting people, and helping them find the joy of loving Christ!

"I usually go to daily mass," I take a deep breath to control my excitement. Jonah frowns in confusion as he starts a stack of clean plates on a clean trolley.

"Daily mass?"

"Need any help?" Peter, Dickie's third born son, married for two years with a two-year-old baby girl asks as he pops his head into the kitchen area. He owns his own construction business after completing business school four years ago. At twenty-seven, his company is going strong and has branched off into home makeovers. His wife is expecting their next baby to pop out any day now, she is due in about two months but it is a high-risk pregnancy so they might induce labor. She's adamant against it and the doctors did say she doesn't need to give birth right away, so she and Peter are waiting until as late as possible.

"It's not too busy yet!" I wave his help away, splattering Jonah with water. "Hey!" I laugh and duck my chin into my chest when Jonah sticks his hand into the dishwater and flicks some soapy suds at me.

"Well stop splashing me!" Jonah laughs and turns his back to me. I slap the water, causing water to spray over his back.

"Don't!" I giggle as he retaliates, water covering my face. "You're gonna make a mess!"

"I'm not cleaning up after you again!" Paul hollers from the cafeteria. I wince as the memory of a food fight two years ago pops up in my mind. Pierre and I had disagreed on a political issue and had decided to settle it with a chicken leg toss. I probably don't need to mention that I won, not him.

"Sorry!" I yell back, holding my hands up in stop signs as Jonah holds his hand out.

"Truce," he smiles when I shake his hand.

"Daily mass, you go to church, that's mass," I explain to him, not going too in-depth because he's probably not prepared for it. Jonah cocks his head. I hand him a plate to dry after rinsing it.

"Do I need, like, parental consent or anything?" Jonah takes the plate and starts drying it, although he pays more attention to me as he waits for my answer. I notice his hesitation. He's eighteen, he doesn't need parental consent but he wants to let me down easily if he decides not to go and no parental consent is the perfect excuse.

"Uh, no. I've always gone since I got the moped but I go to Sunday mass too." I answer. His question had put me on guard. Too many people have called priests pedophiles to my face, telling me people should only start going to church when they are thirty, an eighteen-year-old adult at the youngest. Jonah's question brought those bad memories up. I take a deep breath, let the anger and worry go, and ask Jesus to take care of it.

"Sure," Jonah shrugs. The plate slips from his grasp. We watch as the plate seems to fall in slow motion before shattering on the cement floor.

"Oh, c'mon!" Paul shouts from the cafeteria. Jonah and I make eye contact before bursting into laughter. I can still hear Paul's grumbling about grabbing the broom and the dustpan.

3

Watson Generations

No way!" I throw my head back with a loud laugh as I point between the two old men. "You're Mr. Watson's dad, and your Mr. Watson's granddad?"

"Just call him Dickie," Peter, Dickie's dad, waves my formalities away as I move an end table out of the way to clean, sweep and mop.

"Dickie ain't no Mr. Watson," Patrick, Mr. Watson's grandpa, adds. They'll only see their baby boy and grandson, while I see the grown man I've known my measly fifteen years compared to Peter's seventy-three and Patrick's ninety-four. I shake my head as I laugh again while sweeping the dust bunnies and crumbs out of the corner.

"He's a Mr. Watson to me," I shrug, sweeping the debris into the dust pan. I spend every fourth Saturday of the month cleaning, apparently, Mr. Watson's grandparents' house. I, for one, am surprised. With their "family is everything", I wouldn't expect Mr. Watson would let his parents or grandparents pay for cleaning labour. It's a secret that they don't pay me. They want to but I tell them to put it in the collection at church or some charity. I should have put the elder Watson couple together with Dickie and his wife earlier on in my life. For the past few years, they haven't been in church and it was only the past year I started cleaning for them, after helping them haul groceries one day. The priest drops by to visit them on Sundays to deliver communion and says mass with them specifically on Thursday afternoons. I shrug off my disbelief as I slide the couch off the wall, glad the floor is hardwood plank and that there are slippers on the bottom of the couch so I don't scratch the floor.

"Here honey, let me get that," Pat, as Patrick told me to call him, slowly reaches out his hand for the picture frame I took off the wall to dust.

"There you go, Pat," I gently ease it into his hands. They tremble and shake so it bounces as it hits the floor but he grabs a rag and starts wiping it down. I love old people. They might be bossy and particular about the way they want things done but even in their fragile state they still try to help. "Thanks."

"You do enough as it is," Peter waves off my gratitude. His more stable hands motion for a canvas from his father and late mother's wedding day. I place it in his hands and he dusts it off as I quickly mop the wall, putting so much elbow grease into my work that I start sweating and don't hear the front door opening.

"Oh, Dickie," Marie, Peter's wife, and Dickie's mother, shoo's her son away. "I might be slow but I can walk up the steps perfectly fine!"

"Daisy!" Mr. Watson exclaims, taking his hat off and hanging it on a chair. "That's why I never see any dust bunnies when I check!"

"They help as much as I help," I point to the two elderly men wiping dust off pictures. Dickie smiles lovingly at his ancestors.

"I can help," Dickie takes the mop out of my hands as his mother slowly opens a cupboard. It melts my heart when she pulls out baked goodies. Even though her knees and hips give her a hard time she still finds time to bake at least two times a week.

"Here darling," she shakes the cookie box at me. Dickie had already hung the pictures back up and slid the couch back in place. "Have a break, you hard worker."

"Awe, thanks Mrs. Watson," a big smile slips across my face. I'll sweep the rest of the corners and crevasses so Dickie can mop while I'm resting. "Once I'm done sweeping."

"Take it easy now," Mrs. Watson slides into a padded kitchen chair. I run and slide to the living room, lifting a recliner, a rocking chair, and a cabinet with Dickie to sweep and mop under. He takes down the pictures while I sweep and the elderly Watsons visit quietly with each other. Jokes are passed around, Dickie is teased but his momma defends him, and stories are shared. They make sure they know that the rest of their family is doing okay before sharing more memories and gossiping about friends and the townsfolk.

"Knock, knock," Paul's voice floats up to us from the steps as he opens the door. Two little girls are giggling around him.

"Gamma!" A little girl's voice rings out, making me swoon. What a sweet little voice. Paul had brought his kids to visit their great grandma and great grandpa and great-great-grandpa. I love it.

"Howdy there Polly," Dickie swings his four-year-old granddaughter in his arms. She giggles happily as Paul walks in carrying his two-year-old daughter, Poppy.

"Dada!" She cries in excitement, lifting her arms up for Dickie to spin her around too. Polly looks like her granddaddy from her light blonde hair, sky blue eyes, and big bones to his tall frame and long legs. She's the spitting image of Peter, who is the spitting image of Pat. Watson genes run deep. Poppy's more like her mother, with small bones, short body, skinny and petite with the cutest milk chocolate brown eyes and freckles.

"Nice to see you here, Daisy," Paul trots up the steps with his baby boy in his arms. He doesn't get to hold Aiden long before the baby is in great grandma's arms with what looks like a long cuddle session ahead.

"How's it going, son?" Dickie swings Poppy now as Polly runs to greet Pat and Peter.

"Looks like Daisy and Amy had the same idea, fall cleaning." Paul ruffles Poppy's hair and slumps into a kitchen chair. He yawns and shakes himself. I don't miss the look Dickie and Marie share as I wipe down the bugs and dirt from the window sills in the kitchen. Paul doesn't miss the concerned look either. He rolls his eyes. "Amy's cleaning and Aiden had trouble sleeping last night."

"I didn't say anything, dear." Marie switches arms with holding Aiden. In her old age, it's hard for her to hold onto babies long but she takes what she can and appreciates the small moments she has. Paul mutters under his breath but leaves it at that. I rinse my rag out to wash under everything on the counters. Paul notices and takes everything off the counters, transferring them to the table.

"We're going to the fire," Pat stiffly walks past us, Polly holding his hand. Peter has Poppy in his arms. She's chatting animatedly to him although we can't understand what she says. I wash the counters silently, aware I'm not exactly a part of the family. This time Dickie, Paul, and Marie share worried looks.

"I'll go with them," Dickie volunteers. The old men can't split or saw wood like they used to but they won't stop trying unless someone else is there to obey their orders.

"Thanks, Dickie," Marie smiles thankfully at her son. He kisses her cheek on the way out before limping down their stairs. Dickie doesn't complain but his back injury randomly gives him bouts of phantom pain, it's vicious but he still does what he can to help at his parents' work, and the soup kitchen.

"You cleaning the whole house?" Paul asks me as he sets a bassinet near his grandmother to rest the baby in. Aiden doesn't have blond hair like his sisters, but thick, curly brown hair like his momma. He's big-boned like Paul and has his dad's cute milk chocolate brown eyes too.

"Yeah," I reply, testing the counter for dryness. It's still wet so I move to the hallway to dust the pictures lining the walls. With such a big family, the walls are filled with pictures hanging. They start with Pat, and his wife's parents, and go down to their great-grandchildren. Aiden's the newest addition with Percy's son, Arlo, a couple of months older than him. Soon there will be another picture hanging on the wall. Every birth is celebrated and rejoiced in this family.

"Nah uh," Marie wags her finger at me with a smile. I smile sheepishly as I scurry to the table. I'm starting to tire out. It's early afternoon and I've been here since a little earlier than ten, coming here right after daily mass this morning. The kitchen, the bathroom, and the front porch are all I have left to clean except the hallway. If I sit, I won't want to get back up. "Have some cookies, dear."

"Thanks, Mrs. Watson," I take a sugar cookie from the container. It's so soft it crumbles on contact, making my mouth water. To chew hurts at the wonderful taste overwhelming my mouth. Old ladies always know the best recipes.

"How's your dad doing?" Paul asks as Marie decides it's time to stop cuddling Aiden so her arms aren't so sore later on. I quickly swallow the bite of the cookie in my mouth and wipe my lips before replying.

"Yeah, he's good." I cough to clear my throat of crumbs. My dad randomly volunteers at the soup kitchen with me so he's acquainted with both Paul and Dickie. Aiden cries a little in his sleep so Paul rests his palm on his son's back and the baby quiets down. Outside the kitchen window, I can see Polly and Poppy chatting and giggling, pointing and leaning as they sit on a bench facing a tree. Pat and Peter had stuck an old tractor steering wheel into the tree when Peter had Dickie. Dickie's kids had played with it and now his grandkids are. They practice driving, the boys usually racing as the girls take 'scenic routes'.

"You want anything to drink, Daisy?" Marie asks, slowly standing up as she rubs her knees to relieve the soreness. She can't sit long or have her knees bent for long.

"Oh, no-," at an energetic nod from Paul I switch my answer. "Um, sure."

"Do you drink coffee? I can make you some tea." Marie offers, slowly walking to a cupboard with a slight limp. Her right knee is bothering her today.

"Only water, Mrs. Watson," I smile at her as Paul leans close to me.

"Makes her feel like she can do something," he whispers in my ear when his grandmother's back is facing us to pour water into my cup. "Always say yes," he ends his advice sharing with a laugh. When his grandmother turns around, he speaks up. "If you clean like this at home too I might have to offer you a job."

"How is your hotel business doing, Paul?" Marie asks as she sets the glass on the table near me. Then she sets a couple more cookies on a napkin before placing them in front of me.

"Thanks," I smile at her with my hand over my mouth to hide the half-chewed cookie on my tongue.

"Little slower than usual this time of year but overall still turning a profit," Paul answers, placing his hand back on Aiden when the baby starts fussing again. Cue my swooning. Paul's only ten years older than me and like all Watson's, he's a good-looking guy. I shake myself out of it and focus on eating the three extra cookies Marie set in front of me as Paul rambles on about his hotel business to his grandma. I watch as he appears more animated, gesturing to and fro as he shares amusing stories.

"Does Amy still have post-partum depression?" Marie asks with concern. Paul looks at Aiden, then me with seemingly downcast eyes as he rubs his hands over his face and through his hair. My eyes widen and I stand up abruptly.

"I'll go take the pictures down," I mumble, wiping my crumbs off the table into my palm and throwing them in the trash. It's not a normal black garbage bag, Marie uses flour bags for garbage that she burns in their burn barrel. They stopped buying permits years ago but continue to burn their garbage.

"She's threatening to leave," Paul states quietly but I still manage to hear it as I start at the far end of the hallway with Pat's parents' pictures. He's the last of his generation with his three sisters and four brothers already gone. I let Marie and her grandson converse privately as I dust off the pictures in the back of the hallway, not my usual spot since the lighting is terrible. I tune the two out as I dust pictures, then the wall, then mop the wall, and hang them back in place all the while praying the Chaplet of Divine Mercy for Paul and his wife to reconcile whatever it is that brought a rift in their relationship. I'm done with the hallway and five Chaplets of Divine Mercy for Paul and the whole Watson family when Marie and Paul's conversation comes to an end.

"Thanks, dear." Marie smiles at me as she starts to putter around the kitchen to compile a late lunch for everyone. She's an amazing cook, most likely where Dickie and Pierre get their good cooking skills from and she loves cooking for anyone who stops by. You never leave Mrs. Watson's house without a full stomach. Marie sighs loudly, not out of complaint but just for a bigger breath of air. Sometimes she has to do that. I sweep around her as Paul moves the table and chairs out of my way.

"Thanks," I shoot him a smile, fixing stray strands of crazy hair out of my face. It falls back immediately. Marie hums to herself as she makes sandwiches from homemade bread and homemade raspberry jam from her patch by the garden. It's so sweet and delicious, I've always wanted the recipe but haven't asked because it might be a family one and I'm not a part of the family.

"I'll take this outside," Marie gestures to the platter filled with sandwiches and a jug of cold iced tea.

"Take your time, Grandma," Paul smiles at her but rushes to her side. "I'll carry these down for you and open the door."

"Oh, you don't need to, Paul," Marie shrugs as if to say 'what can I do?'. I chuckle and shrug back as I sweep dirt into the dust pan. There's not too much since she can still sweep at least a couple of times a week if her knees aren't bothering her too much. Even with Paul in front of her, I still watch to make sure she doesn't slip on the carpeted steps. She's dear to my heart. I've moved the chairs back by the time Paul trots up the steps.

"I say we have fifteen minutes to half an hour to finish before she comes back," he laughs and carries the table back into the kitchen.

"Thanks, Paul," I laugh with him as I walk to the mop and pail. "You can clean the bathroom. I'll mop the living room, make my way through the hallway and finish off with the kitchen."

"Sounds good," Paul digs under the sink for a rag and bathroom cleaner. The kitchen sink is actually made out of plywood and painted a serene yellow counter. The Watson house is old but built solidly. It'll stand for generations of Watson's yet to come.

"Thanks for the help Paul, I really appreciate it." I sigh and blow hair out of my sweaty face. I'm probably going to get my period soon, my body is aching and sore, a big indicator that shark week is approaching fast. Paul laughs abruptly.

"She's my grandma Daisy, thank *you!*" Paul emphasizes the word 'you'. I blush as he gives me a hug. "They appreciate you, a lot." He ends with a kiss on my forehead.

"I just see the help needed and give it," I pat his back and step away from him. Paul isn't as built as his firefighter, labour job brothers but he still helps them or Dickie, runs the farm and he works out because every hotel of his has a gym. Since he owns them, he can work out for free whenever he wants.

"Don't worry about the bathroom and the porch, I'll clean 'em spic and span." Paul jogs down the stairs, whistling with the cleaning supplies in his hands. The Watson's are nice people, that's one thing for sure. And they have five generations alive right now, that's beautiful. Pat, Peter, Dickie, Paul, and Aiden, all with the name Watson.

4

Nothing Else To Do

———◆———

I hum in my head as I walk down the Main Street of town on the edge of the bank of the river. With nothing planned today, and it being fall with harvesting all finished, I'd decided to stroll through town to see if anyone needed help. Upon seeing crows getting into garbage bags dumped by the town's playground, I'd walked to the little grocery store and bought bags to pick it all up. On my way back to the park now, I'm picking up stray pieces of garbage floating on the road from the breeze. With autumn rolling around, it's a beautiful day for a walk, not too hot but not too cold. I'm content to listen to the wind whistling around buildings and through pine branches and poplar leaves as I make my way to litter on the ground. It's mostly chip bags and chocolate wrappers with bottles of Pepsi or twisted tea. It being a Saturday, I put the two dots together and deduce that people had partied last night.

My knees are swollen this afternoon, along with my elbows and wrists because of my juvenile arthritis. I know I shouldn't have napped after cleaning the Watson's house but I'd been so tired from running late last night with Jonah and still saying my prayers after that. I'd only gotten to bed around two am and I routinely wake up at five am because I need the first few morning hours of my day to connect with God, talk with Him and pray to Him. I did allow myself to sleep in until six today because the daily mass was in the morning. Picking litter up is slow progress but I'm happy when I look back to find less garbage on the street. I doubt I'll do the whole town today but this is a start. Main Street will look pretty once I'm done. At the rate I'm working, I'll be finished picking up garbage in a couple of hours. There's a bin by the playground I can put the bags in. I'm lucky it's there. I don't have a vehicle to haul the garbage to the dump and I don't have any money to pay the dump person. My last paycheque went to the soup kitchen for cleaning supplies. With my three days a week and five-hour shifts at minimum wage, I don't make too much money. Because I'm still a high school student, they only need to pay me thirteen dollars an hour.

Loud rap music with bass that seems to vibrate the cement makes its way closer to me along with vulgar language. A decked-out truck pulls over to the side of the road where I am picking up garbage. My bag is just about full and my knees are seriously aching. I might have to stop before I finish Main Street, the pain is too great. Usually, I persevere better. "What you doing, baby?" A young man sits at the truck door window. With the pain in my body, I want to snap back at him irritably but I take a deep breath and smile at him.

"I'm just picking up litter," I say, pointing to the bag. Deciding it's full enough, I start to tie the edges together. It crinkles and cracks as I squish chip bags together to tie it lower.

"You gettin' paid?" He asks as his friends raucously laugh in the tinted-out windows of the jacked-up black Ford F-150. I recognize him from school. He'd graduated with a certificate when I was in eighth grade and hasn't done anything else since. Sometimes I feed him meals at the soup kitchen because he spends all his money on booze and drugs, and, I guess, this truck. I hope one day he can take a money management course to spend his money in more productive, healthier ways but all I can do for now is pray for him.

"Oh," I laugh nervously as I try to fold my thick curly hair behind my ears. It pops back out immediately. I hate it when I have to tell people I'm working for free. "No, I just saw the garbage and now I'm here."

"We can give you more work," the guy laughs as he drops some gum, chocolate, and chip wrappers and bags on the ground where I'd already cleaned up. My eyes narrow in disbelief as the driver revs the engine. The guys in the back whistle. "Oh yeah, bend down! Let's see that ass!"

They're looking for trouble. I'd just now put a name to the awful smell wafting from the truck. It's weed. They probably have alcohol in there, too. The engine revs again as I turn around and walk away. It's the best thing to do in this situation. I'm not normally this rude but my patience is wearing thin from the pain in my knees and wrists. *"Oh Jesus, take it. Take it all. I give myself to You. Let Your Will be done."* I whisper the short prayer under my breath as the truck catches up to me. It doesn't look like I'm getting away from them that easily. I offer this upcoming humiliation and degradation as consolation for Jesus's Sacred Heart and His Bitter Passion.

A cherry red Dodge pulls up behind me, cutting off the jacked-up truck from approaching me. They scowl and shout and swear as I sigh in relief and thank the Lord. It's Jonah.

"Hey Daisy Daisy," he smiles at me as he pockets his keys and pushes his door shut. My eyes widen when Col and the triplets get out of his truck. I hadn't realized they were all this close of friends that they hung out on weekends.

"Billy!" Landon shouts, twirling a baseball bat around. My eyes widen as he gets in a batting position and practices a few swings. Harry and Col are having a yelling match with the other guys. "Gonna start counting down, you piece of shit! Get your f—king gutless trash outta here before I make it lose the only thing it has going for it."

"You'll be f—king lucky to live if you do!" Billy, the guy now in the passenger seat, threatens. He'd seen the baseball bat and made sure all his limbs were in the vehicle. Landon only smirks and swings the baseball bat. The driver slams on the gas and revs the engine, smashing into Jonah's truck with his big bumper. I step back as Jonah's truck rocks from the force. Harry picks up a rock and throws it. Landon manages to hit the passenger side of the decked-out truck a couple of times before they take off, burning coal and leaving tracks.

"Oh, baby," Jonah rushes to the other side of his truck. I follow him, forgetting the garbage for a minute. He drops to his knees at the damage he sees. "I just got you back!"

"F—k!" Landon throws the baseball bat down. He still has adrenaline pumping through him as he walks in brisk circles, anger written clearly on his face. I want to console him, tell him it's alright but Landon in an angry state doesn't listen to anyone. We've all learned to wait until he calms down to talk to him.

"Awe, shit," Harry mumbles, kicking the ground and rubbing his hands over his face. He's probably worried Billy and those others guys will report them. Landon just got back from juvie at the end of summer break, technically he's still on parole or a probationary period. One mess up sends him back. Jonah can't report this either, then, unless he tells the whole story because Billy and they certainly will. That means Jonah's insurance won't cover this. His parents will have to pay for it, or they'll make him. He does have a part-time job as a bell boy for Paul's hotel here in town.

"Gonna cost a fortune," Col whistles as he wraps an arm around my shoulders. I sigh in relief and lean into his comforting embrace. I need it after being scared like that by those mean guys. Maybe this is why he and Danae are such good friends. She was always picked on and bullied and he has some sort of hero complex or at least he tries to end wrongs and make wrongs right, even if the vigilante isn't the best way to go. "You okay, Daisy?"

"I smelled trouble when I saw you walking away with a frown," Jonah looks at me, almost completely heartbroken at the damage done to his truck. Dents in the doors, chunks of paint missing, the frame might be bent. I think he'll be able to drive to the shop but he'll have to be careful around corners; a dent sticks out and could pop his front right tire if it rubs against the sharp piece. "But I didn't think it would be that much. Maybe I should have. You never frown. I've never seen you frown before this. What did they say to you?"

"Oh, I'm sure they didn't mean it," I waved his concern away. It turns out to be their concern as all the boys look at me. I look at the scraggly grass on the cracked pavement to ignore their looks. They're probably right to be worried. I certainly was scared, I'm glad they showed up. Thank God for His timing, it's always right.

"Billy's dangerous," Landon bites out. He gestures with his hands. His whole energy around him scares me it's so dark and angry, wanting retribution and retaliation. Landon doesn't know any better, raised in a neglectful, abusive environment. He doesn't know how to properly deal with his emotions but I do have to say they are way better than their younger brothers at controlling themselves. "Deals with my dad. Runs with the McCoy clan. Next time you see him, run the other f—king way!"

"Okay!" I gulp at his anger directed at me. No one is usually angry with me. I give no one any reason to be. It hurts me when people are mad at me, I never set out to do anyone wrong. My goal in this world is to make it a better place for everyone. Harry slaps Landon's shoulder and pushes him back a couple of steps.

"Rose-tinted glasses bro, take it easy." My face burns at his harsh comment but it's nothing I haven't heard before. Too many people have commented on my innocence, how it's bad that a fifteen-year-old girl could believe in a pure, happy world when I should know better. I do know better, but I look past that to try to make this place a safe place for all.

"Are your wrists swollen?" Col frowns at my swollen wrists. They don't know I have arthritis. I keep it a secret, not wanting people to feel pity for me. Landon, Harry, and Jonah stomp closer to inspect, forcefully asking questions and the two triplets cursing. I never lie. I flat out refuse to lie so it looks like four people are going to learn my deepest secret today.

"Yes, but-," I'm interrupted by threats to Billy from Harry and Landon and concern from Jonah. Col nods along to whatever jumbled mess the other three are saying. Exasperated, I tug my hands out of their grip. "No, guys, listen." They don't listen so I sigh impatiently and raise my voice. "No guys! Listen!"

"What the f—k?" Landon coughs as he and Harry share surprised looks. I blush at the shocked look on their faces.

"They must have really scared you," Jonah stares at me in wonder, enunciating his next words. "You raised your voice!"

"I'm sorry!" I blush, looking frantically between the guys. They all just have to be taller than me. Col and Landon look the scariest from Landon's anger bubbling around him to the scar on Col's face. "You just weren't listening! I was trying to tell you they never touched me! They never even left the truck! I have what's called juvenile arthritis! I just don't tell people, well, because... I don't want them, ya know, feeling bad for me. Only in the mornings and evenings and... when the weather changes does it hurt!"

"You have arthritis," Harry deadpans, licking his teeth as he looks at my swollen wrists to my face. Seeing the honesty, he believes me. It might be from rumours about me too, everyone knows I do not lie. "And you still were picking up garbage?"

"I didn't have nothing else to do," I mumble, blushing awkwardly as I fix my hair into a ponytail. The wind has picked up, causing it to fly into my face.

"You didn't have anything else to do today so you were just casually strolling Main Street, picking up trash?" Jonah clarifies. He huffs out a little laugh and mumbles something under his breath. I think it was something about what a crazy, amazing woman I am but I can't be certain. Only I know how unworthy of praise I am.

"Uh, yeah," I smile nervously then point to his truck. "I am so sorry about the damage to your truck!" At my words, he groans.

"Don't remind me..." he looks like he is going to cry at the ugliness of the passenger side of his vehicle. "My parents are going to kill me!"

"I'll help pay!" I speak up, pulling a five-dollar bill out of my pocket and offering it to him. The boys look at me incredulously so I start explaining. "Really, it's my fault your truck is hurt! If I had just picked up the garbage they threw out of their truck they wouldn't have chased me and you wouldn't have intervened. Yeah, they made me uncomfortable but I'm fifteen I should realize by now that guys look at my butt. It's just the way of the world but they shouldn't have been so vulgar about it. I don't put on shows! Why would they think I do?" At my words, I realize how scared I was, and tears well up in my eyes.

"I don't want your money," Jonah gruffly states before enveloping me in a hug. Tears burst out of me as I lean into his muscular runner's body. My cheek rests against his chest and I can hear his quickened heartbeat. We all still have adrenaline pumping through our veins. "I wasn't even going to drive down this street. It's closer if I took Hillcrest drive. Something just told me to drive this way."

"Divine intervention," I wrap my arms around his waist and squeeze. Jonah pats my back. I prayed and God answered, I'm a part of a miracle. Thank the Lord.

"You want a ride home, Daisy Daisy?" Jonah asks as Harry and Landon wiggle their eyebrows and laugh because I'm still hugging Jonah. Blushing, I let him go and dry my tears.

"I gotta go throw the bag in the bin," I point to the park. One bag down, two bags left with all the garbage the crows spread about. Col walks to the door and tries to open it. It refuses to as a result of the damage.

"We can throw it in the box," Jonah offers, gesturing to the bag on the other side of his truck. I shake my head and place my hand on his forearm.

"Thanks for the help, I appreciate it. But I still have the rest of Main Street to do." I follow the boys as they all walk to the driver's side of the truck. Jonah looks amazed at my words as Col climbs in the truck, across the seats to the passenger side.

"I would offer to stay and help but we are going out to the trails to practice for the half marathon." Jonah smiles at me as I watch Harry and Landon try to get in the truck at the same time. They back up in a hurry as Tyler leans out and barf sprays out of his mouth.

"Oh my goodness, Tyler!" I rush to him as he leans on the seat, exhausted. He has a freshly broken nose and black eyes, swollen lips, and cuts scattered across his face.

"It's nothing," Harry holds me back. His voice had gone deadly quiet and the absolute stillness of his body freezes my actions. Harry's pissed off and it's probably because Tyler took a beating.

"Gotta love daddy dearest," Landon scoffs bitterly as he stands in a wide stance to avoid the puke puddle and gently shoves Tyler into a sitting position. He growls in frustration when Tyler's body is limp. "He's already got too much f—king meth in him."

"Walk away," Harry scowls as he carefully pushes me back. His eyes are dark and dilated and I have the feeling someone's gonna get hurt soon. That's one way they release all their hurt and anger.

"I gotta go dump the garbage," I murmur, walking away. I know when I'm not wanted and I'm not going to push it. Jonah pats my head as I walk past him. It's his goodbye as he gets into his truck, running his hand over the dash and murmuring about what a good girl she is. With my back turned, I make the sign of the cross and start praying the Chaplet of Divine Mercy for the triplets, but especially Tyler as I pick up the garbage bag and make my way to the bin.

5

A Day at Work

It's cold in the store compared to outside. Wednesday is the first day of the week I work and I work three days in a row, Wednesdays, Thursdays, and Fridays. The cold is lovely in the heat of summer but annoying in the cold of winter. Sometimes I wear ski pants here during winter, especially if I have to stock ice cream or other frozen foods. If I don't wear gloves, my fingers burn from the cold so much that tears well up in my eyes. I'm a crier, not that I like admitting it. Little things make me cry, like a picture of a three-year-old girl trying to carry Jesus's cross from his statue where he fell. The Third Station of the Cross. Small acts of great love make me cry, like Landon shoving Tyler through the high school's doors even though Tyler has given up on himself. Tyler doesn't see his self-worth, probably because of the mental abuse his father puts him through. Landon and Harry might be arrogant but when it comes down to it, they know that they could be better. I think they help their brother, mainly because they love him, but also because they could see themselves in his place.

Realizing I'd zoned out, I go back to stocking jars of Smucker's jam on the shelf. It's soothing to me, pushing the older jars to the side and putting the ones with a later expiration date in the back. I don't need food going to waste. The store isn't too busy so I make the sign of the cross and start praying the Chaplet of Mercy, my favourite prayer. It's quick, easy, and very contemplative. I'm reminded over and over again of Jesus's greatest act of love: giving His life up for me, for us, for the whole human race. And the best thing of all? He doesn't make us love Him, He gives us the freedom to choose Him or not. God isn't a tyrant.

"Going on break," my co-worker, an adult because they need an adult to close the store with underage workers, informs me. We work great together, mostly because she handles the customers unless she needs me at the till and I work to make the aisles pretty. I always start at the back because she can work in the aisles closer to the till if there aren't many customers.

"Gotcha," I shoot her two thumbs ups. Meandering over to the doors of the store, I see that we must have gotten our drink order early. Snapple, Pure Leaf, and other bottles of juice and different brands of water are ready to be put in the coolers. Kaydee, my coworker, had already started so I continue with the job. It's similar to stocking the jam but colder with the coolers. The chilling bite of the air stings my fingers but I offer my uncomfortableness up for the repentance of souls around the world. It's also soothing work. Like any usual Wednesday, it's not that busy of a day. Humming as I work, falling into a pattern from the beat in my head to a song I can't name, I get a lot of work done. By the time that is passing, I can tell Kaydee is taking a longer break than allowed, which is usual for her. She often forgets the time that passes her by on her break, often getting lost in a book.

"Hi, Mrs. Henderson!" I greet with a smile as I turn around from the coolers. I'd seen her roll her shopping cart up through the reflection of the cooler doors. She's at the till unloading her grocery cart onto the conveyor belt.

"Hello, darling," she smiles, pleasantly surprised when I take over putting her items on the till. She always seems surprised yet I do it every time I see her. What a dear old lady she is!

"I got this for you there, ma'am." I shoot her a wink with a smile. She's an elderly nurse, going to retire any day soon (she's been saying that as long as I could talk), and walks with a cane and a very noticeable limp. She had polio as a kid and aging has only made it worse.

"Thank you!" She breathes heavily, out of breath from this little excursion. She's obese, which doesn't help her bones. After finishing putting the items on the counter, I make my way around to scan them through. Mrs. Henderson animatedly chats about her day as I make my way through her groceries, giving her my discount where I can. I enjoy hearing her stories about the day. It might not be legal, more to the point, ethical, but she tells me about patient reactions and conversations that made her laugh or got her thinking. To be fair, I never know who goes to the clinic and she never mentions names. Mrs. Henderson buys lots of baked goodies, and any in-store bakery items I have a twenty percent discount on. She knows this after the first couple of times she went shopping when I was here. Now it's routine for her to shop every second Wednesday. "How much?" She asks with a grin and leans closer to the screen. With her elderly age, she needs glasses and sometimes forgets that they are hanging on a string around her shoulders. I laugh lightly and point to the eighty-eight dollars and fifty-six cents because she had forgotten to place her glasses on her nose. "And how much without the discount?" Her eyes light up at the fifteen dollars and twenty-nine cents that she saved today, after putting her glasses on. She quickly pays, content with her savings for today's shopping spree.

"I'll take that," I loop my hand through the plastic grocery bags to carry to her car. The bags dig into my skin with their weight but I ignore the pain as the sliding doors open with a clank at the end. They're always slow to open and often get pushed out of their place so the frozen stock guy who also shovels and whatnot has to fix it.

"Thanks, dear," Mrs. Henderson slowly follows behind me. The click-clack of her cane is oddly comforting. My arms burn from the weight but I shoot her a smile as she apologizes. She'd lost her keys somewhere in her big purse and is digging around for them. I sigh in relief when I hear the beep of her doors unlocking and tug open the door.

"You have a good day, Mrs. Henderson!" I shove the door closed with my hip and open her driver's door at the same time.

"Oh, you as well, sweet Daisy." Mrs. Henderson gives me a big hug, taking my breath away as she squeezes tightly. Old ladies might be fragile but boy, are they strong. Turning to the store, I see Pete walking up with a couple of his sometimes friends. I call them sometimes friends because once they drink together they try to beat him up, almost always usually just about killing him. He'll be in here soon and by the looks of his sometimes friends, they are all hungry after a rough night. When they get close enough I can see the extra limp in Pete's lame leg and how he is relying harder on his homemade cane. Upon closer inspection, his eyes are bruised and swollen. Pete longs for any type of human connection because the rest of the townspeople ignore him, not wanting to hang around the town drunk even if he is related to half of them. I mentally remind myself to pray for him, and his sometimes friends, in my evening prayers tonight.

"Pick something, one thing, preferably a meal, Pete. Don't know when you'll get another one." I shoot him a smile and walk in before them. One-on-one with Pete is fine but with the three others guys, with one towering above us all and not all there in the head, it makes me nervous. I shouldn't be. I should trust in the Lord, He will take care of me. "Your friends too," I wave at them all. They all look a little scraggly, maybe they didn't have such a good night. Sometimes the cops rough them up if there aren't other crimes, more specifically, a party at the Smith house. Smith parties are raves, often getting extremely wild.

"Yeah, yeah, yeah, thanks," Pete mumbles as he leads the others straight to the freezers. I know what he's going for. He has a favourite frozen meal. I start stocking drinks with Kaydee, who had finally finished her break.

"You can go for your break now," Kaydee turns me away from the bottles of juice. I laugh and tap her hands for her to release me.

"Soon as Pete comes through the till," I smile at her and start organizing the bandaids and medicine to make them look prettier. Kaydee won't let me stock drinks until I finish my break but she can't stop me from working if I'm not at her arm's length. I don't outright say it but Kaydee knows, she's worked with me long enough.

"I wouldn't do it," Kaydee shakes her head at me as she bites her lip in thought. Then she crosses her arms and shakes her head again. "You're just enabling him."

"Can't enable him when he doesn't have any money," I shrug, not saying my thoughts that disagree. I'm not good at confrontation and I don't want to lead either of us into sin. She herself is religious, not Catholic like me but still, shouldn't all religions show mercy? Kaydee sighs but lets it go, knowing she won't be able to change my mind. I believe I'm doing Jesus's work here on earth, nothing can stop me.

"Hey," Pete greets me, mumbling other words under his breath that I can't hear before chuckling nervously. I scan his frozen meal of steak, potatoes, and corn through the till followed by his friend's meals. One had chosen a sandwich and veggies, one cheese buns and pepperoni sticks, and the last was pretty smart. He was the meanest looking one and he'd grabbed a big box of pizza pops. That's four meals there. I nod in approval, even if it isn't too healthy, it has meat to keep him full. Using my discount on the bakery items, I scan the items through, saving myself four dollars and thirty-five cents.

"It's good," I wave Pete and his friends away as I pull cash out of my pocket to pay for it. The total was less than fifty bucks, which I'm thankful for. This fifty dollars is my rainy day fund and without it, I'll have to catch the bus or rides to school, work, and volunteer. If I go for a run with Jonah, he'll drive me home. Maybe. The shop will probably give him a temporary vehicle while they work on his. The bus will take me to school in the morning and I can walk the ten-minute walk to work and the twenty-five minutes to the soup kitchen. The four men all laugh and tell jokes, all the while looking lustfully at Kaydee as they make their meals in the little microwave by the slushie machine. I look at her so she can see the underlining meaning in my words. "Going on break unless you need help here."

"Go," Kaydee waves me off. I shoot her a thumbs up as I walk down the aisle then take a left at the end. She knows I don't really go on breaks but she can't stop me as I make my way to the aisle I was working on and start facing and stocking items again. I'm on the end of the third last aisle, working with rectangular boxes of tin foil, parchment paper, ziplock baggies, and other similar items. Stacking and organizing them is a slow process which includes falling if I don't do it properly. When I first got this job, this aisle tested my patience and my work ethic.

"Put that back!" I hear a man's voice hiss out angrily, then a smack. My eyes widen in alarm as I duck my head. If I seem like I didn't notice, they will leave me alone.

"I'm sorry!" A woman murmurs. Out of the corner of my eye, I see a black-eyed woman setting some pork chops down and picking up packages of steak instead. The man smiles and waves at me so I shoot him a polite smile back as I face the shelf and continue stocking. Once they pass, and much to my dismay, he still bullies her into buying what he wants, I make the sign of the cross and start saying the Chaplet of Divine Mercy for her and her boyfriend with the intercession of St. Joseph. Soon there is more traffic in the store as it gets busy, as it usually does at the end of the day. People are visiting in aisles, joking with me and their friends, dropping items and placing them back on the wrong shelves, and leaving behind muddy, wet footprints. It had started to rain sometime since Mrs. Henderson had left. I'd expected it with the darkness of the clouds in the sky.

"Daisy to the till please, Daisy to the till," Kaydee calls for my help. Fixing one last row of Glad and off-brand garbage bag boxes, I quickly walk to the till. There's a long line of seven people behind Kaydee's till so I smile guiltily at the customers. The five regulars all laugh, knowing how I am by now.

"I can help you over here," I wave to the second person in line from my till. It's the abusive man and his timid girlfriend. He talks and laughs friendly, flirting with me as I scan and bag his items in a hurry. Something about him sets me on edge and I'm thankful I'm still in prayer. Probably the devil in his eyes. My ears tune out his words as I nod, smile, and laugh along but inside I'm praying for a peaceful night for the couple. He notices the scapular around my neck as I give him my discount on bakery items. Anything to try and get him in a better mood. His girlfriend hasn't said a word, has barely looked up from the floor but sends me a woeful, albeit grateful, look when he asks about a snap back that says 'I love Jesus'. One of the other regular customers snorts under her breath but I cut off her quick comment. "Want me to grab that for you?"

"Yes please, ma'am," he grins at me, showing off the hat to another couple that must know them. The woman is drunk, continuously walking into displays and dropping items with the man picking up after her impatiently. Am I the only one who sees the bittersweet pain in his eyes as he looks at the love of his life that can't seem to stop slowly killing herself?

"It's okay," I tell him quietly with a genuine smile. "I'll pick it up after, don't worry." He looks so relieved at my words he has to take a minute to himself as they wait in line. I use a broom handle with a curved edge on it to take the hat down and pass it to the man. He likes the fit and nods in agreement as I stand behind the till to scan it through. "Your total is three hundred and sixty-four cents. How would you like to pay?"

"Visa," he waves a grey-coloured card at me. I hit a few buttons on my computer, type in the number, and pass him the debit machine.

"Good to go," I wince and make eye contact with the man when his drunk woman crashes into the sunglasses display and knocks it over. The abusive man laughs.

"She needs to leave the premises," Kaydee demands, pointing at the drunk woman as she clumsily tries to put the sunglasses back on the stand.

"Have a good day," I smile at the first couple as the transaction completes itself. She starts pushing the cart out of the store, loading the groceries herself, and waves at me. He wiggles his eyebrows and puts the snapback on his head. Even if he is abusive, I should be happy he believes in God. Maybe he will one day change, if only by God-given graces.

"Oh Paul," the drunk woman mumbles, dry heaving. "I might be sick."

"Let's get you to the truck," Paul, the man of misery, leads the woman out, still bent over. She fights him along the way, tripping over her feet and pushing and hitting him, managing to knock on the sliding doors. I stare wide-eyed when they are forcefully moved from their track and stay slanted. We're going to have to call the bosses to fix it. My heart hurts when I see a little girl seated in the first grocery cart and a little boy standing behind it. I round the till and crouch down to him.

"Hi, I'm Daisy." I smile at him. He grins shyly back, showing me a full set of silver teeth. "What's your name?"

"Nicolai," he murmurs quietly, giggling afterward as he ducks his head shyly. His hair is greasy, indicating he hasn't had a bath in a few days.

"Alright Nicolai, do you mind if I give your dad a head start unloading these groceries on the till?" He shakes his head at me with a bigger smile.

"He's not my dad," Nicolai mutters. It doesn't shock me that Paul isn't his dad, most families around here are broken and two often become one. I know I shouldn't do it, but I reach over my till and hand him a sucker we keep for kids. His eyes light up as I unwrap it for him.

"Hey kiddo," Paul ruffles the boy's hair. Nicolai leans into his embrace. At the love they share, even if they aren't related, I internally vow to pray one rosary a day for them. Paul looks regretfully at the door and back to me with desperate eyes. "I won't be able to pay for that."

"It's been broken before," I wave his concern away. Kaydee clears her throat as her customer leaves, shaking his head at the damage done to the doors. I wince at Kaydee's hardness of heart and spur of the moment I make a declaration. "If our bosses make you pay for it, I have it covered."

"That's not right," Paul shakes his head even with hope brimming in his eyes. I shrug and scan items through, Kaydee bagging them for me. Kaydee stares at me, clicking her tongue.

"I'm going to call Max," she shakes her head before walking away. Paul looks alarmed so I smile at him.

"Just the guy that fixes the doors." I offer as the little girl in the cart whines. She's jealous of Nicolai's sucker. I know I shouldn't, especially with giving others my discount already, but I use my discount for Paul. It doesn't save him too much, but it's something.

"Thank you," Paul sighs in relief, holding the counter and bending over. He snaps back up when the girl starts crying. "Hey, it's okay Mackenzie." He ruffles her hair and picks her up. The smell isn't the first thing to give away her full pamper, it's the size and weight of it that gets to me. He notices what has her crying and looks at me. "She's old enough to have one too," he states, short of pleading with me.

"Okay," I laugh embarrassed. "I wasn't sure so..." I trail off with a shrug of my shoulders as I start a new Chaplet of Mercy for the poor little family. He pops open a sucker for her and she is content to suck on it back in the cart as he loads the first cart up and I scan the second cart through.

"Max and Dan are coming," Kaydee starts bagging for me again. I wince when I can no longer give Paul my discount but he understands. I hate that I'm breaking rules but if my boss, Dan, finds out, I know he will take it out of my check.

"We keep extra pampers in the customer bathroom," I offer Paul. He picks up Mackenzie and nods. The timid woman whose boyfriend is the abusive man walks up to the till with a pack of pads. "I'll help you at the other till," I jut my thumb to Kaydee's till. My coworker had started stocking the drinks, in a hurry now that the end of the day was coming to a close. I take the pack of pads from her arm and scan them through, sad at how much my bosses overcharge for the feminine products. "Twenty-two thirty-seven." The bruised woman silently hands me a twenty-dollar bill. My lips form a line of anger but I accept it and offer her a smile. "It's good," I wave her away as I pass her the pads and throw the receipt away. She smiles in gratitude at me as I dig into the tip cup, only to find forty-five cents. I have to use my toonie to pay the rest of her bill. Now I am officially broke for the next week. I shrug my worry off, glad for the challenge to place all my trust in Jesus.

"Whew," Paul whistles at the price on the computer screen. With two carts, his total had come up to eight hundred dollars and fifty-two cents. "I'll have to make two bills."

"Sure," I put five hundred on the debit machine and pass it to him. Unless people change it, that is the limit and most people don't. Once the money goes through, the total drops to the proper amount and I type it into the debit machine so he can pay again.

"Thank you," Paul meets my eyes to get his point across. I wave his gratitude off. Other people might not have helped him this much but I believe someone would have helped him somehow. There are nice people all over the world.

"Not a problem, really."

"What's your name?" He asks, loading the last of the bags into the second cart. Mackenzie was kicking her legs, trying to find any reason to move or anything to grab.

"Daisy," I smile as Nicolai bites on the sucker. His eyes light up at the crunchy sound, delighting my ears. Crunching, bones cracking (like cracking knuckles, not anything bad), and popping are delightful sounds to my ears.

"Maybe I'll see you here again, Daisy," Paul lifts Nicolai onto the seat of a grocery cart. He's around four years old, and hard to fit but he squeezes in. Nicolai sends me another silver grin as Paul wheels the carts out of the broken sliding doors.

"Prolly," I shrug with a laugh and wave them goodbye. "Have a good night!" And under my breath, with my whole heart believing the words, I add "God bless you all!" Then I walk to the displays she knocked down and start fixing them.

6

One Day Job

———⇒▷•◁⇐———

Morning Daisy," Peter, Dickie's third born son at twenty-seven years old smiles as he toasts me his coffee cup. I smile at him as I climb up into his truck. Unlike his dad and his brother Percy, but like the rest of his siblings that have vehicles, he's a Ford guy. His truck is black. In his opinion, who gets a white Ford? They're either county workers or police officer trucks.

"Good morning Peter," I greet him as I click my seatbelt into place. At the soup kitchen yesterday evening, when I went to wash the dishes after my shift at work, he was there with Paul, sweeping and mopping the hall. I'd mentioned I needed some cash and he said he'd pick me up in the morning for a roofing job. I'd jumped at the chance to earn the extra cash and he was happy to hire a reliable worker even if it was only for one day.

"How was your sleep?" He asks as he signals out of my driveway. Dad fills the potholes every year but with one rain they appear right away again. Peter has to drive slow so I'd just met him at the end of the road.

"Short but good," I nod, yawning. We both laugh at that. Without waking up early for my prayers, I feel like I didn't get a good start to my day.

"Why short?" Peter asks. Unlike Paul, he usually keeps a conversation going. I don't mind, not having friends to talk to about my day or plans. Sometimes I just need another mind to bounce ideas.

"Well I worked until 9:30, then I helped you guys until eleven." I'm interrupted by another yawn. With a sheepish smile, I laugh. "It takes me an hour or so to wake up and I slept in."

"That's okay," Peter laughs as he turns onto the highway. We'd decided yesterday that he'd take the gas money out of my paycheque. I'd insisted where he didn't really mind. It means I'm only making eighty bucks instead of a hundred but I'll take what I can get.

"Went for a run with Jonah after dishes. We're training for the half marathon coming up. I was tired from school, work and volunteering so the run was closer to two hours instead of my usual hour and a half. He drove me home, I had a shower, said my evening prayers, and was asleep by four am." Peter whistles. My eyes widen as I look at Peter. Usually, I don't tell people about my days because they get all proud of me. I don't volunteer and do training for people to be proud of me. I don't want to be placed on a pedestal. "My days aren't usually like that. I've just been busy lately."

"You should have told me," Peter frowns. "I wouldn't have picked you up until nine."

"I literally woke up in time to brush my teeth, that's it. Four hours of sleep is good and I'm a napper. I'll sleep when work is done." I can nap anytime, anywhere. Sometimes sleep doesn't come easily to me, I feel like God wants me to pray so I spend countless nights in prayer and I nap when I have a spare moment during the day.

"You don't need to work today," Peter slows as he enters town limits. It's not too big of a town, maybe a thousand people, and the Watsons are the richer people. They don't act rich like most other people here and are very frugal until it comes to charity. They only have big houses because of their big families.

"I need the money," I shrug. "I spent all my last paycheque and have a week left until I get paid again."

"You might need a money management course." Peter laughs, then takes a sip of his coffee. I'm not a coffee drinker, having despised both the smell and the taste. All the Watsons drink coffee, even the triplets.

"Ah, no, well..." I trail off before looking at him. Should I tell him why I'm strapped this paycheque or will he place me on that pedestal?

"What?" Peter basically barks before he realizes his tone. "Guess I'm a little tired too," he laughs. "Reece started teething. I kept her in the living room so Corinne could get a good night's rest. She's not due for another two months but she's a high risk and has too much fluid. She's on bed rest and I have to keep her there unless she wants to spend the next few weeks in the hospital."

"Awe," I sigh, fingering my scapular. "I'll pray for her."

"We appreciate that." Peter smiles as he slows and pulls into his driveway. Apparently, the roof we're taking off is his. Dickie's truck is parked in the driveway.

"Is Dickie helping?"

"He's watching Reece for Corinne and me. Paul was going to help but Amy needed him at home." I read behind his lines, only because of Paul and his grandmother's conversation last Saturday. "Andrea might drop by to help but it's really only a two-person job."

"It'll be nice to see her," I comment. I know all of his siblings by name and personality but more so the boys. The girls are usually too busy to volunteer at the soup kitchen whereas the boys schedule out time. I haven't seen Andrea in a while. The last I'd seen her was when she'd dropped by after school one day to check on Tyler. She'd been called to the Smith house and he'd fallen off of the roof, drunk and high on meth, after, of course, puking on the Lieutenant. That was last year, beginning of summer, the night Landon was arrested. He'd made bail for two weeks before being sentenced to three months in juvie.

"You aren't afraid of heights, are you?" Peter points to his two-door garage that sits on an incline. There's a lean-to for storage behind it with a root cellar for potatoes and turnips. Peter has a big lot in town, enough for a garden to the left of his garage with ample space in the front yard for the kids to play. It's all fenced in though because they have two young Irish Setters.

"We'll see," I shrug with a grin. My face heats up when my stomach grumbles in the silence of the moment. With only five minutes before walking down the driveway, I hadn't had time to eat breakfast.

"Come inside," Peter invites. "I need to rinse my coffee cup out anyways. Dad will wanna visit too."

"Sure," I shrug, climbing out, careful not to slam his door. Peter's gates are automatic and close as we walk to the back door. Two Irish Setters greet me excitedly, tails swinging and jumping up at me, tongues licking. The younger one is almost chestnut with its dark red but the other is a lighter red, pleasing to the eyes to look at.

"Samson! Rufus!" Peter barks, grabbing their collars and pulling them down. "Down! Stay down!"

"It's okay," I laugh as I pet the energetic dogs. Peter shakes his head.

"It might be okay for you but they are big dogs. I don't want them jumping on my nieces or nephews, they'll knock 'em straight over." Peter explains his reasoning. I nod in understanding. Peter points a finger at them. "Stay."

Once inside, I take my work boots off. I haven't been on a roofing job but figured I'd better have proper footwear. I smile at the sight that greets me. Corinne is in the kitchen, sipping tea at the table and Dickie is playing with his granddaughter, who is in a jumper, giggling and clapping her hands.

"Always helping, huh, Daisy?" Dickie slaps my shoulder as I walk to the kitchen behind Peter.

"You betcha," I respond, my heart melting at the affection Corinne and Peter share. He'd kissed her forehead and is holding onto her swollen stomach. Both of them stare down at the cherished little life in her womb. My stomach grumbles loudly, ruining the moment. I blush as Corinne laughs at me.

"No, no," Peter gently pushes her down. "I'll make Daisy some food, you sit down."

"Oh, Peter, I'm allowed to cook." Corinne rolls her eyes at me, her arms resting on her stomach. I sit at the table, embarrassed at my empty stomach. My dad always taught me to be ready a good half hour before anyone needed my help. I definitely did not do that this morning.

"It's my love for you two," Peter kisses his wife's hairline, his eyes motioning to the baby in her belly.

"Let me tell you," Dickie adds with a grin. Sometime in my walk to the kitchen, Reece had located in his arms. "Peter truly does love you if he's *volunteering* to cook." We all laugh at Peter's expense. He doesn't seem to mind as he takes out a mixing bowl, some measuring cups, and baking ingredients.

"I can help," I offer, standing up. I'm the guest here but I'm also the hired hand. I should be working.

"Go lay down," Peter shakes his head at me. Dickie notices the slightly worried look Peter shoots me. I try to say I can still help but a yawn interrupts me. "I'll wake you up at ten Daisy," Peter continues. "Four hours of sleep isn't enough rest for a day of roofing outside."

"Daisy, go rest." Dickie frowns. "Sometimes you push yourself too hard, little lady."

"Why only four hours?" Corinne asks as Reece squirms in her grandfather's arms. He sings softly while rocking her.

"Work, volunteering, training for the marathon," Peter answers for me and points to the living room. He's not taking no for an answer. "Couch or spare room?"

"Y'all are bossy," I grumble, but I'm happy. The Watsons are good people, they actually care. I love the Watson's, the God-fearing family. It's nice to hang around people that I can talk about God to, not try and hide my faith.

"So?" Peter asks as he puts an apron on. I've never seen him in one, only Pierre and Dickie, the rest of Dickie's boys are too macho for them but apparently not in front of their wives.

"The couch is fine," I roll my eyes and stand up with a yawn. My body is tired and sore, and my period is due any day. Aunt Flow from Red River makes me clumsy and uncoordinated. I hope it doesn't show in my work today.

"Sleep well, sweetie," Corinne wishes me. I shoot her a smile. While Amy and Paul aren't a good match, Corinne was made for Peter. That doesn't mean they don't have their squabbles but Corinne has never kicked Peter out or threatened to leave as Amy does to Paul.

"Thanks," I walk to the couch and flop on it, exhausted. Dickie follows, setting Reece on the floor before tossing me a throw blanket. "Thanks. God bless you guys."

"God bless you too, Daisy," Dickie sits in the recliner as Reece crawls around the living room rug. I make the sign of the cross and pray to my guardian Angel to keep me safe through this sleep. As I am saying amen, my eyelids are closing and my breathing slowing.

"Holy Mary, mother of God, pray for us sinners now and at the hour of our death. Amen. Hail Mary, full of Grace,..." I mumble and rollover.

"Hey, Daisy," someone gently shakes me by placing their hand on my shoulder and pushing. "Hey Daisy, it's time to wake up."

"And blessed is the fruit of thy womb, Jesus." I yawn and open my eyes. Dried eye boogers make my eyes sting as they open and I curl my hands into fists and rub them away.

"You up Daisy?" Corinne asks with a laugh. My thoughts woke me up faster than she did. I'm supposed to be helping Peter take his roof down today! I better get going!

"Uh-huh," I mumbled, sitting up. Once my eyes are clear, I look around. "Um, where's Peter?"

"He's already on the roof," Corinne smiles at me. My eyes widen. I came to work yet I'm sleeping! I shouldn't let others see how tired I am, it shouldn't affect me too much. I love helping people!

"I shouldn't have napped!" I leap off the couch, brushing my hair out of my face. Dickie laughs from the recliner, little Reece napping in his arms.

"It's okay Daisy," he states. "Peter knows how tired you were."

"I came to work!" I dig in my overall pockets for a ponytail. Corinne and Dickie share a look before shrugging. I fold my thick, curly hair into a ponytail, dismayed when my ponytail snaps. Guess whose hair won't be pinned back today?

"Who were you praying for Daisy?" Dickie asks as Corinne takes my place on the couch. She even has a pregnancy pillow to help her relax. If Peter didn't buy it for her, one of his sisters probably did. They're very generous towards each other but not to themselves.

"Haha, what?" I furrow my eyebrows as I make my way to the mud room. I'll put my boots on and run to the garage where I'm sure Peter has half the work already done.

"No Daisy!" Corinne calls lazily after me. I can't deny her as my stomach rumbles loudly in hunger. "Peter left you a plate of pancakes!"

"I have to go work!" I deny it, pushing my feet into my boots. I'd love the food but I came here to work, not eat. Besides, I can work for a couple of hours without eating. I spend Wednesdays and Fridays fasting on bread and water.

"The work will get done on God's time," Dickie calmly says. "In the meantime, the good God doesn't want you getting dizzy spells on rooftops."

"That's fair," I concede, stepping out of my boots. Dickie has spent every Sunday and daily mass since he was sixteen in the church if he could make it. He prays a lot and has read the bible at least fifty times, meditating over passages in the gospels every day. With his prayer life and spirituality, I expect him to be wiser than me, than a lot of people.

"Have as many as you want," Corinne gestures to the tall stack of pancakes on the table. They are still warm even with my two-hour nap as I pull the top one off.

"So what were you praying about?" Dickie asks. Spotting the jam and sugar on the table, yet another Watson tradition. I spread jam on a pancake and sprinkle sugar over it, then roll it up.

"Huh?" I make the sign of the cross and pray over my food, making the sign of the cross over my food also as I end my prayer.

"You were praying in your sleep," Corinne informs me as she turns the TV on. I shrug as I take a big bite out of the pancake-jam-roll. It's delicious.

"Even in my sleep, I pray to God for all the lost souls," I shrug again. "My dad used to wonder what it meant until he decided not to question God. I've always done it since I could talk."

"That's wonderful," Dickie smiles at the little story. I'd love to hear their stories about prayer, God, church, and family. Me and my dad know all of each other's stories by now, after sharing and reflecting on them for years.

"There's a little water bottle you can use while roofing." Corinne points to the plastic purple Contigo water bottle. These people are so generous, no other boss of mine would do this for me.

"Thanks," I toast it to her as I stuff the rest of the pancake in my mouth and put my shoes on.

"Gloves on the counter!" Corinne hollers after me. I spot the yellow leather gloves on the shelf by the door.

"Thanks," I mumble, grabbing the leather gloves and opening the door. Dogs bark and Samson and Rufus run energetically at me. I laugh and pet them as I make my way to Peter's detached garage.

"Good nap?" Peter asks from on top of the roof. He has his truck parked by the edge and is ripping the shingles off, throwing them into the box of his truck.

"Yeah," I mutter, blushing as I spot the ladder and start climbing up. He's already sweating from his work even though it's fall. Soon I won't be able to ride my moped on the roads due to snow and cold weather.

"I'll take the shingles off, you pull the nails out." Peter orders, handing me his hammer. I nod, spotting where he had stopped, and sit on the roof, my legs spread out. Peter laughs. "No fear, girl. Good for you."

"What you mean?" I ask, frowning when I have to lean my whole weight onto the hammer. It still doesn't pull the nail out.

"Most people don't just sit on the roof," Peter walks my way, staying clear of the edge. I see he's afraid of heights. "Here, I'll show you what to do."

"Sorry," I murmur, blushing as I move out of his way. "I haven't done this before."

"No worries," Peter replies, putting the hammer on the nail. He mimes how to pull the nail out. "You hit the handle, it jerks the nail and uses more force to pull the nail out."

"Okay," I take the hammer from him. He watches as I hit the handle, shaking my hand from the pain right after. Peter chuckles.

"It might hurt a little," he warns a little late.

"Thanks for telling me," I dryly reply as I hit the handle softer. The nail doesn't move as much but it still moves, and for that I'm thankful. Hopefully, this work doesn't act up my arthritis.

"Thanks for the help," Peter quickly replies. I roll my eyes. We're both going to try and be humble about this so I decide to say nothing as I focus on pulling out nails. With my thoughts on Tyler and his brothers, I offer my hard work up for the triplets, their brothers and parents, and their whole extended family, including the man on the roof and the pregnant woman in the house.

→ 7 ←

Coupled Together

————=▷•◁=————

"W anna come?" Col asks, twirling his keys through his fingers. I look at my dad to see what he thinks, having just got here after a hard day of roofing. Dickie made us delicious lettuce and tomato sandwiches for lunch and a nice, filling clam chowder with bacon for supper. That being said, Dickie is an amazing cook, that will always be my opinion. Dad gives me a nod to say it's okay.

"Where?" I ask, noticing his arm around Danae's shoulders. It seems to be getting comfy there, although last year he seemed to have broken her heart into a billion shards. He saved her from bullies one day, she grew a crush on him and was working up the courage to ask him out when he started dating April, March's younger sister. They'd lasted all of two weeks before Landon hooked up with her. It had put a dent in Col's friendship with Landon, and they still aren't close anymore but at least they can talk to each other now. April's dating Jett Hendrix now. He never shows up to school but might be voted valedictorian, that's how smart he is.

"Beer run," Col opens the passenger door for Danae. I look to the fire, where my dad is visiting with Romain, Col's parents, and Jonah's dad. With their big family, Betty and Esther often get stuck babysitting for Annakin and his wife's night off. Annakin's wife had decided not to come today unless she was inside the house with Col's mom.

"I'm gonna see if Jonah wants to come too," I state before jogging to the fire. Jonah is having a beer with Angela, her boyfriend, Jesus, Alex Watson, Dickie's youngest daughter, and Col's older brother, Leo, and his girlfriend, Amy, Danae's oldest sister.

"Hey girl," Alex toasts her can of Twisted Tea to me. I wiggle my eyebrows at her, knowing why she's here. Romain invited her. He says with his recent divorce that he doesn't want a girlfriend but he always invites her to gatherings, stops to visit her in town, and shows up at her apartment.

"You made it," Jonah smiles at me, offering me a can of beer. I shake my head and jut my thumb at Col's jacked-up diesel truck.

"Yeah," I shoot him a smile as I nod at the rest of the group. Amy and Leo ignore me, the usual because they think I'm too religious but Jesus and Angela wave. "Wanna come for the beer run?"

"Col asked you to go?" Jonah asks, chugging his beer to finish it. That's my answer there. He doesn't drive with open cans so he's coming.

"Yeah," I jut my thumb to the truck. "They're waiting for me."

"Yeah, sure," Jonah stands up. His arm wraps around my shoulders. Apparently, everyone is coupling up tonight and my partner happens to be Jonah. My dad is always the single guy at these parties. Sometimes, and I cringe to think of it, he hangs out with Aria, Dickie's oldest daughter at thirty-two years old. She's a flight attendant, so it's not often she's in town. "How are you?"

"Kinda sore," I admit. I didn't even go to mass this morning because I fell asleep, I didn't get my morning prayers done either so I'm making myself stay up after the get-together to pray. I need it. I don't want to fall off my own spiritual bandwagon by skipping a day of prayer. I already missed morning prayer time, scripture reading and meditation, and daily mass. How can people survive without God in their life? Without Him, my life would be meaningless, headed for eternal destruction.

"From what?" Jonah opens the door and helps me up. What a gentleman.

"Hey," Col nods at us, putting the truck in gear and driving off before Jonah even closes the door. Col isn't being rude, that's what he does to everyone.

"I spent the day roofing for Peter Watson," I sit in the middle because the seat behind the passenger seat has a saddle in it. He must have gone riding today.

"What's the pay like?" Col asks. He works for the county but wouldn't mind a side job, his RAP program will be over when he graduates.

"Well, it wasn't for his construction business. He just wanted help with his garage roof and his brothers couldn't help." I never answer money questions as long as I can help it. I've noticed money makes people envious, not to mention greedy.

"Have you even roofed before?" Danae asks, fiddling with her fingers in her lap. Col reaches over and takes one hand, lacing his fingers through hers. My eyes widen and I elbow Jonah to look.

"Shh," he laughs, his mouth by my ear. I lean away from him, curling my hair behind my ears. It immediately pops back out.

"Well no, but I'm a quick study." Col catches my eyes in the rearview mirror and holds him and Danae's hands up.

"Keeping this on the down low," he states. I nod as Jonah raises his hands. The interior of Col's truck is grey, with blue and red dotted seats, an older model. He has an aux cord available but no Bluetooth. The front seat has three seats as well as the back, and the middle seatbelts only fasten around a person's waist. I feel bad but Jonah hadn't put his seat belt on and I'd followed his lead. There wasn't a buckle if I'm in the mood for making myself an excuse.

"No judgment, bro." Jonah rests his hand on the back of the seat. If I lean back, my neck will rest on his arm instead. In the front seat, I can see Danae blushing a deep red.

"Been a long time coming," I speak up, teasing the two. Col simply laughs as Danae blushes harder. Neither is on the romantic side so it's nice to see them holding hands. I understand why they aren't telling anyone about their relationship. She's fourteen, he's eighteen. The world would assume he only wants one thing from her. Besides, Danae's dad would flip. Now that she's fourteen she's not even allowed to camp over with Richie, she's only allowed to camp at the Layton's to visit Esther and often uses that as her excuse to stay the night with Col. She even has her own room there so I hope they aren't doing anything like sleeping together.

"Wanna go for a run tomorrow?" Jonah asks, his fingers twisting strands of my hair. I know he's been drinking but not how much. By the way, he's acting, I'd say he's buzzed. That might be why he's being more forward with me.

"I try to have my rest day on Sundays," I let him down softly. He accepts it. That's what I like about Jonah, he's a really chill guy. He accepts what is and lets go of what isn't, not a grudge holder yet a peace-keeper.

"One of the commandments, right?"

"Someone was paying attention during mass," I turn to him, impressed. He'd agreed to come to the soup kitchen with me on Tuesdays and go to mass afterward from now on. I appreciate that he chose me to teach him about God even with my limited knowledge. I'm thinking of taking a gap year after graduation to attend St Therese Institute. It has a nine-month program to delve deeper into my Catholic faith. "I'm impressed."

"You do something, you gotta do it right," Jonah shrugs, opening his window to let the chilly breeze through. Col and Danae have their own little conversation in the front so I turn even more in the seat to see Jonah better.

"Peter said that today," I smile at him, cat stretching. My back cracks as I sigh in relief at the stretch. Roofing isn't that hard of work but it takes endurance to do it all day, bending, pulling, pushing, throwing, and hauling. It's mostly my arms and back that are sore.

"Here," Jonah turns me around so my back is facing him. Streetlights appear as we enter town limits. One is flickering on and off, amusing Col as he proceeds to tell Danae a scary story. I sigh and lean back in relief when Jonah begins massaging my shoulders and back.

"Mmmm," I groan, "thanks, Jonah."

"Yeah, no problem," he kneads his knuckles into my back. I hum, enjoying the slight pain knowing I won't be as sore tomorrow. Col turns onto a side road where the liquor store is located, conveniently by the grocery store and tire shop slash car wash.

"Wanna come in Jonah?" Col asks as he pulls into the gravel parking.

"Sure," Jonah responds, checking his pockets for his wallet. "We gotta buy for Romain, Leo, Alex, and Duncan, right?"

"And ourselves," Col adds with a grin as he hands Jonah some money. It's a pretty thick stack, a couple of hundreds and some fifties. My dad and his friends are partying it up tonight. Col and Jonah both laugh and hop out of the lifted truck. Danae immediately turns toward me with a cheeky smile.

"We already asked Jonah to come before you did," her smile widens as she continues with her sentence. "He said no. The guy is jelly in your hands and you don't even know."

"It's putty," I deflect with a blush darkening my skin. I'm lucky I'm so dark-skinned, blushes are hard to notice. Danae rolls her eyes.

"He likes you," she states bluntly. I love her for it. At least with her shyness, she has confidence underneath.

"I've been getting that feeling," I admit, twirling my hair. Jonah is a nice guy but I don't feel the spark, the romance but maybe we're a couple where love comes softly. Who knows?

"Col told me about a hug," Danae encourages me to spill the story. Maybe she's a romantic at heart, not really showing it to the outside world. People used to say she saw the world through rose-tinted glasses until she met Col, but her family had only moved here two years ago.

"I'm not sure I like him," I state, going the complete opposite direction she wanted me to. I shrug at her shocked look. "He's nice and all, I know a relationship with him would be a good one but I'm stuck on Tyler."

"Perfect way to find if Tyler's interested in you," Danae shrugs as the liquor store door slams shut and Col appears with three big boxes of Lucky if that's a type of beer. I'm not one hundred percent sure but the beer is in a bright red box.

"I'm not going to use anyone," my voice raises a little. Danae smirks as she sips from her water bottle. She is definitely more than meets the eye, why haven't I known her sooner? We'd have been great friends. We will be great friends if I date Jonah or even hang out with him more. I hadn't known Jonah and Col hung out with each other this much but it makes sense if their parents drink together. Dad never pushed the parties on me, letting me stay home alone even at eight years old. I'd matured early for my age. The priest let me accept the Eucharist at six years old, most kids wait until the age of reason, seven years old.

"I know, but you could date Jonah and you might come to like him after all." Ah, my love comes softly thought. I'll talk to my dad and mention my feelings to Tyler. If I do have a relationship with Jonah, it will be because I know Tyler has no interest in me. My life isn't the classic bad boy falls for good girl rom-com.

"That's a thought," I nod my head in agreement. "I'll talk to my dad and pray on it."

"You're gonna talk to your dad?" Danae deadpans in disbelief. I nod as Col puts the three big boxes of beer in the box of the truck. He keeps a little bottle of Jack Daniel's for himself as he climbs into the truck.

"We have an open relationship!" I defend myself. Col looks at us weirdly but shrugs it off as he tucks his bottle under his seat.

"I'm trying to give her relationship advice!" Danae gestures to me. "She wants to talk to her dad, Col! Tell her what a bad idea it is!"

"Her dad might not be as overprotective or overbearing as your dad." He sticks up for me. For that I am grateful. "But rose-tinted glasses, Danae. She'll learn the hard way if she has to." Now I'm not so grateful.

"I just don't want you to get hurt," Danae says pointedly as Jonah exits the store, a big case of Budweiser, a six-pack of Twisted Tea, and three big bottles of Jose Cuervo. He throws the cans in the box and hands me the three bottles. They're heavier in my hands than expected and I just about drop them as he climbs into Col's truck and closes the door.

"Whoa!" I screech, "stop!"

"What?" Col slams on the brakes as Danae yells.

"There's a little cat there!" I point to the street light to the left of the liquor store. Danae rolls her eyes as Col shakes his head. The poor white kitten looks like it's shivering in the chilly night.

"I'm too far away to run over it!"

"But it's a little kitten, lost! No one leaves their kitten in the middle of the road. It's getting cold at night!" It seems like a playful kitten as it jumps and crawls and swats at pebbles.

"Calm down Daisy," Jonah says placidly. "Next time say it calmly. I thought Col was gonna run over someone or something."

"Oh," I blush deeply. I should have thought about that before raising my voice. They did have something to drink already, that's probably why Col was driving more road conscientious than usual. "Sorry."

"Can we go now?" Col asks, putting his truck back in reverse.

"Wait!" I raise my voice a little with that word and lower it again, looking at the other three passengers guiltily. "Can I take it home?"

"You're just going to adopt a stray cat?" Danae deadpans, looking out the windshield at the little white kitten that had veered closer to the store. Light provides heat but now she's exposed to predators.

"Yes!"

"Been more than cats in here," Col parks his truck again. "But if you can't catch it, we're leaving."

"Thank you! Thank you!" I slide over Jonah's lap and open the door. My quick movements make the kitten scamper back but she notices I'm not too much of a threat when I crouch down and walk gently towards her. Soon she is meowing pitifully while purring in my hands. I curl her into my sweater and hop back in the truck.

"Now can we go?" Danae asks, looking in awe at the cute little albino cat. I nod and she nods at Col. He begins driving again as the cat purrs in my arms, crawling about. Even Jonah pets the cute little guy.

"I think it's a girl," I state, laughing when she crawls onto my shoulder and stays there. Apparently, she likes her perch up there.

"Got any names?" Jonah asks, rubbing his hand over her small, skinny body. His fingers tickle my ear.

"Sweetie," I say and laugh in joy when she purrs even louder. She must like her new name.

"I think Duncan said Aria will be here tonight," Col speaks up. I frown. As Catholic as my dad is, he isn't all the way. He's not divorced, only separated but hasn't seen my mother or talked to her in fourteen years. We don't even know if she's dead or alive. The church wouldn't allow him to marry again or have a girlfriend, that's cheating but he's dating Aria anyways, on and off.

"Anywhere I can crash?" I laugh softly, hurting at the pain my dad is putting himself through. I've seen him after nights with her, he enjoys them and loves her but they both were raised Catholic, and both feel the guilt afterward. I pray every day that one day they will get the together ending they want.

"Mine," Jonah speaks up after a moment of silence from the other two. Col's siblings are there for the weekend which means the spare rooms are taken and Danae can't ask her parents without letting them know that she was somewhere she wasn't supposed to be. It sucks because her family is at church every Sunday as well. I hate feeling like a liar when I face them. Besides, both Col and Danae's parents don't allow animals in the house. I know Jonah's parents do.

"Thanks," I lean back into the seat. It's not too far of a drive but I'm exhausted, not used to working with fresh air outdoors compared to the brisk albeit stale air indoors at work or the soup kitchen. Sweetie jumps into my lap, curling into a ball. Her purring makes me drowsy, content now to go to sleep even though I know people will be getting drunk and sinning tonight. When my dad parties, I usually pray that he and his friends don't commit the sin of drunkardness and for any and all other people that might have a problem with alcohol, always with the intercession of St Matt Talbot. Jonah pulls me into his chest and I accept it, my eyes fluttering closed. I'd worked hard today and should be sleeping peacefully in my bed. Col and Danae start another conversation as I make the sign of the cross and ask my guardian Angel to protect me as I sleep. As I'm saying amen my mind is shutting down. Sweetie and Jonah keep me warm enough to sleep until the party is over and Jonah drives me and his dad home. Annakin reassures my dad at least three times that I'm not leaving with Jonah, I'm crashing on the spare bed. My dad kisses me goodnight, leaving in the vehicle after Annakin's with Aria in the passenger seat. Once at Annakin's mansion, Annakin quickly slips into his room where his wife is waiting.

"Goodnight kiddos," Annakin slaps Jonah's back. Sweetie is crawling in my arms, whining and meowing loudly for food.

"Here," Jonah leads me to their large walk-in pantry. He grabs two medium-sized containers for food and water. He fills them up while I try to keep Sweetie calm. She's excited at the nutrients coming her way. "I'll take the spare room tonight," Jonah offers as Sweetie chows down on kitty nibble. "My room doesn't have a rug in case she has an accident."

"Thanks, Jonah but I can't kick you out of your own room. We can sleep in the garage or something." We walk up a large set of stairs and take a left in the hallway. The walls are beautiful sky blue with white trim. Pictures painted by Jonah's younger siblings line the walls, every year they have handprints and footprints plastered onto canvasses to show their growth. It's cute, if I have kids I want to follow this tradition. A voice in the back of my mind tells me I can have this if I marry Jonah. I block it out as he opens the last door on the right.

"You aren't sleeping in the garage," Jonah states firmly, ushering me into his room. "You want some pajamas?"

"Yes please," I'm startled when Sweetie jumps out of my arms. Jonah has a faster reaction than me and closes his bedroom door.

"I'll watch her while you change," Jonah digs in his black dresser for a matching set of pj's. "The door closest to the hallway is a bathroom. Just make sure the other door is locked because I share the bathroom with Betty and unlock it when you're done."

"Okay," I yawn in response. We both laugh as I rub my blurry eyes. I accidentally turn the fan on instead of the light, scaring me into more alertness but quickly switch the light on and flick the fan off. It's a relief to take my bra off. After working hard, it was sweaty and making my skin itch. Jonah's shirt and pants fit nicely on my body, except for the tightness around my curves. I fold my clothes and pile them by the door to change into for the morning. Jonah's family is skinny but maybe one of his sister's clothes will fit me. I need nice clothes for church.

"Okay," Jonah jumps up from his bed. My eyes land on the alarm clock on his nightstand. It's one thirty-one the morning. "I'll let you get some sleep."

"I have to pray first," I mumble, crossing my arms over my chest at the nakedness I feel. I'm sleeping at someone else's house, I should have kept my bra on.

"Uh," Jonah pauses on that word, dragging it out. He looks indecisive but asks me a question. "Want me to join?"

"You want to pray?" I beam at him, trotting to the bed with more energy. "That's great! Do you know any prayers?"

"Uh, the basics?" Jonah questions as he slides onto the foot of the bed. I throw the blankets around me and lean back in bed.

"Wanna say the rosary?"

"Yeah, sure," Jonah falls forward, lying on his stomach. Sweetie jumps on the king-sized bed, making a little nest by my feet.

"Okay," I make the sign of the cross and Jonah follows me. "I believe in God, the Father Almighty,..." I'm not even finished with the Apostles Creed before I'm out like a light. It's the first day since I was thirteen that I missed my daily prayer and the first day in a year I hadn't gone to daily mass. Already I feel the spiritual decline.

8

Not A Thing

———⇒⊳•◦•◁⇐———

"B lessed are thou amongst women and blessed..." I murmur in my sleep. With a yawn and a stretch, I roll over in bed, frowning at the pillow under my head. I'm used to my small, flat pillow, not a soft, thick pillow. Sweetie screeches as my feet push her off the bed and I jerk up, also falling off the bed in the process. I manage to take all the blankets with me.

"I'm sorry Sweetie!" I mumble drowsily, drying my crying eyes with my fists. There are also hard eye boogers which makes it hard to keep my eyes open. She seems to accept my apology as she rubs against my legs. Jonah's head appears above the foot of the bed and I back up farther, wrapping the blankets tighter around me.

"You're cute in the morning," Jonah grins at me, his voice thick with sleep. Was that a come-on? I look frantically between the bed, him and me. Obviously, we didn't do anything but why isn't he in the spare room?! Oh, my dad is not going to be happy. I'm not happy! I promised myself I will not go down this path of tempting myself into the near occasion of sin!

"Why aren't you in the spare room?" I accuse, running my fingers through my thick, curly hair. It's useless when they get stuck in multiple tangles. I'm going to need my hairspray to get them all out, which is the usual occurrence every morning. Jonah stares at me thoughtfully. I know how slow I can be in the morning so I give him some time.

"Uh, we fell asleep praying?" He finally drawls out in a questioning manner. Sweetie jumps in my lap and I hold her there, scratching her jaw and the top of her head.

"I did!" I run my hands over my face, sighing in dismay when I feel dried drool around my lips. I am not a pretty sleeper. Jonah cocks his head at me with another grin as he coughs to clear his throat.

"Does that mean we're still technically in prayer?" He wiggles his eyebrows at me. I sigh deeply. That is not what we should be discussing. Sweetie meows to be petted so I place my hands back on her as I deadpan stare at Jonah.

"Yeah, I guess, technically!" I hiss, hanging my head to catch a breath and get control of my emotions. *Oh, Jesus, I am sorry.* Sweetie sniffs my breath. She's a cute little white kitten, a little on the smaller side than I would like. It looks like she hasn't eaten enough food the past few days, maybe even a week.

"Daisy, it's okay," Jonah states slowly, licking his teeth. "It was an accident."

"I'm gonna, I'm gonna pray," I look at Jonah. He gets the message I'm sending that I want to pray in private.

"I'll hit the shower," he yawns. I content myself to pet Sweetie while he picks out clean clothes from a walk-in closet. I've been in the house before but I hadn't realized the Laytons were this rich before. Annakin and Vanessa have eleven kids and only the twins share a room but the rooms are massive. My dad and I could fit our little cabin in Jonah's room. With the bathroom door closing behind a relaxed Jonah, I make the sign of the cross and engage in my morning prayer routine. Seven Glory Be's to my guardian Angel and seven Glory Be's to the Holy Spirit. Sweetie doesn't want to leave me alone so I stand up to pace the room, the cover sheet wrapped around my shoulders like a cape as I begin to recite the rosary, meditating on the Glorious Mysteries. I can feel my panic drifting away as I surrender my heart to God, accepting the joy that flows from Christ's defeat of death. God knows everything, He knows what is in my heart, that last night had been an accident. I'll still go to confession, of course, but it's going to be alright.

I notice as Jonah walks out of the bathroom, stylishly dressed as usual. He's wearing very light blue jeans with a black button-up. The contrast is striking. Jonah stares at my frozen body with a slightly nervous smile as he dries his hair with his fingers. "You can shower if you want?" He points to the bathroom door.

"I need, um, stuff..." my face burns in embarrassment. I hang my head when Jonah explains the type of body wash and shampoo in the bathroom. Unbeknownst to Jonah, sometime during his shower, shark week attacked. "You wanna watch Sweetie while I shower?"

"Yeah, sure," Jonah picks up my new kitten. His smile is adorable when Sweetie begins purring immediately. "Waters already warm."

"Thanks," I shoot him a smile as I walk skip to the bathroom. When inside, I make sure that both entrances are locked before digging into the cupboards. I feel awful for doing so but he shares the bathroom with Betty. All sixteen-year-olds I know have their periods already. She has to have supplies. I hit gold on the left-hand side of the second sink, closer to her room. Sighing in relief I get everything ready and hop in the shower.

"Jonah!" Betty shouts and bangs on the door. I jump in surprise as I dry myself off with the towel Jonah left by my folded-up clothes. "You don't need two showers! Get out!"

I stare at the door. Jonah's siblings were all asleep when we got here last night. I can't answer. She'll know it's not Jonah but I can't hide stuff. That's not who I am. "Jonah! I really have to pee!"

"I'll, um, I'll just be a second!" I finally venture a reply. Now I'm the one met with silence. I laugh nervously when Betty's bedroom door opens and she races down the hall to Jonah's bedroom door. He answers immediately. Oh boy, this day has not gone off on the right start. I spot the Listerine on Jonah's side of the bathroom and swish some in my mouth as they talk on the other side. I'm giving him time to explain the story so she understands by the time I'm exiting the bathroom.

"Huh," Betty smiles brightly at me. Jonah glares at her. "Mornin' Daisy."

"Good morning Betty," I pick Sweetie up. "Sorry for taking so long."

"Yeah, you really needed to go." Jonah crosses his arms over his chest and raises an eyebrow. It's funny to see. He's not usually bossy but his younger siblings bring it out of him, more likely because Betty was annoying him by peppering him with questions.

"I should have seen this coming," Betty skips past us. I furrow my eyebrows at her then look to Jonah in confusion.

"Should have seen what?" I ask, setting Sweetie down to help Jonah make his bed. It's a big bed, king-sized, with ample space for four people. Jonah's bedding, like his dresser, is black. His bedroom walls are the same light blue but the trim work is black. I never expected all this black from him although it does make sense. If Jonah's pants aren't black, his shirts and sweaters are.

"She thinks we're a thing," Jonah rolls his eyes at me. I stare at him in disbelieving annoyance as we each hospital tuck the end of his blankets in. Jonah raises his hands in mock surrender. "I told her she was grasping."

"Hopefully she listens," I say brightly, trying to cheer myself up. What I did wasn't that bad. We fell asleep praying, that's all.

"C'mon," Jonah leads me to the door. Sweetie scampers behind us, not wanting to be left alone. She's already formed an attachment to us, or me. "My mom probably has breakfast ready."

I follow silently behind him through the grand hallway and even grander staircase. That sentence isn't a strange sentence in itself but to me it was foreign. My mom never made me breakfast, I don't even know how she looks. My dad doesn't have pictures. He won't tell me her name, just that she had a drug problem and couldn't stay clean after I was born. He gave her the option to stay sober or leave because he wanted to raise me in a loving home. She chose to leave. The only other thing I know about her is that she wanted to name me Bambi.

"Penny for your thoughts?" Jonah asks as we round a slight corner and walk through a little hallway. The kitchen is huge with an even bigger dining room. It kind of has to be with eleven kids with friends constantly over.

"Morning Jonah," his dad greets, then takes a sip of his coffee before flipping the page of the newspaper. Old school, how cute. Sweetie lies down by my feet, content for another nap already.

"How was your sleep, honey?" Vanessa, Jonah's mom, asks with a smile. A cute, chubby baby sits in a high chair. A cute brown-haired, light sky blue-eyed, pigtailed, freckle-faced little girl sits in another high chair. I'm not well enough acquainted with Jonah's family to know all his sibling's names. This is the first time I've camped at someone's house, usually accepting the loft in the barn as my bed for the night so dad could have his privacy. It's odd, to have a friend. Jonah might actually be my first friend since third grade. Is it weird to make friends gift baskets?

"It was good." Jonah looks at me. I smile in appreciation. He's giving me the option to tell his parents. And I do.

"I, um, I, well, me and Jonah fell asleep praying last night. I'm sorry." I meet both Vanessa and Annakin's eyes for a second before dipping my head down. Jonah gauges his parent's reactions as he pours himself a glass of milk. Vanessa looks amused as Annakin frowns.

"You're both good kids," Vanessa smiles warmly at us as she places more batter on the pancake grill. Relief flows through my heart. "We trust you." Then she looks at Annakin for him to follow her lead. His frown deepens as he shakes his head.

"Thanks, mom." Jonah half hugs his mother. "Means a lot but it's not gonna happen again."

"Can I talk to you outside, Jonah?" Annakin demands as he folds his newspaper. He has to walk past me to get to the patio doors behind me.

"I'm sorry," I mumble, licking my lips. I pick Sweetie up to avoid looking at him. Annakin nods, accepting my apology.

"I'm not mad at you, Daisy." He gives me a curt nod before holding the door open for Jonah. Jonah's body is stiff as he follows his dad, I can tell it is a slight sense of fear. His body was like that when those guys rammed into his truck.

"Want any breakfast?" Vanessa offers. Two identical young girls run into the room, scowling and waving behind them.

"Mom!" One whines, she has curly long blonde hair that bounces as she walks while the other one has straight blonde hair cut in a bob.

"Sam won't leave us alone!" The shorter-haired one complains, pointing behind her. It's then that I notice the curly dark brown-haired boy hiding behind the corner.

"Sam, be nice to your sisters. Mary Alice and Anne Marie, stop whining. It's two against one, fight back." Betty walks into the kitchen with Esther, pulling her light brown hair into a ponytail.

"Dad's talking to Jonah?" Betty grins and shoots Esther a look. They seem to talk silently to themselves. I frown and bite my lips at what they are insinuating as the twins greet the toddler and baby. It's already starting to get loud. As a single child, I'm in no way prepared for it. Sweetie jumps off my lap and starts walking around the kitchen.

"Girls," Vanessa warns as she gives them a look to stay quiet. She shares another reassuring smile with me as she flips the pancakes. "Jonah is an adult now, he can make his own decisions."

I balk at Vanessa's words. She's on Betty's side, she thinks Jonah and I are an item. We aren't dating, we might but only the future will tell. He likes me and I might be starting to form a crush. "What mom?" Betty asks with a smirk.

"Jonah finally brought a girl home," Esther adds. My face burns a deep red at her comment. I busy myself with finding Sweetie by Vanessa's feet. *Jonah finally brought a girl home.* Apparently, he's never invited... my thoughts trail off. Jonah has female classmates he talks to, sure, but he doesn't make a way to hang out with them. Sometimes he talks to April and May but that's because they're Art's sisters, the same goes for Danae. She's Chris and Karl's sister. They're both on the football team with Col and the two triplets. Danae uses them as her excuse to stay and watch practices, her brothers pick up on her crush but Col doesn't give anything away.

"Jonah's got a girlfriend?" Sam shouts as he runs into the kitchen, looking me over. He grins excitedly as he runs back out, hollering. "Nate! Larry! Jonah has a girlfriend! She's hot!" Pounding feet answer his shouts. Jonah's brothers apparently all want a look at me. Esther and Betty laugh.

"Ignore him," Vanessa sighs with a smile. I pick up Sweetie because she is wrapping her body around Vanessa's ankles. It's a tripping hazard. Once I have her securely in my arms, I make my way back to the barstool of the breakfast niche of the kitchen island.

"Boys will be boys," Esther and Betty chorus. I try to melt into the stool I'm sitting on.

"Stop embarrassing her," Vanessa laughs, stirring chocolate chips into the batter. The door opens and Annakin and his son walk in. Jonah smiles at me although the smile is thin.

"You ready to go home, Daisy?" I nod in relief. Jonah smiles at that, noticing his sisters beside me. They wiggle their eyebrows and shoot him knowing looks.

"Come again!" Vanessa invites me as Betty and Esther sit at the table. One grabs the salt and pepper shaker to place out of reach of the toddler's sticky hands and the other coos to the baby.

"Nate, Larry! She's leaving!" Sam hollers. I deadpan stare at Jonah as I pick up Sweetie. She seems fine for car rides but I don't know how she feels getting into vehicles.

"We're taking Betty's car," Jonah informs me as he rolls his eyes at his brother's antics. "Don't wanna add too many km's to the rental."

"Sounds good," I laugh when the door closes as Nate and Larry are just getting to the bottom of the stairs. They groan when they don't get to spot me, Jonah's girlfriend. I climb into the passenger seat and click my seatbelt into place. Sweetie makes herself at home in my lap. "I think Betty thinks we're dating. Your mom and Esther too."

"Ugh," Jonah groans as he drives around the loop of their driveway. His teeth are clenched. His dad might have reamed him out; quietly because I didn't hear raised voices. "She doesn't listen."

"Does your dad think...?" I trail off as I fidget with the rosary in my pocket. It gives me a light sense of peace but not for long. Does his dad think we are dating or that we did the dirty deed? Jonah shrugs but his lips form a sharper line.

"It doesn't matter what he thinks," Jonah mutters, running his hands over his face. His relationship with his dad is now tense, I seem the most probable cause. Is it because I am fifteen or because I'm Duncan's little girl? I won't be able to live with myself if Annakin doesn't agree with Jonah's decision.

"Hey," I say softly. "Don't let me be the reason you have a rift between your father."

"That's what I like about you," Jonah chuckles bittersweetly. The sadness on his face causes an ache in my heart. Sweetie starts to meow so I scratch her body. She immediately begins purring away. "So sweet and selfless."

He most definitely just hit on me. I'm positive this time.

"We all have the choice," I shrug, my eyes welling up with tears. Jonah notices but thankfully doesn't comment. My eyes are wet for his sake, I don't like any confrontation or burden on relationships and that's what I caused between him and his dad.

"Most don't choose what you choose," Jonah signals to turn onto the gravel road. I stay silent because my humbleness will cause us to argue. I believe anyone can choose the right path, and make a better decision if they put their heart into it. My prayers every day are for peace on earth which is created by selfless people making loving decisions.

"You wanna come in for breakfast?" I ask to divert the question. Sweetie senses the car slowing down and jumps on the dash to look at her surroundings. "We have cinnamon buns every Sunday morning."

"Can't say no to that," Jonah grins, accepting my silence. I can't help but look at him hopefully.

"Does that mean you're coming to church?" Jonah laughs at my question but shrugs with a look of uncomfortableness. He's hurting, he's angry and his dad might be blaming him. It doesn't help that I know Jonah enough to know he's already blaming himself for falling asleep when he should have gone to the other room. I shouldn't have asked him to pray with me. A good intention led to bad consequences.

"My heart and mind won't really be in it," he murmurs after a heavy pause. He always does everything with one hundred percent focus, he's driven. I like that about him so I understand his answer but it shouldn't be an excuse for a one-track mind.

"I understand, but don't let him keep you from God." Jonah laughs at that.

"He's actually the religious one," Jonah shakes his head as he bites his bottom lip, talking about his parents. I give him the time to speak, knowing he doesn't mean to talk ill about his parents but he needs to voice his feelings to think through the events. "Mom doesn't really care so most of us didn't either. I'm glad I met you, you helped me rejuvenate my faith."

"God has His own time." I agree as he turns into my driveway. We all just aren't accustomed to God's time. Everything happens when it happens, not when we want it to but when God is ready for us to experience in that place in time.

"I might bring Larry on Tuesday," Jonah smiles happily at his thoughts. His smile makes me beam joyfully. "He mentioned wanting to go."

"That's great!" I unbuckle as he parks next to my dad's truck. Aria's Jeep is behind my moped. Jonah and I walk side by side in silence to my dad's little cabin. Sweetie had run under the deck. I hope she stays there and marks her new home territory. My dad would warn me to keep her locked up until she knows this is her home so she doesn't run away but I'm hoping she stays. If I keep easy access to food and water here, it might keep her coming back.

"Morning dad, Aria," I shoot them a smile as I kick off my shoes. Jonah had held open the door for me and now he gently closes it.

"Mornin' Daisy," my dad grins at me with sticky fingers and bulging cheeks from a big mouthful of a cinnamon bun.

"Don't you think about it," Aria warns as dad snaps his fingers in my direction! When I was younger we used to get our hands as sticky as possible and rub them in each other's faces and hair.

"Thanks, Aria," I laugh as I slide onto a kitchen chair. Aria and my dad started their 'under the covers' dating roughly four years ago but that's as far as their relationship goes. They're in love with each other, sure, but dad can't get married until he's divorced and he has no way of contacting my mom.

"You slept at Layton's last night?" Dad points to Jonah and holds his hand out for a handshake with a goofy grin. I roll my eyes and slap Jonah's hand away when he goes to shake.

"Yeah," I take a deep breath and look at the couple that is basically my parents. "About that..." I trail off. Here I thought I was confident enough to blurt it all out, and get it over with but now that I'm facing my dad it's harder.

"What?" My dad straightens, looking between me and Jonah. Aria's eyes widen as she puts her coffee cup in front of her face to hide her smile. She thinks she knows.

"We slept on the same bed," I point between me and Jonah. "Me and Jonah," as if my dad needed clarification. Dad baffles me when he walks to the kitchen sink and begins to wash his hands. He's always been a contemplative one. Did I make it clear that we didn't do anything? Jonah looks at me, slightly worried. He's only known my goofball of a father, the man that does dumb things when he drinks. Dad spins around, chewing the inside of his cheek.

"Did you touch my daughter?" Jonah steps back from the force of the words directed at him.

"No." We both state firmly before looking at each other. We quickly look back at my dad.

"We fell asleep praying," I insert, hoping to lead my dad to understand. "It's my fault, I asked him to pray with me."

"It's my fault, I fell asleep while praying with her," Jonah says at the same time. Dad cracks a smile, he could never stay mad for long.

"She's got you on her prayer crusade, eh?" He dries his hands on a towel and stands beside Aria, placing his hands on her shoulders.

"It was an accident!" I stare at my dad. He's raised me since I was born, he knows when I am lying. He knows everything about me, what I have in my heart. I'm very open and honest, I hide nothing. He gives me that same respect now that I'm fifteen.

"I am so so sorry, Duncan." Jonah hangs his head and then shakes himself as if he were pulling himself together. Dad starts massaging

Aria's shoulders and she leans into it. It's hard to believe they are dating sometimes, I can see her as my stepmother.

"What were you praying?" Dad asks.

"The rosary," Jonah is faster to reply than me.

"Joyful Mysteries," I supply when my dad simply raises an eyebrow. He nods, accepting it.

"From now on, just stick to the loft, Daisy," Aria smirks at me as she places her sticky hands on my dad's forearms. She's been through some arguments with me and my dad and knows that we are finished with this conversation, if only for now. He might question me without the presence of Jonah. I don't mind, I'm not a liar.

"Okay, dad," I grin as he sighs and grabs the biggest cinnamon bun on the tray. Without warning, he stuffs it on Aria's face.

"Mmm, delicious," she laughs at the dismay on his face. He uses his pointer finger to take some icing off her nose and puts it in his mouth. Totally cringeworthy.

"Have a cinnamon bun," I kick out the last chair at our four-person table for Jonah. He sits down and catches the cinnamon bun my dad launches at him.

"Good reflexes," my dad nods, impressed. "But are his instincts good?"

"What do you mean?" Jonah frowns between the three of us. I take a bite of the cinnamon bun to avoid answering his question.

"Do your instincts want eternal life?" Dad asks with a grin. Aria rolls her eyes at dad's confusing questions.

"He's asking if you are coming to church," I rephrase dad's sentence to translate his meaning.

"Oh, yeah," Jonah toasts his cinnamon bun before taking a huge bite out of it. I look around the table and I'm happy. I have my first friend since grade three eating my dad's special Sunday cinnamon buns, a Ridel family tradition. My dad is happy even though I know this wasn't his dream. He made what he could out of his life and loves it. I'm even fond of Aria after being standoffish with her for the first year of their relationship but they did keep it hidden from me for a while as well.

9

Self Control

Lord Jesus Christ, Son of God, have mercy on me, a sinner.

- the Jesus prayer

———◦———

O utta my f—king way," Landon shoves past me, Danae, and Col. His lips are in a straight, firm, tightly pinched line. Harry follows behind him with a matching scowl. In Landon's rush, he pushes Danae into the lockers but takes no heed as he marches on, shoving other students out of his way. Harry reaches out and smacks someone for mouthing off to his brother. I stare in wide-eyed disbelief as they continue on a rampage, grabbing a garbage can and throwing it down the hall. The clanging is loud and the mess horrible as they stomp to the math classroom for their first class of the day. Tyler, the quiet triplet, isn't seen. It's an easy guess as to why he isn't here and his brothers are so angry.

"I'm gonna go talk to them," I calmly state, kicking myself in the butt mentally. I had made the janitor's goodie baskets but keep forgetting to bring them to school.

"I wouldn't," Col warns as Jonah and March walk up to the little group. It looks like I might have my first group of friends since third grade but I'm trying not to get my hopes up. I'll know for sure when they choose to hang out with me instead of other people, not that I'm testing them. If people want to hang out with me, they can, but I'm not going to stop them from visiting other students.

"What's got them in a bad mood?" Art asks, raising an eyebrow as Landon slams the classroom door shut. The loud crash reverberates through the hallway. Once the door is completely closed students begin to walk and talk through the hallways again. The whole student body knows to be on edge when the triplets are mad.

"Daisy's going to find out," Danae immediately throws me under the bus. Jonah places a hand on my shoulder. Danae wiggles her eyebrows at me while motioning with her eyes to Jonah's contact with my shoulder. I blush. Since she made her statement about Jonah's crush on me, she does everything she can to point out the promise of her prediction. I stick my tongue out at her. She rolls her eyes. At least she hasn't found out about me and Jonah falling asleep in the same bed the other night. That would definitely prove her point.

"That's not a good idea," Jonah repeats Col's warning. I gently pry his hand off. Jonah has a high body temperature and his hands are like heat packets, perfect for winter but not in the heat of spring, summer, and fall.

"By the time I'm done cleaning the garbage up, I'm sure there will be a teacher supervising the classroom." Art nods along, the only one to do so. He quickly stops when he's the only one agreeing with me. "They'll cool off by then," I add. This time no one agrees with me. That is fair though, they've been friends with the triplets for longer whereas I've only heard the rumours.

"You're going to pick up the garbage?" Danae deadpans with a scoff. She waves at my curvy body, sputtering as she looks at me. "You're so... good."

"That's Daisy," Art pipes up, slapping my back. I grimace in pain. Sweetie had a vicious tantrum when I left her in the barn for the night and her attack had been to jump on my back. For such a young kitten, her claws seem to be big, and the scrapes on my back are pretty deep.

"I'll help," Jonah offers. Danae shoots me an 'I told you' look. I roll my eyes at her as Jonah and I walk side by side to the garbage littering the floor. "I'm not grabbing food or wet stuff," Jonah informs me as he pushes a banana peel away with the toe of his shoe.

"Same," Art adds. They're good people, just needing someone to lead them to what good needs to be done. I guess God chose me to be that person.

"Thanks for helping," I shoot him a smile as we pick up empty gum packets, chip bags, granola wrappers, crumpled lined loose-leaf pages, and plenty of tissues. We have to leave the pencil shavings since we don't have a broom.

"It's not as hard to volunteer if I'm not the first one," Art sheepishly laughs with a shrug of his shoulders. "I don't mind helping, it's just hard to do it when no one else steps up."

"I can totally relate," Jonah adds, winking at me. My eyes widen and I quickly focus my attention on putting the lid back on the garbage can so neither of the boys can see my blush. Now that I know Jonah has feelings for me, I can't help but find him attractive. His spiky light blonde hair, his height, his personality, and the way he helps even when no one else jumps on the bandwagon. My crush snuck up on me yet my mind always wanders back to Tyler. I hate that I've started comparing them in my mind.

"I just see where help is needed, and just, ya know, sort of gravitate there," I stutter out as I pull my backpack straps tighter around my shoulders. Unlike normal teenagers, I have a hiking bag as a backpack. One pocket holds my bible, religious reading material for the day, extra rosary beads, and prayer books while the other big pocket holds my textbooks and binders if they fit. Most times the binders don't fit and I have to carry them in my arms.

"Let's face the fury," Art grins at me before propping open the math classroom door. Vulgar rap music streams out as Harry and Landon growl and complain for us to leave. I walk further in, shutting the music that was splaying out of the speakers on the teacher's desk off.

"Turn the effing music back on," Landon shoots me a withering glare. I shake my head softly, yet firmly. Harry jumps up from his desk and stomps toward me, his eyes blazing.

"Listen to him!" He hisses as he rams his shoulder into mine, spinning me as he starts playing the horrible music again. The beat is good, don't get me wrong, but the words are horrendous. I study the two boys as Harry throws himself back into the desk halfway up a middle row. He's standing there to block anyone from getting any closer to his brother. I sigh and walk around the teacher's desk. They have YouTube open so I type in my favorite song in the search bar.

"What the f—k are you doing?" Landon growls as he runs his hand through his hair, over his face then starts to kick the desks around him. I ignore the screeching and clanging and swearing as I skip the ad.

"You need good music to help you calm down," I finally answer his question as Phil Wickham's song Battle Belongs starts playing. Jonah and Art look at me in confusion, muttering under their breath how this was a bad idea.

"When all I see is the battle, you see my victory!" I bravely sing along to the song. Landon's face morphs into rage. The lyrics are perfect for this moment. Landon and Harry's dad probably gave them a hard time, this is one of their daily struggles, their battle. God sees their victory even if they don't have that sight, that sense.

"I'm gonna go," Art shakes his head at me as he points to the door. I don't blame him for leaving, before tutoring the boys, I wouldn't have stepped in to stop their tantrums but I know them now. They're harmless, they won't hurt anyone. "You should leave too."

"They won't hurt me," I state, praying those words internally to God and surrendering my anxiety of this moment over to Jesus. The Holy Spirit enters me, filling my mind and soul with peace and clarity as Art leaves. I can hear him warning students to stay out of the classroom as Landon marches over to me.

"What the f—k is this?" He demands, shoving desks. They weren't in his way. He's making a mess because it causes fear, it's a fear tactic he probably learned from his father. Jonah steps in front of the desk, blocking me from Landon. Harry is quick to take him out of the way, shoving him back and yelling threats and obscenities at him. I continue singing the song.

"So when I fight, I'll fight on my knees. With my hands lifted high. Oh God, the battle belongs to You!" I mimic the lyrics of the song and lift my hands in the air, raising them in a sort of prayer. Landon jumps over the desk, I flinch back but he pushes me farther against the white boards. The silver bottom used for holding the markers and erasers digs into my thighs. The pain is a sharp reminder that this is very real. *Jesus, take it all. All my worry, my fear, Jesus, I give it to You.* In his leap over the desk, Landon had scattered papers, pencils, and office supplies and knocked over the computer. It finally crashes to the floor, making me flinch. Landon chuckles at the fear I show.

"Sure this was a good idea, Daisy?" He mocks, pressing his arm against my throat. My eyes widen when I can't breathe anymore. Over his shoulder, I can see Jonah raise his hand to punch Harry. They're arguing, raised voices, angry movements. Jonah probably doesn't like Landon laying his hands on me.

"Peaceful Jonah! We do everything peacefully, okay?" I yell at him, cleaning out the rest of the air from my lungs. In Landon's confusion, his hold lessens on my neck. I don't let him know as I make the sign of the cross. Jonah had listened to me but he certainly doesn't agree with me yet, he just hadn't wanted things to escalate any further. "Jesus,"

I whisper, my voice hoarse from the lack of oxygen. Landon stares at me. I can see the demons in his eyes relenting. "Jesus, keep me safe." I continue my prayer. With every word, Landon's anger seems to dissipate. I rejoice to God in my heart. Harry and Jonah also stare at me in bewilderment but I ignore them as I focus on Landon and God. "Jesus, protect me." Landon shakes his head, his snarl falling from his lips. A light seems to flicker on in his eyes. "Jesus, heal my wounds." Tears well up in Landon's eyes at my words. That's the power of Jesus. That's the power of his name. Demons flee in terror. Hardened sinners repent. "Jesus, my Lord, and my God."

"Oh, what the hell," Landon mutters gruffly before pushing away from me. I raise my eyes to heaven when I can breathe properly again, thanking God.

"You ready to listen to some advice?" I ask quietly as I start picking up the teacher's supplies. Landon growls and pinches his nose in frustration but nods. The tears are still in his eyes, and Landon's pride refuses to let them fall. Tonight, during my evening prayers, I'll cry for him, I'll cry for his broken heart. "When someone hurts you," at a sharp look from Landon I rephrase my sentence. "When someone antagonizes you, say the name of Jesus. I'm not going to preach to you, Landon." I laugh at his disbelieving look. "All I want you to do when you feel like you are losing control, getting angry, ready to say 'hell with it', just say Jesus. Say His name and He will take care of it. In your moment of crisis surrender to Him and He will take care of it."

"That's what you did," Landon clenches his teeth together as he leans his butt on the teacher's desk. Maybe I teach by my actions, not my words. Landon knows what I'm talking about because he just witnessed me acting on what I preach. Jonah and Art follow me in volunteering, they need a leader. Maybe I'm the leader that leads by example.

"Yeah, in my moments of fear and anxiety, when I feel like they are taking over my life, I offer them to Jesus. I ask Him to carry my burden so I won't have to. The peace I feel afterward, Landon, it's amazing. There's nothing on earth that can compare." I wave Jonah and Harry away, rolling my eyes at students peeking through the little window of the classroom door.

"Spoken like a true virgin," Landon jokes. I squat down to put the pencils and pens back in the cup. Landon chuckles bitterly when I give him no reaction. I try not to use any negative humour and that was certainly calling me down. Landon doesn't apologize, I don't expect him to. That's not in his character, not that he can't change.

"You want to help me with the computer?" I ask Landon, clicking my tongue when some pieces of plastic around the edge fall. It's noticeably broken. Everyone will know but I don't think they will say anything, other than Jett Hendrix, the whole school population is afraid of the Smith boys.

"I'm not paying for that shit," Landon states with a snarling look to me as he lifts the monitor, and I lift the computer screen.

"I'll pay for it," I offer at the same time he speaks. Landon looks at me, shocked. I shrug at him as I organize the teacher's desk. He will know someone messed with his stuff but hopefully, he won't do or say anything. Just because students are afraid of the Smith boys doesn't mean the teachers are.

"You're a weird one, Daisy." Landon chuckles at me as the tears finally dry in his eyes. I can tell by his voice the ache in his throat is still there.

"Maybe I'm the outdated definition of normal and you all have expanded dictionaries." I grin at him. It takes a second for my bad joke to settle in. He finally looks at me again with regret on his face. The words 'I'm sorry' are written in his eyes but he keeps his lips planted shut; everyone knows Landon Smith doesn't apologize. "I know," I squeeze his shoulder with a smile. "You don't have to say anything Landon, I know."

"Oh, f—k, you are too good," Landon laughs bitterly as the bell rings. Students should be getting to their first class of the day now. Jonah and Harry followed our lead and were lining up all the desks in their proper spots. I fold my crazy hair behind my ears, pleasantly surprised when it stays there for more than a second. I look for any other scattered supplies, hearing a sharp inhale from Landon. I turn to him with a smile.

"It's all cleaned up so I'm gonna get to class," I laugh with a slightly embarrassed look on my face. "I really can't be late again." It's true. I see help and gravitate there, it often makes me late for class. I have one more late pass before my teachers send me to detention. They all loosen the rules for me a little because of all the good I do. I don't like the special treatment, I'm not special. They shouldn't place me on that pedestal.

"F—king hell Daisy," Landon lifts my curly shoulder-length hair away from my neck. I can feel the bruise on my neck, the warmer skin where his forearm had been, and can also tell by the air in my esophagus when I breathe. "I bruised your neck."

"Oh, it's nothing," I jerk my head back so my hair can fall. Landon's eyes meet mine and I hate the new layer of pain, the worst part about this layer? He caused it because he lacked self-control. He hates himself, that's clear to see in the agony of his ice blue eyes.

"I'm going to be better," Landon vows. I squeeze his hand lightly, shooting him an encouraging smile. "That's all Jesus wants from us, to be better, to have our hearts."

"That's all Jesus wants." Landon chuckles behind me as I walk to the classroom door, Jonah catching up. Harry and Landon walk to the back of the classroom, like any stereotypical bad boys they always sit in the last row closest to the door.

"What did you do?" Jonah whispers as we exit the classroom. Students look warily at us but I smile and nod at them. They're worried

Landon is still angry but I encourage them that he's settled down, and their class should pass by without any fighting.

"You can go in," I inform them. Without a word of thanks, they all troop in. Once the hallway is clear, I barrel into Jonah and squeeze him tightly. My stiff shoulders relax as he wraps his arms around me.

"I told him about Jesus," I laugh and sob at the same time. The danger of what happened in there is only hitting me now. I have a bruise on my neck! Dad is going to be angry, Landon's cousins are all going to be mad when I see them tonight to volunteer at the soup kitchen.

I feel comfortable in Jonah's arms like maybe I have a place in them. Maybe Danae is right, maybe my future is with Jonah instead of Tyler but I'm still going to pray on it. I'm still going to pray for the triplets, for the students, for everyone, the whole wide world.

✢ 10 ✤

Jesus Saves

⫸▶◦◀⫷

"Daisy?" Mr. Watson queries when I walk straight to the sinks without my usual routine of stopping to greet his sons and homeless citizens who had arrived early for the supper meal. I don't really care for talking but I love visiting them, hearing their stories of survival, the hope some still have, and sharing with their hopeless comrades. In poverty we find the Spirit, the third Joyful Mystery is proven right over and over again at the smiles, laughs, and love shared between the town drunkards. I love sharing my love with the broken-spirited. My goal in life is to be like Jesus. The Pharisees criticized Him for hanging out with sinners, all the drunkards, tax collectors, and prostitutes but the best thing about His relationship with all of them? They weren't outcasts when His time on earth had ended, when He left them to go heal other people, they were better off, happier, healthier, and healed. "Daisy?"

"Good afternoon Mr. Watson," I quickly shoot him a smile before turning my back to him and facing the sinks. It's just my luck he made soup today, there aren't many dishes to wash beforehand. If that is the case, I'm free to visit. Normally that's what I do but I want to hide what Landon did. I don't believe Landon's uncle or cousins will hurt him but

I don't want them to think he's turning into his father. Landon just has to choose the right path and make the right decision in the future.

"Oh, hey Jonah," Mr. Watson slaps Jonah's shoulder. He had to tie his shoe so he was a couple of seconds behind me. "Becoming a regular, huh?"

"You bet," Jonah stops to visit with Dickie. I like the way he runs his hand through his hair and then shakes it all out of place right after. "Anything you need help with?"

"Yes, always," Mr. Watson smiles and points to the metal storage shelves. Napkins, towels, toilet paper, soaps, and other cleaning supplies are stored there. Dickie must have gone shopping because there are boxes and bags of items on the floor, ready to be faced. "Do you wanna organize the shelves? Put the older stuff in the front please."

"Yeah, no problem," Jonah nods. Pierre meanders over to me while Jonah has his dad distracted. Pierre is one of the only ones who hang out with the triplets, the others being their other cousins BJ and Sadie. Because of the football team, Col has started visiting with them sometimes. They aren't close, especially with the Landon and April history, but the triplets are starting to inherit new friends, just like me.

"What did you say to Landon?" Pierre asks as he places a cutting board and chopping knife beside the sink. I shrug in response. If Landon didn't tell his cousin maybe he doesn't want me to. I'm not a secret keeper but this isn't my story to tell. Pierre sighs as he looks at me. His baby face is the opposite of his cousin's hardened features. He is beautiful, Pierre has God's grace radiating through him. "It's just that Landon has never calmed down that fast before and he's never cleaned up after himself."

"I told him Jesus can help him," I look at Pierre with a smile. No one knows how happy I am that Landon listened to my words. "You know because I see you at church, but Landon, he needed someone to tell him he isn't as bad as he or his dad make him out to be."

"Thanks, Daisy," Pierre laughs lightly with hope burning in his eyes. He has the same honest, warm, milk chocolate brown eyes as his brother Paul. "I hope they start to see their saving grace in Jesus."

"Me too," I can't help my happy smile. Pierre walks to the stove to stir the two large pots of soup. Mr. Watson finishes explaining the stocking to Jonah and makes his way over to me. Behind him are Aria and my dad. I beam at them. "You came to volunteer!"

"Sort of," my dad answers, his fingers flexing. That warns me of whatever he is coming to say next. Did he propose to Aria? Is that why Dickie is with them as they approach me? Did he find my mother? Did she agree to a divorce? Is the church nullifying their marriage? Is she, is my mom dead? "Landon Smith came to visit me."

"Oh," I mumble, blushing as I lift my chin up. If Landon visited him, I don't have to worry about his reaction anymore. He can see the damage. Hope sprinkles in my chest. Landon apologized to my dad. Landon has some sort of hope for a better version of himself. I'll keep praying hard for him and making sacrifices for his brothers. My dad sighs as he looks at the purple bruise on my neck.

"I can only accept and understand your conversion of others to a certain extent. If they hurt you, is it not time for you to rethink? You're only fifteen Daisy." I cross my arms defiantly as Jonah stands up. I shake my head at him. He'd only make my dad angry by defending my actions. Dad doesn't see Jonah as the nice guy next door anymore.

"Blessed are those who endure persecution for the sake of justice, for theirs is the kingdom of heaven." I quote Matthew 5:10 to my dad. He sighs and looks around the kitchen. Pierre and Jonah had stilled to eavesdrop on our conversation. Aria had her arms wrapped around my dad's bicep and Dickie had leaned against a sink, not yet taking a side. In the cafeteria, Percy and Peter are entertaining the homeless. It's getting louder so our conversation won't carry.

"But was it for justice's sake?" My dad asks, his jaw ticking. I understand his stubbornness. I'm his daughter, I was hurt and no father wants to see his daughter hurt.

"He came to you, didn't he?" I softly disagree. Pierre flinches when he drops the spoon into the pot, knowing he's busted now. Aria hides a smile.

"And he's going to church for the next month," dad grins. Relief flows through my veins as we grin at each other stupidly, eyes shining. We may be unscrupulous in guilting Landon to mass but maybe this month will change his life. I'll always try to convert people even if it isn't the normal evangelizing way. Like I told Landon, my normal is outdated.

"Jesus saves," my dad and I high-five each other before my dad envelopes me in a hug. I love my dad's hugs. He doesn't work out, he used to when I was a child but not anymore. He's always puttering around the farm and works construction for Peter's business. Before that, he worked for the county and he's still strong. One of the strongest men I know but all daughters probably say that of their fathers. I feel comfortable in his embrace, safe in the soft hug, and cherished beyond compare.

"Jesus saved me," I whisper as I pat his back. "Demons fled Landon's eyes when I told him about Jesus. I saw it." And that is why I believe Jesus is king.

"So you gonna help?" I ask my dad. He hasn't volunteered in a while. Peter's company has been busy lately and while Peter doesn't have to work because he's the boss, my dad often has to stay late. Sometimes they even have jobs out of town. It's nice to have the cabin to myself.

"Actually, Aria and I are going to the city for a couple of days. I left you the keys to my truck. Emergencies only." I stare at my dad. Did they have some sort of Las Vegas wedding? Has my dad fallen into deeper sin? It's funny how I try to convert other people but the hardest one to convert is my father. I want the best for him, an eternity in paradise, everlasting delight with God. Why does he help me help others but doesn't help himself to God's forgiveness and mercy? He only has to repent!

"Oh, why?" I ask, biting the inside of my cheek. Mr. Watson takes this opportunity to leave since we are no longer talking about his nephew. I'm glad Landon will be attending church, he'll keep more in touch with his maternal family that way. His father keeps the Watsons from visiting their house. Huntley makes sure the Watsons know they aren't welcome but the triplets aren't welcome at the Watson's.

"Family emergency," my dad sighs before looking away from me. His fingers flex again. Whatever he isn't telling me is important. I understand that I might have to wait for the answers. God is helping me learn patience.

"I hope everything is okay," I hug Aria. My dad and I don't have any family but I'd think she or her family would look sadder or more scared.

"Actually Daisy, it's our family." My dad sighs and clears his throat. "I'll explain it when I get back."

"What family?" The Ridel's have always been us two against the world.

"I'll explain when I get back," my dad says firmly. "It should only be four days, tops. AND NO JONAH at the house!" Dad raises his voice with the last sentence. I cover my mouth to hide my laugh. He's pulling Jonah's leg. Dad knows I wouldn't do that.

"It was an accident!" Jonah retorts, shaking his head. Pierre looks between the two of us. I'm glad Betty's theory of our relationship hasn't traveled that fast. But apparently more people than Betty can see. Danae is dead set that me and Jonah will be a couple in no time at all. Aria rolls her eyes at their bickering.

"I'll have a lot of questions when you get back," I huff. Dad has never mentioned siblings or cousins or aunts and uncles. All he's told me of the Ridel family is that his parents passed away, but they were a very loud, dysfunctional family.

"Just wait until then," dad kisses my forehead. "God bless you."

"God bless you, dad." We don't say anything else as he takes Aria's hand in his and walks away. Whenever we have to be apart, we like our last words to each other as remembering God.

"Sorry I'm late," Paul slaps dad's back as they meet in the doorway. He has Poppy in his arms, Aiden in a carrier strapped on his chest, and Polly trailing behind him. "Amy had something come up."

"Uh huh," Dickie picks up Polly to swing around. He does the same to Poppy as Pierre gives Polly a taste of the soup. "Why don't you girls ask Uncle Percy to take you to the park?" Percy had brought his daughters Paisley and Pamela today. Paisley is the same age as Polly and Pamela the same age as Poppy. They'll both be close cousins and even closer sisters. Percy's son Arlo will most likely spend all his time with Paul's son, Aiden.

"Yay!" The girl's cheer and race to their uncle. Once his daughters spot them it's a squealing festival. At whatever the girls tell Percy, he looks to his father for confirmation. Dickie nods and the girls erupt into more squeals when Percy agrees to take them to the park. Polly and Paisley skip ahead, Poppy and Pamela close behind, their little legs running fast.

"Pierre, Jonah, you each wanna tackle a bathroom. Make sure it's clean?" Dickie asks. Jonah nods and tosses me a package of napkins. I shrug and shake my head at him. Dickie clearly wants the kitchen cleared out to talk to Paul in private. Pierre and Jonah make conversation as they walk to the bathrooms. I put the napkins in their place. "Did Amy leave?" Dickie asks his son quietly. They're separating. Paul had convinced Amy to hold off on the divorce for now.

"I'm gonna go sweep the steps," I mutter, pointing my head down. Paul smiles thankfully at me as he bounces Aiden in the backpack. I grab the broom from the counter, nod to the throng of hungry people, and walk out the front doors. Landon, Harry, Tyler, and their younger brothers, Cam and Jim are sitting on the rotten wooden bench visiting with each other. There are a lot of swear words, calling each other down, and negative humour. It's normal for them. Landon spots me first and waves and Harry follows suit. Cam and Jim, the cocky bullies of the Smith family, pay no attention to me. Tyler hesitates before nodding. He has fresh bruises from a new beating. His dad knows he's the weakest, the one that can't fight back. Cam and Jim don't really care, having a fend-for-yourself attitude, but Landon and Harry try to stay with Tyler so they can take the beating meant for him or fight back. Tyler's light green eyes, an indication that he isn't as Indigenous as his father appears to be, are hollow and empty of hope. I one day want to put vitality in those orbs.

I start sweeping to the right of the front doors to give the Smith boys their space. It's not often they are seen together except at their house so it might be important. If they are at the soup kitchen, it means their dad spent all his welfare and drug money on alcohol and they need food to eat. Dust rises from the mostly clean steps. All I am doing is pushing little pebbles shoes tracked in off the sidewalk. When I get to the end of the building, a man with black teeth and red eyes stares at me.

"You think the boys have anything on them?" He asks, his fidgety movements jerky. He's a drug addict. I sigh, knowing Tyler always keeps a vial of something on him and Landon a flask, especially in their winter coats.

"I'm sorry, I don't know if they do but I can tell you what is a better addiction." I offer, leaning on my broom. The man looks at me quizzically. "Jesus," I say simply. "He's my drug."

The drug-addicted man has the audacity to laugh. Embarrassment and zealousness for the Lord make my cheeks burn. I know I'll be faced with callous, indifferent Children of God; but now that I am, how do I respond? I'm not sure how as the man begins to back away, so I speak from my heart, knowing God will put words in my heart to argue His case. "I'm lost," I state so forlornly that the man freezes. Tears come to my eyes as sorrow enters my heart. Sorrow for this man, sorrow for the triplets, sorrow for all the drug addicted, the alcoholics, the hurting, the hopeless. Jesus had mercy on all of them, and so too, can I. "When I don't wake up in the morning thanking God, praising Him, asking Him to help me, I'm lost." I continue. The man rolls his eyes. It bothers me but I push on. "Prayer is my hit or boost or flask, without prayer, I, I'm lost. My day seems so confusing, the sun never rises, and darkness surrounds me. Prayer is spiritual nourishment. It brings excitement to the beat of my heart, encouragement for another day, and hope that somehow, some way, my day won't be as bad as the worst day of my life, even if it was yesterday. Prayer helps me to surrender all my anxiety to Jesus. When my worries are gone, the world seems brighter, my steps a little lighter. I praise God because without Him I'd be drowning in my misery." I take a deep breath. Some of my words seemed to have resonated with the man but the more religious ones stood him on edge. "Without God," I look at the man cautiously, gauging his reaction. "Without Him, I'd be on your dark path and that's why God stopped you today. To tell you that if I can rise from my misery, so can you."

To my sadness and regret, the man only shakes his head with tears in his agony-filled eyes and walks away.

"You believe all that crap?" Tyler asks, pulling a joint out from between his ear and scalp. I shake my head no in warning, silently asking him not to light it as I watch the drug-addicted man teetering away. At least I'd scared him away from a score, that has to count for something, right?

"Yes," I say firmly, plucking the joint from Tyler's thin, faded, dry, and cracked lips. "Jesus saves."

"That's not being very nice, nice girl," Tyler reaches for his joint. I keep it just out of his arms reach. Nice girl? That's a first.

"I like you Tyler," I admit bravely as I hand the joint back to him. He balks at my words before looking at his faded, ripped black skinny jeans and a fuzzy black t-shirt that hangs limply around his bony, frail body. Then he looks at his brothers on the bench. Cam, Jim, and Harry are arguing with each other but Landon is watching me and his brother's interaction. I laugh lightly, my heart hurting as I point to Tyler's scuffed, ripped, holey shoes to his buzz-cut hair so short I can see his scalp. He keeps it cut that way because he doesn't get to shower often. "I like your style, it's not even your style though, is it? You wear whatever you are given second-hand, right? I love that you don't care about your looks as much as Landon. I love that you don't snap at people when you're having a bad day like Harry. I love those light green eyes of yours, how they shimmer with hope even though you deny what could be. I love that you still give minimal effort even though you don't see the value of living, that even if you don't want to live at least you don't try and kill yourself. I love your voice, and how its melody shows the complicated emotions in your soul. I love your music, the sad twang, the excited thrum, the happy beat, the cliffhanger of an abrupt end, the long ending of a wistful tune."

"I try to kill myself," Tyler says bluntly as he rolls up his jacket sleeves. My eyes tear up at the purple marks from needle injections, how his veins are bursts of dark blue against porcelain white skin. My fingers reach up and trace the cigarette burns, the scars from knife wounds, the bruises, and the swelling. Tyler's voice cracks and he huffs out a breath in pain. The back of my throat aches. "I try to kill myself every day."

"I don't believe that," I refute, shaking my head as my hand drops and he rolls his sleeve back down. "Someone who tries to kill himself that often would have succeeded by now. You injure yourself as a cry for help." I fold my hand over his bony hands, his fingers so skinny they are mostly bone. "I'm here to help."

"You are one crazy girl," Tyler says after a large pause. His hand holds onto mine. At this moment, I might be his lifeline to a future. I stare into his chartreuse green eyes as I wait for his reply to my declaration of liking him. No one has ever said that to him, no one even looks at him twice unless he surprises them by actually being sober. Tons of emotions swirl through his light green eyes, fading to lighter green farther from his pupils. "You're pretty cute, too." Tyler continues. "But you're too good for me."

"I expected that answer," I give his hand a final squeeze before dropping it.

"Let me work on myself first, okay?" Tyler's eyes become unreadable at his sentence. I nod. If me liking him helps him fight for a better life, I'm all for it. Maybe I should have told him of my crush sooner.

"I'll wait for you." Am I lying? Will my rising feelings for Jonah break this promise?

"It might be a while," Tyler puts his joint back between his lips. He brings a lighter to the end of the roll. I shoot him a final smile as I walk back to the entrance, sweeping stray pebbles off the sidewalk. He's giving me the option not to wait, it's one I might take depending on Jonah's intentions with me.

⇥ 11 ⇤

River Side Run

———⇒➤·◉·⇐———

R eady?" Jonah grins at me as he jumps up and starts jogging on the spot. He'd just finished tying his shoes tighter. His younger sisters Betty and Esther are with us along with Landon and Harry and their cousins BJ, Bianca, and Sadie. Col is here with Chris and Karl but no Danae. She doesn't run and can't make an excuse to come. The last person in our group to run for the day, to train for the half marathon, is Art. I look around the group, at Art's light, basically white, neck length thick blond hair and thick, tall farmer's build to Betty and Esther's petite, ballerina bodies and so on. Sadie is the smallest and skinniest but don't let that fool you. She's a dancer, a scholarship to some dance academy. If I were to join the track team, we'd be partners for the relay. Landon and Harry are at the back of the group, not ones to stretch and not at ease with half of the group. They are good with their cousins and me and Col but not the rest. Chris and Karl are visiting with Art and Col at the head of the pack. Out of the four, only Art isn't competitive but he works out every day. I suspect my challengers for winning are Jonah and Art. Sadie might give us a tough time also. Quarterback Col will be troublesome as well. The rest will be at the back of the pack. Chris and Karl weight lift more than run. Their lungs aren't equipped for the fresh mountain air and hills. The group as a whole had decided to run the river trail. It leads us to the top of the hill and loops around the wide part of the river. That leads us to just under the twenty-six miles for the half marathon.

"Y'all ready? Let's go!" Chris, Danae's older brother with the bossy persona, shouts, and waves at us to follow him. He starts off at a slow jog for a warm-up, Karl and Col in line with him. Betty and Esther are a couple of paces behind them with BJ, Bianca, and Sadie behind the sisters. Art waits for me and Jonah to run with. Landon and Harry take up the tail.

"May and Junie mentioned something Betty and Esther said to keep a secret," Art grins at Jonah and me. He so knows what they were gossiping about. I roll my eyes, keeping my focus on my breathing and running form.

"Betty and Esther don't know anything," Jonah mutters. I enjoy the scenic view, and the different types of trees passing us by. The pine, poplar, spruce, willows, some wild Saskatoon, and raspberry. The moss and soft forest floor with some roots make us trip occasionally. The sky is a beautiful hue of dark blue, fluffy light grey clouds spattering the blue. Art laughs.

"Why are you and Daisy hanging out all the time now?" He asks. Just because Jonah and I are hanging out more doesn't mean we are a couple. I let Jonah speak, not one for talking, especially not during my runs.

"We're just friends," Jonah states. I feel a little awkward stuck in the middle of the two tall boys as they disagree but I ignore it. This half marathon is important. The more runners, the faster times, and the more money raised for cancer research and medical help for the sick.

"Yeah," Art looks at the both of us but shrugs his concern off at his next words. "Apparently Pierre mentioned Daisy and the Trips threw a fit."

"What?" I bark out in shock. Art looks at me in surprise at my raised voice. I usually never raise my voice so he knows this has tilted me off my axis. "When?" Was it because I mentioned my crush to Tyler on Tuesday? Lately, Landon and Harry have been nodding or waving at me, saying hello when we pass in the hallway, and actually carrying a conversation with me during our study session or visiting at the end of mass and not flirting.

"Thursday, I think." Art shrugs again. "Chris overheard it."

"They have taken more of an interest in her," Jonah agrees with Art. I keep facing forward, my chin held high. They really shouldn't be saying this in front of me, nor gossiping. Stories are how rumours spread.

"They probably don't like the rumours Betty and Junie are spreading." Art adds. He trips on a root and just about faceplants but we both react quickly. I grab his shirt and hold him while he lands on his hand.

"You good?" Jonah asks, slowing down for us to catch up. Behind us Harry and Landon cackle at the fall. They can be a bit shamelessly rude.

"Just embarrassed," Art laughs it off, ever the good-natured guy. We all have vices, theirs seem to be gossiping and mine must be judging. I don't need to criticize them in my mind, they are free to think and say what they want.

"Think the Trip's heard Betty's insane idea yet?" Jonah seems tense at that idea. Students have learned the hard way to be afraid of the Smith boys. He doesn't want any trouble.

"Insane?" Art scoffs and looks between us. "Sane, you mean. We all see the chemistry."

"Let's not gossip, boys," I finally speak up. The rumours might make my relationship happen with Jonah sooner than either of us wants. I'm only fifteen, too young for a boyfriend or to be thinking that way. Our parents wouldn't agree either.

"Go at your own pace!" Chris hollers behind us, picking his pace up. We all speed up, some more than others. Sadie and BJ pass Betty and Esther. Soon Art, Jonah, and I are, then Harry and Landon. I can feel the burn in my calves as we start the incline of the hill, it's a slow rise so it will take a lot out of us. Jonah, Art, and I soon take the lead. Our faster pace will slowly take us farther ahead of the others. We had all agreed to go out for ice cream afterward as a sort of team sportsman-ship function. Ice cream is a worthy motivator.

"You hear about the Watsons?" Art asks. Is this what having friends is like? Talking about other people? I trip on a stick but thankfully catch myself. With the cold nip of the air, my arthritis is acting up. Of course, I'm not going to complain but will Jonah catch on? He knows.

"What's up?" Jonah asks, looking behind to keep an eye on his sisters. Except for Landon and Harry, they were at the back of the pack. The only reason the two of the triplets are there is probably because of the girls in front of them. Landon had slept with any girl aged sixteen to twenty-six in this town except for Betty. That is an exaggeration but you get my drift.

"Phillip was wounded on tour. They're sending him back and the Watsons are having a prayer vigil." Paul had told me last night after his talk with his dad. We spent the hour from six o'clock to seven praying with Peter. Jonah, Pierre, and Dickie took care of the soup kitchen during that time. Then Dickie, Jonah, and Pierre and I went to daily mass while Peter and Paul watched the soup kitchen.

"Oh yeah," I smile. This is good news, not gossip. I can share it. "Paul invited me and my dad to join." It will be amazing to pray with others. I get emotional when praying in a group, and hearing the heartfelt prayers of others. Tears of joy fall down my face as unimagi-nable joy bursts out of my heart, filling my body.

"I'll join," Jonah looks at me before shrugging. I shoot him a smile of gratitude, the more prayers, the better. Art hides a grin.

"I might too," Art laughs lightly. "I gotta see what y'all see in this God person."

"Really?" I beam at him, my heart thrumming in excitement. Another person might come to know God, how beautiful!

"Yes," Art says. "If that's true, ain't nothing better to do." I love his answer, and his newfound enthusiasm for God and religion. I'm glad he has an open mind and willing heart to find the true reason for life, why we were created. Art reminds me a lot of Jonah, maybe that's why they get along so well.

"Wanna take the long trail?" Jonah asks with a grin as he points to the trail veering to the right. It will take us through some hills and turns; the trail is called the Biathlon for a reason.

"Sure," Art veers to the right. We follow him until we are in line again. My right knee is starting to get an ache in it from my arthritis but also from the shock from landing. This is why I have perfected my running form, the better my form, the less pain I cause myself. "You hear the McCoy's got little Carlos involved in their business now? Something 'bout he threw dirt in a guard's face so his uncles could hold them up."

"Carlos is Larry's age," Jonah tuts. "Can't imagine a ten-year-old doing something like that. They probably gave him a cut, too."

"Like, crime?" I ask, missing a step because of the pain. It reminds me of when my horse, Honey, trips or steps wrong. Her nose just about hits the ground but she continues at her pace.

"Yeah, you know, the McCoy clan?" Art asks me after both he and Jonah make sure I am okay. I can no longer hear the rest of the group's pit-pat of footsteps. They must have taken the shorter way. I don't blame them. I might have pushed myself a little too hard today.

"Everett, Calvin, Daxon?" Jonah explains and rolls his eyes when I shrug, still not knowing those names. Art laughs outright.

"Jett Hendrix, his dad, and his uncles. The McCoy's. They steal a lot, rip a bunch of people off but also to launder money they let the homeless 'rent' the apartments next to Paul's hotel." Art explains. We decline on a hill and it speeds our pace up. I smile at the next hill that starts at the bottom of this hill when all I want to do is stop and catch my breath. The boys have longer legs than me. I have to work harder to keep up with them. Whatever aches and pains I suffer from this run, I'll offer up for the half marathon for cancer awareness. I put it in God's hands. Whatever happens, happens. I don't need to worry.

"At least they do some good," I speak into the silence. Art and Jonah share a look before laughing.

"Always positive," Art laughs. The next half hour of the run is silent as we focus on ourselves. During my run, I pray the Chaplets of Faith and Divine Mercy and offer prayers for whatever God needs. I may have slowed down the pace a little but the boys don't mind as we all catch our breath. Both boys train seriously for running, they won't be the first to break. They know how to push themselves even when they think they can't continue. I'll be the first to quit but I can't, I'm not wired to give up. I push myself past my breaking point, over and over again; sometimes I don't even know why I do so when I do. Soon we are close to the river loop, the waving of the stream soothes us with the chirping of birds and rustling of brush animals. The serene day is broken by the splash and screams of a young child. Jonah and Art look at each other before taking off amidst the cries of what can only be the child's family. The boys are going upstream but the current will take the child downstream so I take a deep breath and build up my speed, veering right instead of going to the commotion. I'm on an incline that only gets worse. The river bank is steep from here on out, the child will only be rescued by boat unless I can get to him by a path carved from moose hooves from summer crossings. I'd dressed for the chilly day, a windbreaker over a thin hoodie. As I am running I whip the jacket off. My lungs burn from the continuous effort but adrenaline pumps through my veins. The child has stopped screaming but I can still hear him crying as he tries to fight against the current taking him deeper into the water. I rip my sweater off and scan the rising shoreline. The river often has logs in the water by the bank due to ice breaks. Gauging where the boy might end up and where I need to jump to pull him to shore I spot a three-second area and take the leap. *Jesus, keep me safe.*

The brisk water freezes my body and I hold my breath as I go under. I know how to swim but I'm not very good, just good enough. I'd landed five meters behind the boy but he's twenty meters away from shore. Once I'm accustomed to the chill of the water, I begin swimming toward him. It takes a couple of minutes, the rigorous activity keeping me warm in the cold water. I latch onto his clothes. His teeth are chattering and his lips are blue.

"Can you swim?" I ask calmly, unzipping his thick fall jacket. The water will only weigh the jacket down.

"No," he bursts into tears. I wipe water from his face after letting his jacket float down the river, taking this time to regulate my breathing.

"That's okay," I point to the bank. "There's a little trail there. The water is pretty deep straight to the bank but I'll pull you. Okay?" He nods so I turn around and wrap his arms around my neck. Jonah and the boy's dad had raced down the bear trail and are a couple of steps into the river. I take a deep breath and start swimming, the boy weighing me down. Breathe, left stroke, right stroke, breathe. I repeat the process, discouraged at the little progress I make. I can hear shouts of encouragement the closer I get. The child's dad wades in further, just about falling from the sudden drop of the river floor. My dad takes me here on Sundays, that's why I know this area so well. It's a Ridel tradition to spend Sundays outside admiring God's beautiful earth. I slow down closer to the boy's dad's feet, knowing I'll hit the slightly sharp bank. It's sand so it's soft but hitting it hard will be like running into a dirt wall. When I am close enough, the father leans down and grabs his son. I crawl on the river bottom until I reach Jonah. He drags me the rest of the way out of the water, talking as he looks over me in worry. I laugh at the shirt I'm wearing today. Often I make my own shirts or steam or sew vinyl on them. My shirt today has a quote from St. Francis de Sales, 'There is nothing small in the service of God'. Guess Jonah won't be letting me take the humble way out. I stand up, shivers racking my body as I wring out my clothes as best as possible.

"Take my sweater," Jonah offers, pulling his hoodie over his shoulders. The dad is taking the clothes off the son so I close my eyes instead of turning around. Jonah laughs. "I'll turn around, and take your shirt off. Put my sweater on."

"Thanks," I wring my hair out before taking the hoodie from his outstretched arm. Coughs wrack my body from the chilly day, cold water, and wet clothes. I'll probably get a cold from this. I make sure that I'm not facing anyone and quickly switch my shirt to Jonah's warm sweater. Like his pajamas, they fit comfortably except around my curves. I cough some more as I completely ring my shirt out and tuck it in my sweat pockets. The father is taking his son up to the bank, probably to the hospital. He won't stop thanking me and worrying over his son.

"Let's get you somewhere warm," Jonah throws an arm around my shoulders. He shakes his head as he looks at the two males walking away, the river, then me. "You are one smart chick, me and Art didn't think of all the moving variations."

"Nah," I deny, "my dad takes me here at least once a month."

"Humble too," Jonah shakes his head but laughs bittersweetly.

→ 12 ←

Night Visit

———◆▶◉◀◆———

"Daisy, Daisy," my dad's lowered voice wakes me up. It's surprising that his voice wakes me up, not the door opening, his luggage rolling on the floor, the motor of Aria's Jeep, or our dog barking. I'm usually a very light sleeper. I must be exhausted from the run and the river. Sugar doesn't bark unless it's a vehicle she doesn't know, though. Aria has been coming here for so long Sugar knows her car.

"Huh?" I blearily yawn and stretch, rolling into a sitting position.

"I'm gonna turn the light on, Daisy," Dad warns. It's not a simple flick of a switch. We have a well hooked up to plumbing so we don't live too much off the grid but we don't have electricity at night. Solar panels collect sunlight and store it for use but if there isn't any sunlight, which there hasn't been in the past few days, we resort to our kerosene lamps. I hear the flick of a match before flame bursts into the darkness. Soon my dad has his bedside lamp lit. With a groan, I shield my eyes. Dad laughs as he sits in his rocking chair, he has to turn it to face me and the bed. Usually, it faces his wall of windows and he can peer into the sunrise or sunset, or the darkness of night if he can't sleep. Every shelf has a votive candle, statue, or picture except for the four windows the rocking chair faces. "Daisy," dad looks at me seriously but a smile forms on his lips as he shakes his head at me. "Just because I said no Jonah doesn't mean I said no boys."

"Ahh," I sigh, running my hands over my hair to get it out of my face. It might be weird that I am in my father's bedroom but I'll have to explain the story. It's simple enough. Dad's thick cotton blankets with a patched jean quilt on top are heavy and warm. I enjoy the warmth when I sleep, the heavy quilt keeping me warm throughout the night but when I'm awake, it's just too hot.

"Why are the Smith boys sleeping on the couch?" Dad asks, crossing his arms over his chest. He's not scary, at least not to me anyways, but he can act pretty tough when he has to. This appears to be one of those times. Dad cocks his head. "Is the third one in your room?"

"Yeah," I yawn deeply, shrugging some of the blankets off. "Tyler's in my room so I took your room. I'm sorry dad, I didn't know you were gonna be home tonight."

"Is that why they are here?" Dad demands, flexing his fingers on the rocking chair armrests. He's hurt, upset that I went behind his back. "Because I wasn't here? I didn't raise you to keep secrets, to hide what you do, or to do it in secret. They have no right to be here when my fifteen-year-old daughter is alone. If you had to, you could have given them the loft-."

"-Dad," I interrupt his rant. He can go for hours when he starts. At least he isn't monotone. "Tyler's dad beat him up bad. He can't walk. The loft only has a ladder with a square opening. I did think it through. I'm sorry I didn't tell you but we don't exactly have a landline to call on."

"Does he need medical attention?" Dad shoots up, striding toward the door. I roll my eyes at the quick change of attitude. That's my dad for you, but I'm happy. It means my dad trusts me.

"Landon and Harry won't let him," I sigh as my dad continues. He won't hear whatever I have to say now that he's worried about Tyler. I slip my knitted slippers on, wrap a throw blanket around my shoulders and follow. The throw blanket is a little touch of Aria. She makes my dad's bed in the morning and thinks it looks better with the throw blanket folded in half the long way to cover the foot of the bed. In the deepening darkness of the short hallway, I decided to turn back and grab the lamp. My room is the same as dad's, although it lacks a wall of windows. I don't mind. When I pray to watch the sunrise, I climb into our little attic and sit on the small balcony.

"He's breathing slightly shallow," Dad hums and motions me closer. "Thanks for the light, Daisy."

"No problem," I reply, saddened at what the flickering light shows of Tyler's thin body. His whole head seems to be one big bruise. Harry and Landon had refused to talk about it but I might have overheard that Huntley really went overboard this time, shoving Tyler's head on the floor. Smashing his nose, his eyes are swollen and bruised. A cheekbone might be cracked, there are plenty of scratches and cuts, some still bleeding through the stitches I put in earlier. I don't think it's okay that he slept through me gently washing his face, icing the swelling, and closing the cuts but Landon said he was high on meth. He didn't know what all was in Tyler's system so we never gave him any pain medication, not wanting to overdose him. Huntley is abusive, I know that, but this is a ridiculous new level. Some of Tyler's knuckles are scraped, and one was popped out of place. His stomach is swollen, I think it is a cracked rib or two. The worst part? Well, maybe not the worst part but the thing that probably hurt the worst were the long, thick black and purple swelling lines on Tyler's back. Harry may have mentioned a baseball bat. Who gets this angry? Who loses that control? Who hurts his son so badly he might be disfigured for the rest of his life? The baseball bat might have hit Tyler's kneecap. They think it's okay but no one will know until Tyler gets x-rays.

"Did you call Dickie?" Dad's voice is hard as he surveys the damage done to Tyler. I mutely shake my head. Landon and Harry had made me promise not to tell anyone, my dad wasn't part of that promise. How could I anyways? Only Tyler out of the four of us teenagers has an electronic and he only has a small, smashed, cracked screen iPod that only works on wifi. Here's a little hint: me and my dad don't have wifi. Another thought pops into my head, why I couldn't fall asleep easily tonight? It's the prayer vigil for Phillip. The Watsons will all be there, phones shut off or left at home. Dad seems to read my thoughts. They won't do what my dad wants to do. I can tell by the glint in my dad's eyes. Huntley pushed it too far and dad's going to take it into his own hands. "Get the three oh three ready for Col," Dad spins on his heel. I stand in stunned surprise. My dad, he's talking about... guns... violence. It strikes fear through me.

"No, dad!" I race after him. God is the only judge of justice, not us.

"There was a cougar nearby," dad laughs at me. Shame on me for judging. I knew my dad wouldn't do something that drastic. Why did I doubt it? "Col's gonna hang out here just in case it comes back. See if you can lock Sweetie, Buck, and Honey in the barn."

"Oh," my face flushes. "Okay."

"Shut the light off, we don't need to wake these guys up." Dad takes out his iPhone and scrolls through his contacts.

"Landon's passed out from drinking," I state, not talking back but informing my father. I blow the flame out and pad back to his room as he makes a phone call to Col's stepdad.

"What's happening?" Harry asks, his voice thick with sleep. I glance at the clock on my dad's phone, surprised at the time. It's two am.

"My dad got home early," I speak into the dark of the night. Near the kitchen, I can see clearly because of the big window and the cleared front yard so I sit at the table. Harry follows me, his shins knocking into an end table. I hide a laugh as he swears and grumbles then sits in my dad's spot. On the ledge of the windowsill is a little battery-operated candle so I turn it on. It creates enough light to see Harry's face. "Got some drool there," I point to my face to alert him. Harry glares at me as he leaves it alone for now.

"See you soon, Annakin." Dad hangs up the phone. He turns to us as he leans against the fridge, staring at Harry. "Col and his dad will be here in fifteen. Col will help Daisy get the animals in the barn and Abe and I will go to town. You can stay here as long as you want, Harry." The triplets all look alike for the most part but have very defining features. Harry's is his thick wavy, shoulder-length brown hair. He has the top half in a cute man bun with some falling into his face from turning and tossing in his sleep. He clasps his hands together in front of his face, elbows resting on the table. Unlike Tyler's thin, knobby fingers, Harry's are thick, strong, and tanned yet with callouses like Tyler's. Does he also play the guitar?

"What are you going to do?" Harry finally asks after we sit in a moment of silence. I shrug, telling him I didn't betray his confidence if he wants to tell the story. All I said was that Tyler's dad hurt him badly. Everyone will know by the next couple of days. Huntley enjoys bragging about 'teaching his unruly boys a lesson' in respecting their father.

"Just give him a warning," dad shrugs. His fingers are still flexing back and forth, showing his anger. I can tell he isn't telling me the whole story, just like his unknown reasoning about not telling me about our family. He'll explain it to me when he's ready, not when I demand him to.

"Lots of people have," Harry shrugs with a bitter laugh. I hate the lack of hope in his eyes. Cold seeps through the floorboards. I curl my legs into my chest and cover them with a blanket. A cough surprises me with its intensity. They'd been coming and going, more so when I lie down or stand up. The cold air is bringing them out now.

"You haven't been dressing for the weather, have you, Daisy?" My dad shakes his head at me with a half smile. "Guess I'm gonna have to start reminding you again." I cut a look at Harry, pleading with him not to say anything but he only smirks. His explanation will get the heat off him.

"She went for a swim," Harry laughs at my dad's disapproving stare. I wilt in my seat, covering my face.

"Daisy-," dad's soon-to-be lecture is cut off from Harry.

"She rescued a little boy from drowning in the river."

"I'm still sorry I interrupted our run," I smile apologetically at Harry. He rolls his eyes. They probably heard my apology over a hundred times.

"What? Daisy!" My dad exclaims, stepping forward. I groan in embarrassment when he places a hand on my forehead to check my temperature. Harry coughs to hide a chuckle but there is joyless pain in his eyes. The hurt I see makes me reach forward and squeeze his hand.

"We have lots of love to go around," I inform him as my dad sighs in relief.

"No fever, that's good. At this time of year, you could get pneumonia!" He's right but that's not the problem. I'm safe and healthy and I was sleeping peacefully until he showed up. If my cough gets worse, technically I could blame it on him.

"Where's Aria?" I deflect his overprotectiveness. He doesn't usually arrive this late at night without her.

"Prayer vigil," Dad deadpans with a roll of his eyes. Welp, this is why I don't lie. I'm horrible at it. Dad looks at me seriously. "I'll tell you about why I went to the city in a few days. I still have some things to set up."

"Sure, dad." I nod, tucking the blanket around me to prevent the chill from seeping in. Harry looks between to the two of us but doesn't question it. He knows how to mind his own business because he wants people to mind their own business when it comes to him and his family.

"Why do you have to put the animals in the barn?" Harry asks. Honey's pen is our whole front yard year-round. He'd balked at the size of her especially without a halter or rope to control her. It doesn't help that she walks behind you hoping for a treat or that she's a Percheron Quarter Horse cross weighing up to one thousand pounds and stands at fifteen hands high. I love Honey, she's calm and gentle and mostly used for pleasure rides or plowing the field. When I go into rodeos with her we often place last but it's more for fun than anything else. My dad has a horse too, another Percheron Quarter Horse, a buckskin gelding. They can partner in pulling the wagon or we can ride them separately.

"Cougar was spotted," dad answers simply. Lights appear in the kitchen so dad gets his boots on by the door. "You kids don't need to wait up."

"Okay," I reply. Harry had stayed silent as dad gently closed the door. Even with Landon drunk and Tyler high, he still doesn't want to wake them. I'm content with silence as I sit on the chair, waiting for Col to help me put the horses in the barn. With them just arriving, the horses' curiosity is peaked so they'll be making their way from wherever they were. Harry isn't as comfortable in the silence, he keeps looking around and tapping his fingers on the table.

"So...." He trails off as he peers into the living room. Landon had started snoring and it was pretty loud. "You got a crush on Tyler?"

"Yes," I reply honestly but my face burns. Harry laughs bitterly, runs his fingers through his thick wavy hair, then hits the table.

"He wasn't drinking lately." His fists slam onto the table again. The pain in his eyes hurts me. My eyes water. Harry doesn't usually speak about his feelings, he acts on his feelings. If he's angry, destruction comes from those hands. If he's happy, pranks and jokes from those hands. When he's hurt, they find someone else to hurt or control. "Huntley noticed. Wanted to keep Tyler in that stupor. Knows Tyler isn't as weak when he's not drunk. Actually stands up for himself. Tyler refused, would not drink." Harry looks at me, really looks at me, unshielding his always-shielded eyes. "You gave him hope and that's what happened!" He surges up and points to my bedroom door before pacing the small kitchen. I startle in surprise, hurt at his words but I refuse to apologize for giving someone hope. The door opens and Col walks in, carrying my dad's gun. Col notices the slight tension between the two of us but like his usual self, doesn't comment. He only gets involved when violence becomes a problem.

"You ready, Daisy?" Col asks, nodding at Harry. Harry repeats the gesture.

"Yeah," I stand up, leaving the blanket on the chair. I have a jean jacket hanging by the front door that I shrug on around my shoulders. Col double-checks the safety on the gun as he holds the door open for me. It's dark outside, misty and foggy. The cold sends shivers down my back.

"Here," Col snaps on a headlight, illuminating our way. We walk side by side.

"Honey! Here girl! Honey!" I'm startled when she suddenly appears in the darkness. I pat her nose, grab onto her mane, and swing up. Col hands me the gun so he can jump on Buck. Not one to like any weapon, I give it back as soon as I can. Col isn't afraid of the dark unlike me so he takes up the lead as we take the short ride to the barn. My dad and I have about twenty cows and a bull, if they stay together they'll be fine. I jump off Honey, open the barn door and flick the light on. Buck and Honey walk right in, not afraid of the dark enclosed space. We only have a bare lightbulb in the middle of the barn since we only run electricity through our battery-operated solar panels. Me and my dad live off the grid, with no TV, and no satellite. Landon and Harry weren't very impressed, at home they have a TV in their room. I walk to the cat house, grab the food container and shake it. Sweetie knows the sound of food but she doesn't come when I call her name. We're getting there though. At the sounds of bush rustling, Col takes the safety off and loads a bullet in the chamber.

"Get close to the wall," he orders as he stands behind a panel. It's not full coverage but it's better than nothing. I sigh in relief and Col chuckles when my Alaskan Malamute Chocolate Lab cross dog enters our view. She wags her tail in greeting but stays at the doors, Sweetie has made it clear the barn is her turf now.

"Hey Sugar," I coo as Col lowers the gun and clicks the safety back in place. Sugar is a pretty tall dog I got from the reserve near here a couple of years ago. One of my sort of friends gave me her as a gift for helping her sister out of a tangle. Sugar has an all-black coat like a Lab's with the bone structure of a Husky and Husky bright blue eyes.

"Your dad mad?" Col asks, scouting the wooded area near the barn for a cougar. As quiet and lethal as they are, we won't get much warning of an attack.

"Well, yeah, I guess," I shrug, wrapping my fingers around Sugar's collar. If my dad took Abe and Annakin, it's serious. If it was just a talk, he'd have grabbed the triplet's uncles. He might put his "talk" into action with only Annakin and Abe with him and both of them would feel inclined to do the same.

"Your dad is a good guy," Col throws an arm around my shoulder as we walk back to the house. "He'll be fine."

"Yeah," I murmur, flinching at some twigs cracking. Col laughs at me.

"And Harry knows you're good too, he'll come around," Col adds, almost as an afterthought but I know him better than that. During our short ride and now our slightly longer walk to the house, he'd thought his statement over in his head before speaking out loud. He's not very good at helping until violence becomes a problem.

13

Guest

———⟫•⟪———

Let's call it a day," Peter pats my back as he picks up my pail of nails and slips the hammer into his light brown leather tool belt.

"We've only been working for an hour," I roll my eyes as I stand up, thankful to straighten my back. Peter had nailed plywood on this half of the roof so I was helping him nail shingles on.

"Good day work done," Paul grins and stretches from his perch on the edge of the rafters. His back had been bent for a while as he hammered little pieces into the rafters to hold the plywood that we will be putting on tomorrow evening after Peter is done work, we are done volunteering at the soup kitchen and daily mass has ended.

"Thanks for the help," Peter gestures for me to go down the ladder first. I grab the big water bottle leaning against a stack of shingles to take with me, not wanting Paul to carry it with his hammer and nails since he doesn't have the good fortune of wearing a tool belt. He'd forgotten it at his house, technically, but really he had come over to visit his brother while Amy watched the kids at her mom's house. Probably to rant, but I'd ended up being here, so he was put to work.

"You need a ride, Daisy?" Paul asks as he climbs down the ladder next. Peter gives me a playfully annoyed look because he was supposed to climb down second.

"Nah, going for a run with Jonah," I respond, wiping shingle debris off my sweater and jeans. The black particles might just stain my bright pink sweater. At my words, Paul and Peter glance at each other before wiggling their eyebrows with grins. "No guys, not like that." I deadpan. They ignore me as they ask how long 'this' has been going on, and by the blush on my face, they start teasing me some more. Boys.

"Jonah, huh?" Peter grins, taking the ladder down. He accidentally knocks it against an eavestrough, bending the flimsy metal. Paul rolls his eyes at me as year-old black water with leaves and twigs slips out the side. There is moss on top. It's a pretty nasty-looking nature soup.

"He's pretty good looking," Paul wiggles his eyebrows and slaps my back. I lurch forward from the unexpected force and catch myself against Peter's truck.

"Hardworking too," Peter laughs at my burning face. I wilt into myself as they put the pail of nails, their tool belts, and other tools back in the garage to shelter them from the weather.

"Comes to church now," Paul adds, ruffling my hair much to my dismay when he exits the garage. He stands with his hands on his hips for a little after-work chat.

"Uncalled for," I step away from him. A laugh bubbles out of him. It's good to hear Paul laugh, he hasn't been as joyful since Amy said she was leaving him, and even before that he was tenser. It has to get worse, maybe even to rock bottom, before a beautiful married couple calls it quits. Paul won't call it quits though. Dickie raised his sons to be one woman men so Paul will continue to work things out with Amy and stay single if she moves on.

"We're just teasing you," Paul shoots Peter a look to stop teasing me. Peter is a pest if not controlled, Paul grew up with him and knows that so I'm thankful for his intervention.

"God willing, right?" Peter huffs out a laugh as Paul slaps him, rolling his eyes. Peter raises his hands in the air for the universal sign of surrender. "Okay, I'm done." The look I give him tells him I don't believe his words. "I promise," Peter laughs, closing the garage door with a press of a button. He quickly runs outside so the doors won't lock him inside even though there is a human door he could walk through.

"Here they come," Paul laughs as Rufus and Samson notice the garage doors closing and run over, barking and yipping excitedly.

"No jumping!" Peter warns them with a grouchy shout. I burst into laughter as I kneel down to scratch Samson's belly, he'd flopped on the ground for a good ole belly rub. He doesn't stay down long, being the younger one and still slightly over energetic. He runs in circles around me, knocking into Paul's legs as Rufus sits on my lap. "Stop crowding her," Peter clicks his tongue.

"Jeez," Paul complains good-naturedly. "You never stop being bossy."

"Go home already," Peter retorts with a grin as he pokes Rufus off of me. I stand up with a laugh and try to fold my hair behind my ears. The thick curls immediately pop back out.

"Thanks for the visit, Watsons. Jonah should be here soon so I'm gonna wait by the curb." I jut my thumb to Peter's automatic gates. There's a side gate close to it for people.

"Why don't you let him in?" Peter smirks, meeting Paul's eyes. Mischievous trouble glints in them.

"We can do a lil' hazing since you don't have any older brothers to do it for ya." Paul agrees with his older brother. I don't need them to do that, it would be way too embarrassing. Besides, Jonah and I aren't a couple. If I feel the timing is right, I'm going to tell him about my crush on Tyler. That's only fair to him and the answer I received from my prayers, I think, I never really know until the moment arrives. Anyways, I just know that I should be upfront and honest.

"It's not like that!" I defend myself, quite uselessly as my burning face denies my proclamation. Since Danae and Betty put the crush into my mind, it hasn't left.

"Wear a dress," Peter waves at me before scooting in the front door. He hid so I couldn't shoot back a witty reply.

"It's not a date!" I holler a reply anyways. I don't own any dresses anyways. Growing up with only a father, dresses were never part of my life. Aria has mentioned them on and off for dances and anniversaries but my dad and I always pushed it off.

"Don't change who you are for anyone," Paul smiles sadly at me. With his personal problems in his life, I readily take his advice. He's learning from his mistakes now, his wife is leaving him because he isn't the five-star, suit-wearing, overachiever business type. Paul wants the simple things in life, a good wife, beautiful children, a happy family, God, church, homegrown food, the great outdoors, and teaching his children how to appreciate the land and all its blessings.

"Not gonna happen," I wave at him as I walk away, slightly skipping down the sidewalk. Things are moving forward with Jonah, I do have to admit, but I don't think I like it too much. We only started getting closer after Tyler rejected my feelings toward him. Does this mean that Jonah is my rebound? It's best overall to come forward with my feelings, I decide.

My heart stumbles in excitement as a smile forms on my lips. Jonah is pulling up to the curb as I lock the gate so Peter's dogs won't get out. Jonah still doesn't have his truck back, the shop said it would be a while, so he's using the rental SUV. He waves in greeting, a smile lighting up his face. I reach out to the door handle and pull only to hear the lock clicking down. My deadpan eyes roll at Jonah's cheeky smile.

"Oh, you're so funny," I mutter loud enough for him to hear. The lock clicks back open so I tug on the handle as fast as I can but Jonah had immediately locked the doors again. I roll my eyes and try to act grumpy, crossing my arms and trying to pout my lips but they can't stop smiling.

"Well get in!" Jonah cheekily smiles at me. I pull on the locked handle.

"You need to unlock the-," the doors click as I am speaking so I quickly yank on the handle. He manages to lock them before I can open the door. Jonah chuckles in amusement.

"Hurry up!" The doors unlock again so I quickly pull the handle. Thankfully the door opens.

"Thanks for unlocking the door," I dryly comment, sliding in and buckling up.

"Oh, no problem at all," Jonah grins as he puts the car in drive and slowly exits the parallel parking spot. There isn't too much traffic at nine at night. I kind of like it. The sun has already set for the most part in this beautiful brisk fall weather. I enjoy the cold, and the dusk. Most people overlook the beauty of the end of the day, the birds chirping, the wind whistling, the hustle and bustle of the town slowing down, and the world coming to rest as the night animals wake up.

"Oh hey," I point to the stop sign. "Is that Pete?"

"Um, yeah, I think so," Jonah peers through the windshield with me. Pete is lying on the ground by the stop sign, probably passed out. He doesn't look too good with vomit on his dirty, stiff, stained clothes and greasy hair filled with dandruff barely covered by a worn-out baseball cap.

"Do you mind if we take him to my house?" I ask, my heart going out to the poor guy. Not much is known about him but a lot of the towns-people mention the ballad of Ira by Johnny Cash as him. Something about he went to war, his mind can't handle it and now he drinks himself slowly to death and it's a painful experience for everyone.

"Yeah, sure," Jonah answers even though he is taken off guard. Since we're already stopped he puts his hazards on and we get out. Pete smells of urine and his snores are deafening.

"I'm gonna put my sweater on the seat just in case he's wet," I inform Jonah before placing my sweater on the seat. It doesn't cover much space on the leather interior so I hope it manages to catch whatever may leak out of Pete.

"Oh, that's nasty," Jonah covers his mouth and turns away, hunching over. I lean over Pete and turn him on his side so the vomit can fall out of his throat. The stench is horrendous, overpowering my nostrils.

"You got any gum or tic tacs for him?" I ask Jonah, following his lead and stepping away.

"Uh, let me check in the console." Jonah jogs to the driver's side of the SUV and peers in. Pete groans and heaves, a new burning-nostrils vomit stench wafts through the wind.

"You okay, Pete?" I crouch down and pat his back. My nose wrinkles at more barf spraying out of his mouth.

"I, what, huh, where my?" Pete mumbles, wiping his cheek with the back of his hand. I cringe at the sticky vomit now spread across his hand and chin.

"I'm going to take you to my place," I smile gently at him. "Get you a shower and some food."

"Yeah, uh-huh," he mumbles, holding his hand up for me to take.

"I got it," Jonah softly pushes me out of the way. I hide a smile when he takes Pete's hand in his sweater sleeve-covered hand. Jonah grunts when he has to haul Pete's full weight up by himself, Pete being no use at all.

"I got the door," I open the door as Pete wobbles. He ends up hitting his head on the edge.

"Should we put the seat belt on?" Jonah asks.

"No," I reply, gently closing the door. Pete leans on it. "If he needs to puke, it's faster to get out."

"Smart," Jonah opens my door for me.

"Thanks," I slide in. Pete burps loudly in the backseat as Jonah closes the door. I peer in the backseat, worried about Pete. He's a drunk, like a lot of people in my small town but he's worse off. He can't hold a job, can't stay sober for the life of him, he's lost full control of one of his legs and limps around town with a cane.

"You're amazing, Daisy," Jonah says as he buckles up. I shrug, looking out the window. "Have you picked up Pete before?"

"Uh, no, not really. Usually, I just sit with him until he's fine to walk to his shack." I answer as Jonah looks both ways before crossing the street. It was a four-way stop sign.

"See!" Jonah points to me. "No one does that!"

"Jesus did," I reply quickly. "I think, probably, the bible doesn't go into detail. But Jesus helped the outcasts and the drunkards. I'm just following what Jesus did."

"Just take the praise," Jonah rolls his eyes with a huff of laughter. The rental SUV's motor is quiet, a silent purr compared to his truck or Col's loud exhaust.

"Thank God for the good He does through me, in me, and with me." I laugh at the slightly irritated expression on Jonah's face.

"Fine," he groans, looking in the rearview mirror to check on Pete. He'd gone pretty quiet back there.

"C'mon Jonah," I grin, elbowing him.

"What?"

"Thank God for the good I do," I smile cheekily at him. Jonah stares at me to see if I'm being serious. I nod my head, grinning.

"Thank you Jesus..., for helping Daisy..., help Pete." Jonah quietly stutters.

"Awe! There you go, Jonah! Easy peasy."

"I guess," Jonah murmurs, his fingers tapping the steering wheel.

"Too soon? Okay." I still smile at Jonah when he nods at my words.

"Let me just get used to this whole God thing first." He shoots me a polite smile.

"Sorry, I'll have more patience."

"You don't need to apologize. You're, like, zealous or whatever for the Lord. Never apologize for that." The words I love you pop into my mind but Jonah would take them the wrong way. I don't love him in a romantic way, I love him as a brother of Christ. I love that he lets me act upfront with God, he doesn't get uncomfortable and hide the Lord in his life. He's come a long way in the few weeks since I've asked him to believe with me.

"Thanks," I shoot him a grateful smile.

"See, there? Gratefulness!" We both laugh, laughing harder when Pete startles awake. Pete mutters something we can't hear and leans his head on the window. Jonah cringes when we hear a screeching sound from all the oily buildup on Pete's face from lack of showering.

"I'm happy for your faith," I smile at Jonah, becoming serious as he pulls into my driveway. "You've come a long way."

"Only with your help," Jonah shoots back. He frowns at my dad's little log wood cabin. "Is that Landon on the balcony?"

"Is he praying up there?" I ask excitedly, peering out the windshield. My shoulders slump in dismay when I see him drinking from a flask. The balcony is my and my dad's little chaplet room! "He's not praying up there!"

"What is Landon doing here?" Jonah asks as he parks the car.

"Tyler's hurt pretty bad. They brought him here last night." I reply, getting out of the car. "That's a holy place, Landon! Please don't drink up there!"

"Oh, sh-, sorry! I'll get down!" He hollers. I wince when he stumbles against the wall, knocking into our framed picture of Jesus's Divine Mercy.

"Hey, Daisy!" Harry waves at me, sitting in my dad's rocking chair. Sugar is laying on his feet.

"Hi, Harry!" I wave back at him.

"Hey Jonah," Harry greets Jonah.

"Hi," Jonah mumbles back.

"I don't think he heard that," I open the back passenger door, squealing when Pete falls out. I jump back, my reflexes surprisingly fast. Pete groans, spittle dropping out of his lips and down his chin.

"Oh, that's nasty," Harry wrinkles his nose.

"Here, help me." Jonah waves Harry over as he struggles to stand Pete up. Pete is trying to fight him.

"He stinks of piss."

"I'll help," I offer, closing my eyes when Pete's loosely curled fist aims for my face. For a drunk man, it lands pretty accurately. At least he didn't have much power in the punch. "Ow," I feel my cheekbone.

"Here," Harry mutters, pushing me out of the way. "I know how to deal with drunks."

"You okay, Daisy Daisy?" Jonah asks as they hold Pete's arms to his body and carry him to the house, his feet dragging.

"Yeah," I skip ahead of them and hold the door open. Harry whistles and murmurs something to Jonah.

"Oh yeah, I know," Jonah replies.

"Be nice," I gently scold.

"We are," Harry deadpans. I close the door and squirt around them.

"Let's get him in the shower," I open the bathroom door.

"Yo," Harry slaps Pete. I gasp. "Wake up. Get your ass in the shower."

"Hey!" Pete shouts when Harry drops him. Jonah grunts when he catches the full weight of Pete.

"Not cool," he mutters.

"I'll get him some clean clothes."

"Have you done this before?" Harry and Jonah stare at Pete's dirty body in disgust.

"Sort of. It's just my dad's old clothes." I leave the bathroom to Harry and Jonah arguing and Landon stumbling down the steep stairs that are more like a ladder. Deciding I'll worry about Landon later, I quickly grab Pete some of my dad's clothes and race back to the bathroom.

"What do you do to us?" Harry mutters, setting the clean clothes on the toilet seat.

"Make you a better person," I grin at him.

"Go, we'll get him in the shower." Jonah sniffs. Harry nods along although he looks disgusted.

"Do small things with great love!" I shut the door to the words of Mother Teresa. I lean my back on the door, fist-pumping. "Yes!" I whisper shout. I helped two boys, one pretty not nice, to do a kind act.

Thank you, Lord!

"Hey Daisy," Landon smirks at me. He stumbles a few steps before crashing into me. We end up hugging each other so he won't fall.

"Where'd you get the alcohol?" I frown, taking the flask out of his hands. I'm dismayed when it's empty. He drank all of it.

"You'll never know," he laughs, pulling us onto the couch.

"No!" I shoot up, wagging my finger in his face. "We all have boundaries. Do not cross them!"

"Is cute, little Daisy, mad?" Landon coos.

"Do you want something to eat? I can make you some food." I've been around enough drunks to know food takes the buzz off, if that is the right saying.

"Can you make me some chocolate cake?" Landon closes his eyes, sighing in delight. "Cream cheese icing, too."

"Yeah," I sigh and stretch, looking at the clock. It's near ten pm. It's going to be another late night.

14

Newspaper Famous

———➤➤-◇-◄◄———

So...?" Betty grins at me, looping her elbow through Esther's. I was at the back of the pack. The sister's Betty and Esther were in front, then the friends Asia and Mimi, then the sisters Danae and Leanne walking on the sidewalk. Betty and Esther are walking with interlocked elbows, giggling and gossiping. Asia is walking with her arms swinging. Mimi is busy wrapping a piece of chewed and dried sour gum back into its wrapper. Danae has her shoulders hunched in and her hands stuffed into the pockets of her black sweats. Leanne is the one talking out of the pair and she is a hand gesture person.

"Jonah came home late," Esther giggles. I roll my eyes. Jonah stayed late to eat some of my amazing chocolate cake. He said he didn't care for cream cheese icing but he ate it up real quick and had three more pieces drowning with the amazing icing.

"See, I'm not the only one." Danae laughs at my exasperated groan. This bunch of girls jumped on the Daisy and Jonah love train.

"The Trips were there too," I defend myself and my chastity. Why won't these girls get it? They don't understand that I'm not interested in dating, but I guess that's what most teenage girls think about. Girls can have boy friends that are only friends, I'm the prime example.

"Ooh, did they stay the night?" Esther giggles. I think sometime during the riverside run Landon had flirted with her and now she has a big ole crush. Poor girl is going to get her first broken heart when Landon screws around with a different girl.

"All three of them?" Leanne elbows Mimi, wiggling her eyebrows. The Trips are the bad boys of the school. They probably want to change them, and prove that they can become good. I don't buy into the bad boy romances. Only the Holy Spirit can move a person to become the best version of themselves.

"Yeah," I answer, taking a Twizzler out of Danae's pack of sweets. Col always fills her locker at school with sweets, her words quoted from him 'I'm sweet for you'. Cringe moment. He won't admit to saying that in front of the boys.

"Was there a party?" Asia asks, grabbing Danae's last candy. "Col left last night and didn't come back 'til five am."

"No," I stifle a laugh as Danae's eyes widen. A blush flows across her face as she zips her lips. Oh boy, she's sneaking out with him now, not even pretending to camp at the Layton's. She is going to get caught soon with how daring she is acting.

"Funny," Leanne giggles and elbows her sister. Danae shoots her a nasty look to shut up which Leanne completely ignores. "That's when Dani got home."

"Ooooh!" Betty whistles. She's a sucker for relationships. Betty always has to butt into relationships, give them a ship name, and see the couple together before they see themselves as an item. Betty could make a career out of matchmaking. "Tell me more!"

"Dude, that's my brother!" Asia complains, crossing her arms and kicking some pebbles at Danae's feet. No girl likes her friends dating their older brothers. I'd feel like trust was broken between the two of us as she went behind my back. I understand where Asia's anger is coming from.

"I met him first!" Danae exclaims, kicking the pebbles back. Just because Danae is an introvert doesn't mean she is pushed around. With three older brothers, three older sisters, two younger sisters, and a younger brother she's had to fight for her position in the family.

"Did you ever hear the story?" Leanne wiggles her eyebrows at me. I shake my head to indicate I hadn't. Before this school year, before tutoring Landon, Harry, Art, and Col, before hanging out with Jonah more, and being introduced to his family; I had not hung out with these girls this much before. Asia is a given, our dads are drinking buddies and since Danae started dating Col, she's become a friend to me. Betty and Esther seem to really want me to date their older brother. I guess it's good that they like their brother's potential girlfriend.

I just can't get Tyler out of my mind, out of my heart. Good girls can't change the bad boys, as movies and books depict. As I know so, but I want him to come to church with me, to believe with me. I'll have to pray for his conversion. I'd rather have him as a friend than lose him altogether.

"She doesn't need to hear," Danae moans, covering her bright red face with her hands. Their dad is white and their mom is native, she's the perfect mix of Métis with not white skin but not brown skin and light brown hair and eyes.

"It's sweet!" Esther speaks up, high-fiving Leanne. The story of how Col met Danae, I've heard something about it. Col's dad lives in the city not far from here with his new woman and he had to live with his father since he was only seventeen, being allowed to spend weekends with his mother on the farm, which he and his siblings prefer. Danae's dad drove the school bus and that's how they met, at least from what I heard.

"Yeah, totally meant to be." Betty seconds. She points to the grocery store and murmurs to Esther. The United States sells alcohol in grocery stores, but why am I so baffled that the liqueur store is the building next to the grocery store in our small town?

"Danae was always picked on by Kevin and his cousins-," Mimi starts the story. I guess I'm finally hearing the true story firsthand. It will be nice to hear from the girls, nice to learn some history of the group, of the people in this town.

"The Martel's," Asia speaks up. She squints angrily ahead of her, making me chuckle at the cute twist of her lips. Angry is bad but it looks cute on some people, usually, the people who are so laid back that they never get angry. Asia is one of those people. Or I just find people getting worked up funny, most angry people make me laugh and that makes them even angrier.

"Norman and Martin." Mimi grinds her teeth when she says the two names. I've heard of those two boys, and seen them around school, they are in some of my classes now that I'm in high school. They usually just ignore me, ignore everyone. I haven't seen that much bullying at my school, but lots of students are nicer when around me. The comments I've heard are they feel like I'm too holy to be in their presence and try to be better people around me. I laugh internally at that, I know I'm a bigger sinner than them because of my judgment and hypocrisy. We are all works in progress and I have to train my mind not to judge and act better than thou.

"That rich, fancy equestrian family." Esther nods at Betty's whispered words while looking pointedly at me to get her point across. I don't mind rich people, as long as they are nice to me and others, I'll be nice to them. I do have to admit it's hard to be merciful when you are rich, material items soon take over to showcase your wealth.

"Bullies, the lot of them." Leanne sniffs. I softly chuckle at her British or Irish accent.

"That was totally, like, a Peaky Blinders accent." Danae squeals and hugs her sister. I've heard of the show but refuse to watch it. Apparently, the main character in it tries to be like God and that isn't cool. We are only human, created by the Creator. I firmly believe you are who you look up to, and what you put into your mind and I refuse to be a part of that ungodliness.

"Loved it," Mimi joins the hug. I smile at the three sisters hugging but sadness alights in my heart. I'm an only child, I don't have the bond that sisters who grew up together share. I've only just started making friends. People smile and wave at me, asking how I'm doing but they don't get too close to me. As a Christian, as a Catholic, I make them uncomfortable. I try to do good and be a better person than the person I was yesterday, an hour ago, even a minute ago. When people hang out with me for a little bit they don't like that I make them live consciously, not by force or authority but by example. There are good people in the world, plenty of them, but many good people don't incorporate the spiritual and corporal works of mercy into their lives, and those are what Jesus wants us to do. Clothe the naked, feed the hungry, visit the needy, those are why I stopped and helped Pete even though I was repulsed by his stench and dirty, greasy figure. Every person we meet, we should treat that person like Jesus.

"Speak of the devils," Asia mutters. She and Esther flip the three Martel cousins off as they enter the grocery store. The boys weren't facing them so they don't even notice the gesture. I wince at the vulgar gestures the girls younger than me are making. Every little act, every word, every thought in our mind is a spiritual battle for our soul's eternity. We all grow at our own pace, I shouldn't be judging them. In years to come, they could be more faithful, more zealous for the Lord than I am. I pray that that is the case.

"No judging, guys." I gently say. Should I say that? I don't know but if I don't teach them, who will? I know the Faidleys are Sunday mass regulars but their parents aren't here to guide them. The Laytons go to church at Easter and Christmas, they need a Godly influence in their life. I'm not perfect, I don't think I am, I'm not better than anyone but if I have knowledge that they don't; especially if it be about God, I want to pass it on. God judges us on our judgment or mercy of others, I want the whole world to act in mercy. Think about the peace that will bring to the earth!

"It's true," Betty huffs, popping a bubble with green 5 Gum. It's a Layton thing, they always have gum in their lockers, backpacks, and cars. Everyone bums pieces of gum off of them and they don't mind because they seem to have an unlimited supply. I guess it is beneficial to have rich parents that give them a hefty allowance each week. For all their money, the Laytons don't act snobbish or uppity. It's something I'm sure everyone appreciates. Betty's shoulder-length brown hair is in a French braid on top that stops halfway to allow a ponytail. It's a cute hairstyle, I like it. My wild hair would never let me do that. I have too many flyaways, split ends, and curls. The tamest my hair gets is if I loop a ponytail every inch to keep it under control. My hair looks like that guy off of Moana. Esther suggested cornrows but no one I know knows how to put them in hair.

"Just gossip with us," Esther urges. From her grumbling early in the walk - which I don't know how I was invited because I was strolling the streets picking up garbage - she had complained about Betty's laziness. After dolling up Betty's hair, she expected the favor to be returned. It wasn't so she had a classic, cheerleaders high ponytail in her classic blonde cheerleader hair.

Lord, forgive me. I so just judged her in my mind, pretty harshly too.

"I've heard this story tons of times," Asia exhales loudly and grabs Mimi's elbow. "Let's get some Yop." She's also leaving because it is her brother and she probably doesn't want to hear a group of girls giggling about him.

"And cheese," Mimi adds. She has an obsession with cheese that all the Faidley girls share. The older, the better. Cheese makes me fart, milk makes my stomach hurt, and dairy products mess my digestive system up pretty badly. I might be lactose intolerant.

"Get me some Twizzlers!" Danae pushes Leanne forward. The sisters are only a year apart, close to being Irish twins and Danae tries to act bossy but Leanne is bossier than her. Funny how that works but it's probably because Leanne is very much an extrovert while Danae prefers solitude. Danae is pretty tall for her age, taller than the rest of us girls, and insanely skinny. She looks like she's all bones but if you've ever played football against her, she's also insanely strong. Her bones must be titanium. Before the Faidley's moved here, their dad ran a dairy farm.

"Get them yourself," Leanne retorts, laughing as she races to catch up with Mimi and Asia. Mimi is two years younger but they are closer because they share a room, Danae used to share with their older sister, Helen, until she moved out last year.

"C'mon," Danae squeezes between Betty and Esther. "Let's get some Twizzlers." It's nice to see her talking with other girls, usually she tends to herself. She's not quite the middle child, but she was often the forgotten child. Chris and Karl chuckled as they told me all the stories of Danae being forgotten because she was so quiet as a child.

"Nerds too," Betty adds, placing a hand on her lower stomach. "Period cramps suck."

"A Coffee Crisp will help," Esther says. But then she groans. It's science — women and girls that live together, their periods line up. "Chocolate always helps but I'm synced with you so we gotta buy some for me too."

"You know Jonah will run to the store for us," Betty grins at me, trying to butter me up. I'm happy she likes me, but she needs to slow the Jaisy train down. I'm torn between Jonah and Tyler and need God's guidance on if I should choose one to be my life partner or if I should focus on being single, study at St. Therese Institute or become a nun. "Just so you know if you need him to buy you pads, he will."

"We aren't dating," I mutter, glad my dark skin hides my little blush. For the majority of my life, I wasn't around boys, except Col, Leo, and Richie but none of them are my age so we never hung out. I've only ever talked about shark week supplies with my dad and since he'd let me meet Aria, she'd been my go-to.

"Uh-huh," the three teenage girls knowingly say. I roll my eyes at them, something I've been doing a lot lately since they got this Jaisy idea. And yes, they've made some jokes about our ship name and sung some Jay-Z songs to me.

"You coming, Daisy?" Danae asks, looking back. She'd let go of Betty and Esther's arms to talk with me privately and knowing what it is, I decline. She wants to list the pros and cons of both boys but I don't agree with that, there seems to be too much judgment in that. I like them both for who they are and won't pit them against each other, even if only in my mind.

"Nah," I wave them off. Danae nods in understanding. She's a private person so she respects her friend's privacy. They're cut off by a Ford Expedition that I recognize. It's Phil Watson's. I haven't seen him since he got back, it'll be nice to talk to him. I also want to visit with Phil. If he's driving he can't be physically hurt so they must have sent him back for his mind. He needs a break, hopefully, war memories don't break him. That's probably why the Watsons had the prayer vigil.

"Daisy!" Phil's oldest daughter, Paris, shouts when she sees me. I laugh when she and her younger sister, London, barrel into me and hug me tight. When Phil is on tour I rarely see them at daily mass or the soup kitchen. Phil and Arlette have four girls and two boys ranging from ten years old to just a baby so Arlette has her hands full. Dickie or Phil's cousin Francis always helps her get them to Sunday mass on time but now that Phil is back, he'll be helping Paul because Amy is leaving him. My thoughts remind me that I have a lot of praying to do.

"Hey girls," I hug them tight. They both have thick Watson blonde hair and hot chocolate brown eyes. London recently went through a growth spurt, she has her father's tall height in her genes while Paris seems to have their mother's shorter stature. "How are you guys?"

"Daddy's back!" London squeals, dragging me to her father. He leans against a cement block, arms crossed over his chest, squinting against the bright sunlight. Like every other Watson, his muscles are defined against his body but even more so with his military service. The Watsons are traditional Catholic men, preferring the Latin mass. Their wives and daughters wear veils to mass, a promise to God to stay obedient to Him; I don't even do that.

"We're so happy," Paris smiles at me, rolling her eyes in a very Watson-like fashion at her younger sister's antics. At ten years old, she thinks she has to act more composed and as the oldest child, she is, of course, the bossy child.

"I'm happy for that too," I respond as London holds my hand and Paris leans in for a side hug.

"Hey, Daisy," Jasper, the eight year old boy, waves at me as he stands beside his father. He is the spitting image of his father, from the lanky body, the thick blond military cut hair, and sky blue eyes, the only one out of his siblings to do so. The rest got their momma's brown eyes that are a strong Watson feature. Only Dickie, Phil and Payton have blue eyes out of the large family. Jasper always tries to act macho and cool so I always burst his bubble by pinching his cheeks and pulling him in for a bear hug. "Awe, c'mon!" He whines when I squeeze him tight. "You saw me, like, two days ago."

"Actually, it was three," I ruffle his short hair, so basically his scalp as London and Paris wrap their arms around me again. I'm loved. They are my church family, my Catholic family, spiritual family. With them,

I never have to hide who I am. I try not to with classmates and citizens but some small part of me is very careful about my speech in front of them.

"Whatever," Jasper huffs, squirreling out of my grasp.

"It's so good to see you!" Arlette smiles widely, albeit tiredly at me. While I was greeting Jasper, Phil had gotten a cart and she sets the car seat over the width. Phil and his brothers were raised right, they know how to treat a lady. They do all the heavy lifting and hard, outdoor work and help their ladies inside when needed. Arlette must be so grateful and happy Phil is back. Poor baby Savannah was born while her father was on tour, her father is a stranger. Vienna doesn't remember him and is shy around him. Denver doesn't respect his father as much as he should, but that has to be earned anew with his father's arrival. Philip has his work cut out for him.

"If you need help, let me know." I smile at Arlette as the two toddlers start yelling from the back seat of the Expedition. Denver is four and Vienna is two years old. Their mother pushes the cart into the store, slowly walking behind.

"London, Paris, go help your mother," Phil orders. The girls are happy with Jasper chasing them around and bugging them. Phil rubs his hands over his face with a deep sigh before leaning once again on the cement block.

"I take it kids are hard work," I grin at him, standing facing him with a couple of feet between us. Jasper is busy running between us to the car, shouting through the open door. Denver isn't too happy staying buckled up and his wailing is contagious with Vienna.

"I better take them out," Phil yawns, then stands up. "Arlette will be a while."

"I'll watch Jasper," I offer. Dads often don't have eyes in the back of their heads like mothers do.

"Thanks, kid," Phil responds before climbing into the backseat to unbuckle his toddlers. The Watsons nicknamed me kid a while ago, it's a serious day when they call me by my name.

"Catch me if you can!" Jasper shoots me a grin before taking off. A smile makes its way onto my face as I start running after him. Jasper forgets that I love to run and train for marathons. Soon my smile turns to a frown and my heart stutters in my chest. Jasper had veered toward the road and wasn't paying attention to where he was running, which is straight into traffic, and the road is busy.

"Jasper, stop!" I shout, sprinting toward him. He thinks I'm chasing after him and speeds up, giggling. Drivers honk as they slam on the brakes of their vehicles. We aren't in a school zone, they're going a little over the speed limit because they are going down a hill. Phil shouts at Jasper to stop, his face frozen in fear. Denver can hear the fear in his voice and cries in response. My breathing seems loud in my ears, and blood rushes through my body, pounding in my heart. I'm gaining ground but will it be in the short time frame to get Jasper out of harm's way? The squealing brakes alert Jasper to the danger ahead of him and he jerks to a stop so suddenly that he loses balance, flying forward. I reach forward, grasping onto his shirt just in time to pull him out of the way of a passing minivan. The driver honks, the passengers glare at us as I wrap Jasper in my arms. Not usually one to cry, he sobs into my chest, his heart beating fast. "Hey, you're okay." I hold him tight, hearing the flash of a camera amidst his sniffles and raggedy breathing.

"You have to look where you're going, Jasper!" Phil runs up, Vienna and Denver in his arms. He sets them down to look over his elder son when Jasper launches himself into his father's arms. I leave them alone for the group hug, walking to the stores front doors that my friends if I can call them that, are strolling out of. The girls all have nosy, excited profiles on their faces.

"What happened?" Betty asks, biting into a KitKat. The crunch is a soothing sound to my ears but my thoughts wander to a different, deeper meaning of the crunch. Jasper could have easily died if he was hit by that van, his bones would have been crushed, and the crunching amplified from the crunching of the KitKat.

"Jasper just about ran into oncoming traffic," I state the truth, hoping they won't delve deeper to find my involvement in saving him. I thank God he gave me the ability to catch up to the eight-year-old. If Jasper had died, I would have to relive that moment every time his name, or the Watson name came up.

"Is he okay?" Leanne asks, hesitating to walk over there. I see why when I look back. A crowd had formed around the war hero and his son.

"Yeah," I reply, shrugging as we all start walking in the direction we came from. Betty had driven to the park, I had ridden my moped, and Asia's parents had dropped her and the Faidley girls off there. They had all made plans to hang out together when I stumbled along. Even if I wasn't in the original invite, it was nice of them to invite me along spur of the moment.

"Bet he's shook," Esther shakes her head, a hand on her heart. "That's scary."

"No shit," Danae rolls her eyes, eating a strawberry jam Klondike ice cream. Esther has a Coffee Crisp, her favorite although she doesn't drink coffee or even like its taste. Asia and Danae are sharing a pack of Twizzlers and Mimi and Leanne are sharing a small block of cheese. I'm not kidding. It's old cheddar, Cracker Barrel.

"Excuse me, ma'am," a man shoves his camera in my face. I startle back, blinking my eyes in surprise. "Can I get the name of the young lady that saved that young boy's life?"

"Daisy!" Betty and Asia exclaim, shooting me amazing looks. Esther and Betty squeeze beside me to get into the picture, Danae ducks her head and the other three girls don't really care as they eat their sweets, waiting for me to respond.

"Daisy Ridel," I sigh, elbowing Betty and Esther away from me as I avoid the camera lens and walk passed him.

"She was the girl that saved the boy from drowning last week," Betty smiles into the camera. The reporter slash journalist keeps the camera on her, probably knowing he will get more out of her than me. Danae is the only one to slip past the camera and reporter, the others too enraptured with the thought of being in the next week's newspaper print. I avoid it. I didn't rush to save Jasper to be written and photographed, I pulled him back because I love him as a brother in Christ.

15

New Fam

———⟫•❖•⟪———

"Oh, hey Tyler," I jump up from my perch on the sofa. Landon's feet had been in my lap and they fall to the floor with a loud thump as I set my bible on the coffee table. With nothing to do at the moment, having done my homework and helped the Trips with theirs, I'd been reading my bible, meditating on what I thought the passage was trying to tell me. Dad had asked me to stay home from school today because he wanted to talk to me. That was after he left at five am this morning for the city with his truck and a trailer. Aria went behind in her Jeep. I'm really curious as to what they are doing and what my dad plans on telling me today but I'm trying to stay patient.

"Hey Daisy," Tyler croaks, leaning on the little hallway wall to catch his breath. His gait is very pronounced with his limp yet he still refuses to go to the hospital. I walk up to Tyler and wrap my arms around him, giving him a gentle hug.

"I'm so happy you are up. Praise God!" Tyler chuckles, which turns into a coughing fit as he reciprocates the hug. I don't mind when he doesn't let go right away. He needs loving in his life and I don't mind being the one to love him.

"I think I'm gonna shower," Tyler states after his coughing fit ceases.

"You want help?" I ask, wrapping my right arm around his waist and looping his left arm over my shoulder, careful not to put too much pressure on his bruised and sore body. I hate feeling each rib in Tyler's anorexic-looking body, every vertebra on his spine. What I hate worse is the swelling of his flesh and inflamed bruises. At least we know he doesn't have internal bleeding, he would have died by now.

"Ooh, Daisy!" Landon whistles, lifting his feet back onto the sofa. Dad had tried making him and Harry go to school but they refused. The compromise was me tutoring them on their homework dad picked up from school. Landon wasn't too happy about that but Harry seemed happy to have algebra occupy his thoughts.

"I was offering your help," I roll my eyes as I help Tyler turn. He leans heavily on the wall for support. "I'm keeping my eyes and my mind as pure as I can until marriage if that is my vocation from God. Even if that isn't the case, I'll remain chaste forever."

"Sheesh woman, I was kidding," Landon grumbles, rolling off the sofa to help his brother shower. Landon had taken advantage of our meager facilities every day, showering, styling his hair, and shaving. He's pretty vain.

"That's exactly my problem. You don't take my virginity until marriage seriously." At the V word both boys cough in embarrassment, Landon's cheeks tinging red. I love using the word around them to get this reaction, hopefully, it makes Landon think before he sleeps with another girl.

"I take it seriously!" Landon groans, squeezing passed us to open the bathroom door. "Just stop saying that!"

"What?" I smirkingly grin as I carefully let go of Tyler. They all think they can tease me, they should be able to laugh when things are reciprocated. "Virgin until marriage?"

"Yes!" I laugh at Landon's uncomfortableness and Tyler joins in. It soon makes him cough again. Landon scowls at me from the hacking cough which makes Tyler grimace in pain. "Stop making him laugh!"

"Why would I stop making him happy?" I retort, causing Tyler to laugh some more. Apparently, I'm the only one willing to argue like this with Landon, per Harry's words. It amuses Harry to no end, to see us bicker. Landon sends me a death glare. "I'll stop, I promise."

"Get out of here unless you want to see him naked," Landon shoos me away, obviously because I just won that argument. He needs to pout in private while I gloat in public. Just kidding, I don't gloat. Gloating causes pride to rise and I want to remain a humble person. At least I think I'm humble.

"Who do you think has been giving him his bed baths?" I take a towel out for Tyler and set it on the closed toilet seat, along with a face cloth, some body wash, and shampoo.

"What?" Tyler asks, eyes wide as he stares at me in shock.

"I only did your arms, upper body, feet, and calves," I inform him, waving my pointer finger in his general direction. "I don't need to see or feel anything else. VTM."

"We know!" Landon throws his head back with a groan. "Get out!"

"Take your time, we have well water." I close the door because I saw Landon picking up a pair of socks. They hit the door with a thump. "Love you too!"

"You are pretty loveable," Harry pops his head out from the top of the fridge. I jump in alarm. While Tyler was resting in my room and Landon was complaining about the lack of TV, X box, and wifi Harry had been enjoying the outdoors. I hadn't expected him inside so soon. He's cuddled with Sweetie, played fetch with Sugar, went spruce chicken hunting with Sugar, and even pet Honey!

"You too," I reply, unable to take a compliment without dishing them back. Harry rolls his eyes before digging into the fridge again. He's also a sweets and dessert person.

"Landon ate all the damn cake," he grumbles, shutting the fridge door only to open it right away. I laugh at his actions as I walk around the fridge door and stand beside him, peering in. No leftovers, thanks to the three boys but dad went shopping yesterday and bought a boatload of food. I'm not sure how we are supposed to eat this all before it goes bad. I might have to give up my fasting days so food won't go to waste.

"I can make more if you want," I ask, moving some grapes and avocados out of the way to see if he bought any desserts. Dad bought all Aria's healthy food too. What a bummer.

"What about cookies?" Harry asks, looping his arm over my shoulders and pulling me back so he can close the fridge door.

"Sure, what kind?" I respond, reaching into the upper cupboard beside the fridge. Because of my short height, I have to stand on my tippy toes. My tongue makes its way to my top lip in concentration. We keep our baking supplies and spices up here. Sometimes mice are a problem so we keep food items in the upper cupboards and dishes in the lower cupboards, being careful to wash them before use. It's a pain.

"Here," Harry pulls me out of the way. "Let me get 'em."

"Thanks," I blow my flyaways out of my eyes and point at the ingredients even though I'm behind him now. "That white bag of sugar, the brown sugar too. That little tub of baking soda. Oh, perfect, you already got the vanilla. Do you want chocolate chips or peanut butter?"

"Chocolate chips," Harry responds, setting all the items on the counter.

"Oatmeal too?" I ask as I turn the stove on. In the daytime, I can use our small, electric stove but in the nighttime, I use our wood stove. That's a pretty neat experience, cooking on top of the wood stove, smelling the food slowly cook. When I made my chocolate cake, I used the wood stove because it was late at night. Harry and Jonah thought it was pretty cool too.

"No," Harry snorts. "You only like oatmeal in your chocolate chip cookies if you are crazy."

"Do not!" I retort, spinning toward him. He glares at me, trying to hide a smile. All of his hair is in a man bun today but some strands have escaped. I reach up to fold them behind his ear, knowing they must be itching his cheek if his hair is like mine.

"Don't touch me," Harry snaps, squeezing my wrist tightly with his fingers. My eyes widen as I lose control of my fingers, and the tips begin to turn a purple-ish pink. "You got it?" He shoves my hand away from him before twirling away and storming to the door. He doesn't get far when the door opens and my dad appears in the doorway, a baby in his arms.

"You and Aria adopted a baby?" I cry, racing over with a smile on my face although Harry's actions and words have me shaken. Harry stops his march. In the bathroom I can finally hear the water turn on, covering up Landon's grumbling. "Why didn't you tell me?"

"Daisy," dad speaks up with a heavy sigh, looking me straight in the eyes. He means business. "This is your cousin, Philomena."

"Cousin?" I ask, stumped. It's always been us two Ridel's against the world. Even when he told me we had family, I didn't think he would let me meet them. Most people don't just take in their family that they refused to acknowledge for years. But I have to remind myself that we aren't normal people, we are Ridel's, and Ridel's take care of each other. What happened to my family for my dad to pick them up? Aria and some young men are unloading the trailer. Through the door, I can see some dressers, mattresses, and bed frames with garbage bags squeezed in to maximize space.

"Yes, your cousin," Dad says patiently, holding the baby out to me. She's so tiny, has to be under a year old. She can support her neck, smile, and grasp onto the soother in her mouth. "Harry, do you mind helping Aria and my nephews unload the trailer? I have to return it to Romain tonight."

"Sure," Harry murmurs, his face impassive. I make a mental note not to initiate physical contact with Harry, it seems to set off the demons in his mind. He's just another person that will be added to my prayers.

"She's so small," I whisper, wagging her hand. Dad smiles down at her, love brimming in his eyes.

"You want to hold her?" He asks, "I'll go help your cousins and them get everything out and set up. You want to watch the kids?"

"Kids?" I ask, curling Philomena in my arms with my dad's help. I've held kids, but never really any babies under six months. It's a new experience, one filled with love.

"Philomena's siblings," dad ushers me outside. "Where is Landon, he can help too."

"He's helping Tyler shower," I reply, my eyes widening at the seven more kids ranging from preteens to toddlers running around in the front yard. "I have eleven cousins?" I ask in bewilderment. Why didn't dad ever tell me about my big family?

"Four. Sally Anne and her three older brothers. Philomena and her four siblings are your cousin Lawrence's kids and the other two girls are Louis's (Lou-ey) girls." Dad slaps my back. "Go introduce yourself."

"Will do," I make my way to the oldest girl sitting on my tire swing. I guess it isn't just my swing now, but my cousins' as well. Dad built it for me when I started to walk. Philomena is asleep in my arms even with all the shouting and giggling from the rest of the kids as Sugar energetically chases them around, racking up a loud bark. When I get closer to the swing I notice another baby on her lap, this one about a year old. She looks grumpy from being woken up from a nap. "Hi, I'm Daisy. Your cousin."

"Obviously," the preteen girl snappily responds. My eyebrows rise in shock at her attitude. She sighs. "Sally Anne, this one is Tikara."

"Your niece, right?" I ask, more so to make conversation than to really know. I'd pieced together that knowledge from the information my dad gave me.

"Yeah, my bro Louis's baby," she responds, her eyes lighting up at the fact that she can school me in something. "Tinsley! Get over here!" She shouts. I'm concerned when the baby in my arms doesn't flinch from her loud, abrasive tone. A tall, skinny, thin-boned girl with long hair runs toward us, smiling with rounded-off teeth. It shows that her parents let her suck on her soother too often for too long. Her thin, long hair is a light brown color. When she reaches us, with a little boy and girl following her, she smiles sweetly at us.

"I'm your-," Sally Anne interrupts my words.

"Tinsley, this is your aunty Daisy."

"Hi," Tinsley smiles and wraps her arms around me. I love the hug she gives me, the immediately given trust.

"Buddha, butt, boo," the young boy smiles at me before pushing into my legs. I just about fall from the force.

"Sorry. I didn't catch that," I smile down at him.

"He said he wants to swing," the little girl speaks up, surprising me. She speaks better than the boy who looks older than her.

"The boy is Conan," Sally Anne speaks up. "And the girl is Kennedy. Guys, this is your aunty Daisy."

"Let Buddha boo," Conan yells, pushing against Sally Anne on the swing.

"Let him swing!" Kennedy shouts with her brother. Her voice is louder than his, deeper too. When she talks it is loud but when she yells, boy oh boy, it's *loud*!

"Patience you two!" I raise my voice to overcome theirs. "We can all take turns." Kennedy and Conan don't agree with my words and vocalize their feelings. Tinsley takes off, running to the other two kids as they run to us.

"Kennedy, Conan, stop shouting!" The girl running at us shouts, bossy and annoyed. Out of all the girls, her hair is the shortest, resting on her shoulders. It's also probably the thickest hair here, besides mine. I have my dad to blame for my Maui look-alike hair.

"That's Makayla," Sally Anne juts her chin to them. "And Windsor."

"Hey Makayla, it's okay." I smile at her. She looks at me dubiously before walking off, Tinsley following. Conan and Kennedy keep yelling together, pushing at Sally Anne's knees curled from the swing seat. Philomena is still sleeping.

"Oh my God, fine!" Sally Anne bursts out, jumping up. Conan and Kennedy immediately climb on, happy now. The smiles are a big contrast on their tear-streaked faces.

"Please don't say that," I gently talk to Sally Anne. She rolls her eyes crankily before thrusting Tikara at me. I barely manage to shift Philomena in my arms before catching Tikara. She stares at me, her lips wobbling and her face turning red as Sally Anne stalks off. "Makayla!" I call out, frightened at the prospect of holding a wailing baby and a sleeping one. Philomena will certainly wake up with her close proximity to Tikara.

"I got her," Makayla says, pulling Tikara roughly out of my arms. The one-year-old stops crying once she is in familiar arms.

"Hold her better, please." I gently say, miming how Makayla should hold her cousin with Philomena in my arms. Makayla just sets the little girl on the grass.

"That's all you gotta do," Makayla rolls her eyes before running off to chase Windsor. My next hour is spent playing with the two small girls, lying in the grass, watching Tikara crawl around and Philomena trying to eat grass while lying on her stomach. They don't really make noise, the silence is worrisome. Shouldn't babies cry? Isn't that how

I tell if they need their pampers changed or a bottle? I also keep my eyes on Conan and Kennedy, they argue with each other but if anyone interrupts them they have each other's back. Sometimes Conan just needs alone time so while he is off doing his own thing Kennedy plays with Tikara, pulling grass and showering herself and the babies with it. Makayla and Windsor get in the way of Dad, Aria, Harry, and my cousins hauling the stuff in. I'd spotted three bunk beds, one had a double bottom. There were four dressers, two tall ones, and two shorter, wide ones. Aria, as a woman, was designated the clothes to haul in. Lee got the dresser drawers while Harry and my dad partnered to haul dressers and Lawrence and Louis partnered to haul beds in. Sugar was having a fun time with my cousins' two dogs, one a small grey and white Shih Tzu, the other a young black and white mutt. The small dog is an inside dog, something I'm going to have to get used to. Dad is a big believer in no dogs in the house but winter is coming so we will have to get used to inside animals. When all the work is done, Aria wants to leave quickly to spend the rest of the day with Phil. Tomorrow she leaves for two weeks for back-to-back flights with only two days off at separate times for a break. She'll make a load of money but is not going to church worth it? That's a question I ask myself but can't honestly answer until I become an adult myself and see how much supporting my living habits actually costs.

"Lawrence, Louis, come take care of your kids!" My dad shouts to the house from outside as he sits on the lawn with me, holding Philomena, whose pamper was heavy and wet. With the long drive, Tikara's is most likely as well. Dad lowers his voice to talk to me, looking around to make sure none of the kids are within hearing distance. "Don't let them use you, they will."

"But I will help them," I state stubbornly. Even if they abuse my help, is it not worth it? The spiritual and corporal works are completed when acting upon mercy.

"I know, my darling girl, just make sure they put in the work as well. Kids are tiring, I only had one and there seems to be a dozen here now." Dad sighs, running a hand through his balding hair. "Those men don't have jobs or driver's licenses. They barely get any child support to get by. I'm going to have to work overtime as much as possible, but I'm not going to ask you for monetary help. What you do with your money is up to you, all I ask is that you spend it responsibly."

"If you need help, I'm down," I offer anyways. My cousins walk out of the house, shoving each other with curse words and smiles. My dad and I sit in silence as they each pick up their daughters, complaining about the full, now funky-smelling diapers with more vulgar language.

"I got some explaining to do, huh?" Dad chuckles bitterly. He throws his arm around my shoulders and pulls me into his side. I lean my head on his shoulder, curling into his embrace. I love my dad's hugs, he doesn't give them often, being raised in an authoritative home where emotions were frowned upon and physical touch denied.

"Yeah," I respond forlornly. "What happened to it being just us two Ridel's against the world?"

"My parents, they had their troubles." Dad begins, licking his lips. I let him take his time. A story this hidden must be painful to tell, to remember. The least I can do is give my dad a safe place to tell his story. "My dad, I loved him, ya know? He brought joy into my life and loved me even with all the trouble in the family. He'd made his mistakes, and owned up to them. I have a half-sister from him, it's hard for me to believe that I have a fifty-year-old sister. But he is the one who taught me my faith, brought me up Catholic."

"Stop getting sidetracked," I wave my hands in front of his face. "Tell me about my aunt I've never met." What a wild day. I become an aunt and learn I have an aunt, that's way more family than I knew I had.

"Her name is Jade, Jade Hamilton. She's European, happily married as far as I know with two daughters. Kaitlyn is fourteen and Andrea is ten. Jade got along well with Joseph, my brother, but that was because they were drinking buddies. I still have to talk to her, but she might be taking custody of Sally Anne since she got along well with her girls."

"Only Sally Anne?" I ask with a frown. Dad shrugs.

"She's worked in a grocery store since she was nineteen, only four dollars up from minimum wage. Her husband is the stay-at-home parent."

"How do you know all this?"

"We talked at the funeral, traded numbers, and are keeping in touch now since Myriam died."

"Whose funeral? Why wasn't I invited? You've been talking to her for how long and haven't looped me in? Who in the world is Myriam?" I ask, putting a fist over my mouth to stop more questions from barreling out, showing my bafflement at the boatload of information my dad is dumping on me.

"My brother Joseph's funeral," dad sighs. "Jade called me the day of and that's why I took off so suddenly with Aria. You never met him, I didn't have the mental stability at the time to explain everything. The night I got back, I was already stressed, and seeing Tyler so banged up just put me in a bad mood. I'm sorry to admit I took it out on Huntley."

"Tyler didn't deserve the abuse from his father but you shouldn't have thrown hands, dad."

"I know, Daisy, I know."

"Who's Myriam?" I ask, getting dad back on track.

"Your grandmother." Dad sighs, his muscles stiffening. "She, uh, she wasn't very nice. Myriam immigrated from Salvador, Brazil from the state of Bahia. Got a work visa as an author, met my dad, married him to become a citizen, and pretty much used him. Her books went nowhere because she tried writing them in English and her grammar wasn't good, for that matter, her plots sucked." I laugh at the tone in my dad's voice, annoyance laced with laughter but a slight bitterness trails behind.

"Did you know your brother well?" I ask. Windsor and Makayla race out of the house, laughing and shouting as kids do.

"He was ten years older than me, shielded me from mom's abusive ways. Was a lot like my father that way, was who he was named after, so that showed in his character but his mind couldn't handle it. Started drinking, and slowly became a drunk. When he drank he became like our mother so we grew distant, Jade preferred to stay in a stupor as well so they got along but I felt... abandoned, and got some trust issues from that now. Decided to take a step back from them when I got the chance and filed emancipation papers as soon as I turned sixteen. Turned to this good Catholic family for support but I made my own mistakes. They helped me get a job for the man who used to run Peter's construction business. I married your mom, got sucked into her lifestyle, and went downhill from there. When your mom became pregnant was when I snapped out of my downward spiral. I didn't want to be the father my father was and I didn't want your mother to raise you as my mother did, so I gave her the ultimatum. She left, I stayed."

"I know this, dad, you've told me more than once."

"It gets pretty complicated from here," dad sighs and squeezes my shoulder. "My brother divorced your cousin's mother soon after Sally Anne was born. They were raised with a drunk for a father and a manipulative woman for a mother, so take it easy on your cousins. Joseph married Kaitlyn Burger, a woman twelve years his senior with two daughters. I met her at the funeral. It's a terrible thing to bury your second husband. Both of your step-cousins had different fathers, opting to stay single and enlist in the navy. Jade, confusing I know, to have an aunt Jade and a step-cousin Jade, who is actually only a year younger than me. Amanda is thirty-eight. They're Black. Jade will probably never contact us or think about us again; she didn't really care for your uncle but Amanda agreed to keep in contact. I guess she enjoyed drinking with Joe, her mom, your aunt, and your cousins."

"This is wild, dad."

"Yeah," dad exhales deeply. "That's enough for today, I'll let it sink in with you for a few days. Once you have it handled we can talk more but I need to think about other stuff."

"Sure dad," I respond, "just one more question."

"Shoot."

"Why'd you take them in, if you never met them?"

"They're family," dad shrugs. "I got out of the stigma, the inter-generational trauma. I'm giving them the chance, especially the young ones. With your example leading them in life, they'll go places."

"Jesus is my example," I state confidently as I stand up. My right leg fell asleep and I was just about to fall when I don't feel it touching the ground.

"Jesus is a good example," my dad admits sadly. I know where his thoughts are going because I've thought them myself so I speak up.

"It's never too late to accept God's mercy." They are words we all need to hear, a lesson of love.

16

Winner

————➤◦◅————

C'mon Lee!" I urge, pulling him up from the double mattress bottom bunk bed. "It'll be fun."

"It's also what a way to introduce me to your friends," he grumbles, shaking my hands off. In the few days since he moved in, he'd mentioned joining the military and training for it in his spare time. Free time for him is uneasy to get, Landon, Lawrence, and Louis all sneak off to party and are either drunk or hungover pretty much daily. That left me and Lee in charge of their seven kids. To sum it up, Sally Anne hates it here with absolute fury. She's just waiting for Aunt Jade's paperwork to come through so she will be in the custody of the non-strict, fun-loving, easy-going aunty. So yeah, she's been a little grumpy towards me... and my dad... and Lee when he needs her to help out because their brothers are too intoxicated or headache-y. Windsor and Makayla love it here, the cat, the dogs, the horses, the cows, the freedom and they are enjoying it while it lasts because Monday morning dad is putting them in school, along with Tinsley. Conan will be going to the head start program every weekday morning except Fridays. It saddens my heart, and my soul to see the negative ways Conan and Kennedy interact with each other and the rest of their family. I can tell they were neglected and I hope to change that. I've learned the babies are terrified of car seats, usually, Rennie and Louis's girlfriends would leave them buckled up throughout the day so they could party.

"I don't have friends," I roll my eyes at my cousin. He's definitely my favorite one so far, seems to have his life together. That just proves that the others are the ninety-nine I need to go look for.

"Who the hell are those two?" Lee retorts, waving at Landon and Harry behind me. They look uncomfortable in the small living room with Conan hitting and pushing on their legs, Sally Anne complaining about too much light this morning, and Windsor and Makayla chatting to them. What's even funnier is that I put Philomena and Tikara in their arms to get Lee up for the marathon today. I know Harry goes from girlfriend to girlfriend and Landon sleeps around. Holding the babies is a consequence of their actions if they get a girl knocked up.

"Oh," I hum in thought, looking at two of the Trips behind me. They haven't called me their friend, but they have talked to me more lately since I've been tutoring them and dragging Landon's butt to church. He's become a much nicer, sweeter guy since praying the highest form of prayer, where heaven meets us here on earth during mass. "Are you guys my friends?"

"I'd hope so," Landon scowls at me. "We've been living here for a week." There's also that. With only a two bedroom, one bath cabin, and sixteen extra people living here it's getting hectic. Landon and Harry are going back to Huntley's when Tyler is able to walk without getting winded. Dad thinks it is some sprained ribs, if not broken so it will take the better part of two months.

"No," Harry deadpan retorts in all seriousness. I really set him off when I reached out to touch him, which baffles me because he can touch me. Something bad must have happened to him for him to have that reaction. Harry has to initiate contact and he can't receive contact. How does he interact with his girlfriends? When Philomena farts in his arms he gives me a withering stare.

"Call her dad," I equally as seriously retort, jabbing Lee with my fists to get him up. He's joined me for runs around the perimeter of the fields and I know he's fast, a better sprinter than a marathon runner but any extra legs to raise money is worth it. If his brothers weren't so out of shape, I'd get them to join as well. Running is raising good money for a good cause!

"Rennie! Come get your kid!" Landon shouts for his non-communicative brother. Harry has been snappy with me lately. I've taken it in stride, mostly because I know I set off the demons in his mind, but it was an accident! "Louis too!"

"I have two friends," I smile at Lee. "Danae will be here soon. Her boyfr-, her friend will be driving us to the start line."

"Do you have a secret from your dad?" Lee gasps dramatically, having noticed my close, open and honest relationship with my father.

"That's her lying voice," Landon snickers. My two older cousins are still hungover and refuse to get up, annoying Landon and Harry.

"I can do it," Makayla takes Philomena from Harry's arms.

"You're only eight," Lee sighs, waving his niece to bring her sister to him. "I'll change her pamper, and Tikara's, then we'll go enter the marathon."

"Thanks, Lee!" I smile enthusiastically at him, looking triumphantly at Landon and Harry. They made a bet that I wouldn't get him to come. I don't gamble but I just won!

"No one can say no to you Daisy," Landon rolls his eyes. Makayla is grabbing the diaper bag and Windsor is taking Tikara from his arms. Since they moved in, I've missed my solitude. I'd even had a headache yesterday and all the yelling and fighting put me in a bad mood. Offering up my pain for those who need it usually helps but because I was in a bad mood, my heart wasn't in it and I was being selfish.

"People do all the time," I frown, "especially when I ask them to come to church or pray with me."

"I agreed," Landon sniffs.

"You felt guilty and I and my dad used that guilt to get you into the church." I cheekily grin at Landon. Jesus saves!

"What did he have to feel guilty for?" Lee asks, rapidly changing the diaper. He must have experience with this, having to take care of them for his drunkard of brothers. Poor dude must have missed a lot of teenage things to do growing up. Windsor is ten, Lee is eighteen, and Makayla is the age Lee was when he probably had to step up to watch his nephew.

"Uh, nothing." I back away, my eyes wide. I don't like showcasing others' mistakes. Landon's lips form a straight line. He still doesn't like thinking about how he hurt me, it reminds him of his father but at least Landon knows he can choose to be abusive or be a better man. Landon is trying, that already means he is a good guy.

"I effed up," he growls, running his hands through his hair before storming outside. Harry glares at me before following his brother, slamming the door. He's a grudge holder, something that will change with how much he is hanging out with me and my dad and his Watson family.

"What did he do?" Lee asks, setting Philomena on the floor to have some belly time so he can change Tikara's pamper. Conan and Kennedy's energy had sparked from the slamming of the door. I smile in amusement as they find some markers and begin drawing on their father and Uncle Louis's faces. Lee smirks and shakes his head but leaves them to their devices. My cousins shouldn't be this hungover, to not wake up with the cool, moist tip of a marker coloring their faces.

"He choked me," I say very quietly. I'm not going to hide what Landon did but it's clear to see he regrets it and bringing it up hurts him.

"He shouldn't have done that." Lee glares at the door. Great, I'm Lee's younger cousin. We did just meet but he says I'm too innocent and naive and that he has to protect me. He graduated high school last year and spends his time watching his nieces and nephews. Louis and Lawrence always manage to find part-time jobs. Dad is going to see if Peter will hire them on the condition that they agree to stay sober.

"It's cool," I pat Lee's back. "We're cool. You two can be cool. He's actually a really nice guy once you get to know him, past all the walls he puts up."

"He's a drunk like Rennie and Louis," Lee hisses through his teeth.

"Me and dad are trying to change that but his role model, his dad, is a drunk. They started drinking and partying at a young age. We have to show them by example that they don't need to drink with how hard life can be. They won't listen to advice."

"Not many people do these days," Lee sighs, setting Tikara on the floor and throwing the plastic shopping bag of dirtied pampers and wipes into the garbage. We can't set it outside yet because it's still bear season but the stink is filling up the house. Dad is going to order a diaper genie with his next paycheque but for now, we are strapped.

"Col is here," Harry opens the door a sliver and shouts to us before closing the door just as quickly. The Trip's mood swings are worse than mine, but I grew up in a loving, nurturing environment, they did not. I'll have to show them nurturing ways to engage and interact with their family and friends.

"Col is your friend's secret boyfriend?" Lee asks with a raised eyebrow, pulling on a pair of socks and his runners. He sleeps in sweatpants because he doesn't have pajamas. Lee, along with his brothers and the Trips, usually sleep with only shorts on but dad doesn't allow it. Frankly, I don't care to see it.

"Shh!" I shake my head at him. "Secret means they haven't told anyone else yet."

"Just you, because you are such close friends, right? Miss. Friendless."

"They told Jonah too!" I'm quick to say.

"Ah, they told your boyfriend too. Do they want to go on double dates?"

"Jonah is not my boyfriend! Why do people keep saying that?" I groan, slapping my hands over my eyes to cover my burning face.

"Is he running in the marathon?"

"Yes-," Lee interrupts the rest of my sentence as we wave goodbye and shut the outside door.

"So he's running because you asked him to."

"He's on the cross country running team! He's racing in the marathon as practice for the finals coming up." I huff, climbing in the backseat. Landon has this thing about always sitting in the passenger seat, Danae is in the middle and Col is driving. I'm going to be squished in the back with Harry, Lee, and Leo, who always joins the race. Leo doesn't usually do anything with Col, or to support our town, but he always races in this marathon. His new girlfriend - we have to be careful because Dane's older sister, Amy, is his ex-girlfriend from very recently - insists he run the race and they were best friends since sixth grade so it's an ongoing tradition of theirs. She will be in the marathon as well. Last year they beat me, along with three other people (one of them, Jonah, and one of them Paul Watson). Sixth place isn't bad for a fourteen-year-old but I've been training for the whole year, I'm aiming for first place. It will be a shock to the town, but a good one, if I can do it. Jonah, Art, Paul, and Lee are all pretty fast.

"Hey Daisy, Daisy's cousin," Col greets as he puts his truck in gear and backs out of our curvy driveway.

"Lee," Lee introduces himself. He doesn't buckle up, and neither does Harry but I'm not intimidated as I clasp my seat belt ends together. Safety first, even if it is only a short drive. I set out in life to lead by example and this is one of those times where action catches people's attention. With a huff, Landon stretches the seatbelt across his body and buckles in. The constant dinging of the seat belt indicator may have also been a factor in his safety. The annoying little bell dinging gives anyone not wearing their seatbelt the attitude to buckle up, even if it is only to get the mechanical dinging to shut up. Leo jumps out of the truck to open and close the gate at the end of our driveway, the gate keeps the horses in and trespassers out. I'm stuck in between Harry and Lee, otherwise, I would help him since it is my gate, my property. Well, my dad's.

"Nice to meet you," Col depresses the signal button as he waits on the approach for his brother.

"Same," Lee replies, not one to talk much and even less so in front of people he doesn't know.

"Jonah said you're going to his house after?" Danae asks her statement, trying to be nosy. When will they get it that I'm not hanging out with Jonah to date him?

"Yeah, me, Art, Pierre, Sadie, and BJ."

"Wow," Landon scoffs. "He invited our cousins but didn't invite us."

"Oops," I cough slightly in embarrassment. "I was supposed to send you the invite but forgot."

"Getting tired of us already?" Landon scowls, his muscles stiffening. "We can leave."

"No!" I cry, "I just forgot! You guys are welcome as long as you want."

"No, they aren't," Lee mutters quietly. With a small, two-bedroom house this full, we should really ask them to go home where they at least have a bedroom to themselves instead of sharing a living room with eleven other people. I won't let them go home as long as I can help it. Tyler will only be hurt more, and probably get drunk and high to become immune to the pain. At least at my house, with all the chaos and crowdedness, he can actually live, be himself, and struggle with his addiction but know he has a support system to fall on if he needs to.

"Jonah invited you guys as well, and Col and Danae. His parents took Nate and the rest of his younger siblings to their grandparents for the weekend." I speak up, shooting Lee a look to be nice. "It's just a small get-together, please don't invite anyone else. Especially any drinking buddies."

"Yeah, let me party without having to worry about my brothers," Lee adds.

"Yeah, they get mean when they're drunk. Try beat the shit out of me," Landon chuckles. "Fools."

"Hey! Please don't call anyone that!" My voice is slightly raised. "No one is a fool."

"Stop dissing my bros," Lee scowls.

"I got more bros than you." Landon retorts, "kick your ass."

"Cut it out," Danae rolls her eyes, curling closer to her boyfriend. She doesn't want to be in the way of any punches thrown. Lee is to my left, diagonally opposite Landon. I'm in the middle of them, dread seeping into my stomach. I have first-hand knowledge of how violent Landon can be. He would never hurt me again, he promised. Lee won't hurt me either, even with his dysfunctional family they still ingrained in his mind the motto that a family sticks together.

"What? With your handicapped brother?" Lee snickers, causing Harry's hands to form fists. I shake my head at him, wanting to place my fingers on them to hold his hands down and his anger at bay but he is angry and he doesn't react very well to contact from other human beings when he is in a good mood.

"Watch your mouth!" Landon swivels in his seat, sending a death glare at my cousin. I slide back into the seat to avoid the mean gaze, squishing between Lee, who doesn't mind, and Harry, who shoves me away. Leo keeps his eyes locked on his phone, avoiding the drama. Most of the time he just doesn't give a care, he's a lot like Col that way. Or I should say Col is a lot like him that way since Col is the younger brother.

"Cool it guys!" Col raises his voice to be heard. "I'm not afraid to kick you guys out if you start fighting. My truck, my rules."

"Whatever," Lee scoffs but he doesn't respond to Harry and Landon's muttered threats.

"At least you guys can burn all this anger off during the run," I chirp, clapping my hands.

"Oh my goodness, Daisy. Shut up!" Leo shouts at me. The sudden outburst shocks me into silence. I stare at Leo, hurt at his anger towards me. I've never done anything mean or rude to him, always been myself, helpful, kind, and hopeful.

"Uncalled for," Danae shoots him the bird. It's a ballsy move, Leo doesn't like her either.

"Wasn't asking you, jailbait." Leo scoffs, grabbing her finger and bending it backward. Danae screams which cause Col to swerve as he hits his brother to stop hurting his girlfriend.

"Your friends are crazy," Lee mutters, swearing under his breath when Col's truck crosses over the yellow line into oncoming traffic.

"Let her finger go Leo, or we all gonna crash!" Col yells, adding expletives in there that I refuse to repeat.

"Slow down!" Landon clutches onto the oh shit handle to brace himself. Harry ducks in front of me, pulling on my seat belt to make sure it is around me tightly. I don't understand him, at all. He's trying to protect me while he's treating me badly. Leo shouts some swear words as he lets Danae's finger go. Drivers honk at us as Col swerves back into his lane.

"Thank the Lord we're safe," I breathe out in relief. Landon, Lee, and Harry all swear at Col and ream him out as we enter town limits. My fear is forgotten as I look at the busy streets, moms and tots ready to cheer us on, some kids and dads I know stretching to prepare for the race. "Let's go make some money for cancer research!"

"Yay!"

"Woo!"

"Fun!" Landon, Lee, and Leo all cheer half-heartedly.

"It's Jonah," I lean into the front seat as we pass Jonah, Art, Esther, and Betty.

"See, you like him!" Danae taunts with a grin. Col is driving slowly, trying to find a spot to park in the crowded streets of the usually empty town. We have to drive quite a ways back because the competitor's parking is packed full. That's a good sign, one I enjoy.

"No, she doesn't!" Landon and Harry snap, defensive because they know I like their triplet brother. Col manages to find a parking space in the post office parking lot, but as he circles in to take it, a little car zooms forward, taking it over. Danae honks at them as Col waits for pedestrians to walk over the crosswalk safely. It's Phil Watson and his family. I wave to them and they see because Danae had been honking. London, Jasper, and Paris's faces light up when they see me. Phil is carrying Vienna in a backpack carrier and pushing Savannah in a two-seater stroller. One seat is empty as Denver walks beside his mom, Arlette keeping a firm grip on the energetic toddler's wrist.

"She can like Jonah and Tyler at the same time," Danae rolls her eyes. Harry and Landon both shoot me dirty warning looks to deny Danae's words. Col circles around a housing block, finally just parking between two people's houses.

"I like Tyler, I'm tired of saying I don't like Jonah," I say to placate them. It's Danae's turn to shoot me a dirty look. I widen my eyes and shake my head at her to get her to stop pushing Jaisy. "People shipped us together without even getting the facts straight. I don't like Jonah. He's just a cool friend."

"You ever think they started Jaisy because the J of Jaisy let people know he liked the -aisy?" Leo scowls at me before jumping out of the truck. What is his problem with me?

"I just don't understand why he doesn't like me," I shake my head sadly. Then my eyes widen as an understanding of his words dawned on me. "Jonah started Jaisy?"

"No," Danae denies as Harry and Landon glower at me one more time before exiting the truck. Oddly enough, Lee follows them. I take it the tough words earlier were just them testing each other out, seeing if they'd be compatible as friends. Lee's answer must have been a yes. I wait for Danae to finish her answer, slightly scared at Col's fingertips running over Danae's forearms and his whispers in her ear.

"Uh, that's it?" I frown when Danae giggles and pushes Col away. They act like they are doing the deed but what do I know?

"What else would I say?" Danae shoos me out of the truck. "Leave us alone, we'll look for you at the finish line."

"Col is racing, too." I remind him just in case he has other activities on his mind.

"I'll be there." He assures me. I jump out of his truck, used to the isolation of being by myself as I walk to the registration people. During the short walk, alone with the street filled with people, I ask Jesus to work through me in the run. *Lord Jesus Christ, help me to persevere in this long run. Keep me offering up the ordeal of this race for the conversion of souls around the world, peace on earth, and the repentance of sins. Let me reflect on Your Passion as I push myself to my limits, remembering Your Agony as You filled Your deepest desire - to give us eternal life. Amen.*

"Hi, Daisy, ready to kick some butt?" Paul grins at me, sitting behind the registration table. I return the smile as he jots down my name and the number of the bib I'm designated. Our town is still small enough that we don't digitize registrants even with neighboring towns joining the competition. In a few years, I expect this race to be countywide. The benefits of that step up are tremendous, the more runners, the more registration fees, and the more money raised donated to charity.

"God willing," I sigh, signing my signature on the paper with the clipboard and pen Paul hands me. I clip my twenty-dollar bill onto my sign-up sheet. Affiliated sports players, like Jonah, have registration fees paid by the school. "Where are the kids?"

"Dad has them at the finish line, ready with water, crackers, and chocolate milk." Lovely, I always drink chocolate milk after the race. My ski coach taught me that. He wasn't really my ski coach but since I was eleven years old I worked at the ski shack just passed my place and if it was a slow day he'd take me out on the trails. He still owns and works at the ski shack, slowing down in his old age but he always shows up for the races. The whole town is amazed at his perseverance but I'm not. When you are close to someone and hear their story, you understand their drive a whole lot more. He'd served in the Vietnam war - for Vietnam. The country had made it mandatory that all their sons fight. He served his year and immigrated out of the country, forever damaged from the horrifying experience. He's an atheist now, and always asks why I carry that cross around my neck, but he's a good man. I pray I can get him to believe one day.

"Good man," I hand the clipboard back to him. Paul hands me my white bib with big block numbers. I slip it over my head and tie the strings around my waist. I'd come dressed for the weather, a loose windbreaker easy to take off once the sun's rays warm the earth, a light zip-up sweater to throw off when the midday sun warms my body temperature, and tighter fitting sweat pants so less wind drag will slow me down. Most suggest also wearing a baseball cap but my wild hair refuses any sort of hat on my head. "Thanks, Paul."

"God bless your run, Daisy." Paul shoots me a smile as he waves the next racer forward. I love the community of our church and the universality of the Catholic Church. It's hard to be Catholic when the other religions and atheists outnumber you but when there are more than one of us Catholics in public, we feel safer, more comfortable. We aren't afraid to say God, to talk about Jesus and Mary, and meditate and reflect on our faith to push each other to be the version God destined us to be.

"You ready, Daisy?" Art grins at me, jogging on the spot. His long blonde hair bounces with his steps and the little ponytail tying it back makes me laugh. At the mention of my name, Jonah and his sisters turn to face me. I can tell the difference in their class between me and Art. Matching running clothes and fancy brand names compared to me and Art's mix-matched second-hand, thrift store clothes but I'm not jealous or envious. The Laytons donate to charities and they help out at the soup kitchen and volunteer when our town needs them to step up. If they decide to spend money on themselves, that's okay too. Most times poorer people spend the little extra money they have on take-out food as a splurge on themselves. Betty, Esther, and Jonah buy designer clothes or wear their mother's high-end clothes. She gets shirts and pants, any type of clothes from competitors or start-up companies hoping for a shout-out. Vanessa gets her children to model them, or their friends, and gives them to the second hand store to sell at a steal.

"Ten minutes until the race starts!" Someone calls out with a speakerphone. I smile at Art and wiggle my eyebrows.

"Ready as I'll ever be," I respond to his question, beginning to jump around to get my blood flowing. Once my body is nice and warm, I'll do some stretches. Stretching when I'm cold hurts my muscles for some reason and because it is fall, this morning is just above freezing.

"Partner?" Art grins, shooting a look at Jonah. Awe, he's on the Jaisy train too, trying to get a rise out of Jonah by partnering with me.

"Sure," I roll my eyes, playing into his plan. I'm not dating anyone yet, I'm too young. I'm not doing this to upset Jonah or create drama.

Jonah will probably run with us, his speed matches ours. It just sucks that I have to work harder to maintain that speed because of the advantage of their long legs.

"Hey Daisy, Daisy," Jonah smiles at me. When my eyes linger on his face, his sisters giggle. It's really not my fault, he either has an extra birthmark from the other day or he has some chocolate or pepper on his face.

"Hey Jonah," I return his smile, reaching up to his face and rubbing my thumb over the extra birthmark on his cheek. "Did you have Nutella for breakfast?"

"Your tone was different there," Landon throws shade at me, appearing from within the crowd with Harry and Lee behind him. Esther's face turns red when Landon stops his walk by her and throws his arm over her shoulders. Betty squeals in delight. Poor girls, they're going to get their hearts broken by him.

"No!" I deny, my voice high in pitch. Harry scoffs at me.

"Nutella and peanut butter," Jonah answers my question with a slightly embarrassed profile as he scrubs at the rest of his face.

"That's not a very good breakfast for a half marathon," I frown, reaching for my backpack to find a granola bar for him. It's useless, I'm not at school so I didn't bring it with me.

"At least he had breakfast," Lee hotly retorts.

"Get up earlier," Betty snipes back, sticking up for me. I shoot her a smile of gratitude.

"This wasn't in my plans," Lee scowls at her, rolling his neck and shoulders to warm them up for the run.

"It should have been," Betty responds. "This is for a good cause!"

"I moved here three days ago, no time to prepare and no knowledge this even existed." Lee snaps back, rolling his ankles now.

"Who even are you?" Betty queries as the announcer shouts into the microphone, informing us we now have five minutes left and to make our way to the starting line.

"Daisy's cousin," Lee sighs, shaking his head at me. "I thought you said she was your friend."

"Um, I, uh," I stutter out. I told the group of kids I now hang out with about my cousins. Of course, I didn't get into too much detail but the reply I was going to shoot back to Lee was harsh on Betty. I actually never called her my friend and I don't want to hurt her feelings now. Besides her annoying Jaisy attitude and nosy personality, Betty is a really good friend. She cares about me, she brings me out of my bubble, she tries to get me into some more fashionable clothes, to talk with her cheerleader and dance club friends, and to be more outgoing. The more friends by association I have, the more chance to spread the good news of the Gospels.

"She did tell," Betty coughs out, blushing as she waves over Lee's body. "I just didn't expect all that."

"Ooh!"

"Uh oh!"

"Woo!" Landon, Harry, and Art all cheer.

"That is my little sister!" Jonah raises his voice as he squares off with Lee. "Do not say anything inappropriate."

"That's my little cousin," Lee raises an eyebrow at Jonah. I purse my lips, everyone seems to be talking about me and Jonah as an item and we aren't. Frankly, it's getting on my nerves. My patience is being tested.

"Hey guys," I speak up, breathing out to calm myself down. It's probably the lack of sleep and exhaustion from watching my cousins that have my walls wearing thin. "Let's focus on the run, burn all out angry energy there and visit lovingly afterward, okay?"

"Whatever," Harry bites out. The group gradually disperses with the last glares slanted at specific people. Betty mutters something about too much testosterone as Landon leads Esther to a spot on the starting line with him. He'll probably run at her speed to tease and flirt with her but I hope they keep their distance. She's only fourteen and he is a well-known playboy. Art smiles sympathetically at me before we walk to the starting line side by side.

"No Paul this year," he comments, checking his shoes to make sure they are tied tightly.

"Weird, huh?" I start some leg stretches in between Art and someone I'm not familiar with. It looks like they are from one of the next towns over. I'm happy about that.

"He's probably tired of winning." Art laughs, holding his straight arms back. I grab his wrist and gently pull them together, stretching his arms.

"He did have a five-year win streak," I laugh, turning around so Art can stretch my arms to get the blood flowing and muscles relaxed. Then Art looks at me seriously, with sadness in his eyes.

"He and Amy really split? Man, I really appreciated their rock steady, I looked up to them a lot, especially Paul." Seeing the sadness in Art's eyes, I bring him in for a hug.

"It's just a separation. They could get back together yet." I try to comfort him. Paul refuses to get a divorce, they got married in the Catholic Church which frowns against divorce. They don't have a valid reason for divorce, relationships take effort, not resignation. Paul was also raised to choose one woman and remain faithful to her no matter the ups and downs. I really hope Amy doesn't stomp on his heart too much.

"Runners get ready!"

"Good luck," Art shoots me a competitive grin.

"God bless your run," I wish the Catholic version of what luck means. We believe in luck but also miracles and blessings from God. Time seems to slow down as adrenaline pumps through my body, the beat of my heart is an echo of the whooshing blood flow. The announcer, our town mayor, is counting down the seconds until she blares the horn. It seems like I can count a full ten seconds for one of her seconds before the horn screeches in our ears and we are off. I push myself to get out of the crowd, Art breaking the wind in front of me. A smile slips onto my lips as I settle into my running routine, staying at the beginning of the race, but not first place. Lee has that spot right now. With a brisk breeze juxtaposing the warm sun beating down, my juvenile arthritis is acting up. With a grimace at the pain, I turn my frown upside down, offering my pain up to God for whoever he wants to use it for. The pace is steady, slower than my normal speed. I don't mind, firstly because the pain would worsen if I sped up, and secondly, I can save my energy for the last leg of the race. Art smiles at me, jogging by my side now. A runner ahead of me stumbles and falls, holding their ankle. I slow down, stop and stay with them until medics arrive. Art had kept running at our chosen pace, we (the group I trained with) had planned for something like this because I can't resist helping people. If I have to burn too much energy to catch up to him, I won't. It takes some stamina to catch up to Art and my aching bones scream at me for doing so but I push on. Jesus was dehydrated and badly beaten, blood loss galore, probably dizzy from the pain, my aching joints aren't that much suffering. If I do it with a smile, others will receive grace. That is my goal, and so I push on. The one-and-a-half-hour run seems to drag on as we tackle a hill, run through a dirt path in the forest, on the sandy bank of the river, pass by cheer stations, and water stops. At the halfway mark, Art speeds up the pace as planned. Now we find out who our competition is. Paul usually finished the run in an hour and thirty-eight minutes. I'm hoping to finish in an hour and thirty minutes exactly. We catch up to Jonah, who is listening to the book of Romans out of a Bluetooth speaker. I absolutely love it and enjoy the narrator reading scripture when he keeps pace with us. Soon the only people in front of us are the town-er and Lee. Leo actually smiles at me when I pass him. He's as confusing as Harry with his mood changes concerning me.

"Let's speed it up again," Art points at his watch. "We wanna beat Paul's time, we gotta keep up the hustle now."

"On it," Jonah replies. I save my breath as we speed up again, gaining ground on the out-of-town-er, who is in second place right now. We pass a cheering station, making us smile with the tiredness seeping in, giving us a boost of energy. They are appearing more frequently as we get closer to the finish line. We veer onto the highway heading into town. My heart thrums in excitement, especially when we pass the second place. Jonah and Art have longer strides than me but I slowly push myself ahead of them, taking it easy. Once I finally pass them, they cheer me on, showing amazing sportsmanship. I'm in the zone, the runners high as I continue my elevated pace. I get a boost of energy when I see the fifty kilometres an hour sign, indicating the last quarter of the race is here. My bones hurt, and when I look down at my wrists they are swollen and red. Inflamed.

"You've been holding back on me, haven't you?" Lee shakes his head at me. I shrug as he kicks up his pace. I follow along, glad to have the challenge. The wind is against our backs now, a relief in the end stretch. The sun has peeled out of the tree line, sending hot waves over us. My body is sweating but with the finish line within my sight I keep my jacket on, taking it off would only throw me off my pace. Lee hisses out a breath when he lands on his foot wrong and starts hopping to accommodate the pain. "Don't you stop!" He yells at me when I slow down. "Win this thing, cuz." I enter town limits, people on all sides. The exhaustion from the constant movement is taking its toll on me, I want to slow down, to stop running but I push on. The cheering encourages me as I get a stitch in my side but I pick up my pace still. I train to push myself at the end and it helps as I start sprinting even if it is a little early.

God let me win this for Your glory. In everything I do, let me do it with a willing heart to make my will Yours. Amen.

It seems like I can't breathe with how fast I'm running, the fastest I've ever run before. My aching joints and spasmodic lungs, my tired calf muscles and stitched side, everything in me is screaming for me to stop.

Jesus, carry me. Like how You carried my sins on that heavy cross.

As soon as I break through the finish line, classic red ribbon, I fall on the pavement, gasping for breath with a smile on my face.

"You okay, Daisy?" Paul asks, offering me his hand for help. "Walk it off, kid."

"Time?" I ask between huffs of breath, hands on my hips as I walk in little circles to the cheering crowd shouting congratulations. Peter pulls me into a hug, laughing happily.

"Praise God, Daisy! Best time yet!" He leads me to his dad's after-running station.

"God bless you, Daisy," Dickie smiles as he hands me my chocolate milk. It's a tradition by now. Unless there are new runners, he knows exactly who drinks what after their run.

"Here," Paul walks up to me, shaking his head with a bittersweet smile as he holds the timer out to me. "See for yourself, kid."

"God willed it," I laugh as tears sprout in my eyes. The time is 1:31:31. All glory to Him.

→ 17 ←

Friends

———➤•●•◄———

T ook you guys darn near long enough," Lee mutters as a greeting
   when I walk through Layton's front door. I stick my tongue out
at him before hanging my sweater and jacket in the closet and setting
my shoes to the side. My nose wrinkles at my stinky body odor more
present without layers shutting it in.

"The mayor needed more help than we thought," Pierre shrugs,
following my lead in hanging up his hoodie. When I had caught my
breath after finishing the race, I'd high-fived every participant and
helped Dickie and Pierre hand out bottles of water. With the activity of
the day done and all the runners returning safely, the Mayor had asked
the volunteer team of the day and any stragglers to clean up the garbage
off the street. Then she'd somehow gotten a flat tire so Pierre stopped to
help her. I passed him the tools and lent him my strength when needed.

"She probably didn't pick up any trash herself," Landon scoffs.
Their dad causes the most mayhem in town so the mayor makes life
difficult for him and his brothers. We shouldn't be judged on the actions
of our parents, as children, we are our own people.

"She helped," I defend the mayor. We all make mistakes and judge
rashly and harshly. We all need forgiveness and mercy. Landon stares at
me defiantly as I sigh and shoot him a smile, throwing him off balance.

It isn't premeditated. I just don't want to argue, my house has been too full of that stuff lately and I'm exhausted from the half marathon. I simply don't have the energy right now to convince him that looking through the world with a lens of mercy is better than a lens of judgment.

"Ugh, Daisy," Betty wrinkles her nose when I sit on the couch beside her and Esther. Col and Danae were cuddled on a love seat, Danae on Col's lap as she giggled and they conversed together. Harry, BJ, and Landon are on another couch, Jonah sitting on the stairs, and Sadie lying on the floor. "You stink."

"I haven't had time to wash up yet," I admit, standing up to back away. It gives them space from my stench to breathe better. Running a marathon will make a person sweat, and constant movement causes the temperature to rise.

"You can borrow my pajamas again," Jonah offers, jumping up. "Have a quick shower." Harry and Landon look at each other before glaring at him. I close my eyes, wincing at the thoughts probably swirling through their minds. People judge based on their personal experiences, Landon and Harry sleep around, I know where their minds went even if that's not where my mind goes or what I do.

"What the hell is he talking about?" Landon demands, jumping up. Harry clenches his fists together. He's not afraid to fight or to hurt someone when he's angry to get the antsy energy out of his system. I'm wary of just how tall he is now, how muscular he appears to be. Harry and Landon might not have the best of diets but they work out daily and tackle rivals in football games. Their dad beats them and they know how to punch from that and how to take a punch. Jonah doesn't have any cousins his age, his brother closest to his age is twelve, he never wrestled much growing up being surrounded by girls. Even if Harry and Landon don't double-team him, he doesn't have much going for him. Should I be worried about a fight breaking out? Landon has gotten into drunken brawls with my cousins but Harry has yet to release the tense energy of Tyler's beat down from their father.

"Daisy didn't tell you?" Betty grins at the triplets, wiggling her eyebrows. Since Jonah is out of their sight, up the stairs, they turn their glowering looks on me. "She stayed the night a couple of weeks ago."

"Dad was pretty upset with Jonah," Esther adds, smirking as her eyes light up at the gossip she is ready to spread. Teenage girls will be the death of me.

"Seriously Daisy?" Harry scoffs, crossing his arms over his chest as he sits on the top of a couch. I've noticed that that is his habit, rather than sit on the couch seats, he sits on the top where a person's head and shoulders usually rest. It's a part of who he is, his character, it's a little tweak to him not others have. I'm not sure if he even knows the habit himself.

"What happened to the whole chastity thing?" Landon hotly accuses. I sigh and pinch the bridge of my nose before responding. The devil attacks those who are on the right track, not because we mean something to him, but simply because he doesn't want God to win. Here's a little hint though: Jesus will always win. Always. I can't let Landon's accusative tone get to me, that would be allowing the devil to win. People cannot always control their environment but they can control their attitude in their environment.

"They're making it sound worse than it was," I speak up calmly to defend myself. "My dad and Aria were drinking. I was gonna sleep on the couch but me and Jonah fell asleep praying. That's it. I already feel bad enough about it, okay?"

"Oh, you feel bad?" Landon coughs and runs his hands through his faded haircut. "Tyler just about died 'cause you gave him hope and you just hide the fact you spent a night with Jonah!"

"We didn't do anything," I say calmly, breathing through my nose because I wanted to snipe at him. *Jesus, give me patience. Please.* "I'm not perfect Landon, I can make mistakes too."

"And keep it secret," Landon bites out.

"I wasn't planning on keeping it a secret," I hold my hands in front of me, then clasp them on my knees when I feel awkward and out of place. The triplets are making me uncomfortable and I'm fairly used to awkward and tense situations. "But how do I approach the subject to Tyler? We aren't dating. He made it clear so what, I'm just supposed to be loyal and obedient to him when I'm not even intimate with him?"

"Uh, Daisy," Landon coughs. I duck my head to hide my smile when the tables have turned. I've somehow made them uncomfortable now. "You talk so mature-like but act so naively."

"I'll take that as a compliment," I smile at them as Jonah trots down the stairs, hands in his black Matrix sweat pockets. He has a white Champion shirt on top with black lettering, a size too big.

"Pj's are on the sink," he smiles at me, snapping his fingers and clapping his hands as he sits on the second bottom step.

"Thanks, Jonah," I shoot him a grateful smile. He blinks in surprise and shakes his head before running a hand through his hair. His lanky runner's body seems thinner than normal, than Landon, Col, and Art's thickly built bodies. Jonah is still thicker than Tyler, everyone will always be bigger than Tyler unless he turns his life around.

"Don't take too long," Betty calls after me. "We have some drinking games planned!"

"Col, stop telling that one story!" I holler over my back. He breaks off a kiss with Danae to laugh.

"Uh, ya boring!" He retorts, then begins my one drinking story again, overdramatizing it. I roll my eyes as I jog up the stairs and into Jonah's room. His bathroom doesn't have a door that swings into the hallway. I make sure both his and Betty's doors are locked before undressing and hopping in the shower. Shower caps are useless for the volume of my hair so the group downstairs is going to be seeing some even wilder hair today. Betty's bottles of shampoo and body wash are low so I use Jonah's Old Spice, wrinkling my nose at the powerful scent springing forth. With my body clean and smelling fresh, I dry off and pull on Jonah's pajamas. The pants are forest green and dark grey plaid, the shirt has a picture of a sailboat on it. I fold my dirty clothes and set them on the floor by the sink before exiting the bathroom. The bedroom air is brisk compared to the foggy bathroom.

"Hey Daisy Daisy," Jonah smiles at me by his window. He has a bookshelf to the right of his window and has some playing cards in his hand.

"Crib?" I ask, bending over and letting the towel fall off my hair to dry it.

"Yeah," Jonah coughs, shuffling the cards from one hand to the other. I dry my hair with the towel, frustrated with the knots in my curly, crazy hair. It's never-ending. I have to brush my hair when I wake up and before I go to bed. "Betty swears she's gonna beat Art's butt."

"Competition runs in the family?" I ask, running my fingers through my tangles. There are multiple knots. If I have the time, I'll have to pick them apart strand by strand. Keeping my hair nice is a pain.

"Hey! I'm not that competitive!" Jonah laughs, shuffling the cards to his other hand. If that wasn't apparently showing off, I don't know what is. Jonah walks toward me, folding the cards lengthwise in the palm of his hand. His fingers must be very dextrous with how skillfully he shuffles the cards about.

"Hurry up Jonah!" Betty hollers from downstairs. I laugh at the tone of her voice, and the bond they share. Sometimes sibling bonds make me lonely, I have no brother or sister to share memories with. No one to smile at an inside joke, no one to taunt and tease or help and grow. At least with my cousins here, I have a chance at some sort of sibling connection.

"See ya down there," Jonah cracks a smile, reaching for my hair. My eyes widen when he tucks my hair behind my ear, then smiles when it pops back out. Jonah's making his move on me. I'm going to halt his progress soon, at fifteen I shouldn't be interested in anyone but my mind and heart won't get over Tyler. We have a connection, a bond, Tyler and I, a zap we feel when we gaze into each other's eyes, when we stutter in our conversations, when we blush from unexpected contact living in such small quarters.

"I'm gonna hang the towel up," I murmur, my heart skipping a beat at the look Jonah gives me. He's making a move. I have to stop his progress. "Um, hey," I turn around, looking seriously at my friend. His honest face, his happy eyes, his blonde hair starting to get longer than he likes it, his tall, lanky body; I like him but not that much, at least not right now. I hope I don't hurt him too much but it's easier to break it off before we start a relationship. "We need to talk."

"We'll find time tonight," Jonah smiles at me, then rolls his eyes when Betty hollers at him to hurry up again.

"Yeah," I nervously fiddle with the towel as I respond. Jonah is a levelheaded guy, his reaction won't be as dramatic as Landon or Harry's but I'm already dreading hurting his feelings. "Okay."

His reply is drowned out by old country music blasting through the house. I walk to the bathroom, asking God for the courage to have this conversation with Jonah. With the towel hung up, I make my way to the hallway, trying to untie my knotty hair. I walk slowly, my arms burning at the awkward angle I have them up in as I try to undo every single small knot. Landon is in the hallway and whistles when he sees me. "Looking good, shawty."

"Thanks," I blushed, ducking my head. Landon, as always, is acting like a big flirt but he's harmless, especially now that he knows I have a crush on his triplet brother. Tyler has never been a happy-go-lucky guy and Landon is grateful for the happiness I bring to his brother's life. They won't believe me, but I've learned so much about perseverance and hope from the three brothers, I pray one day I have a chance to tell or show them that their lives aren't as bad as they think, that they are actually good people even with the murky circumstances surrounding their lives.

"Tyler's a lucky brotha," Landon drops a chaste kiss on my forehead and loops his arm around my shoulders. If I date Tyler and marry him, Landon will be my brother. With Landon's interactions I know he will be a good brother but he needs to work on his slight OCD compulsions. Landon has learned from his father the antic to control every outcome of his life even if that isn't possible. I frown, side-eyeing the supposedly best-looking triplet (only I seem to think it's Tyler, but again, I'm biased with my feelings and hormones).

"You not mad no more?" I laugh when he rubs his knuckles on my wet hair. It doesn't hurt too much because my thick hair is soft padding against his bare knuckles. Landon stops giving me a noogie when I show no reaction, huffing at me irritatedly.

"Tyler's still messed up 'cause of you," Landon sighs as we trot down the stairs. His jaw clenches, showing me the pain he is hiding in his forced carefree attitude. "It'll be a minute... but you aren't that bad."

"Thanks," I pat his back as we reach the bottom step. Landon drops his arm, spotting Esther cheering Art on. Apparently, Jonah has won too many arm wrestling competitions in the family and she can't bear to see him win another. "That's all I ask."

"That doesn't even make sense, Daisy," Landon rolls his eyes, departing from my side. Art is slowly winning the arm wrestle but Jonah is putting up a hell of a fight. Col and Danae are making out, which saddens my heart. She's so young, he should have stronger self-control. They should both remain chaste until marriage. Betty, Esther,

Sadie, and BJ are cheering the competitors on, Pierre in front of Jonah and Art's red faces, eye level against the table to make sure they tap out to win. Alcohol bottles are already opened, some that even I can't name from experience with my dad's raging weekend alcoholic tendencies, there are Red Solo cups in everyone's hand except Col and Harry. Col must be DD'ing and I've learned Harry doesn't drink. He wants to be the generation that puts a stop to alcoholism in his family. Their older brother, Simon, also doesn't drink but Tyler, Landon, Cam, and Jim all already have alcohol problems.

"Dance with me, Daisy," Col bows and holds his hand out to me. Danae huffs at his absence but she's not a jealous type and smiles when I accept Col's offered hand. "M'lady."

"I can only two-step," I laugh when he twirls me into his chest. Landon immediately slides up to Esther, making her blush when he presses against her body. Jonah doesn't like it too much but when he moves to intercept Betty blocks him.

"Works for me, partner," Col grins. I laugh at his puppy dog eyes. Col and I get along well but we don't hang out too often, usually only on the farm or at rodeos. I have a feeling he's sucking up to me for help on the farm or he's in need of a rodeo partner.

"Rodeo coming up?" I ask, knocking into the coffee table. My heart has a mini heart attack as I feel my feet knocked off the floor but Col dips me to catch my fall, transitioning it into a smooth, low dip with my forehead close to level with the floor. Harry and Landon whistle, they are friends with Col so the dancing is allowed. I doubt they'd allow me to dance with Jonah, claiming some excuse but really it's because everyone knows Jonah likes me. This reminds me, I need to steal some alone time with Jonah to let him down softly.

"Zhao can't come," Col admits, sliding us by Danae on the couch. He pauses our dance to bend down and peck Danae on her nose. I find his charming action cute but dread makes me want to confront Danae, and tell her to reevaluate her relationship with him. She's so young yet, only a year younger than me and I'm way too young for a relationship. "And Danae can't ride."

"I'm your cheerleader," Danae sticks her tongue out at Col. I ignore the lust in his eyes when she uses her tongue to lick her lips in a very sensual way. She's fourteen! Where did she learn that? There is too much porn in this world, that's one reason I'm thankful my dad doesn't have a TV or internet. It'd cause me to sin way too much.

"So you need a header?" I avert my attention wholly to Col. His eyes are on Danae but he jerks his eyes away. The big swallow of Adam's apple makes me aware of the battle he is fighting. If anyone finds out, he could be charged with statutory rape. I hope he makes the adult decision to walk away after a pure kiss goodnight.

"Short notice, no one else can come." Col smiles cheekily, twirling me into his chest before dipping me again. He can be a charming flirt when he wants something.

"Let's go Col!" BJ hollers, the rest of the boys with him as they troop to the garage. Landon taps the door frame as he trots down the steps to the garage. BJ is waving Col forward, Pierre on a bench as Jonah spots him. The weight is seventy-five to start off, Jonah and Pierre won't last long but they aren't the type of guys to be embarrassed or ashamed about it.

"What?" Col let me go to bend down and kiss his girlfriend. He barely touches her before backing away, muttering something under his breath. I pray he uses the self-control we all can possess, that I know he has.

"We're gonna see who can lift the most!"

"Y'all know it's me!" Col shouts before running after the boys with a whoop. With the garage doors closed, Esther flops on the couch beside Danae. They both groan, sliding further down the couch to gain extra comfort.

"I think I'm in love," Esther sighs dreamily. I choke on laughter when Betty chucks a throw pillow at her younger sister's face, snapping her out of her daydreaming.

"No," Betty groans, slumping into a single-person couch chair. I swipe the throw pillow from Esther before she can reciprocate the harsh gesture of chucking the square, fluffy object at her sister. Betty will thank me one day when she isn't too busy telling Esther to stay away from the oldest Smith triplet. "Not Landon."

"He's not bad on the eyes." Danae cheekily grins. She knows she's fuelling a fight, a sibling war of dominance. Betty will win, older siblings tend to, but if she doesn't she'll get Jonah and Angie on her side. Esther and Danae are both much too young to be thinking these thoughts. Has my generation always been this sexualized? Am I only now noticing it with a group of friends to finally call my own?

"Stark blue eyes." Oh great, here's a list of Landon's hotness attributes. This one comes from a dreamy Esther.

"Dark brown hair," Betty admits. Sadie pretends to gag. This is her cousin they are talking about.

"Curly too." Esther again, her face a bright apple red at her unspoken thoughts flitting through her head. Has she drunk anything? She's only fourteen!

"Okay, guys," I roll my eyes to stop their list of what they like about Landon Smith, the oldest triplet. It made me uncomfortable, thinking I had stepped into the judgemental territory. We should spread love, not gossip.

"You're looking pretty cozy there Dani," Betty grins as she pops some popcorn in her mouth and sips it down with a mixed drink. "With Col."

"Anything happening?" Esther wiggles her eyebrows, cuddling up to her friend. They weren't particularly close classmates until Danae's friendship with Col became apparent. Until now Danae always had her own crowd of friends, her two younger sisters, Col's younger siblings, and a couple of her sibling's classmates. Danae hadn't really cared if she had friends or not but her sisters dragged her with them.

"I'm thinking tonight," Danae smiles before hiding her face behind her beer bottle. Her comment makes me blanch, she's excited and she's only fourteen. I take a deep breath to calm myself, placating my mind with the thought of Mother Mary's young age when she bore Jesus. Some theologians or historians suggest Our Blessed Mother was only fifteen when she accepted God's fiat for her. That's my age now, and I know I'm failing miserably at agreeing to God's destiny for me but the point for me right now is to keep landing on my feet and walking the narrow path even when I fall off again and again... and again.

"Awe no, Dani," Sadie sighs and shakes her head sadly. Bianca agrees with her cousin silently but rests a hand on her shoulder for comfort. Sadie and Bianca are Watsons, regular Sunday mass Catholics with a not-so-steady prayer life outside of school and church. While Dickie's family is the most religious out of his five siblings, the least his siblings do is come to church on Sunday. It's a Catholic thing or a small-town thing. If you are in a town where your parents are, you go to mass with them on Sunday. I've noticed it with Sadie and the triplet's older cousins who have graduated and left town for travel, studies or just to get out of Dodge. They fall off the spiritual wagon when they don't have their parents' routine and I notice it when their responses or reactions are slow in mass but I'm so thankful they come with their parents. Believing in God is a beautiful struggle.

"Shhh," Esther puts a finger on her lips. She wants to hear more, enjoying any gossip she can hear and spread.

"Col will wait if I want him to," Danae states confidently.

"So wait," I say quite bluntly, getting angry at Danae's flippant attitude and lack of respect for her body. She grew up Catholic, we've been going to the same Catholic Church for a year, and she knows better. She was raised to follow in the Lord's footsteps, her family isn't perfect, two of her older sisters shacked up and her oldest brother sleeps around but at least they are all adults, moved out of their parents' house. I would never dare to go behind my father's back, I know the sacrifices he's made out of his love for me and I'm not going to show him that disrespect he doesn't deserve.

"You're only fourteen," Sadie sighs again, shooting Esther a look to shut up when she opens her mouth. Esther does so, knowing she isn't the winner of that fight, especially with the look written on Bianca's face. "Don't do it."

"I second her," I speak up. "Making love is intimacy privileged for marriage."

"You're too old school," Betty rolls her eyes but I spot the concern flickering through them for Danae. And sorrow, Betty's mom raised them to be independent women but sometimes she makes headstrong decisions she regrets. We all learn by our mistakes.

"Go for it, Dani!" Esther cheers before we hear scurrying feet and the conversation comes to an abrupt stop. I'm happy to see Danae mulling over Sadie's words and the warning look in Betty's eyes.

"Hey," Jonah pops back into the living room.

"Lost pretty quick, huh?" Betty laughs as she teases her brother. Competition really runs in their family.

"I'm a runner, not a lifter," Jonah rolls his eyes. I like how he isn't uncomfortable in his skin, he knows who he is and what he can or cannot do. That attitude draws my mind to him but my heartstrings tie into Tyler. Jonah pours another mix of Pepsi and alcohol into his red solo cup. I don't drink, but I don't mind if other people do, as long as they don't get drunk. Drunkenness sets me off.

"Weak," Esther scoffs under her breath. She's upset at her brother for protecting her from playboy Landon. I hadn't realized she'd seen the warning talk Jonah gave Landon in the garage, it was hard to see from my angle, near impossible for Esther unless there was a mirror which is most likely the case. Most gyms have mirrors so you can make sure your form is correct.

"You stay away from Landon," Jonah dips his cup to his younger sister, a warning glare on his usually easy-going face. "I'm a snitch."

"No!" Esther pouts, throwing her head back. I've been living with Landon for a while now, should I tell Esther that reaction, that pouting angers him, or should I let them find out for themselves? Am I overstepping if I speak up or am I creating drama by keeping quiet? Will Esther even listen to me? Unlikely, not to judge or be rude, so I stay silent.

"C'mon, Jonah," Betty rolls her eyes, picking her nails. She's saying the words Esther wants to hear but I don't catch any conviction in the words' altercation. "Momma raised us to be independent."

"Right, not stupid," Jonah smirks, wrapping his arm around my shoulders. It's so nice to have friends, and physical contact but man, my shoulders are sore. Everyone seems to use me as a resting block.

"I'm a snitch," Betty raises an eyebrow. Danae averts her eyes. Sadie coughs as she disperses. The chips on the table catch her attention and I nod, impressed at her choice to mix Cheezies and Lays salt and vinegar.

"We just talking," Jonah laughs. The alcohol on his breath stinks with a slight sweetness added on. Jonah doesn't drink much, stopping his intake for the night when he gets a buzz on. I hope my words tonight won't trigger drunkenness in him.

"It's Daisy," Sadie speaks up, defending me. It's a Watson thing. They've accepted me as part of their family for helping the triplets out and Watsons stick together. I'm charmed at the inclusion, never having an extended family of my own until recently. "She has the whole chastity thing down."

"It's called VTM," we share a grin as we dap, the quiet Bianca following suit.

"And you two are too young to be here," Jonah points to Danae and Esther. He's stating his authority as the man in charge with his parents out of the house, Esther can't disagree when Betty nods along. It is a small get-together but I think they are right, the two girls are too young to be here. I'm too young to be here but I've grown up around this stuff, these two haven't.

"I've been to more parties than you," Danae retorts, pulling her iPod out and smiling at a text she reads. Her whole face melts into a love-sick expression. The text must have been from Col even though he is ten feet away. Oh, to be young and in love.

"He's talking about your age," Betty defends her brother, turning the tide. Besides their independence, their mother also raised them with the family stick together mentality. Esther ducks her head in a pout.

"Get to bed Esther," Jonah points up the stairs. Esther groans but obliges her brother.

"Night Esther," I shoot her a sympathetic smile. I'm only a year older than her, they could be treating me like that if they wanted to.

"You too, Dani." Jonah pushes. I wither, stuck in their staring match.

"Whatever," Danae snaps, jumping up. "Col's ready to leave." The weightlifting competition must be over. Col might have been cocky about winning but BJ and Landon would have given him a run for his money. They're all on the football team, all tackle people while Harry is the quarterback. I don't really know which is better or stronger or what, not attending one football game. I'm always too busy volunteering or working to go to school sports.

"Stop being so rude to all my friends," Betty sighs, taking a sip of her drink. Sadie shares the chip bags when Betty reaches over. The two get along well, both on the dance team. Sadie is the captain but Betty and her mom design the dresses or outfits and Bianca follows Sadie around everywhere. Out of all the Watsons their age, they are the only girls with seven guy cousins as well. Payton, Luke, Simon, the Trips, BJ, Pierre...

"Let's go," Jonah turns us around and tugs me forward.

"Uh, see ya then Danae," I wave over my shoulder to her. I only promoted her chastity, I hope she appreciates me not trying to kick her out or feel too young.

"Don't go," Betty rolls her eyes. "Jonah's not top dog."

"Neither are you," Jonah retorts.

"We need to talk," I nudge Jonah as a reminder. I've seen them bicker before, shots fired so close together I could barely keep up. The Layton's are fierce, having Viking heritage.

"No smooching," Betty and Esther laugh, Esther quickly trotting up the stairs at the look her brother shoots her.

"Not likely," I respond, allowing myself to be led into the kitchen by Jonah. The garage door is open and I notice Harry spotting his brother. Col is laughing with Art and BJ teasing his cousins. Apparently, he can lift more than them which puts them in a not-so-good mood.

"So Daisy," Jonah interlocks his fingers with mine and pulls me into the kitchen. Pierre and Lee were starting to bake something and take it to the living room when they see the serious expression on our faces. Lee winks and wiggles his eyebrows at me, I wrinkle my nose and shake my head. He's a player like the Trips. The girls can still see us from the living room so Jonah sits on a kitchen counter, patting the space next to him.

"No thanks," I shake my head, tugging my hand out of his grip. My heart hurts at the sadness on Jonah's face but breaking it off now is better than leading him on.

"No, Jaisy, huh?" Jonah smiles bitterly.

"I'm sorry, Jonah but I like Tyler. He's not interested in me but I don't want you to be my rebound. I care about you too much as my friend to hurt you like that." It didn't seem like I was making any excuses, was

I? Jonah drags his hand through his hair, muttering something about a haircut.

"That's why Harry and Landon have been snappy with me lately," Jonah hums, looking in the direction of the garage. I nod at his words, I'm an open book, probably too honest for my own good. He gulps down the rest of his drink. I wrinkle my nose at the burp that bursts out of him. Jonah himself looks surprised. "Excuse me," he taps his chest.

"Friends?" I ask, holding my pinky out to him. Jonah stares at it, thoughts rolling around his mind that I can see written on his face.

"Friends," Jonah agrees, schooling his features and pinky promising me.

✈ 18 ✦

Holy Spirit in
the Fam Jam

———————⟫•○•⟪———————

Thanks for driving us," I smile at Jonah. He drove out of his way
to pick me, Tyler, Landon, Lee, Sally Anne, and Windsor up for
church. The backseat of the rental SUV is small and because Tyler is
injured, he got the passenger seat. That didn't make Landon happy,
especially sitting next to Windsor squished against Sally Anne and Lee.
When things got too hectic from the cranky Sally Anne and Landon, I'd
decided to climb in the hatch. Landon followed suit. Dad drove the rest
of the kids, two car seats and one booster seat filled the back seat. Harry
got the front seat with Conan and Tinsley and Makayla had to sit on the
floor. Dad is looking into buying a van with Rennie and Louis's child
tax money. We badly need it if we all need to go somewhere.

"He drove too slow," Sally Anne rolls her eyes.

"I'm not getting stopped with two people in my hatch," Jonah
retorts, shutting the SUV off with a press of a button. Lee is out of the car
before he even puts the car in park. Landon and I have to wait for Jonah
to open the hatch to let us out. On church grounds now, Landon stares
defiantly at me but does not speak. He knows he's prone to swearing and

he's trying to stop it. I admire him for his resolve, knowing how curse words manage to slip out of every sentence he speaks.

"There's a lot of people here," Harry cracks his knuckles. Dad and Lee both have a baby in their arms, the kids are all running up and down the steps, seeming obnoxiously loud in the holy land.

"God-willed," I laugh at Landon's nervous expression at the Ford Expedition, the three trucks, and another car here. Phil is here, his dad, and his brothers Percy, Paul, and Peter. It's nice to see all of them here. Usually, it's just Peter or Dickie or Paul so the other ones can run the soup kitchen but they must have closed early tonight. If they brought their kids, there will be thirty people at this daily mass. This blessing is heaven sent, God's children have listened to His calling.

"It's quiet time," dad puts a finger to his lips as he warns the children in his soft voice. My dad is a good dad, that's for sure.

"Okay!" Kennedy replies loudly in her deep voice with a smile. We all can't help but chuckle at her cuteness. Surprisingly it's Harry that swings his arms down to pack her in his arms. Tinsley runs to me, hugging my waist. I grab Conan's hand to keep him still. He constantly moves, and probably has ADD. We all troop into the church, Conan tugging me and his cousin forward. My dad usually sits in the pew in the back but Makayla and Windsor take that option away when they race to the front. Watsons sit on the right side pews, a tradition since before I was born. They like being close to the tabernacle so Windsor and Makayla turn to us with smiles as they slide into the left-hand pew. I give them a thumbs up before stopping by the holy water font and dipping my hand in it before making the sign of the cross, showing Tinsley and Conan what to do. Harry does the same for Kennedy as Landon helps Tyler walk to the front. Dad and Lee make little crosses on Philomena and Tikara's foreheads, blessing them with holy water as well. They go on ahead while I wait for a sulking Sally Anne to follow suit. She's pouting because we made her come since her brothers aren't here. Rennie and Louis absolutely refused to enter this sacred building. Dickie makes his way to his nephews, radiating happiness that all three of them are here. His happiness is not joy, though, when he sees how beaten up Tyler is. Landon sat him in the second pew so the kids won't bump into him and Sally Anne had used that as her excuse to sit as far away from my dad and Lee as she could.

"Good evening Daisy," Dickie smiles at me, ruffling Conan's hair. Conan sticks his tongue out and runs off to his older siblings, Harry sitting Kennedy on his lap. I find it cute how Harry has taken to the three-year-old. "You wanna read today?"

"Sure," I genuflect, stay kneeling to show Tinsley what to do. She smiles shyly, sucking her thumb. I gently pull it out of her mouth and hobble between the floor and kneeler to pass my dad, Lee, the babies, Harry, Kennedy, and Conan. My heart is soaring in joy, the first two pews on either side are packed, and the second pews are each half full. Usually, there are only about five of us at daily mass, thirty is an exceptional number and I praise God for His goodness. It's when I'm kneeling, praying to God, and finally settled down, Conan in front of me so he has fewer distractions, do I realize that Jonah has managed to disappear. We are five minutes early, the Watsons already finished praying the rosary and Phil is going to confession so Jonah still has time to make an appearance. At the start of mass, as we are singing "Peace is Flowing Like a River", he appears with his little brother Larry. They squish in beside Makayla and Windsor. Tears fill my eyes as we all sing and pray together, and when Fr. John walks up to the altar, I'm reminded of Jesus ascending the Mount of Olives with His disciples. When our priest bows, then genuflects before the foot of the altar I remember Jesus sweating in Agony on Gethsemane. As Fr. John kisses the altar over the relic of St. Bernadette I think of the Pharisees taking Jesus prisoner, how Judas betrayed our Saviour with a kiss on the cheek. *Lord have mercy, Christ have mercy, Lord have mercy. Glory to God in the highest...* We celebrate mass to remember Christ's greatest sacrifice for us: His death on the Cross and the mercy we receive from His bounty. He is King of all but was led as a prisoner in front of human leaders to be sentenced to crucifixion. I go up to read the reading of the day, my heart and soul are so happy I can't help but sing the psalm even if I can't carry a tune perfectly. The sound of our voices resonating together makes me smile so wide and continuously that my cheeks hurt as I begin the Alleluia for the gospel proclamation. The children can't sit as still as the Watson children and they talk and fidget but they are here, we brought them here and introduced them to God and that's what matters. Stillness and silence will come when we make the church their wonderful habit when they can feel the peace of God. Fr John says a quick homily, but it really sinks into my mind with its simplicity: take time for hospitality. With all the new mouths to feed I've been too busy cooking and cleaning and worrying about time. I haven't taken the time to actually see how the children are settling into our life. They look fine to me but I don't know them and I haven't been personalizing our relationship. When our voices join together in praying the Apostles Creed I reflect on our profession of faith in contrast to the lowness of Jesus being led as a prisoner back to Pilate to judge. We kneel for the liturgy of the Eucharist, accustomed to the Watsons' Latin mass habits at daily mass. I like it, believing that the wine and bread are turning into the Blood and Body of our Lord Jesus Christ and that He is God so we should be kneeling to show the proper respect. A jolt runs through my body when I clue into Fr. John washing his hands as Pilate did, allowing the people to hurt Jesus. I hadn't put that together before. *Hosanna in the highest, blessed is He who came in the name of the Lord.* You take away our sins when You carry our sinful cross up Calvary. My eyes tear up again, my heart and soul so thankful for the Lord's great sacrifice of scourging when Fr. John raises the chalice in the air. It also sends zealous anger coursing through me, at this point in Jesus' condemnation, He was mocked as a powerless king. Fr. John raises the Host high as well, and the crucifix behind him is what we should be thinking about: how Jesus was raised on the cross to hang between heaven and earth. We all stand for the Our Father, joining hands to remember Christ resigning Himself into His Father's hands. *Lamb of God, You take away the sins of the world, have mercy on us. Lamb of God, You take away the sins of the world, have mercy on us. Lamb of God, You take away the sins of the world, grant us peace.* Jesus is taken down from the Cross and laid in Mother Mary's arms. Our Lord's sacrificial self-giving is over. We must retain hope and faith in His promises. When we receive communion, I imagine our bodies are the tomb for Jesus to lay to rest until we can celebrate mass again. Going up for communion saddens me when I see all the children unable to receive Jesus and vow internally to start baptism lessons with them. Once I get them all baptized, I can start on reconciliation and First Communion lessons. Within the year or two they live with us, they will be able to receive Jesus, it just depends on how badly they want Him. I whisper the Anima Christi prayer to Conan when we are back in the pew. He struggles to get out of the pew but I refuse to let him run around and be loud. To distract him I point to Fr. John covering the chalice once again. The tomb of Jesus is closed. When the last prayer is said, the exit song is sung, and our personal gratitude prayers are said I think back to Jesus' disciples and friends walking away from the tomb, one last sad and loving glance before they return to their homes.

Axel, the altar boy today, along with Jasper blows the altar candles out. I let Conan go, who was mumbling some complaints about Kennedy walking around. I am the first to exit the pew despite the children raving to get out of the church. "Hey all," I speak up, getting everyone's attention as I point to Tyler. "If you guys don't mind, let's all take a moment to pray together over Tyler. He's hurting pretty bad and could use God's healing love." Then I turn to the priest nervously. "If you don't mind leading, Father."

"Of course not," he smiles warmly and strides to Tyler. "Let's get you up to the tabernacle. Dickie, get me some holy water please." The priest helps Tyler walk up to the altar and sits him gently in a chair. The children race up first, excited to be where they weren't allowed during mass. When I get there, I kneel, feeling the power of Jesus in the Blessed Sacrament. The adults and older children follow my lead as the priest blesses an uncomfortable-looking Tyler with holy water and lays his hands on him to pray. We follow his lead, raising our hands to Tyler as Fr. John leads us in making the sign of the cross and prayer. Dickie has to stand because of his back injury and he holds a prayer book out for the priest while keeping a watchful eye on Sally Anne, who had refused to come up here. Seeing all the children's reactions, the only one we won't bring next time we come to mass is her. Makayla picked up on the prayers right away and Windsor said great big loud amens after each prayer, so excited were they to pray! Conan, Kennedy, Tikara, and Philomena didn't really care as they didn't know what to do or what was happening, but they liked the ringing bells and singing and walking up for communion as it was a change from sitting and listening. Tinsley and Larry were quiet, the more introverted out of the children, but Larry was awestruck with the powerful pull of mass stretching him toward God and Tinsley looked in splendor at the sacrament hoisted in the air even if she didn't understand its meaning. Fr. John ends his healing prayers over Tyler with a serene amen. The children hear the word and jump up, excited to run around after an hour of quiet time. I let them this time, placating myself with teaching them to genuflect and bless themselves with holy water at the end of mass next time we come. I'm one of the last ones out because I hang back to sit in a moment of silence with Jesus. We, humans, get lonely when no one comes to visit us or when our visitors are distracted, so too, Jesus longs for our love when we are in His presence.

"Do you always have to sit on the tallest object?" I jokingly ask Harry, who was sitting on the roof of the pickup. I was sitting on the edge of the box and Landon leaning on it on one side of me, closer to his brother and Lee on the other side of me. Jonah and Phil were watching the kids climb trees as the rest of us were visiting in the parking lot. Dad, Percy, Paul, and Peter each have a baby in their arms, rocking the fussier ones for comfort.

"Whatever," Harry sneers at me but a smile soon replaces it. Someone mellowed out after praying. Praise God he is no longer angry at me.

"We need to do this more often," Tyler grins, a sight rarely seen on his face. I blush when Dickie catches me gazing at him for too long and my dad catches on. My dad simply rolls his eyes at me, knowing when I'm ready to confront my crush and talk to Tyler, he'll be there for me to lean on.

"Musta been faking it," Landon laughs, slapping Tyler's back. His younger, underweight brother winces from the force as it jerks him forward. When coughs start to hack out of Tyler I step forward and gently rub his back, careful not to put too much pressure. Paul and Peter catch on to my blush from my hands touching my crush but don't tease me at this moment. They have the courtesy not to in front of my crush, it would embarrass both of us.

"Just cause God healed his leg doesn't mean God healed his ribs," I frown at Landon, biting my lip. The healing prayers miraculously cured Tyler's knee injury, one of the more serious injuries he had. We'd all silently assumed he would walk for a limp forever but his walk is no longer lilted. I scan the Watsons, wondering who the saint is in their family so that God allows healing to come from their praying heart. My guess is Paul.

"Ah, he can toughen up." Landon rolls his eyes, never one to apologize.

"Got that right," Harry jumps down as the children all race toward us. They must have made plans from the grins they all share as they crowd their respective guardians.

"We wanna-,"

"Dad, can-,"

"Lee!"

"Uncle Duncan-,"

"Camp-,"

"Rosary-,"

"Pray-,"

"All of us!"

"Friends now-,"

"Hang out-,"

"Okay! That's enough!" My dad raises his voice slightly. Half of the children quiet down but half continue to talk, unable to hear him from the talking still going on. "Quiet down everyone. We all have a voice, let's just use some patience to all speak in turn."

"I'm going to drop Larry off," Jonah pulls me aside, Larry behind him. "I'll be back soon."

"See you," I turn my attention back to Tyler, whose coughing fit had ceased.

"I'm fine," he backs away from my touch. I smile sadly at the space between us, and not just physical. Tyler doesn't like Jonah, probably because he knows Jonah likes me. My crush is watching the guy that might be my other crush drive away, I don't like the anger in his eyes. When I tune back into the conversation with the adults and children, I see Peter and Paul taking Paul's three children to his truck and buckling them in. Phil and Dickie are doing likewise with Phil's four oldest children, and Percy with his five children, Pierre helping them out. Dad and Lee are buckling the babies in their car seats and Kennedy in her booster seat. Makayla, Conan, Tinsley, and Windsor claimed the front two seats. Dad scratches his head with his baseball cap and points to the box of the truck.

"You might as well all jump in there," he shrugs. Harry opens the tailgate for Tyler as Landon lifts Sally Anne over a wheel well. Lee stabilizes her although she seems upset at being treated like the young girl she is.

"But Jonah-,"

"Get in and have some fun," Harry rolls his eyes, holding his hand out for me to climb up.

"Forget about lover boy," Landon huffs, slamming the tailgate closed before easily hopping into the box.

"He said he was coming back," I murmur softly, chewing my lip. Jonah will probably be concerned when we aren't here when he shows up.

"Get up Daisy," dad motions for me to hop in the truck. I finally take Harry's offered hand and step on the wheel to climb up. Dad drives conscientiously all the way back home, extra safe with six of us in the box. We really do need another vehicle and I can't wait for us to find one. We'd still be squished because there are so many of us, but at least we'd all be able to fit in the vehicle.

"What did the children want?" I ask. Looking mainly at Lee since his nieces and nephews were asking him their questions as well.

"They made plans to pray with the Watsons," Lee shrugs, the wind blowing his hair back.

"Oh wow," my smile brightens. "That's amazing!"

❖ 19 ❖

Gift Baskets

Now in the building after running to Jonah's rental with him, I look over my gift baskets for the janitors once again. I'd been meaning to give them these for a while now but it hadn't happened as soon as I intended so now it's more or less a Thanksgiving and thank you basket. "Chocolates, gift cards, a yearbook from last year, signed thank you cards from each class, a personalized coffee cup, and some beans to go with it."

"I'm sure you have it all." Jonah rolls his eyes, holding open the school doors for me. We both have a basket for the two janitors, as big as the baskets are.

"Thank you," I scrub my shoes off on the mat.

"I should thank you," Jonah cheekily grins, opening the second set of doors. "The janitors are gonna think I helped too."

"You did," I frown but soon smile again. "You helped pack them and carried them into school."

"Thanks," Jonah laughs with a roll of his eyes. He knows I won't take all the credit. I may have come up with the idea but he and Art dropped in some funds and Jonah and Betty picked some of the items up. It was a team effort.

"Hi, Debbie!" I smile at the tall female janitor with long grey hair down her back in a braid. I like Debbie; she always has a smile for everyone and a kind word to say.

"Hi, Daisy," Debbie smiles at me as she leans her broom against the wall. It's a big one, for commercial purposes and she might be getting carpel tunnel from using it all these years. Last year the school gave her an award for twenty years as their janitor.

"This is for you," I shyly smile as I hold out the gift basket I was carrying. Debbie's eyes flicker with gratitude and wonderful surprise. "A little thank you for all your hard work."

"Oh, Daisy! You are so sweet!" Debbie pulls me in for a hug. "Thank you!" She places a hand on her heart as she peers into the gift basket. "You have some of my favorite chocolates in here."

"Lucky guess," Jonah smiles when I simply nod in agreement. I had no clue the chocolates I chose were her favorites, I'd chosen some of the more expensive kinds as well as personal favorites. I'm not much of a chocolate eater, rather than splurging on myself I often buy Pete his essentials instead.

"I'll drink this on my coffee break," Debbie toasts the basket to us to point out the Tim Horton's coffee beans in a pod we put in there. Everyone except my dad seems to have a Keurig these days.

"Have a good evening Debbie," I say, waving goodbye to her as she grabs her broom again. She smiles at me as we walk to the other end of the school. Debbie starts on one side and Jerry, the other janitor, starts on the opposite side. They meet in the middle.

"That felt pretty good," Jonah admits, passing me the second gift basket before running a hand through his blond hair. My eyes catch the bulge of his bicep from his movement. The muscle is there but it isn't as pronounced as Col, Art, or Landon. I quickly look away before Jonah notices my attention. It's not attention I want to give, or receive. I'm only fifteen, I don't want lust to sneak up on me, and gazing will only enable it.

"Every act of selfless love results in that good feeling," I laugh when Jonah looks confused for a second, mulling over my words. I like his thought process, and how he wants to understand everything. Jonah wants to live his whole life at one hundred percent in every moment. It's a quality of his that others don't have.

"What if someone doesn't appreciate the good gesture?" He finally asks. I stare at him, now the confused one. He just flipped my whole argument. How could anyone possibly not be grateful for a kind act? I don't do good deeds for pity unto others or for others to praise me, I enjoy helping others. Selflessness is a good feeling, something Jesus taught us when He hung on that cross, crucified for our sins. He was selfless enough to give His life for us, the least we can do is make gift baskets for janitors.

"Who wouldn't appreciate a gift basket?" I frown, staring at my shoes in contemplative thought. Would Jesus appreciate a gift basket? I'm reminded of Martha and Mary, Martha cleaning and Mary sitting and listening to Jesus's preaching. If I was there in that time and place, and I had given Jesus a gift basket; would He have acknowledged it, shared it with others, or simply given it to those who needed it most? Should I be reevaluating to whom I give gift baskets? I don't know anyone's personal lives, Jonah here beside me could be in more need of a gift basket than Debbie but I don't know for sure. Now I'm getting into the semantics of judging.

"Just a thought," Jonah waves my concern off. He has to stop walking abruptly when the door in front of us opens. Art walks out, pushing his hair out of his face and curling his fingers through the ends to get tangles out. His mullet is so out of fashion but it suits him completely with his old soul personality and old-shaped face. Some people look old and some people look young but it doesn't mean they look bad, it's usually their character that makes them a good or bad person. Art's smile widens when he sees us.

"Hey guys," he grins, shutting the bathroom door. "I'll come with, can't exactly have a tutor session without you," he looks pointedly at me with a friendly smirk.

"Yeah, sorry Art." I grimace before shooting him a small smile. As per the recent usual happenings of my life, I'd double booked or overbooked, which seems to be happening more frequently. I'm over-extending myself and something is going to give soon. It'll probably be my prayer life because I'll fall asleep praying to catch up on all my late nights or early mornings of missed sleep. With the race over, I don't need to run with Jonah any longer but I enjoy the activity, the longevity, and the determination involved. Realizing I'd zoned out slightly, I offer the boys another small smile, still directed mostly at Art. "As the tutor, I should be accountable and respectful of my learner's time."

"It's cool Daisy," Art rolls his eyes, elbowing me. "You don't have to take everything so seriously."

"I guess," I concede, chewing my lip in thought. "But I'm trying to live every single moment consciously. That takes serious consideration."

"Is that why you don't have a phone?" Jonah butts in, cocking his head in curiosity as Art holds open a set of doors for us to walk through to get into the primary wing of our small school.

"No," I laugh, my face burning red as I sheepishly smile at the boys. "I can't afford it."

"Don't you have a job?" Jonah frowns, waving at the second janitor. Jerry glances behind him before returning the wave. He's young, only his third year here right after graduating. Jerry loves athleticism, often helping volleyball and basketball coaches train us.

"So... maybe I need to budget better." I wince slash grin in Jonah's direction as we pull up beside Jerry.

"Got you a gift," Art gestures to the big gift basket in my arms. Jerry's eyes widen in surprise as he looks at all three of us before staring at the basket.

"For all your hard work," Jonah adds as I hold the basket out to Jerry. He finally leans his broom against the wall, both hands wrapped firmly around the gift basket as he takes it out of my arms.

"What's all this for?"

"Just a little appreciation for all the work you do, cleaning up after all us kids and whatnot," I smile at Jerry, sticking my hands in my pockets. My thumb and pointer fingers pinch the crosses in my pockets from the many rosaries I carry on me. The three of us don't know Jerry too well and now it's getting awkward, touching my rosaries brings me comfort.

"Thanks, guys," Jerry smiles at us, setting the basket on top of the primary student's shelves. "My little fam will enjoy this."

"Awesome, we gotta go. Thanks again for all your hard work and we'll see you around!" Jonah waves goodbye before throwing his arm around my shoulders. Art reciprocates the gesture on the other side of me. As an only child with a single father, I bask in the comfort of human contact but as a recent auntie and cousin, I'm tired of the human connection. My brain is tired from endless conversations, loud background noise, children screaming and running and laughing, Sally Anne complaining and arguing with her brothers, Rennie, Landon, and Louis's drunkenness.

"Hey! Put me down!" I laugh when Jonah and Art scoop me up, hands under my thighs.

"You sure you want us to?" Jonah asks, his eyes twinkling in amusement.

"Uhhhhh," my stuttered answer is interrupted by Harry and Landon lounging by the library doors.

"Toss her here!"

"Oh no!" I squeal, twisting and turning to get out. Art grunts when I accidentally elbow him in the cheek, losing his grip on my leg for a second before his grip is tightened. "Don't do it, guys!"

"One!" Jonah and Art taunt, swinging me back and forth. I stop fighting, pushing my legs with their movement. They aren't listening so I might as well have some fun with it, live more at the moment, vicariously.

"Two!" Harry and Landon smirk as they brace themselves to catch me.

"You guys better not drop me!" I warn as all the boys shout three and suddenly I'm flying through the air. My screams trail behind me, the boys laughing at my fright before I awkwardly land mostly on the flirty triplet and we topple into the wall.

"Harry! What the hell man?" Landon coughs as our bare arms screech against the wall.

"Blame Art and lover boy!" Harry retorts, grasping me under my arms and swiftly pulling me up. It takes a second for me to get my bearings straight, having been tossed and tumbled down a wall.

"I said not to drop me!" I huff, wiping dust and dirt off my clothes. My elbows are red and my skin is slightly peeled off. The pain makes me clench my teeth together but I force myself to relax as I offer it up to God for all those who have been physically abused in their lives.

"You landed right on me," Landon deadpans, still sitting on the floor. "I took the brunt of the fall."

"Jonah and Art threw me," I throw the two boys under the bus. We're not kids anymore, it's not easy to do the birthday bumps with teenagers and full-grown adults.

"You didn't say we couldn't," Jonah smirks, high-fiving Art. I give him a look that sarcastically asks him to rethink his defense.

"Pretty sure I did," I retort, offering Landon a hand up. His dead weight is unexpected and I groan when I fall on him again, our heads knocking together roughly.

"Useless woman," Landon grumbles, shoving me up. Harry stabilizes me.

"Why are you so heavy?" I retort, offering him another hand up.

"It's called muscle, baby," Landon flexes, showcasing his thick bicep muscles. I roll my eyes, poking at some flubber left on his arm.

"That's exactly what this is."

"You little shit," Landon swipes at my feet. I dance back with a grin, bumping into Harry, who wraps his arms around my waist. I forgot about the triplet bond. Unless they are fighting with each other, even when they are fighting with each other, they always have each other's back. Always. You pick a fight with one triplet, you pick a fight with all three.

"Oh no," my smirk fades into worry. Landon wiggles his eyebrows as he stands up, cracking his knuckles. "Oh no!"

"I gotta get to work," Jonah carefully steps around the Smith boys. He shoots me a thumbs up before waving goodbye. "Have fun studying." It's a gentle reminder of what we should be doing instead of what we are doing.

"Art, you gotta help me, man," I shoot Art a pouty look.

"I mean," Art smirks at me as he takes a step back to enjoy the show. "You did just insult the guy."

"He fell because you threw me!"

Blueprints

⬥━━━◦━◦━━━⬥

"You never answered my question," Col sends a charming smile my way. He's sucking up again. I'm not that good at rodeos so he must really need a partner.

"Which was?" I arrogantly smirk back. I remember, I'm just making him ask again. It's fun having friends, and teasing them. I'm thankful for the relationships God has given me this year.

"I need a partner for the rodeo," Col rolls his eyes. Once a person gets to know Col, the scar on his face deflects from his character. To strangers Col is quiet, scary, and dominating, to his friends he is caring, protective, funny, and driven.

"Can I use Dancer?" I answer his question with a question. I'll give Col a straight answer, I just want an answer to my question first, it's rude holding this information back but I don't have any other bargaining chip. "I'm broke so I need to try to place in the money this time."

"Yeah," Col replies, turning into my dad's driveway. "So you in?"

"Yeah," we dap. I frown when the gate is already open. Dad must be home early from work, which is rare but a good thing and he must have the horses in the barn or with the cows.

"Looks like you have lots of company," Col states. I nod along, spotting the two extra vehicles in the driveway. One is Dickie's and one is Peter's.

"Huh," I agree, it's also rare for us to get visitors. Our house isn't big enough to host coffee dates or friendly dinners, especially not now with all the extra people. It's a fend for yourself for a spot at the table to eat, the children usually sit there. My dad had rounded up two more chairs and a high chair so the children were covered but Harry ends up sitting on the counter and the rest of us on the couch, beds or floor.

"I'm coming in," Col states, turning his truck off. "See if I can get another practice session with your dad before the rodeo."

"Maybe together," I add, "get in the groove of working together."

"Yeah," Col replies, leaning on my shoulder. "Can you give me a piggyback ride?"

"Boy," I snort in disbelief, looking between us at his large body to my smaller, lighter one. "You're too heavy."

"What happened to the Daisy that would accept a challenge?" Col retorts, walking behind me with a knowing grin. He had spiked my competitive gene. I'm slightly hardheaded when it comes to doing what others think I cannot do.

"Fine," I groan, bending my knees a little. "Jump up."

"You the best," Col smirks, climbing onto my back. My knees come close to buckling under his weight but true to his words, I refuse to give up and totter toward the front steps. Behind the house, in the tree fort, my dad had made me as a child, I can hear the older children playing, screaming and hollering, running through the trails, probably with a stick in their hand. The war games appear to be on. It's a pleasant surprise when Harry races around the edge of the cabin, a branch in his hand as he leans against the siding, panting to catch his breath.

"Little terrors they are," he gasps for breath, sneaking a look around the corner. Then he turns back around, laughing as I topple from Col's weight. We land on the grass, Col jumping off my back so our limbs weren't tangled together.

"Told you you were too heavy," I huff, brushing grass and leaves off my clothes and picking them out of my curly hair.

"Your turn," Col offers, kneeling on the ground. I whoop with a grin and climb up, enjoying the carefreeness of our friendship.

"Got you!" Windsor skids to a halt next to Harry, his own branch pointed at Harry's chest. It's shaped like a Viking war axe.

"Give that to Daisy and climb on my back," Harry offers, not wanting to lose the game. What trickery! Windsor's eyes light up in understanding and he tosses me his axe before jumping on Harry's back.

"We can take 'em," Col states confidently, firmly wrapping his hands around my knees, interlocking his fingers in front of his ribs.

"Die, peasant!" Windsor declares as Harry charges toward us. I deflect a stab, soon Harry and Col are running in circles as Windsor and I parry, all of us running out of breath. Charges, hollered threats, back steps, sword thrusts, leaning dangerously close to falling off their shoulders, it's an intense workout but I've never had so many laughs burst out of me at one time.

"My turn!" Tinsley squeals, the first to spot us. Col groans as he sets me down, rubbing the back of his neck.

"We have to go talk to Uncle Duncan, Tinsley, but maybe after?" She pouts at my words but Windsor races off, Makayla hot on his heels. Tinsley, Conan, and Kennedy follow them, all with swords (a little twig for Kennedy and a branch way too big for Conan, it drags behind him).

"That was pretty fun," Harry admits, stretching his back. "Windsor is a chunk though."

"Hey!" I defend my little cousin. "We all grow through fat stages!"

"At least you didn't have a full-grown woman," Col retorts, trotting up the three steps into the cabin. Harry and I are behind him, quickly closing the front door to avoid the brisk air nipping its way inside. With all the body heat we don't need to have the wood stove running during the day but we like to preserve the warmth inside. The drawback to that - the air gets stale quickly.

"Rude," I scoff, kicking my shoes off.

"Hey, my girl," my dad grins at me before taking a sip of tea. My dad is a huge fan of tea, always drinking any kind he can make naturally. For the past four years birthday presents from Aria to him have been David's tea collections.

"Hey dad, hey Watsons," I hug my dad, and lean on him as I peer around his shoulders. A bunch of blue papers covers the table. Harry busies himself with grabbing a glass of water as Col sidles up to me.

"How are you doing, kid?" Peter asks. Dad frowns and backs up his chair, Col and I have to jump to avoid our toes being stubbed.

"I'm pretty good," I reply, ruffling my dad's head full of thick black hair. The children are heard before they are seen, a big commotion as they troop in, voices loud and breathing hard, laughing and arguing with each other.

"I already warned you guys to stay out," dad warns, shaking his finger at the children. Sally Anne glares at him, baby Philomena on her hip as Kennedy starts crying and Tinsley whines about lack of water.

"Uncle, we dying of thirst, man," Windsor cheekily grins at my dad.

"Share a cup and back out you go," dad juts his thumb to the door. "I told you guys we need space with the blueprints."

"Blueprints?" I butt in, peering at the tabletop. It's then that I notice some house plans and my heart leaps in my chest. Dad's building a bigger house? Sixteen of us won't be cramped in a tiny two-bedroom cabin anymore?

"Whoa Duncan," Col whistles, flipping some papers to get a closer look. "That's damn near a mansion."

"I suddenly find myself with fifteen children," my dad retorts, turning the blueprints back to face him. I open my mouth to correct my dad, Rennie, Lee, and Louis are adults but I realize why he said that. We have to yell at them to come to eat, pick up their dirty clothes, and clean up after themselves and their children.

"We can leave," Harry scowls, his fingers white with the amount of pressure he is squeezing his glass with. I'm very surprised it hasn't shattered.

"You are fine here," Dad waves Harry's anger off. Harry's glare doesn't waver, he's the grudge-holder of the Trips. "In fact, please don't leave. You distract the children so we can clean the house or do the outdoor chores." Harry's glare turns into a flicker of a smile but all he does is set the cup down to walk back outside. It's more of a storm outside. He's still angry, it worries me how long he can hold onto anger.

"Where's Landon?" I ask, peering through bunk beds and over dressers to spot him in the jungle gym that has become our living room. Harry pauses his exit to hear my dad's answer.

"Took off with Louis and Rennie," dad sighs, crossing his arms over his chest. "Bunch of freeloaders."

"Landon wasn't drinking when those idiots weren't here," Harry retorts, his grumpy face back on. I wince in his direction as an apology. The door slams on his way out. The Watson's all share a look before Phil stands up with a stretch.

"I'll go talk to him," Phil states, chugging the last of his tea. The shortest boy in his family, but by no means short, he ruffles my hair on the way out. The oldest of the family always seems to be the shortest. Col is taller than Leo, Betty and Esther taller than Angie, Danae taller than Amy, well, taller than all her older sisters. Danae is freakishly tall, all limbs and bones.

"Oh, c'mon!" I groan, my fingers feeling new knots in my hair. I shoot Phil the stink eye, along with Peter and Paul because they have a tendency to mess my hair up. "You all know what a pain my hair is."

"What?" Peter smirks at me, mock surprise written on his face. "Did Daisy Ridel just complain?"

"No!" My voice rises in pitch, indicating my embarrassment as my face flushes. The Watsons and dad chuckle heartily.

"You just did," dad laughs at my dismayed expression.

"Did not!" I argue back, sticking my tongue out. He isn't mad, I'm not mad, it isn't disrespectful, it's playful.

"Did too," dad retorts, rubbing his hands together. He has a prank coming, that's one of his signs so I step back from him, curious but worried. Last time I ended up with tree sap all over my clothes and hair and with how difficult my hair is, I had to chop a lot of it off.

"Hey Duncan," Col speaks up, his fingers tapping the counter. "Sorry to interrupt but I don't have much time. I have a rodeo coming up next week, do you think you can schedule a practice with me? And Daisy?"

"Woo!" Peter whoops. "Go Daisy!"

"Last one of the season," Col adds, putting pressure on my dad's response. My dad looks at Col, contemplating.

"I'll teach you," dad is interrupted by Col's cheer of yes! "But," my dad speaks up in a warning tone. Col covers his mouth, realizing there is a catch. "You and Abe have to help me build this house."

"Oh, totally," Col agrees. "I only have English this quad. I go to school in the morning, then my hands are yours."

"You can't miss any classes?" Dad frowns, probably expecting Col's help all day every day until the house is up and running.

"I'm not failing again," Col snickers. Betty is convinced he didn't get enough credits so he could spend another year in school with Danae. That idea is preposterous to me.

"I see. Half a day is better than nothing. If you stop by before school I can probably fit it in," my dad looks at Peter who nods his head slightly. Peter is his boss, the roping lessons will probably make him late. I love this small town, the loving atmosphere, and the easy-going Watson clan. "Monday work?"

"Yes sir," Col finds the brownies Makayla and I baked last night and shovels one into his mouth. "Thank you." And with that, he walks out of the house, crumbs trailing behind him.

"Bring me a brownie," Percy nods his head in the direction of the counter. As the only female in the house, and the only one standing, I walk to the tray and bring the whole thing to the counter. All five men take a piece, leaving crumbs in the tray. Food doesn't last long in this house and we'd tripled the brownie recipe for all the children to have a piece last night. Crumbs fall out of Peter's mouth when he hollers goodbye to Col.

"Always the messy one, this dude," Dickie teases his son. I set the tray on my lap as I take Phil's seat. Paul is on my left side, Percy on my right.

"Where're all your children?" I ask, nodding at what looks to be a large kitchen in the blueprints. Plenty of cupboard space, and two little cupboard pantries on either side of the kitchen. A large double sink, no kidding with all the dishes we have to clean every day, but still no dishwasher. My dad is a big believer in old school traditions, mainly because while dishwashers are time-saving, they increase laziness and that's something he doesn't want to see in his daughter, or his 'fifteen children'.

"Audrina's watching mine," Paul runs his hand over his face with a sigh. The separation must still be hurting him so I offer him the tray of brownie crumbs. Paul shakes his head with a little pain-filled smirk before digging in.

"Arlette's watching Corinne and Reece," Peter speaks up about the whereabouts of Phil's children. "Kaitlyn might be there as well."

Is it weird they call their mother by her first name? I never call my dad Duncan but I'm young yet, they are all adults.

"When can our children," - I point between my dad and me when I speak. Peter and Percy laugh at that. - "Go pray with your children?" Then I point to Dickie's three sons, who all have children. None of Dickie's daughters have children yet but the oldest four boys, ranging in age from twenty-four to thirty-four all have children.

"Two weeks," Dickie taps the paper in front of him. "We're having a Watson family reunion. You guys are welcome."

"Because we're helping the Trips," I smirk at my dad, "or cause my dad's admitting his relationship publicly?"

"Whoa, kid," Paul coughs out a laugh.

"Better be a perfect house," Peter joins in on the teasing. "Can't have Aria living in an overstuffed cabin much longer."

"Aria has her own apartment," Dickie side-eyes my dad. My dad winces and focuses his attention on the blueprints in front of him. Percy and Peter snort at their dad's words, muttering something about Aria spending nights here. I guess you're never too old to throw your sister's boyfriend under the bus. At least they like my dad, it wouldn't be fun right now if they hated him.

"Jeez Duncan," Percy adds, playfully chiding my father, "when are you going to put a ring on our sister?"

"He needs to find my mom first," I say, looking at my dad to see if he wants me to stop talking. My mother has always been a touchy subject, that's why I think he just told me she was dead. "See if the church would allow them to divorce, or maybe she's, uh, maybe she's no longer with us."

"Why don't you just ask-," Dickie frowns but my dad interrupts him. Paul and Dickie share a look, the two men also love through broken marriages so they have an idea of what my dad doesn't want to talk about. This just means I have to pray about it, for them.

"How many bedrooms? I was thinking five. That's roughly four to a bedroom." Dad twists some papers for us all to see. "We might be able to add another bedroom or two here."

"That's a good idea," Peter nods along. "With the fireplace right there you won't need to worry about lack of heat. Besides the bedrooms with their own wood stoves, those would be the warmest rooms come winter."

"And winter's coming fast."

"I can come early Monday morning," Percy suggests. "Borrow the fire department's CAT, knock the trees down and flatten out the building site."

"Then me and Duncan can measure the floor plans out, tape it off."

"Try not to make the trees kindling," my dad catches Percy's eye. "We can save the wood to burn, dry out the green trees."

"For sure." Percy nods along.

"Paul and I will handle all the permits," Dickie looks at his son. "You still have those connections at the county from your hotel work?"

"Yeah," Paul answers. "But this is Duncan's land so we'll need him with us as well. Sometimes they take a while so we should head in Monday morning."

"We can do that right after the roping lessons," dad agrees. Paul sets the empty brownie tray on the table to look over the blueprints.

"With sixteen people living here, you might want to add another bathroom." I clutch the tray in my lap, already feeling overwhelmed at their plan-making. They lost me already, I'm confused about times and working and stuff.

"I'd suggest to the left of the mud room." Dickie points to the front door which is to the left of the kitchen when facing the house. "Just a toilet and a sink even so the children have quick access to it if they need to poop. The outhouse might be too far away for little children to run to in time."

"That is a good idea," dad admits. "This is going to be expensive."

"I can give you some supplies from the hotel," Paul offers. "Outdated windows that our permits won't allow but can be used in a private property. Sinks, toilets, we have some floorboard planks and rugs."

"That's too much," dad waves Paul's offer off. I'm always giving things away, objects, money, and help. It feels weird to be on the receiving side but with all the new Ridels here I've been needing help rather than giving help. Who's picking the children up from cross country practice, who's cooking them supper and snacks, grocery shopping, driving them to church, stitching cuts, holding ice packs on swellings, making sure they don't bother the cows because the cows are scared of them, not having seen this many children before, stopping arguments that turn into fights, sobering up their dads. It's taxing looking after so many people.

"They're just sitting there," Paul shrugs. "Might as well put them to use."

"I can't thank you enough," my dad shakes his head. The children's voices are loud once again and I spot the irritation on my dad's face so I stand up and put the tray in the sink.

"I'm going to take the children for a wagon ride," I inform them. My dad always took me for wagon rides when I was a child. I'd fall asleep from the lull of the wagon and the jingling of the bells on the harness, the sweet smell of the fresh air, and the breeze whispering across my face.

"I'll come with you so you have an adult with you," Percy jumps up. I hide a smile at the relief on his face. Percy isn't a planner when it comes to houses but he can tell where the wind will blow and what to do to stop a fire. It's a sense to him, a God-given gift he uses to save lives when he's out in the bush.

"Thanks," I hug my dad goodbye as they all tell me to be careful. I've been riding horses since I could walk and driving them since I was eleven but I adhere to their advice.

"Call Phil back in," Dickie gently orders his son. Percy quickly leaves to find his brother so he could hook up Buck and Honey. They are a traditional family, girls in the kitchen, loved and respected and cherished, while they do the heavy lifting. It melts my heart but I grew up alone, I know I can hook up the horses without them and drive them myself. There is a certain independence to an only child.

"Hey Daisy," Paul looks seriously at me. I return the stare. His face is serious and he used my name, they never do. It must be important.

"Yeah?"

"Take Tyler with you," Paul lets a grin slip out. Peter guffaws as he elbows his brother. I roll my eyes but steer my body to my bedroom, where Tyler rests when he isn't rocking in the rocking chair on the stoop or lying on the grass. It's getting too cold out there to do that. I'm not taking Tyler because his cousin asked me to but because I want to check up on his sobriety. With the medicine he has to take for his healing ribs, he hasn't had as bad of withdrawals but it's still going to hit him hard one of these days.

⇻ 21 ⇺

Thrown Off

———=▷-◉-◁=———

"W oo!" Danae hollers, clapping her hands. I clap along with her, smiling at the clear win of Col's barrel racing ride. In a small town rodeo like this, he entered everything for the extra competition. Usually, he only rides bulls and broncs, saddle broncs, bulldogging, and team roping (where he needed my help).

"Jailbait," Leo scoffs, his new woman hanging off his arms much to Danae's dismay.

"Slut," she coughs out, her elbows resting on the railing of the fence. Then she nods to Leo's new girlfriend. "Slut's STD." Even I can't stop a laugh at Danae's deadpanned words but a fierce glare from Leo shuts me up. And guilt, I shouldn't have laughed at her rude statement. I offer a quick prayer to the Lord for forgiveness and think about a nice quality Leo's new woman has, whose name I cannot fathom. She isn't rubbing her relationship with Leo in front of Dani, she's on the other side of him, trying to keep her hands off her boyfriend. Leo's new girlfriend has respect for his old girlfriend and her family. Does Danae even see that?

"Take it easy there, tiger," Landon squeezes himself between the two, earning a shove from Leo but Danae curls into his body. He has a flask in his hands and offers the fourteen-year-old a sip. Harry scoffs to my right and shakes his head bitterly. We both can't believe Landon or Danae's ease as they take turns sipping from the flask. A year ago Dani would never have touched the bottle but since she'd been hanging around with Col, Zhao, and the rodeo crew, she's become quite adept with large loads of alcohol in her system. I'd really wanted Tyler to come, to watch me in my events but he'd begged off an excuse about resting. We couldn't afford to bring all the children and Lee wasn't too interested in the rodeo so he stayed home to watch the pouty, cranky, and sleep-deprived children. Conan, Kennedy, Philomena, and Tikara would probably have naps, Tinsley, Windsor, and Makayla are maybes, insisting they were too old to nap.

No one is too old to nap, ever.

"And that ends the rodeo events for the day, the dance starting at eight. For any who placed, please make your way to the registration booth for your winnings." The amplified noise from his speaker grates on my ears but I offer my annoyance to those who don't have the chance to hear the sound here on earth.

"Let's go, Daisy," Landon slaps my back with a grin. Using Col's horse, Dancer, and my skills learned from the best roper in the county, I'd placed number one in all my events. My dad will be so proud of me when he finds out, seeing his passion brought to life in his daughter. Sometimes I feel bad knowing I'll be taking that away forever if I do become a nun, but he can keep teaching others, like Col, and be like Tim Fleming on Heartland if that's even possible. Before Col's barrel ride he tried persuading me to go pro with him but that will take me away from daily mass and meditative nature walks. I simply can't give up on God that way.

Going to a mass a day sends a demon away.

"There'll be a lineup," I shrug his arm off me. "I'm going to go brush Dancer down, cool her off."

"After you get your money meet me at the beer gardens," Landon smirks, slyly winking at Leo's girlfriend. What a playboy, her man is right there. Since Landon started living with me and my dad he has stopped a majority of his womanizing ways but it seems to be second nature to him when he sees a female. I'm proud of his progress but I'm saddened at his disrespect for the fairer gender.

"That's where my sister wanted us to meet," Leo's girlfriend tugs on his arm. "You don't mind walking with Landon, do you?"

"No," Leo scowls, shooting the bird to Danae. She wiggles her eyebrows and makes a vulgar gesture back to him. I'm not sure what it means but I have an inkling it's rude and sexual when Harry bursts into a snickering sort of laughter.

"I know he's not worth my anger for how fast he ditched Amy," Dani sighs as she scowls in Leo's direction. If looks could kill, he'd be dead. It's not an amusing thought. "But she's still living at home because they were shacked up. I see her broken heart."

"I'll pray for her," I offer, linking my arm through hers. Dani smirks at me, a mischievous grin on her face as her eyes twinkle.

"You should pray I don't scratch his truck and ram a baseball bat into it, smashing the headlights."

"Calm down Carrie," Harry rolls his eyes as he throws his arm over my shoulder. His fist knocks into the side of Danae's face and she snaps her teeth at him.

"Watch it, Smith," she snarls at him with a grin. "I bite," Harry responds by wrapping his arm around my neck, his fingers now on my other shoulder.

"Do I have to tap out?" I question with a smirk, elbowing Harry. He scowls at me before his arm falls off my shoulders. "Thanks, friend," I chirp.

"I'm not your friend," Harry gruffly retorts, falling out of step with us. He cracks his neck and fingers. Is it a nervous habit? "I'm going to the beer gardens," he mutters before stalking off.

"I always seem to push his wrong buttons," I sigh, reminding myself to pray for the Smith triplet that refuses to let me in. They all refuse but Harry makes his independence obnoxiously clear.

"Don't worry about it," Danae waves my concern off. "Harry likes you, he's just afraid because he actually likes you so he's pretending not to tolerate you."

"Yes, Mrs. Expert," I roll my eyes. We've reached Col's horse trailer and Dancer steps back to turn around. Danae squeals at the horse's big back end facing her. "You grew up on a farm," I deadpan, slapping Dancer's left hindquarters. She steps to the right to create a path to her head.

"Good girl," Danae runs her hand over Dancer's belly. I hand her a brush. She starts on one side and I start on the other, brushing anything off Dancer's coat before rubbing her down and checking her hooves. She was a good girl today and deserves the best treatment, all God's animals do.

"Trip's waiting for you at the beer gardens," Col informs me before waving his envelope full of cash at his girlfriend. Dani squeals and jumps on him, wrapping her arms and legs around his upper body.

"Thanks," I say, my reply drowned out by Danae's voice. I hope the triplets didn't order beer and put it on my tab, I'm not even allowed in there because I'm underage and I already have plans for the money. A new volunteer at the soup kitchen stole the funds for the next few meals so I'm giving my winnings to Dickie. I'd personally rather have the money for myself as savings if Pete or someone else needs something but God will provide out of his abundance. The worst people can say is no if I ask them to help him out.

"What you gon' get me?" Dani cheekily laughs, kissing Col's cheek. He spots my wide eyes at their interaction and shakes his head at me. I lower my eyes and busy myself with loading Dancer into the trailer, happy to see he did not have his hands on her butt, but rather on her thighs close to her knees. Col is a gentleman.

"I need this money for my truck, princess," Col kisses her forehead and then sets her down. "Got to get me some new winter tires." When Danae whispers something in his ear, he clears his throat and holds his horse's reins out to her. "Wanna hold him while I untack?"

"Sure," Dani pouts, his rejection is soon forgotten when the horse is nibbling treats out of her palm. She acts like a young child sometimes but a full-grown woman the next, it's scary that she is trying to grow up fast. I want to retain my innocence as long as possible. I stuff my hands in my pockets, caressing my rosaries as I walk to the registration table. The grass is ripped and torn by horse hooves, there are plenty of horse craps lying about, tread tracks from tires from the dewy grass earlier today. Col had to spot me my entree fees for the day since I had zero dollars to my name, in agreement that I'd pay him half of what I won. He'd get his winter tires and the soup kitchen would get some money for at least an extra meal. It's a win-win situation. When I reach the registration table the lady quickly counts the money in the last envelope, explains the winnings I am receiving, and closes up the shop to head to the picnic tables close to the beer gardens. Even though she hasn't asked for help, I take the time to fold the table and lean it against the outbuilding for the workers to clean up tomorrow or tonight. She thanks me for my help, not too interested in conversation before hightailing it to the beer gardens. Dreading that my hard-earned money might already be spent, I drag my feet in that general direction.

"Hey Daisy, Daisy," it's Jonah that greets me from the beer gardens. Surprisingly he's surrounded by the Trips, Col is hanging out with his rodeo crew. I must have wasted more time than I thought if he had his horse untacked, cooled down, and groomed by now.

"Hey Jonah," I slap his back in greeting as I sit beside him. Harry scoffs but doesn't say anything else, still peeved at me from earlier. And well, because it's Jonah.

"What you doing with the money?" Landon grins at me, his arm wrapped around a girl I don't recognize. Esther is going to be so hurt by this if she finds out. Am I not helping a friend if I don't say anything or would I be creating drama by telling her? I hadn't realized friendships would be so hard.

"Give it to Dickie," I answer. When they frown in confusion I find myself clarifying myself when I usually don't. Has gaining friends changed me into a bad person? I don't need to justify myself to anyone but God. "Someone robbed the cash stash he kept for this week."

"I thought you'd give it to your dad," Harry stares at me, gears spinning in his brain. His fingers clench on top of the table and when he notices my gaze on them he shoves them under the picnic table. Harry doesn't like anyone knowing who *he* really is. It's as if he's afraid someone will find out he is actually a nice person and will take advantage of him, probably his father.

"He doesn't let me give him money," I reply. My dad has always been proud of money. One of the few things I've learned about his family is that they were sure he wouldn't amount to much. Boy, the Ridels were wrong, my dad became the best roper in the county while raising a daughter as a single dad and running a small yet income-earning farm.

"Not even for those big house plans?" Landon frowns. The house is massive, with five bedrooms, now two and a half bathrooms as they are extending his and Aria's bedroom to fit in a bathroom as well. Both are hopeful for future babies and with the rest of the house full, they decided to have enough space in their room for a crib and trundle bed. "How can he afford that?"

"Have no clue," I shrug my shoulders awkwardly. I don't like talking about money with anyone. Aria is also pitching in some of her hard-earned money, she's been saving her money for years; but dad will only use the money she was saving since they have been together, saying she can use the rest how she wills because it was her money before they were a couple.

"You should give it to your dad anyways," Landon says. The girl on his arm is losing interest because he isn't paying enough attention to her. It makes my heart melt, Landon cares about me and my dad. He wants the best for us even if his ways and words are quite blunt. "It'll be your house when he's dead."

"Who knows," I refute his answer with a shrug. I know everyone dies but his words hurt, my dad will live for years down here on earth. He's healthy, not too many accidents occur around this small town. He can survive in the wilderness if he somehow gets lost. Finding my mind trailing, I dwell on Landon's statement and my answer. "One of my cousins could get the house."

"You're his daughter," Harry deadpans.

"I might become a nun," I shrug again, feeling nervous at the boys' reaction. Jonah stiffens beside me, Landon coughs and shakes his head before turning his attention back to the girl, Harry stares at me, gears still turning in his brain. "If I become a nun, I'd be living in a convent."

"And your dad is okay with that?" Landon turns back to me. The girl sighs loudly before stomping off. His attention on me is direct and fierce and makes me wobble in my thoughts. I want to back down, and say it's just a thought but becoming a nun has been many thoughts to me. A sister of Mother Teresa's religious order is what I've always wanted to be since my dad told me about her. I silently ask God for the courage to explain how my dad doesn't mind me becoming a nun if I am following God's will for me.

"Yeah," I state simply. "God's will be done."

"A nun," Harry repeats.

"Poor Tyler," Landon snorts, rubbing his hands over his face and through his hair. "The only girl to like him wants to be a f—king nun."

"I'm not sure," I speak up after clearing my throat. My face is burning. I feel attacked right now but I know it's because I'm sort of embarrassed by telling my deepest dreams to the boys and their hard-hearted reactions.

"If that's your dream," Jonah speaks up, shooting me a smile with his pinky raised. "Carpe diem, Daisy Daisy."

"Thanks for understanding," I smile at Jonah, interlocking my pinky with his. We shake our words that way. I shouldn't be afraid of what I want in my relationship with God, and shouldn't let human opinions affect me. *Jesus, send your Holy Spirit to counsel me and keep me strong in faith. Amen.*

Not Another Dog

————➤━◉━◄————

Thanks, Mr. Faidley," I beam at Dani's father. He returns my smile but looks worriedly out the doorframe where Col is waiting in his truck for me and Daisy. I'd been uncomfortable asking him if Danae could visit me when I know she and Col haven't told her father about their relationship but I'd made sure they weren't using me to sneak her to his house before agreeing to their plans.

"You sure seem to be hanging out with him a lot," Mr. Faidley frowns. Danae cuts a sharp look for me to make an excuse but I've never been the cunning type of figure. A moment too long of silence stretches before us. Dani can't manage to look her father in the eyes, I clear my throat and Mr. Faidley crosses his arms over his chest.

"He's my neighbor," I finally speak up with an apologetic wince. "I usually bum rides from him after school in the winter if we both don't have anything to do."

"I hang out with Richie and Asia when I'm there," Danae adds with some bite, making me raise my eyebrows. I've never spoken to my dad that sharply. Mr. Faidley looks his daughter in the eyes with a frown and after another too-long stretch of silence he backs off.

"We'll have a talk when you come home, Danae," he states firmly. I wince at the angry tone of his voice but Danae simply spins on her heel and stomps off. She has a few headstrong years ahead of her, Drake and his wife are going to have some migraines in the near future with her upcoming attitude.

"Thank you, Mr. Faidley," I shoot him a small smile. "Have a good night."

"You as well Daisy," he closes the door, shaking his head at his daughter. With the door closed, I trot down the steps and jog to catch up to Dani. She has her arms crossed over her chest with an angry look printed on her face. I bite my lip, feeling frustrated at her attitude toward her father, a father that only wants the best for his daughter and to protect her.

"You see how he is?" She stomps her foot and throws her hands out. "He doesn't trust me!"

"C'mon, princess," Col slaps the side of his door from his unrolled window. "Have you given him a reason to trust you?"

"You're supposed to have my side," Danae pouts, running around the hood of the truck. I climb in behind Col, sending him a look he reads perfectly. He mouths sorry to me and shrugs. Apparently, he knows she's prone to these moods and still likes her. Dani angrily climbs up in Col's lifted truck and slams the door shut. He visibly winces at the force used as I gape in shock at the fourteen-year-old girl. I've never witnessed this side of her before, with becoming sort of friends, will I experience their bad sides too? Do I show my bad side to my friends? I'm rarely ruffled, barely ever angry or lashing out at anyone but I do have my bad days like everyone else. I'd just try not to get them involved.

"What are your plans for the day?" Col asks me, his eyes meeting mine in the rearview mirror, silently pleading with me to pick up some sort of conversation so it isn't as awkward in the tense quiet of the truck. Sometimes his radio doesn't work and this seems to be one of those days.

"Nothing really," I respond, tucking my hair behind my ear to no avail. "Just play with the nieces and nephews, maybe go for a wagon ride. They really love them, love the horses."

"If any are interested in rodeoing, I'll prop them." Col offers, signaling out of town. That's where we see Art, Jonah, and Pierre walking on the sidewalk with a dog trailing behind. Col seems to have the same idea as me as he pulls over and unrolls Dani's window. She huffs and crosses her arms over her chest, but doesn't say anything even though she is clearly still pouting.

"They would love that." My sentence is completed just before the three boys greet us with smiles, taking in Dani's sulky countenance.

"What's up?" Col asks, checking the roadway in front of him, then his side mirrors for any traffic behind him. Being a small town, and early afternoon, there is no traffic on the barren black top.

"Anyone wants a dog?" Jonah laughs, spotting me in the backseat. His smile perks up but true to our friendship pact, he doesn't say or do anything to flirt with me. I appreciate it.

"Dog's sorta just been following us," Art laughs, flipping his overgrown mullet top to the back of his head. His hair isn't as thick and wild as mine but it still flops back in front of his eyes. "I can't take it home, there's already too many."

"Awe," my eyes water at the timid short-coated dog shyly wagging his tail at us from a safe distance away. He's probably been abused and knows to stay back now. Dani, still in a mood, huffs and picks at her fingernails.

"Can't keep it," Pierre smiles ruefully with a sad little shake of his head. "Izzy and Eddie are already too many dogs for a town lot."

"I'll see if I can take him in," I slide to the passenger side and open the back door. The movement startles the pit bull look-a-like dog back a few steps but his tail wags when I sit on my butt and buttscooch toward him. With what seems like a smile, he bounces over, tail wagging.

"Be careful Daisy!" Jonah warns, "he hasn't let us touch him yet."

"Awe, he's fine," my voice melts into the tone we all use to talk to dogs and babies, especially when he practically sits on my lap and tries to lick my face.

"Someone's made a new best friend," Pierre teases me, leaning against Col's truck but jumping back when he realizes how hot the engine is. Col's diesel has been overheating lately, running out of cooling fluid with each trip into town. His replacement part is coming in tomorrow, until then he's been going through a crazy amount of antifreeze to keep his engine cool.

"We gotta go," Dani mutters gruffly, arms crossed against her chest as she slouches into the seat.

"Can we catch a ride?" Jonah asks. Danae's face clouds over in more anger but Col's shoulders slump in relief.

"For sure," he replies amicably, setting his palm on his girlfriend's knee. She slaps it away. Art shakes his head with an amused grin as he hops into the backseat, Jonah following him.

"You wanna help me get him in the box?" I ask Pierre.

"You bet," he replies, scooping the thick dog into his chest, his arms wrapped around the dog's legs. The pit bull whines as I run around Pierre to open the tailgate.

"You sitting in the box?" Col asks, rolling Dani's window up and unrolling his. With a grin I look to see Pierre's answer; we won't say no to riding in the freedom of the box.

"You coming to the reunion?"

"Dad and Aria are going public," I smirk at Pierre, accepting his hand for help. He's a gentleman when he remembers. Kaitlyn tried teaching her children higher standards of etiquette but Dickie doesn't mind if they only say please and thank you.

"Finally," he laughs with me. I pull the stray dog closer to me. He's shaking in fear so I rub his back, hugging him close.

"Four years 'under the covers' is long enough." I roll my eyes, kissing the top of the dog's head. He uses that as an opportunity to quickly lick my face.

"You think your dad will let you keep him?" Pierre asks, jutting his chin at the dog. I shrug, the wind picking up at the faster speed Col is going. With us, in the back of the truck, he won't go more than sixty.

"We did just take in a whole bunch of kids," I laugh with another shrug. "Don't see why he won't take a dog but we already have three and dogs are different than people."

"Whoa Daisy," Pierre laughs and looks at me, and this time he really studies me. "You're gonna be my niece-in-law."

"Huh, guess so, eh?" The dog falls on me when he tries to step on the wheel well, drool flying from the wind. I wrinkle my nose at his saliva hitting my cheek and gently shove his face behind me.

"We'll be able to pass on Grandma's recipes," Pierre smiles sweetly at me. "You're pretty much family already."

"Awe, thanks, Pierre." I smile at him, grunting when the dog falls into my chest at the turn Col takes into my dad's driveway. As per usual, dogs barking and kids screaming and laughing greet me as I hop out of the box of Col's truck. My smile strains and flickers away, sadness at Danae's still simmering temper keeping my mood low. Col is trying to chat with her but she's having none of it.

"You okay, Daisy?" Pierre frowns at me, rosary beads clenched between his fingers. My lips twitch at the picture, he's a lot like his dad and his older brothers. I shrug in response, not wanting my worry to weigh him down. I should be resting in God's embrace instead of worrying about fallen humanity. "Wanna say a Hail Mary with me?"

"Sure, yeah," I smile and make the sign of the cross. The dog whines in my arms, pushing me over as it tries to sit in my lap. My heart soars when Pierre's voice mingles with mine in the silence. Sometimes even I need encouragement to pray, sometimes even I run away from God.

Snarls interrupt the end of our quick prayer as Sugar and my cousin's dogs greet the stray, but his hackles are raised defensively. I shoot Pierre a smile of thanks as I race to the pit bull surrounded by the children and drag it back from our dogs. Dad is making his way out of the cabin with Lee, Louis, Rennie, Landon, and Harry.

"Why do we have another dog?" Dad raises his voice over the loud, excited tone of the children. I smile at him, urging a chuckle from Pierre and Jonah at the suck-up action.

"A stray," I answer hopefully with a cheeky smile. The children don't understand my answer because of the lack of words but they aren't far behind me when they start begging my dad to keep it.

"We already have three dogs, my girl." Dad sighs. "They're gonna start chasing Romain's cows and sheep soon, just make too much of a ruckus in general." He stares at me when the dogs begin growling at each other as if to prove his point.

"I understand dad," I smile to show I'm not mad even as tears come to my eyes. I'm very soft-hearted and not giving this stray dog that I've absolutely fallen in love with a home already hurts.

"I'm sorry," Dad pulls me in for a hug and kisses the top of my head. He knows me since a baby, knows how sensitive I am. Most call me naive.

"I know," I swallow the ache in my throat as Jonah hauls the pit bull back into the box of Col's truck.

"We'll probably take the evening to drive it out to the veterinary practice next town over," Pierre speaks up, wiping his long, chubby fingers on his jeans. "Hopefully they can find a good home for him."

"I guess I'm stuck babysitting," dad grins at me but I see the tiredness in his stance. He's a light sleeper. Every time Landon, Louis, and Rennie clatter into the house he wakes up and he's been working twelve hours for Peter so we have more money for the house and groceries and bills. I wish he'd let me help him.

"I can stay," I offer, waving at Col and Dani arguing on the driver's side of his truck and Pierre and Jonah standing to the side of me. Art had followed the triplets to the ATVs. "We don't need six people to drop off a stray dog at the shelter."

"No," dad gives me another hug, one I'm grateful for. Conan always hugs my dad and it's warmed him to physical contact with everyone, especially me, and it takes the edge off the memories of authoritarian parents. "Go, have fun, enjoy the time you have with your friends."

"Thanks, dad," I'm interrupted by a clang. Harry and Landon point and laugh caustically at Col, whose truck now has a dent on the hood. Danae is stomping angrily into the passenger seat.

"We're leaving!" She hollers angrily, slamming the truck door shut. My eyes widen in shock as I look at Col in concern. He shrugs and runs his hands through his hair.

"Danae's too damn young for him," dad huffs under his breath. Jonah glances at me, seeing my frozen face. If my dad put Col and Dani together, their parents certainly will.

"They're just friends," Jonah speaks up. His complete lie to my father baffles me. Dad simply raises an eyebrow, accepting his answer. He'll talk to me later to get the truth.

"So are you and Daisy," Pierre chuckles, slapping Jonah's shoulder with a grin. Jonah's eyes widen and he cuts a quick side eye to my dad.

"Shut up," Jonah rolls his eyes, his face flushing when my dad catches his side eye.

"Didn't I say no more Jonah at the house?" Dad frowns, stepping protectively in front of me. He has his very serious, very unimpressed face on when he stares Jonah down.

"Only when you aren't here," I cheekily grin, spinning around him to skip to the truck. The pit bull whines from the box. Danae punches the window, the stray flinches back from the abrupt sound.

"Get in!" Dani's face is livid as she violently points to the back seat.

"I think I might just ask to be dropped off at home," Jonah laughs, opening the door. Like the gentlemen he is, he lets me climb in, then Pierre.

"Grow up!" Col finally yells, his lips pressed in a firm line. "You wanna smash my truck you can f—king walk!"

Lee and Landon snicker as Louis and Rennie uncover the quads. Art groans as he climbs in behind the cranky girl. Dad probably asked my cousins to check the fence line and count the cows. Harry is already chilling on Honey's back, sitting like a pro with the measly two lessons I gave him. He's a natural, with animals and children and the outdoors. Harry is a good friend but I have a feeling this time together will make him a great brother.

"So, um," I clear my throat as Art and Jonah busy themselves with putting their seatbelts on. It's more to avoid the tension in the truck than the safety aspect. "Anyone wants to pray?"

"Yes," Pierre states immediately, handing me his rosary. I love his rosary, he made it himself when he was twelve years old. It took a lot of tears and blood and sweat to make it. The tears because of his impatience and frustration at messing up the work, the blood from carving the beads with a knife and accidentally cutting his fingers, and the sweat from making it in the hot summer. He used deer sinew from a buck he shot, skinned, and butchered himself.

"No!" Dani screeches, crossing her arms over her chest and throwing herself back into the seat. I want to snap at her, get mad and tell her she's acting a lot like my eight-year-old niece but I refrain from doing so. If I can't say it nicely I don't need to say anything at all. I also shouldn't be judging, but alas, I am human too.

"Right now doesn't seem like the best time," Jonah whispers in my ear. I shiver involuntarily from his breath tickling my neck.

"It might help," Col speaks up, pulling a rosary off his rearview mirror. I'd put it there years ago when we first started driving around together and he hadn't minded my faith showing in his vehicles. It's a perk for him now. When he rides those ornery bulls he blesses himself with it and says a Holy Trinity Chaplet asking God to keep him safe. That's the only time he prays but my hope is that he'll pray more often eventually.

✦ 23 ✦

The Extended Watson Family

———◦———

"That's too formal," my dad groans, his hands on Aria's shoulders. The look Aria sends him should have shut him up. "We're not in high school."

"It's the first time I'm introducing you as my boyfriend to my father," Aria snaps quietly as a hoard of Watson children run toward us. It's very loud, with laughter and giggles, raised voices to pretty much-screaming greetings as Lee and Harry take Philomena and Tikara out of their car seats and Sally Anne helps Conan and Kennedy out of their booster seats. In the bundle of children, I miss my dad and Aria's few sliced words. Many hugs are passed around, greetings issued, and kisses given. It doesn't surprise me when Windsor runs away from the contact. He calls it mushy stuff, having grown up in a household that doesn't show affection. Jasper runs after him, as well as Axle, Percy's oldest son.

Katie, Chloe, and Amelia, Dickie's nieces around Sally Anne's age surround the group next. It's the first time I see a carefree smile on my cousin's face as they drag her away, gushing about their clothes and hair. Paris, usually one to stay back with the younger children, trails after them. I find it endearing Dickie's oldest granddaughter is as old as his youngest niece. It shows just how pro-life the Watson clan is, something I can appreciate.

"Cake!" Kennedy yells loudly, a happy shine to her eyes. I can't help but smile at the cuteness overload. Conan grabs her hand and they are off as fast as they can with their little legs to the food table. To my surprise it's Jilly, the triplet's mother, manning the table. She handles the handful of children well. Denver, Paisley, and Abel had joined the Ridel children in chanting for cake.

Near the fire but far enough away for a couple of blankets to lay on the grass are Arlette, Audrina, and Andrea, Dickie's daughter and daughters-in-law. They have their babies in their arms and the toddlers on the blankets, a neat little fence keeping them in. It makes me wonder if we should put Kennedy in there, but given how independent she is, she wouldn't take too well in the enclosed space. A chuckle worms its way out when I see Corinne notice all the children crowding around the food table, she's unable to help when Andrea shoos her back and Arlette and Audrina share in scolding her. She should be resting. Corinne takes it easy but I see the sadness in her eyes when Arlette has to pick Reece up because she's crawled her way out the fence. I make a mental reminder to ask Corinne to help me with a silly little task. It will lift her spirits.

"Here," Harry holds Philomena out to me. The surprise plasters itself on my face. Daily mass really mellowed Harry. He's freely talking to me, something he hasn't been doing with his grudge holder ways.

"Where are you going?" I ask, folding the sleeping baby gently in my arms. Harry glances at me, an angry undertone to his softer profile around his extended family.

"Hang with the boys," he mutters after a moment, quickly turning around and walking away. Lee follows him after setting Tikara in my other arm.

"You should go to the girls," Lee slaps my shoulder before jogging after Harry, who'd caught up to Landon, Tyler, BJ, Pierre, and Luke,

Dickie's brother's college-aged son. Shrugging everyone's dismissal of me, I begin the walk to the toddler fence. Tikara is old enough to crawl around and she's starting to wiggle in my arms to get out. I've been around babies but I still label myself as inexperienced, especially holding a six-month-old baby and a fourteen-month-old.

"You look like you need some help," Shawn, Dickie's older sister's son, swoops in. He's BJ's older brother, volunteers with me at the soup kitchen, and works for his cousin Peter's construction business. Shawn is a prankster at times but he enjoys the simple things in life and his wife is even simpler than him. Some people would call them hippies.

"That I do," I laugh in relief when he takes Tikara out of my arms, throwing her in the air.

"Boys, huh?" Shawn tuts with a grin as he rolls his eyes at his cousins. When I turn to face him for our conversation, I see his wife, Roxy, their one-year-old daughter in her arms standing by Julia, Rory's oldest daughter, and her husband with her three boys beside her. Surprisingly the Ridels weren't the last to show, as late as we were. "Wanna hear some news before it falls down the grapevine?" Shawn grins at me with a wiggle of his eyebrows. I shrug.

"Sure," as long as it isn't gossip. Shawn steers me to the fenced-in area for the toddlers. It's going to be packed with Tikara, Tonya; Shawn's one-year-old, Reece, Pamela, and Henri, Julia's one-year-old.

"Roxy and me are gonna have another baby!" Shawn's grin turns into a lovesick smile.

"Awe! Congratulations!" I smile brightly. He pulls me in for a hug.

"You're the first to know," Shawn laughs at my surprised face. "We're telling everyone today."

"What an honor!"

"Hey!" He shouts, an edge to his voice. I jump in shock, he was just releasing me from his hug. "Tanner, get your hands outta her food!" I turn around to see what got his attention. Shawn's three-year-old son had thought it would be a good idea to take Kennedy's plate of grapes away. I wince, knowing how loud her cries are from living with her for the past few weeks. Nick, Julia's middle son, had taken a seat on the grass next to Tanner and they were both obliviously munching on Kennedy's lost grapes. Big tears well up in her eyes as a scream rips through her throat. Conan notices first, and being the aggressive little boy he is, he tackles Nick and Tanner with a bellow. I never understand his words, mumbled and mispronounced as they are, but I'm pretty sure he's mad at them for taking away Kennedy's purple grapes. Kennedy joins her brother, flopping on Nick. The grapes are lost in the process, Marie and Peter's long-haired collie gobbling them up.

"Conan! Kennedy!" I holler at them, my voice drowned out over Shawn's louder one. Even with Tikara struggling to get out of his arms he still pulls Kennedy off. I block her with my legs, hearing actual cries coming from Nick and Tanner. Conan threw hands, something horrible he learned from his drunken father. Dickie is the next to reach us, swooping down to pick up a ferocious Conan. My nephew won't stop screaming or hitting anything in his reach as tears stream down his face. Dickie holds him like a baby, securely holding his arms and legs against his body. Kennedy hits my legs, her screams matching her brother's. She's yelling something about Dickie hurting Conan. Philomena is waking up, her face red and lips curled into a cry. Roxy and Julia are by their crying sons, comforting them while shooting nasty looks at my niece and nephew. "It's okay Kennedy," I try to soothe. She can't hear me over the din of their cries.

"Here," my dad picks up Kennedy. "Stop crying," he states firmly as he dries her tears with his hands. "We'll get you another plate, simple as that."

Philomena erupts into screams. My headache is back with a vengeance. I walk away from the chaos, rocking the baby in my arms. Dad has to hold Kennedy like Dickie is holding Conan because she won't calm down. I'm halfway to the truck when I break down, sobs falling out of my chest and tears streaming down my face. Someone runs passed me, opens my dad's truck and pulls the diaper bag out that I'd been walking to, and jogs back to me. Philomena is still crying, ear-piercing screams that make me wince with the headache exploding in my brain. It's Paul who sits next to me, takes my niece out of my arms, gives her her bottle of milk, and rocks her gently in his arms. It's Paul who wraps an arm around my shoulders and pulls me in for a hug, not saying a word.

"I don't know why I'm crying." I blow a big breath of air out and dry my tears. "I'm sorry."

"We've all been there." Paul shrugs. He has purple bags under his eyes, showing the stress he's been under. Even with his wife leaving him with their children and having to run his hotel business as a stay-at-home dad he still is the first to come to help. I can't help but burst into more sobs. God really is good. "Happens to the best of us."

"God got plans for you, mate," I say through some sniffles. Paul smiles bitterly, so much pain in his milk chocolate eyes.

"Kinda finding it hard to connect with Him right now." He blows out a breath of air, adjusting Philomena in his arms. He's going to have to burp her soon.

"I'm sorry," I say, my watery eyes catching his. My lips tremble as I try to hold back another wave of sobs. "It's none of my business and I'm trying to stay out of it but you must be hurting so bad. And you still help out, still have hope." The sobs burst out of me and I shrug and shake my head, not knowing why exactly I'm crying now. "I was talking to Art the other day and he mentioned how much he looks up to you for guidance. Jonah too, the Trips. You aren't that much older than us but you're still so good, ya know? I don't know what I'm even saying. You're good, that's all, I guess."

"How much sleep have you been getting?" Paul diverts the theme of the conversation with a bittersweet smile.

"Between Sally Anne fighting to stay up late, feeding Philomena and Tikara so my dad could rest, and Landon, Louis, and Rennie getting home at all hours, Conan and Windsor randomly waking up terrified," I shake my head, yawning. "Maybe, four or five hours of interrupted sleep."

"Here's the plan," Paul shoots me a tired smile. "I'm going to take Philomena in for her nap, you're gonna come with me and have a nice, long nap."

"I came to visit," I interrupt with a frown.

"There's plenty of time to visit," Paul begins to burp Philomena. "Catch up on rest while you can. You don't know when you'll get the chance to again."

"Hey, my girl," dad steps into view. It's then that I realize the crying has stopped and everyone went back to visit. "You okay?" Dad crouches down.

"Yeah," I laugh, slightly crying as well. Dad looks at Paul. He shrugs, folding Philomena in his arms after her burp and sliding the nipple of the bottle on her lips.

"I think Daisy could use some sleep." Paul looks at dad. "You're both pushing yourself too hard. Duncan, Peter told me you're falling asleep at work. Daisy yawns constantly at the soup kitchen and sometimes falls asleep in adoration. You both need to take a step back from something. Your whole lives you've been helping other people, let us help you."

"But who am I supposed to help?" I ask with a frown. Paul is going through a rough time, Phil has war memories waking him up at night, Dickie's busy helping Corinne and his parents, and everyone else doesn't really notice.

"Yourself," Paul states firmly, albeit gently. "Yourself and your family."

"Who's gonna help us?" Dad asks, running his thumb and fingers over his jaw.

"Me, dad, Aria," Paul shrugs. "You got us Watsons if you don't get anyone else." Paul manages a cheeky grin. "You finally came out with Aria so you're fam." Dad rolls his eyes at that and offers me a hand.

"Go have a nap Daisy," he says in his supposedly stern voice. I accept his hand for help.

"I'll make sure she lays down and shuts her eyes," Paul grins at my dad. My face drops at the silent conversation they seem to share, eyebrows raised, lip twitches, the little hand gestures.

"Sleep well, my girl," dad kisses my forehead. He shakes his head when he spots Kennedy and Conan sharing a plate of grapes next to Nick and Tanner.

"See ya dad," I sigh, failing to hide another yawn. I look over my shoulder, focusing on the younger children to find Paul's, frowning when I can't. "Where're your kids, Paul?"

"Amy came and took them," he sighs, holding the door open for me even when he's the one with his hands full.

"At least let me take the diaper bag," I divert the conversation, hating the pain in his eyes.

"She has a new boyfriend already," Paul says, motioning for me to go up the stairs first. I comply, shrugging yet again. Most people don't open up to me so I'm not sure how to react. "Some cop Andrea can't stand to work with. I know things weren't perfect but she left so fast. She should still be breastfeeding Aiden but she never had any interest in things maternal. She used to go for walks with me, helped dad out on the farm, and baked and cooked with me. Especially when we were engaged, used to pray the rosary with me, and go to daily mass when she wasn't working. It all changed when we got married. It's like she slowly stopped caring, more so she went back to the person she was before we started dating. Guess it's true you can't change someone."

"I'm sorry Paul," I pat his shoulder. "I don't really know what to say or how to help."

"I don't want to tell my family yet, just Andrea knows she already moved on... I'm so... lost." While he is speaking I pull out the pull-out couch, fluff up some pillows and unfold some throw blankets. The pillows go on one side near the edge. Philomena can barely roll over but better safe than sorry.

"Wanna pray?" I ask when he carefully lays Philomena down. Paul looks out the window, at his brothers and uncles and dad and grand-fathers visiting, the women manning the food table and toddlers, the children running about and laughing. His jaw clenches so I stand up beside him, leaning my head on his shoulder. "You feel like you're on the outside, staring in, huh?"

"Yeah," Paul snaps out of his blues and steps back, shoving his hands in his pockets.

"Sometimes it bothers me," I meet his eyes for a whisper of a second before looking away. "And sometimes it doesn't 'cause Jesus had twelve apostles and only one stayed with him through His Crucifixion."

"John," Paul smiles sadly. "The disciple whom He loved."

"I'm going to pray the Chaplet of Faith to fall asleep," I crawl onto the couch bed with another yawn. "You can join if you want."

"In the name of the Father, and the Son and the Holy Spirit. Amen." Paul leads the prayer with the sign of the cross. I let him lead the prayers, happy to have someone to lead me in prayer. Lately, it's been me leading the children because of dad's crazy work hours. Sometimes I just want to follow in prayer, and with what Paul said about Amy not praying with him, he probably wants to lead someone. Honestly enough, I don't mind. We haven't even finished the first decade of "Jesus, Mary, I love you, save souls, save the consecrated" before I'm asleep.

When I wake up, Tinsley, Makayla, and London are coloring on the floor. London's are scribbles all over the page, Makayla is using markers and getting some all over her fingers while Tinsley is coloring with pencil crayons, carefully in the lines, and trying not to use too much pressure. In the split seconds I take all this in, they catch me waking up.

"Aunty!" Makayla grins, jumping on the bed. Surprisingly enough London calls me Aunty as well. I scoot to the edge of the bed before they can bump into Philomena, wiping eye boogers from my eyes. Instead of feeling refreshed, I feel even more tired. It will take me a minute to wake up so I'm content to embrace their hugs.

"Wanna color?" Makayla asks, quickly jumping off the bed to show me her picture.

"Wow! Good work Micks!"

"Look at mine!" London falls off the bed in her hurry to show me her scribbled page. The loud bang does nothing to slow her advance or wake up a slightly snoring Philomena.

"That's a lot of purple!" I trace some of her scrawled lines, all grape purple.

"Aunty, look at my pony." Tinsley thrusts her coloring book in my face. Of course, hers is the horse page. She catches as many rides on Honey as possible, annoying Harry with her same question over and over again: can you take me for a ride? Puh-lease!

"That looks a lot like Honey," I smile at her. She nods energetically.

"I'm gon have a horse like Honey someday." She states, the dream taking root in her mind as she all but belly flops on the floor to finish coloring.

"I'm bored," Makayla groans with a smile.

"Go play outside with the boys," I nudge her with a smile of my own. "Or go watch the babies with the ladies."

"Daisy look!" It's Sally Anne's face that pops out from the kitchen wall but not the hair I'm accustomed to her having.

"Thought we'd do a little makeover," Alex shoots me a generous smile. She works at Dickie's sister's hair salon, the only one in town.

"You look beautiful," I smile widely at Sally Anne. She looks happy, something she hasn't been around us. Maybe she just needed girl time. Lord knows I'm not that capable with hair and makeup and fashion stuff.

"Thanks," Sally Anne blushes and giggles. "You should get your hair fixed too!"

"My hair is pretty hard to work with," I begin to shake my head no. Sally Anne looks up to Alex, a pout on her face. I can tell by the gleam in Alex's eyes that she also wants to work with my hair.

"Me and Aunt Bobbi will put cornrows in your hair," Alex decides, pulling me up off the couch. "Let's do this."

The kitchen is a mess, not in the usual sense but someone has gotten a haircut, chunks of hair litter the floor, and brushes, combs, sprays, and other hair care items are spread about Marie's usually food-filled table. Savannah and Arlo are asleep in a bassinet close to the kitchen sink, a close eye being kept on them by Julia, who is rocking Henri in her arms. Roxy is in the rocking chair, Tonya snoring lightly in her lap. All the babies must nap around the same time, to have five of them sleeping right now. It's the first time I think the Watsons have too many children when London, Tinsley, and Makayla run downstairs, knocking over Nick and Tanner.

"Okay, that's it!" Woody, Bobbi's husband, raises his voice. "If you're five and older, get outside and stay outside!" He points specifically at London, whose lips fight valiantly not to cry. I feel sympathy for her, Woody is being harder on her because she knows better but it was probably Makayla that started the race.

"You five outside as well," Alex shakes her finger at Chloe, Katie, Amelia, Paris, and Sally Anne. Bobbi stands with her hands on her hips and a raised eyebrow.

"We weren't bothering anyone!" Sally Anne argues. The four Watson girls nod along with her words.

"Sally Anne, please listen to them," I ask quietly. Conan and Kennedy already started a kerfuffle, I don't want another Ridel bringing drama here. A spark ignites in her eyes, defiance written on her face.

"I said get out!" Woody hollers up the steps.

"Who's not listening?" Harvey asks his brother-in-law. At the sound of their father's voice, Amelia and Chloe shoot each other worried glances. A fire is seemingly lit behind them as they hustle out of the house.

"I don't need to listen to them," Sally Anne raises an eyebrow, undaunted. Paris, treated as a great-grandchild with less responsibility than the grandchildren, swallows stiffly before she scurries in a big circle out of the house, murmuring something about playing tag with her siblings.

"Why don't we go to the basement?" Katie suggests, looking hopefully at her aunt.

"Don't make me get your dad, girlie," Harvey calls up the stairs. He gives me a nod and a smile when he spots me, waiting patiently for his niece.

"Grandpa's sleeping in the basement," Bobbi shakes her head.

"Yeah," Sally Anne hollers down, crossing her arms across her chest very defiantly. "Well, you can't go get my dad!"

"It's not worth the fight Sally," Katie tugs on her friend's hand. "Let's just go sit in the truck or something."

"I was just fine before you guys picked me up," Sally Anne sends a frosty glare my way. There is so much I want to say to her, the scripture I want to quote but the words that come out of my mouth aren't what I'd been thinking. They must be Holy Spirit God-given.

"I love you, Sally Anne." I profess simply. "I'm gonna do my best by you, even if you think I'm an awful human being. I'll make mistakes, I'll hurt your feelings, and it will be messy. I don't want to be your mom, I want to be your cousin that you can talk about boys with, gossip with friends, cry together, and praise God in the rain." I notice I'm ranting so I stop, leaving an abrupt silence in the house. Harvey is wagging his finger for Katie to get outside. Sally Anne stares at me, tears welling in her eyes.

"Whatever," she snaps, hanging her head as she trots down the stairs. I sigh deeply, falling into a kitchen chair.

"You seemed to handle that pretty well," Julia smiles at me, switching Henri to her other arm for a change in position.

"You think?" I yawn and lean my head on the table. "I try to do that but most times I end up yelling at her. God's really sanctifying my patience with her."

"I think it was mighty damn fine," Bobbi smiles at me before tilting my head to start on corn rows. "Poor baby, you ain't have a mama and you tryna raise your cousins. Aria wasn't lying when she said you guys were having a tough time."

"Bobbi," I look earnestly at her through the reflection of the window pane. "There's sixteen of us in a two-bedroom cabin smaller than Marie's kitchen and living room."

"Sally Anne got along well with Amelia and Chloe," Bobbi says. "Get Duncan to ask Harvey to take her sometimes."

"Or Uncle Andy," Roxy speaks up. "Katie and she are closer than Amelia and her."

"Don't move," Alex laughs when I go to shake my head. They have my hair parted in seven sections, clips and ponytails holding the sections they weren't using out of the way.

"Sally Anne won't go for it."

"Why's that?" Bobbi asks as Philomena starts crying. When I move to get her Alex freezes me.

"I got it," she runs to the living room with bobby pins in her teeth.

"Well, my aunt Jade is filing for custody of her because her two daughters get along well with Sally." I'm interrupted from saying more when Marie enters the house. She's helping Corinne up the steps although it might be the other way around. Bobbi's hands move fast in my hair even with her eyes watching her elderly mother and heavily pregnant niece-in-law climb the stairs.

"The heat was just getting too bad for me," Corinne smiles at us with a rosy, flushed face. Roxy exits the rocking chair, already knowing it is her grandmother-in-law's favorite seat.

"You're finally taking some time for yourself," Marie smiles at me and pats my knee, her hazel eyes lighting up in happiness. "You deserve it."

"Why? What all do you know about Daisy?" Bobbi asks, quite nosily as Alex walks into the kitchen with Philomena.

"Wanna toss another bag of hotdog buns down?" My dad stands in the open doorway, swatting at mosquitos. Only my able hands aren't busy with all the babies the ladies are watching and it seems like we all freeze when Corinne waddles to the end of the stairs and lightly tosses the bag down. Dad frowns up the steps, at my head squished on the table because Bobbi had got to the end of one row of cornrows. "You okay, my girl?"

"Getting my hair braided," I smile a no teeth, polite smile at him.

"Exactly," he deadpans. My face flushes as Roxy, Julia and Alex laugh.

"Go to the men, Duncan," Bobbi shoots him a half-hearted stink eye. "We ladies are having fun."

"Daisy with her hair braided." Dad shakes his head in confusion as he slams the door shut. If he doesn't slam it, it doesn't close. We've all learned that with Pat's house.

"Don't worry about him," Alex pats my shoulder.

"Every girl's gotta grow up," Julia smiles at me, adjusting Henri in her arms again. The door opens again, seemingly constant with how many people are there. I hadn't realized just how big the Watson family is.

"Why does my mom think you deserve a break?" Bobbi asks again, pulling tighter on my hair. The pulling isn't to get me to talk, it's so the braids stay in longer.

"Oh, Paul told me," Alex grins wickedly when I say nothing.

"I told you what?" Paul himself asks. I wouldn't say he is smiling but the expression on his face is happier than earlier.

"Why Grandma thinks Daisy deserves a break." Alex's grin widens. Paul's eyes light up as he leans against the kitchen sink, placing a comforting hand on Savannah's back; she had started whimpering in her sleep.

"Daisy does," Paul confirms. "Been working too hard."

"How so?" Bobbi asks as she finishes off another cornrow. With Alex helping her again that's three done, Marie had taken Philomena in her arms to rock. Bobbi and Alex are surprisingly fast with their nimble fingers.

"Nursing Tyler back to health," Paul starts listing items on his fingers with a prideful glance directed at me. "Helping Peter roof his garage, training for and winning the annual half marathon, working, tutoring after school, volunteering at Dad's soup kitchen, cleaning Grandma and Grandpa's once a month, not to mention she cleans the church once a month as well, taking care of Pete when he is drunk, watching after her drunk cousins and seven nieces and nephews." Paul takes a deep breath. The uncle he'd walked in with, Rory, slaps my shoulder with a nod of acknowledgment. "I didn't miss anything, did I?" Paul raises an eyebrow at me. Sometime during his rant, Savannah has located to his arms and is snuggled contentedly on his chest.

"You bragged me up way too much," I frown, my face red from Paul's speech of thankfulness for me. "Sometimes I don't even do all those things or I do them without the proper effort."

"She's such a sweet girl," Marie adds on. My face burns from compliments and gratitude. I don't help people for them to place me on that pedestal!

"She comes and cleans grandma's house once a month," Alex chews her lips as she looks at me, quite stumped. "You come and clean my grandma's house," she repeats. I guess Paul hadn't told her that part.

"That'll be the thing you drop," Paul decides on a whim. "I'm sure my siblings, cousins, aunts, and uncles will step up for that."

"We will," Bobbi confirms. Marie tries to wave them off but they have none of it. It's more so Pat and Peter that will fight them, they're more stubborn than sweet, lovely Marie.

"You can drop volunteering at Dickie's soup kitchen too," Rory adds. "Louis will be back from tour soon and will need something to occupy him until he finds a job."

"And the half marathon is over so no more running so extensively," Julia adds to everyone's agreement. I wilt in my seat. They're planning my life out for me, deciding what I should and should not do because I broke down in front of them. Dad raised me better, I know better than to act so dependently.

"You don't need to take odd jobs with me anymore," Peter adds. Bobbi is just starting the last braid in my hair. She'd watched while Peter had ascended the stairs, while I'd only heard the walk she saw who it was.

"I need the money," I state quietly. When they all speak up to try and get their input across, I try to shut them down, sending Paul a grateful smile for not saying anything. "Rennie and Louis spend all the child tax on booze, dad is spending all his savings on the mansion, and Rennie and Louis don't work."

"Duncan doesn't know you've been buying groceries, huh?" Paul blows a big breath of air out. Marie smiles sadly at me, pity in the way she gazes at the baby in her arms. Bobbi and Rory stare at me in disbelief. My dad and I aren't as close to them as the others so they hadn't heard of our struggles.

"He thinks it's Aria stepping up," I admit quietly.

"Well, why hasn't she?" Paul barks, surprising me at the anger in his tone. I balk at his raised voice as Peter places an arm on him to calm down.

"She just hasn't thought about it," I shrug. Bobbi pats my head with an impressed smile at her handiwork.

"Looking good, girlie."

"Maybe someone should put the idea in her head," Peter suggests. He and Paul share an unspoken conversation that the women can't understand but Rory gets the gist.

"No," I say softly, wincing at the drama in the Watson family because of my Ridel family. "She's been a good sport with dad spur of the moment taking in a whole passel of kids. We can't possibly ask any more of her."

"Am I interrupting something?" Patrick, the young one, grins up the steps. The Watsons all greets him with smiles and hugs, it's a slow ascent of the stairs for him. I laugh at the extra big kisses on the cheek Bobbi gives him when she notices his hand holding onto the girls.

"You have a girlfriend?!" I grin excitedly, joining the hug train after he passes Alex and Julia.

"Drew, meet Daisy, Daisy Ridel, family friend, Drew Jendryck, girlfriend," Patrick grins, pulling his girlfriend forward with their tightly clasped hands. I envelop the cute little lady in a welcoming hug.

"It's so good to meet you!" I give her hand a squeeze, spotting Rory, Peter, and Paul heading outside. "I'm sorry, excuse me, I have to run after Paul for a quick word."

"Have at 'er," Patrick laughs, pulling his girlfriend to his grandma. It makes my heart happy. Patrick's always been content to be alone, even in the midst of friends and family. If he's bringing his girlfriend home, it's serious.

"Never saw that coming," Peter laughs as Windsor leads a pack of kids past us, all racing and hollering and giggling.

"Bet you Payton knew," Paul grins cheekily. He stops walking when he spots me trailing behind.

"Patrick has a girlfriend," Rory shakes his head with a disbelieving smile. "Who gave him that idea?"

"What you need, kid?" Peter nods at me to talk. I'm old enough to wait until the adults are ready for me to talk, and since I wait, they let me talk.

"Is there some random couple-week job you can hire Rennie and Louis for? Keep them busy from drinking?" I look at Peter, who owns a construction company, and Paul, who owns a chain of hotels. "I'm hoping they'll get a taste of real living if they stop the booze and see what they can make from their own hands." Paul and Peter share a look and my heart sinks into my chest.

"I can't have customer's complaints again," Paul states forlornly. "When I hired Pete for that stretch business slowed and that can't happen again, especially with everything going on." He's talking about Amy leaving him.

"It's a safety hazard," Peter shrugs in a what can you do manner. "Already gave Pete the job I would have given them and I can't take back my word. I'd be able to hire one of them when Pete goes on a binge but that's promising work that might not be there."

"I'll hire them," Rory speaks up. "The wife's brother needs some guys to pull roots, shovel grain, and haul wood. I was going to get Louis and Luke but they're well enough off they don't need the money. Luke can enjoy his summer break from school and Louis can find a different job or help his grandparents out. They're getting up there in age."

"Do you mean it?" I ask with a smile and tears in my eyes. Rory nods with a shrug.

"It's not much but it's what I can offer in the hopes it helps." Peter and Paul nod along, thinking it is a wonderful idea.

"Thank you!"

24

The Ridel House

I'm usually the first one up, but not this morning. It isn't even the smell of dad's coffee brewing that wakes me, it's the sound of heavy machinery and trees splitting. Percy is already here with his CAT, clearing the brush away from dad's chosen plot of land for the mansion. I'd stopped using an alarm clock when it kept waking everyone else in the living room up, but my internal alarm routinely wakes me up at five am sharp. Today is no different when I glance at the clock hanging on the living room wall, on what little space there is not obscured by bunk beds. Sally Anne is still asleep next to me. My skin is cold because she steals the blankets in the night and tucks herself in good and secure. Lee's eyes are open on the top bunk bed across from me. I shoot him a smile. He rolls his eyes before slamming his pillow over his head, covering his ears. Windsor and Makayla are on the other top bunk, Tinsley and Kennedy on the bottom, with Harry and Tyler taking up the double bottom bed. Conan was throwing a tantrum last night so dad put him down in my room. Landon, Louis, and Rennie hadn't made it home last night; or if they did, they finally listened to my dad's advice and slept up in the barn loft.

With a yawn I roll out of bed, crossing myself and mentally praying as I brush my teeth and change in the bathroom. Three Hail Marys for Mama Mary's intentions, seven Glory Be's for my guardian angel's protection throughout the day and seven Glory Be's for the Holy Spirit's guidance. Throughout the quick time it takes me to get ready, more vehicles arrive and voices of people greeting each other and planning the groundbreaking are heard.

A lot of people means a lot of food being eaten so I decide to spend the day baking, even if I should be going to school. Dad has a major sweet tooth so he won't say no, especially with his excitement for the mansion being built hyping him up. With my short prayers done I start a five-decade rosary, meditating on the Joyful Mysteries. I pull out dad's recipe book and start on beet and carrot cake bread. With garden harvesting finished only a couple of weeks ago I have tons of fresh veggies to use up. Dad and I always plant an extra large garden, giving the extras to the soup kitchen or families in need. This year our family ended up being the family in need but we don't have big enough storage for it all. We're working on digging a bigger root cellar. The four loaves are in the oven when I finish mentally praying my first rosary of the day so I start on the St. Michael Chaplet while I bake zucchini muffins. The noise outside is a constant buzz in the background. Harry is the first one up and when he sees me baking the first words he says are: "Can you make me some zucchini patties?"

"Sure can," I respond, humming and smiling as I whip up the muffins. Harry wanders off to the bathroom, shaking the sleep from his eyes. The muffins are ready to go but our oven is small so I start washing the dishes that had piled up throughout the night. Water cups, baking utensils, and bowls, someone had clearly snacked on some of the leftover beets and another made use of the last bit of Saskatoon squares Makayla helped me bake. During this time I say the quick Chaplet of

Divine Mercy for everyone in my town and parish who need God's love and the Chaplet of Faith for my family.

The loaves are finished baking as I wash the last dish so I quickly switch them out for the muffins to the sound of blankets shuffling and pillows being tossed. Everyone is waking up but they don't want to start their days yet. When Philomena wakes up crying I bring her to the kitchen and change her wet pamper and give her a bottle of warmed-up milk.

"Here," Harry motions for the baby from his perch on the kitchen table.

"Thanks," I beam at him, gently setting Philomena in his arms. She is content to fall back asleep now that she is dry and getting full.

"Make my damn zucchini patties," Harry grumbles with a roll of his eyes. His attitude is simply him trying to show me he was being selfish in holding Philomena but I shrug it off. On the whim that the men outside want Mrs. Watson's zucchini patties as well, I quadruple the recipe. Harry gets a bottle ready for Tikara when she starts fussing in the bassinet. Lee is the next one awake and he jumps off the top bunk, puts his runners on, and is out the door. Tyler is next and he carefully walks to the bathroom to take his medicine. Dad hid all the pill bottles and leaves Tyler's designated amount in the sink cupboard which the children can't reach. The door opens when I am clearing up counter space and keeping an eye on the frying patties.

"Heard you got some food," Peter Watson grins at me, a thermos in his hands. I cross myself, ending my prayer as Peter sits at the table. His clothes are full of bark and sawdust, leaves, and dirt. It wouldn't surprise me if he had ants or spiders crawling around his jean jacket.

"You want some beet and carrot cake?" I offer, holding the fresh loaf out for him. The smell is delicious, urging my stomach to growl. I'm glad it was quiet because I can wait until everyone else is done eating to help myself. The cook should always eat last.

"Yes sirree," Peter smiles his goofy smile. I know a smart Alec response is coming with the flash of his crooked teeth. "Fair trade for the pancakes."

"Then you owe me for the zucchini patties," I shoot back, cutting a still-warm piece of cake for him.

"You got me there," Peter shrugs, accepting the piece. His eyes light up like a child's when he feels the warmth. I laugh when he has it gobbled up in two bites.

"You need help out there?" Harry asks, still holding Philomena in his arms. Her bottle is empty but it's stuck to her lips, acting as a soother in her sleep.

"Only if you feel like it." Peter shrugs. "Got my two crews working and the whole fam came out to help."

"Really?" I ask my voice almost a squeak. "We don't have enough food!"

"Kaitlyn is gonna watch the kids with some of the other moms-in-law so Audrina and Arlette can come to help you out. Aunt Bobbi's coming too, Alex and Andrea." I stare at Peter's words in shock but he isn't finished. "Paul finagled all the permits that you guys needed, with both my crews here we'll have the mansion up by the end of the week."

"Wow," the surprise is evident on my face. "I never imagined not living in the cabin."

"Now you're gonna be living in a seven-bedroom mansion," Peter grins and wiggles his eyes. I'm not quite thinking as I cut up the beet and carrot cake. Tyler nabs a piece, smooths back Philomena's hair, and sits on dad's spot at the table. I'm lost in the healthy flush to his skin, the lack of purple bags under his eyes, and a slight tilt to his lips that show he isn't as sad as he was. I thank the Lord for that as my stomach twirls in my stomach. Peter caught me studying Tyler, blush on my face.

"There he is, the lazy dog," Percy not so gently slaps the back of his brother's head before hollering to someone outside that the boss man is having a coffee break.

"Get ready for school Daisy," dad is the next in the house. A troop of men follows him in. I smile sweetly at him while handing him a zucchini patty. "That's not gonna work," he laughs in between chewing the greasy, crunchy sweet tasting food.

"But the muffins in the oven will," I widen the smile on my face, trying to school my features into innocence. Harry snorts at me as Tyler shakes his head with a laugh.

"You're burning muffins," Paul speaks up. With all the men crowding in I hadn't spotted him walking in. He quickly scoops on an oven glove and takes the last pan of muffins out, abnormally dark.

"I'll still eat it," one man speaks up as he raises his hand. Dad looks at him, then the children all waking up in the living room.

"Thank you!" I chirp, smiling thankfully at the stranger in my home. He must be a guy from one of Peter's crews.

"Men outside!" Dad hollers, snagging the last cooked zucchini patty of the moment. "Harry, Daisy, can you guys get all the kids ready for school?"

"Yeah," Harry mutters, glaring at me. I squint at him, wondering what I did to make him angry this time. It hurts my heart and weighs me down when he shows this sublime negativity toward me. I have no clue what I did to make him hate me!

"Out," dad slaps the friendly stranger on the shoulder. He nods while stuffing a full muffin in his mouth. It jolts me into reality. The men will need water with all the work they'll be completing. "Get the kids ready for the bus and drop Kennedy and Tikara off at Percy's. His mother-in-law will watch them for the day and pick up Conan when she picks Paisley up from headstart."

"Okay Dad," I wave at him when he closes the door. Harry hands Philomena to Tyler and turns to me. The look on his face says he means business.

"Don't stop making those patties." He juts his finger at the stove. "I'll handle the kids." And he's off, shaking the bunk beds, pulling pillows and blankets away, and shoving their shoulders. I'm impressed, he's not interacting too roughly with them in the process. Tyler is another story. He's staring in fear at the baby sleeping in his arms.

"You'll be fine," I smile at him as I throw a blanket over Philomena.

"Just don't leave me alone with her," Tyler laughs nervously, then winces from his still bruised ribs.

"You're fine," Windsor grins at him, flopping into a chair at the table shirtless.

"Put a shirt on, Win." I gently order, chopping up some fresh beets. The easiest thing to make for a large group is stew and with all the veggies stored in the cellar, it's the healthiest option.

"Sally Anne's in the bathroom," he complains with a good-natured grin. I've yet to see him complain seriously or throw a tantrum. Windsor loves life and enjoys making the rest of us laugh with his jokes and teasing.

"You don't need a different room to put a shirt on," I deadpan with a laugh.

"I'm out of clean clothes," Windsor smirks at me, his light brown eyes lighting up jovially.

"Oh," I say, looking around the mess that is in the kitchen with my cooking and baking covering up most of the counters. I'm feeling claustrophobia setting in with everyone getting up. Kennedy is running around in her underwear, asking about Conan. Makayla is tucked under blankets, failing at fake sleeping with a huge smile creeping onto her face. "I'll wash laundry while you're at school."

"Awe, do I have to?" Windsor whines but my attention is caught on his cousin. The expression on Tinsley's face melts all hardness in my heart when she holds open my old children's bible. Every morning and night I read to them and to see her soul on fire for more scripture makes me thank the good Lord generously.

"Yes," I say to both of them.

"Don't stop making my patties!" Harry points his finger at me with a squint in his eyes. My eyes widen in dilemma. I told Tinsley I'd read her the bible but I'd told Harry I'd cook him breakfast. I can't do both by the time the bus comes around. Should I be Mary or Martha in this situation?

"But-," I begin to speak up.

"I'll read her the damn bible," Harry interrupts me. Really, I truly am glad he is talking to me but it hurts how angry and negative his words are. I shut my mouth, internally offering my sadness for Harry to find love for the Lord in his time spent with us. With fresh patties flipped, I run to the door and peek out. One of Peter's crews is unloading two-by-fours since our yard isn't big enough for machinery. The other is clearing trees that Percy knocked down. Voices float around me, both from inside and out. Harry clears his throat obnoxiously, warning me with a glowering look to get back to the kitchen. I manage a hidden laugh. Someone is super hangry.

"Col's here! Awesome! Even Abe and Romain." I peer out the door once more, squinting at the sight. "Is that Jonah? And his dad? Everyone came! Wow!"

"Jonah?" Tyler's eyes become even sadder, a downcast appearance rupturing the anxiety covering his face.

"Plate's empty," Harry glares fiercely at me. I'm unsure of whether it's from the lack of food or the presence of Jonah. I don't even know how or when he got a plate because Kennedy is sitting on his lap, Conan is perched on his shoulders, and Tinsley is leaning against him with Windsor and Makayla sharing a chair right next to him.

"Sorry," I smile sheepishly at him. "I got distracted."

"Yeah, being nosy," Sally Anne snaps, flipping her hair over her shoulder as she slides into the last kitchen chair.

"That's true," I shrug as I busy myself flipping patties and organizing the little mess from oil splashing. Harry speaks up, cutting off any other conversation as he reads the passage Tinsley opened the bible to. I'm content to listen, as seems to be the case for the group sitting around the table. While Harry is reading I portion out the plastic plates for the children and spread my fresh baked goodies on them for their breakfast. Conan and Kennedy's I rip apart, Tinsley's I cut in half and then I mash some up with milk for Tikara. We've been giving her soft foods lately and it's shown in her digestive system much to the dismay of the children and her dad. When I serve the children's plates the small room overfills with voices that I don't tune into as I hastily clean up the kitchen and pack their bags for the day. A muffin and a slice of cake for each child and a bottle of water, some carrots and peas from the fridge, and ham and lettuce sandwiches for their lunch. It's hard to get them all into clean clothes and brushed hair before the bus comes but we manage it all in a flurry.

"Daisy!" Dad hollers at me from the rectangle of men by the recently cleared spot for his mansion. "We'll pray before we start building!"

"You heard him," I shrug to Tyler and Harry, who had followed me to the end of the driveway. I have Philomena in a cloth carrier strapped to my chest, Harry has Kennedy perched on his shoulders and Tyler holds Tikara in his arms.

"Dickie," dad slaps Mr. Watson's shoulder. It's his way of showing respect to the eldest man here, also the one who leads us in faith.

"Your house, son, you sure?" Dickie asks, looking happy to call my dad son. It makes my heart leap in my chest. When Dad and Aria marry

I might not be as lonely. Even now with just announcing their relationship the Watson family has taken great strides in trying to include me in their lives. Dad nods, so Dickie begins with the sign of the cross. "Thank you, Lord, for this beautiful day. We thank you for the night's rest that we received and for the grace to begin this day with a strong work ethic and companionable spirits. All that we do, may we do it to praise You. Please bless the people here today and the people who set foot into the house and may their words upon entering any house be "Peace unto you", we ask this through Your son, Our Lord Jesus Christ. Amen."

"Amish vibes," Harry laughs when the men begin to work. I don't know how to respond to the comment if it is him being rude or not, so I ignore it.

"I have to plan some meals and prepare snacks." I clear my throat as I grab Kennedy's hand. I know how to drive but it doesn't mean I like to without my driver's license, only old enough to have a learner's license but dad said to get the children over to Peter's, so I should.

"I'ma check-up on Landon," Harry points to the barn. Then he grins mischievously as if he hasn't been holding a grudge against me. "Heck of a time getting them up there last night."

"I slept through that?" I raise my eyebrows, impressed. Harry shrugs and ambles off, leaving me alone with Tyler. Well, we have the little girls but that's not the point. Tyler isn't the best at making conversation and I'm slightly awkward around him with my crush. "Want to come with me to drop them off?

"Sure," Tyler shrugs, chewing on his fingernails. He can't manage a bite when Tikara keeps flopping about in his arms, wanting to crawl on the ground. I exhale loudly, my patience with babies crying has drastically become a desert and by the look on her face, she's ready to bawl. Kennedy races ahead, the Shih Tzu nipping at her heels. Ear-piercing wails greet me when Tikara cries to be let down. We can't outside because the ground is too cold for her so I run to the door and Tyler jogs behind me, wincing at the pain he feels from his healing body. Suffice it to say he won't be helping much with the houseraising.

"Oh hey," Paul smiles in greeting at us as he wipes crumbs off his face.

"Missed some," I tease, pointing at his dimples. Tyler shakes his head to tell his cousin he doesn't actually have anything on his face. Tikara's cries get even louder when Tyler sets her on the floor to roam around. I wince and lean against the fridge, curling my hand around Philomena's soft head. Her dark brown eyes flutter as she fights sleep, wanting to see what has her cousin upset.

"Awe girlie," Paul swoops into Tikara and throws her gently in the air. "What's up with you?" He coos, tickling her under her chin and on her stomach so her cries turn into laughter. Tyler leans on the fridge next to me, shaking his head.

"How's he do it?" he asks in amazement.

"He's got the magic touch," I laugh, leaning my head gently on his shoulder. Tyler's whole body stiffens at my action before he relaxes, accepting my nearness. We watch in silence together at Paul playing with Tikara, bubbling laughs and shrieks of glee spilling from her lips as a shine appears on his face. It's a glowing look of love, one I've seen plenty with his interactions with his family, especially his children and Amy. As if on cue the shine fades. He's probably thinking about the trials in his life so I speak up, hoping to distract him. I really need to pray for him. "We need a ride to drop the girls off."

"Just take my truck," Paul digs in his pockets for his keys. At my surprised face, he rolls his eyes. "You're responsible, kid."

"Thank you for your trust," I smile, stepping away from Tyler. He murmurs something under his breath, looking super sad but relieved to have me walking away from him.

"You wreck it you buy it," Paul cheekily grins but there isn't a lot of sass in the action.

"You wanna get Kennedy in the truck, Tyler?" I ask. He nods with a groan, knowing how difficult it is to catch her in the first place. Maybe I shouldn't have let her go. When the door closes after his exit I set a hand on Paul's shoulder. "I'm here if you want to talk Paul."

"Thanks for the offer but I probably won't," Paul states, clearing his throat after it cracks in his speech. "I'll talk to my brothers or grandma. If I talk to you, or any other woman, it could lead to some sort of emotional affair."

"That's fair," I concede, ignoring the urge to give him a hug. Maybe I shouldn't have been hugging him as a married man. I can hug Peter because Corinne is cool with our relationship but Amy is a different case. I'm no one to be jealous of but sometimes she is, even of Paul's relationship with his sisters.

"So you're getting comfy around Tyler," Paul diverts the conversation with a grin. My blush answers for me but I pack the girls' diaper bag to avoid answering his comment anyways.

"He made it clear nothing is happening," I sigh, deciding spur of the moment to come clean with Paul. He probably needs this little dilemma to ignore the drama of his life. "And I don't mean to act any different around him. It just happens because of my feelings."

"Did you tell your dad?" Paul asks, bouncing Tikara on his knee. She smiles up at him adoringly, drools falling down her chin. "He should know this if Tyler is living with you guys."

"Yeah, he does," I reply, scratching my head. "I think he does, I told him Jonah likes me so Jonah isn't allowed over anymore but he didn't say that about the Trips so maybe I didn't? I'll mention it to him again anyways."

"Good plan," Paul says as the door opens. Harry, Cam, and Jim are dragging a pale-looking Landon into the house not too gently. Jim is kicking the back of his heels as Cam cusses him out.

"Tyler's waiting at the truck," Harry motions out the door. I don't like the way he squints at Paul and me, as if deciphering if we were doing something we shouldn't have been doing. I quickly pick up the baby wipes out from under the bed Paul is sitting on and step back from him, feeling self-conscious. I'm reminded that not all minds think as innocently as I do with Harry's suspicious look.

"Okay, thanks," I murmur, my face flushing hotly. Living with the Trips and my older cousins has really disturbed my innocent mind. I would have never thought the kneeling thoughts if I hadn't heard such crude jokes from their mouths. I send it from my mind, tell the devil to leave my mind by invoking Mama Mary and her Beloved Son Jesus Christ.

"You boys come to help?" Paul asks, frowning at me.

"Naw," Cam straddles a kitchen chair as Jim stops bracing Landon against his body. His brother drops to the floor, his senses too deadened to stop the fall. I quickly say a prayer for Landon and remind myself to pray for him sometime today, as well as for his drinking buddies, my cousins. "I came to sit on my effing ass."

"Language," Paul frowns at his younger cousin. I wrap the straps of the diaper bag around my shoulders and pull Tikara's car seat from near the indoor wood box. Cam rolls his angry eyes and shoots the room in front of him with two middle fingers. Jim slaps them away before kicking Landon's limp form on the floor. Landon groans as I buckle Tikara into her car seat. She opens her mouth to scream and I brace myself for the loud sound while chastising myself for not showing mercy unto Landon.

"I came for the food," Jim shrugs, cracking bubbles with gum in his mouth.

"I'll be cooking when I get back," I wave to the counter. "You're free to eat what leftovers we have." I slide on the floor to Landon, stretch out my leg to rock Tikara in her car seat, and roll Landon onto his side. It takes quite a bit of strength for me to move his knees into a curled position and bend his arms under his face into the recovery position. "Can you make sure he gets some Tylenol and water?"

"He did it to himself," Jim shrugs, tossing zucchini pattie pieces at his brother, hoping to land them in Landon's slightly open mouth through his sleep.

"Effing a-hole for the shit he did last night," Cam jeers scornfully, not to be outdone by Jim's lack of concern for their older brother as he kicks Landon's stomach.

"That's enough," Paul's voice is the hardest I've ever heard it. "All three of you were drunk last night."

"F—king kick him again," Harry warns with a sharp slap to Cam's head. The force knocks his nose into the table. I pat Landon's shoulder, tell him how much I love him, and pray for him to get better, and quickly leave to avoid the rising tension of the twins against Harry.

"How do you do this?" Tyler sighs against the passenger door of Paul's truck. He runs his skinny fingers over his bony scalp. Inside I can hear Kennedy screaming and banging on the windows to get out. It's nothing compared to Tikara's screams. I fear it is PTSD with the stories Windsor has told me.

"With great love," I answer my favorite triplet. "Can you buckle Tikara's car seat in and I'll get Philomena settled in hers?"

"Yeah," Tyler leans down as I walk around the hood of Paul's truck.

25

Fight, Fight

⟫•⊙•⟪

I'm confused about the homily last night," Jonah appears behind me and leans his shoulder against the locker next to mine.

"How so?" I ask, stuffing my textbooks and binders into my hiking bag. It's weird for me to be going straight home instead of volunteering but like the Watsons said I can't be everywhere at once and now I have a family that needs me to look after them.

"How is Jesus the new Moses?"

"That's a good question," I beam up at him, happy that he was still pondering the priest's homily from last night. Lately, I've been too busy to do that. It's mentally exhausting having children constantly talking and playing around me and with me. I finish stuffing all my homework into my backpack and pull the straps around my shoulder, laughing to myself when I can't seem to get them on properly because I'd tried putting them on like the diaper bag straps. Teenage mothering at its best.

"So...." Jonah trails off. His hand reaches out to my face before he clenches his fingers and drops his arm. I send him an understanding smile. He wants to act on his feelings and sometimes he forgets, I can't blame him for that.

"Moses parted the Red Sea and saved God's chosen people from the hands of the Egyptians, right?" I begin the explanation as we walk to the doors. I need to catch the bus with Sally Anne, Windsor, Makayla, Tinsley and Conan so I can't dawdle or I'll be walking home. Who am I kidding? Jonah would give me a ride free of charge.

"Yeah...." Jonah trails off, his eyes darting from the clock on the wall, to the couple making out in the boot room, to me putting on my outside shoes. I'm the only teenager who tries to wear inside shoes, and outside shoes outside. I can see the couple now and recognize them as April, Art's sister and Jett, the supposed valedictorian even with his lack of school attendance.

"Jesus is our Red Sea," I say, opening the boot room doors. Some jocks smirk at me, none saying thanks as they squeeze past me into the boot room. I think some purposely brush against my body but it is a tight space so I leave it be, waiting for a space in the line to hold the door open from behind it. "Jesus is the New Covenant Moses."

"Okay...." Jonah hops up onto the railing. I smile at a cheerleader who thanks me for holding the door open. Just in the hallway, I can hear the Triplets laughing raucously, probably about the girl that just walked in. They haven't been sexualizing girls in a while so I thought they'd been better. It hurts my heart to think they only don't do it in front of me.

"Jesus died on the Cross, right?" I let the door go, ready to leave until Col and Art wave at me behind the Trips.

"Right," Jonah shoots me a look that tells me what I said was common sense. I laugh lightly with a half-shrug.

"So Jesus was scourged before He carried the heavy Cross, burdened with our sins. Think about how bloody that was." I shoot Jonah a look to see if he was following my train of thought as I wave to Col and Art to show them I'm waiting for them.

"Painful," Jonah sighs, his eyes watering. His soulful reaction makes me smile in gratitude for the Holy Spirit opening his eyes.

"Blood is red. Jesus was pierced in His heart and water and blood sprouted from the lance hole. That is Jesus's the Red Sea. His Death is our Red Sea, the example of what we should do to pass through the Egyptians." Jonah stares at me, a lightbulb popping off in his brain. I see it when his stare isn't the one he usually has of 'you look nice' but of one that says 'God is good' to which I wholeheartedly agree.

"God is so damn good," Jonah's voice cracks as he runs his hands over his hair before jumping off the railing.

"All the time," I beam at him. He grabs the door I'd been holding for me to walk through.

"Get your tongue out of my sister's throat!" Art complains, quite loudly. The boot room is bursting full of the jocks, the Trips, Art, Col, Jonah, the cheerleader and Jett and April. Somehow I'd ended up between Jett and Art. Maybe it was God's plan to diffuse the situation. Art's hands are curled into fists. "She was supposed to leave you the first time you f—king hit her!"

My eyes widen at Art's insinuation. Jett is abusive? I look to April, at her tightly fitting turtleneck with long sleeves, and think back to every time I've seen her. She was always dressed provocatively, with minimal clothing. Art's allegations might be true with how she covers herself up now but it isn't my place to judge. I make a mental note to pray for her and Jett and their relationship. "Maybe we should take a deep breath?" I place my palm on Art's chest as a physical reminder to calm down. His angry eyes flash down at me. Suddenly I hate being short. Everyone takes me less seriously when they can look down on me. I make the Sign of the Cross and pray internally, for Art to cool down, for Jett not to antagonize him, for April to speak for herself but most of all so the students in the boot room can interact with each other with love in their actions.

"Listen to the Bambi," Jett smirks coldly, turning around to face Art. April was sitting on the top boot rack, her legs around Jett's shoulders with his face tucked into her stomach. A fight is brewing, I can feel it with the tension deepening in the overstuffed room.

"You haven't bandaged her up in the middle of the night, Daisy," Art's expression is loathing in his downcast way of glaring at me. Col shakes his head, asking me silently to back off. *Jesus, keep me safe.*

"Mercy Art, everyone deserves mercy," I speak up, coming chest to chest with him and back to chest with Jett because they'd both squared up to each other. Col is at Art's side, always ready to defend his friends. *Jesus, protect these boys. Mother Mary, wrap them in your loving mantle.*

"Watch out!" Jonah warns me, worry flashing through his eyes. Col places his hand on my elbow, nodding in the direction of the doors. He wants me out of here. *Jesus, send Your Holy Spirit to counsel us.*

"Let's do this peacefully, okay Art?" I cough when he and Jett both squish into me, facing off macho-like as testosterone-filled boys do. *Jesus, open our eyes to Your Love poured out on the Cross.*

"We made up," April shoots her brother a glare to stop egging her boyfriend on. Her fingers tremble as she squeezes them into balls, the pressure causing her skin to whiten. She's clearly lying but whether she is protecting Art, protecting Jett, or protecting herself I do not know. "I sort of lied when we broke up."

"Bruises don't f—king lie." The bodies around us crowd in, and teachers' curiosity is peaked as the students cheer the argument on. Jett often looks spoiling for a fight and Art has given him the perfect reason. *Jesus, I love you.*

"I had to show her what she could and could not do as my girlfriend," Jett smirks at Art, cocking his neck. I envelop my friend in a hug, fearing the fight that is bound to break out. The jocks are chanting *fight, fight, fight,* around us and the clamouring noise grates on my ears. Col tries to pull me away from Art but I hold on tight. *Jesus, send the Holy Spirit to comfort Art from Jett's evil words. Mother Mary, by the power given to you by God the Father, scare the demons fighting for Jett's soul.*

"Yeah, that's why she was at my house last night." Landon sniggers, high-fiving Harry, his ever-present wingman. I stifle a groan. Of course, he would make that remark. The only ones spoiling for a fight more than Jett are the triplets.

"What the f—k did you say?" Jett swirls to Landon, his jock buddies lining up around him. They aren't chanting anymore but bracing themselves for a fight. Jett against Art was okay but now they have to back up their buddy because no one messes with the Trips.

"I f—ked April last night," Landon smirks, taunting Jett to bring it on. April winces and ducks her head. Her reaction shines truth down on Landon's words. Art pushes me off him, cussing Landon out. Jett hollers threats as he reaches behind him to take a swing at Landon. He swings just as Art pushes me in front of him. Everything happens too fast for me to comprehend what happens until I'm sliding down Col's body, stunned by the pain rupturing the centre of my nose. Threats are shouted, fists are swung and people are shoved as a result of Jett's action.

"Lord Jesus Christ, Son of God, have mercy on me, a sinner," I mumble as I gently caress my tender nose and wipe the blood off my lips. April is screaming, thumps are loud from fists landing on flesh and sharply inhaled breath is released just as quickly from the next punch thrown. Through the midst of bodies, I catch a glimpse of Tyler, fighting beside his brothers with a pain-filled expression on his face. As an acquaintance of mine would say, a double whammy. He's already bruised and sore and broken. I stand up, squirrelling my way through everyone to get between Landon and Jett, who is really fighting compared to the rest of the group. It's vicious, their fists flying at fast speeds. I see blood on Landon's cheek from a cut because of the silver knuckle buster that appeared on Jett's hand. Jett has a swollen eye, already turning purple.

Shoving through the students not fighting very enthusiastically I keep praying the Jesus prayer. Everything is a jumble of noise, loud taunts, thumps, the squeak of shoes on the floor and curse words until I reach the main two troublemakers. "Stop please," I heave myself between them. "Landon, we do things peacefully, right?"

"Outta my way, Shorty," Landon glares at me. His hands reach out to pull me out of the way but he ends up catching my body when Jett cracks a good one between my shoulder blades. My breath catches in my throat as tears come to my eyes. "What the f—k is wrong with you?" Landon glowers at Jett while dragging me out of the boot room. Two teachers rush past us to break up the fight as I gurgle for breath, staring at Landon looking down at me. He's scared, it's easy to see in his grimace as he cradles my head in his lap. Harry is next out of the boot room, kicking at some jock behind him while half-carrying Tyler. My chest hurts, and my lungs expand for oxygen I can't suck in.

"Watch your back," Harry spits at Jett. The amount of hate in his eyes frightens me. The PE teacher is holding Jett back and pushing him around the triplets.

"Breathe Daisy," Landon shakes me. "F—king breathe!" My eyesight starts getting dizzy, and silver and black spots appear so I'm not sure if what I'm reading on Jett's lips is right or some figment of my imagination. He's calling me his cousin, saying I should be able to take a hit if I'm related to him.

"Ahh!" My ears pop painfully as I can finally inhale. Tears leak out of my eyes but I don't care when Landon hugs me tight and kisses my forehead.

"Thank God," he breathes out shakily. "You dummy! What were you thinking? You don't step into fights!"

"Yeah, you idiot," Harry huffs as he glares at me but I see the hate drain from his eyes, replaced by relief.

"Peacefully," I gasp out, my heaving chest slowing down as my breathing regulates. "We do things peacefully guys."

"Not when someone's f—king beating you," Landon snorts, pulling my back up into his chest. My back spasms in pain but Jonah and BJ appear from around the doors, in good shape considering they were in a fight, so no one notices my reaction to the pain. April sprints around them to run after Jett, shooting a middle finger in Landon's direction.

"You said you wouldn't tell, asshole!" I close my eyes, fatigued from the drama. Sally Anne threw a fit this morning when Lee and I wouldn't let her wear Daisy Duke's to school and a crop top tank top. Where in the world did she even get those clothes?! It's setting a horrible example for Makayla who already wants to wear crop tops and training bras even though she's too young. Kennedy had a screaming match when we left her home with Lee, along with Philomena and Tikara. She absolutely did not want to leave Conan and it took a lot of patience on my end just to get him in the headstart doors because he was terrified of leaving his siblings behind. Windsor got into a fight at lunch, being the new kid and slightly overweight makes him the perfect scapegoat for bullies but Windsor isn't one to back down or take the hate.

"Your peacefully might just get you killed," Jonah huffs out, nodding at the triplets. BJ nods in agreement with him. Harry nods back to Jonah, a thank you or a peace agreement between them now. They're on the same side when it comes to Jett Hendrix.

"It killed Jesus," I smile wanly at them, worriedly checking Tyler out. He's standing on his own but I see he's favouring his bum knee again. Harry huffs and puffs about my answer but in the end, ultimately says nothing of substance. BJ winces, knowing where exactly I'm coming from because we spent all our Catechism classes together.

"Jesus' Red Sea, right?" Jonah asks, stuffing his hands in his pockets. He flips his head to get his hair out of his eyes. Then he stares at me defiantly. "You want to join His Red Sea?"

"It would be an honour," my loving smile takes all the boys aback. I tap Landon's curled hands, which hadn't left my stomach as if he was holding me together. I'll be sore but I'll be fine. Any pain I have I'll offer for the Lord and His Will to be done down here on earth.

"You're f—king crazy," Landon huffs, digging his nose between my shoulder and neck. Tyler furrows his eyebrows at his brother. I can see Jonah stiffen at the way the oldest triplet is interacting with me. Frankly, I'm confused by it as well, he's really pushing boundaries.

"I'm fine Landon," I state firmly, albeit gently and tap his hands again, noticing the scraped and peeling skin, the discolouration and crooked gaps. This certainly isn't Landon's first rodeo. Art slaps Jonah's back with a good-natured grin, valiantly hiding the worry in his eyes from his sister running after Jett.

"We got detention, boys." Col throws his arms around Art and BJ with a grin. With his scar, and just out of a fight, adrenaline pumping through him, he looks every bit as scary as the rumours say of him. Harry, Jonah, BJ, and Tyler all huff and complain with proud grins as the jocks trail around them. Another round of threats and taunts are issued but the teacher separating everyone keeps it civil. The social teacher stays back when the jocks enter the classroom and surveys us.

"Do you need medical attention, Daisy?" He frowns. The blood on my face is already dry, and my nose doesn't hurt as much as my back so I don't think it's broken.

"Daisy wasn't doing anything," Harry speaks up, glowering at the teacher defiantly, daring him to try something.

"She was trying to stop the fight," Jonah adds. He's labelled as a good kid like me so his words go a long way with the teacher.

"Goody two shoes doesn't deserve detention," Col sniggers and runs his hands over his face and shakes his body. "Wasn't her fault no one listened to her shouting 'peacefully'."

"We all deserve whatever comes," Landon points between all the boys then sets his hand on my head. It's weird I can actually feel it with my thick hair in corn rows. I usually have a good cushion on my head from my Maui-like hair. "But Daisy doesn't."

"I was in the fight," I speak up. Landon squeezes me to shut up as all the boys glare at me. Col kicks my toes. "I didn't hit anyone but I could have done a better job of de-escalating. I froze when Art said Jett is abusive. That's my fault for believing and judging Jett and April without seeing them for themselves."

"Shut up," Landon says scornfully. It hurts my heart to feel that emotion directed at me. Only Jonah and Col catch on and all they do is offer me half-shrugs.

"You live in a bubble," BJ sighs, crossing his arms over his chest and wincing at the pain he feels.

"Rose-tinted glasses," Harry mimes sliding on shades.

"We all know it's true," Art shakes his head at me. He's clearly still angry, the emotion tensing his muscles. "He basically admitted it."

"I know Daisy wouldn't fight," the teacher intervenes. "You boys get in the classroom. Landon, to the office. Daisy, you are free to go home."

How is it that Landon is being sent to the office when the fight had more to do with Art?

"Thank you, sir." Jonah waves at me, the only one to acknowledge me before the classroom door closes behind them. Tyler stares at his feet, looking so small and hopeless with his hunched shoulders, stained shirt and ripped shoes. My heart goes out to him. I want to wrap him in a hug, kiss his hair and show him all the ways he's loved. Landon helps me up. I should say Landon pulls me up and basically carries me down the hallway. He even throws my backpack over his shoulders. He's a sweetheart underneath his hard exterior, I so knew it. I can see the Martel cousins through the window by the classroom door and they send me hand gestures that I assume are vulgar, even if I don't know

what they are. Of course, they were with the jocks in the fight. The
Martels have some kind of vendetta against the Smith triplets and vice
versa. Landon doesn't notice them as he turns the corner of the hallway
and barges into the office. Jett and April are squished beside each other
in two chairs. April shoots me a look to mind my own business and Jett
waves cockily at me.

"Asshole," Landon coughs, dropping my backpack on the floor and
sliding into a chair. I don't get a choice of where to sit when he pulls me
onto his lap. He's making me uncomfortable. I've never been this close
to anyone before unless I count my days as a baby and toddler when my
dad would hold me close. I don't like it, don't think it is right for a single
girl to be sitting like this. Especially when Landon leans his forehead
on my shoulder.

"I'm free to go," I say quietly. The Holy Spirit is telling me to handle
this delicately. Something is haunting Landon from his traumatic life
and I don't want to trigger his response by hurting him in any way.
Landon's hands tighten around my body when I try to stand up. It's
frightening when he won't release me. Landon is strong, not just from
working out and playing football but also from his job in construction
and the abuse he tolerates at home. "Landon," I whisper close to his ear
and hug him tight. "I'm okay, it's okay, you are okay."

"I know Shorty," he twists in the chair, his hands dropping to his
legs before he tucks them under his thighs.

"Jesus saves." I shoot him a sad smile when I stand up. I wince when
I lean down to pick up my backpack, my shoulder blades scraping my
bruised spine together. It's a pain-filled process to put my heavy bag on
but I offer it up for Landon, to whom my heart goes out, for healing and
comfort. "Peace be with you, Landon."

When I walk past him on the other side of the glass separating the
hallway from the window I see him revert back to the guy he was before

he lived with me and prayed with me. A stoic, hard boy who's lived a long life in his short years.

When I exit the building the last of the buses is disappearing around a bend. Looks like I'm walking home. I don't mind the setback, it gives me more time to pray in solitude which is really hard to come by. Lately, there doesn't seem to be enough hours in my days.

26

Harry's Secret

It's a nice day for fall, perfect for nature with the cool breeze but blazing sun. It's a quiet day too. The Watsons are having a birthday party for Katie so Sally Anne, Windsor, Makayla, Conan, and Kennedy are over there, hopefully having the time of their lives. The Watsons specifically picked them up to give us a break, which is super nice but without the children home I'm kind of lonely. I'm accustomed to all the people and the energy a bunch of children brings. It was a delight to see that Louis and Rennie did not go drinking so I'm free to leave their babies with them. Lee apparently has a secret girlfriend and is spending the day with her. He knows he's leaving soon for basic training so he wants to spend as much time with her as possible. Landon is visiting his dad, and Cam and Jim helping him distract Huntley so Tyler can spend some time with their mama. It leaves me at the house with Harry, who is the only downside of this beautiful, serene day.

"I'm a dumb native," Harry complains from his perch on Honey. I'd felt slightly betrayed when I had to hop on Buck, who isn't used as much as Honey so his bad habits have become more developed. That meant I needed stirrups which meant a saddle when I'd rather ride bareback.

"You aren't dumb," I shoot back, patting Buck's neck as we pause at the edge of the cow's pasture. It's beautiful here, with rolling hills, birds chirping, and fluffy clouds. "And aren't you Métis?"

"Yeah," Harry scowls. "But Métis still hunted and trapped and spoke a different language than English."

My eyes widen in shock. Harry really is in a mood. *Lord guide me, I don't know what to do.* I stare at Harry, studying him hard. He doesn't even squint under the scrutiny of how angry he is. He simply stares back defiantly. I turn my attention to the hills, spotting some of my dad's cows grazing, a hawk perched on the tallest pine, and a doe frozen from the wind blowing our scents her way. Rabbits bound in the periphery of the bush, a woodpecker beats on a dead tree, Sugar is chasing a fox through the meadow, disrupting the peace of the animals. The cows snort, the doe bounds off, and the rabbits scurry into hiding. The hawk calls out a warning which causes Sugar to cut back on us. She barks freely, her tongue lallygagging with a smile on her snout. It's so cute when animals smile.

"I can show you how to hunt and trap," I finally speak up. I shot my first gun when I was seven years old. It was Col's old pellet gun and I'd missed the cardboard box but it was my start with guns. Dad got me a bebe gun when I was twelve and I'd hit a couple of prairie chickens and rabbits and had them for supper, but the queasy feeling in my stomach every time I took a life put an end to that.

"You know how?" Harry's voice is gruffly directed toward me.

"I'm more of a berry picker," I shrug with a sheepish smile, reflecting on the hunts I went on with Col. We'd end up empty-handed because I'd say it was too beautiful a life. Thinking back on it, I guess Col has been my friend my whole life, probably my best friend even if I was a second thought to him because of his rodeo crew. After I could walk Col was always chasing me around and throwing me in the river, playing soccer and baseball, riding ponies, mud bogging and racing at the town's not legal but not illegal track, sledding in the winter evenings to keep boredom away, quadding to the cabin for weekends out with his family, canoeing on the river. We only drifted apart when he started drinking at fourteen years of age and I didn't want to see him intoxicated. "But I can hunt."

"Berry picker," Harry snorts, lying down on Honey's back. He's so relaxed with Honey compared to when he first moved in I want to snap a picture and show him the before and after shots.

"It's hard to take a life." Harry looks sharply up at my words. I roll my eyes at his misunderstanding. "Animal life."

"Of course, you've hunted," Harry exhales loudly, showing his displeasure. I furrow my eyebrows at him, confused and hurt by his words. Instead of speaking up, I breathe deeply, letting my hurt and defensiveness float out on the wind away from me. Just because Harry is in a bad mood doesn't mean I need to be, too. *Lord Jesus, send your Holy Spirit to comfort us.*

"Let's go get the .22 and come back here," I offer Harry. "Rabbits are plenty and that fox just scared some prairie chickens." I turn Buck around. He walks at a faster gait when he knows we are going home. I enjoy the ride and pray a Precious Blood rosary for mercy on the way back, enjoying the scenery, and all the different trees. Pine, spruce, poplar, willow, a few maples, the underbrush, the sliver bushes pretty flowers. My favorite are the Old Man's Beard when we pass the swampy part of my dad's back forty. I start a Chaplet of St. Michael for Harry, for protection against the demons haunting him. Robins fly around us, squirrels crawl up trees, and the hawk soars over the canopy of branches covering our dirt path quad trail. God's earth is so beautiful, I laugh to myself when I get a spider web across my face. God's animals are beautiful, even the buzzing of the insects that really test my patience. Sugar lopes beside me, chasing after rabbits ahead of me before doubling back to walk beside me and getting distracted by the next rabbit.

"Thanks," Harry gruffly states when we reach the barnyard. I smile at him to show him I wasn't bothered by his mood swings as I tie Buck to the hitching post. Harry loops Honey's rope on the railing but doesn't actually tie her up. She's not a flight risk, unlike Buck. "No," Harry speaks up louder. I bump into his shoulder as we walk to the house. The mansion's skeleton is complete, with a cement floor underneath. Dad had vetoed the seven bedrooms but kept the extra bathrooms. Peter and his crew got the electrical lines and sewage pipes all hooked up but it's a waiting game to get the sewage cistern built. They don't want it too close to the well just in case it cracks and leaks. With Peter's cousin's birthday party, they'd only come to work for the morning. Half the house had outside walls put up. It was fun looking and trying to claim the bedrooms with the children and seeing how big the living room and kitchen are. There is even a separate open spot for the bigger dining room table! "You weren't listening, were you, Daisy?" Harry sighs, wrapping an arm around my shoulders. I wrap an arm around his waist cautiously. When he doesn't react I sigh in relief.

"Sorry Harry," I send an oops smile his way. "I was thinking about the mansion."

"I'm sorry," Harry pats my shoulder. "Sorry for my mood swings, for taking my anger out on you. All you have been doing is helping me, helping us and I let my mistrust and my past get in the way of my future, especially with an honest, loving girl like you. I'll probably mess up again but I'm going to try not to hold onto it."

"I appreciate that," I smile at Harry. He opens the front door for me. With no one but dad home I don't have to trip over the pile of shoes. We should be cleaning the house, washing laundry, baking snacks, and freezable meals but this is my and my dad's first day off in a long time. He's spending it catching up on sleep after a long-distance phone call with Aria. I'm spending it teaching Harry how to hunt.

"Hey cuz," Rennie shoots me a quick smile. Louis grunts. They are at the kitchen table, playing Go Fish. Philomena is laying on the floor, staring at the ceiling with the Shih Tzu close to her. Tikara is crawling around, picking up crumbs as she goes.

"Hey Rennie," I smile at him but continue walking to my dad's bedroom. He keeps the guns there in a safe while the bullets are stored upstairs.

"Haha! Go Fish!" Louis chuckles heartily as Rennie doesn't get the pair he was hoping for. I knock before entering my dad's bedroom. Harry had stayed with my cousins.

"Hey, Chester, you're back," my dad grins at me from his position on his double bed. He swaddles himself to sleep, blankets tucked under his toes up to his chin.

"Didn't mean to wake you," I smile at him, closing the door. His gun case is behind his door, hidden slightly from the kids that way. He keeps it locked but I know the key is nailed to the wall behind it.

"I was already up," dad waves my concern off as he sits up with a big yawn. I feel the wall for the key and stick it in the keyhole when I find it. "What do you need the gun for?"

"Teaching Harry how to hunt," I answer, grabbing the smallest gun out of the case. It's the old .22, my dad gave Abe my Bebe gun for Richie when I stopped using it.

"Only the .22," Dad states, wiping his eyes with his palms. "Be careful out there, my girl."

"We're taking the horses. Won't go too far. We'll probably scare the animals with the target practice first," I inform my dad as I carefully hold the gun in my arms and lock the safe back up.

"I can't believe Jett gave you black eyes," dad scowls, carefully studying my face. My eyes aren't swollen anymore but they are still purple and ache fiercely. It makes me wonder if Landon craves this pain with all the fights he's been in. It's probably a better pain than dealing with the mental pain from their abusive father. Harry is standing outside my dad's door when I open it.

"Gun's unloaded, the safety is on. Point it to the ground anyways. I'm going upstairs to get the bullets."

"I've held a gun before," Harry rolls his eyes, holding the .22 much more casually than I appreciate, especially with babies crawling on the floor. Maybe I shouldn't have told him to keep the barrel to the ground. *Jesus, keep everyone in this house safe. Amen.*

"Have you shot it? Loaded it?" I asked, climbing up the steps that Conan loves to jump off of. I'm afraid he's going to jump from the top soon and break a leg. That little boy is fearless in certain aspects.

"No...." Harry admits after a moment of silence. I leave him at that while I dig in a desk cupboard for the rounds, analyzing the space. We could fit a bunk bed up here and a cot by the slant of the roof. Lee, Harry, and Tyler could all sleep up here then while the mansion is being built. Before I climb back down the ladder-like stairs I go into our little chaplet room and kiss Jesus' feet from the large crucifix we have hanging on the wall. *Keep us safe, Lord. Your will be done.*

"We'll go back to that meadow," I tell Harry my plan, tucking my miraculous medal in my shirt and stuffing the box of bullets into my overalls bib pocket. "Aim away from the cows, just get some target practice in. I can show you how to track animals."

"You know how to track," Harry deadpans with a shake of his head.

"I'm not the best," I chuckle. "Just good enough. After this lesson, you'll probably want to go out with Col. He's the best our age."

"Why am I not surprised?" Harry rolls his eyes. His tone isn't as negative as it could be but I still ignore his statement. I've become a more pessimistic thinker hanging out with him, his brothers, and my cousins. It's hard to be the only person with a hopeful countenance.

"We have a gun holder thing for a saddle," I motion to Harry to the barn. Honey is munching on some of the last green grass of the year,

Buck is trying to sleep with Sugar under his belly. Those two sure do trust each other.

"I'll take the gun," Harry decides out loud. I wince, pausing in my step. Sweetie is munching on cat food. I'm happy to have spotted her. She's a pretty wild cat, especially wary of the children so she doesn't come around too often anymore.

"I, um, I have more experience," I speak up haltingly. "It might be best if I take it."

"This can't be much different from a handgun," Harry rolls his eyes. I grab a hunting knife to tie to my saddle as well as the leather rifle gun holster to tie to Buck's saddle. Handguns, somehow Harry has fired a handgun. Those are pretty much illegal.

"Would you mind praying before the hunt?" I ask, tying the straps to Honey's saddle. She's the calmer horse, better for the gun to be with her. I'm asking Harry because of the Amish comment he made the other day. Since then he hasn't been to daily mass, even when Kennedy begs him to come. "To teach people to respect the life given to us by the animals we stop to pray. We utter a simple prayer before the shot if we have to kill it when we already shot it, when we are skinning and butchering it, and after the work is all done. It's just a reminder to thank God for the food and the gift of life the animal gave us."

"Makes sense," Harry shrugs, climbing up on Honey while I tie the hunting knife to Buck's saddle. The gelding whips his tail at me to show his displeasure at being used on such a beautiful day. He does it on purpose, I know he does because there aren't enough horse flies to whip his tail that hard.

"A treaty man showed me that," I add, swinging up on Buck. The gelding does a little hop and dance to try to scare me out of the ride. I turn him in circles until he's ready to listen to me.

"Who?"

"My dad's friend," I shrug, clicking my tongue and my heels to Buck's flank. He plods on, taking slow footsteps. "Haven't seen him in three, four years. He's the one that taught me and Col how to hunt respectfully, the native way, I suppose. We use almost every part of the deer and moose, their tongues and bones as well as the meat and hide."

"Is there anything you don't know?" Harry laughs. I roll my eyes, happy to hear no jealousy or annoyance in his tone. He's teasing me as a Col would, as a friend would, maybe even a brother.

"Plenty," I confirm. "I'm not the best driver. I mess up on half the meals I make. The house could be much cleaner but I'm lazy. I should be teaching Conan how to spell and Kennedy the alphabet but I put holding the babies before that or helping Win and Micks with their homework. April could probably use a girl friend to talk to and I haven't been acting with a lens of love and mercy to anyone I meet because I'm too exhausted to begin."

"Sounds like you need to go up to the mountain to pray," Harry urges Honey on. She picks up her pace to a trot so I kick Buck's flank, clicking my tongue. The old horse doesn't want to switch gears. He only speeds up when Honey is just about out of sight and knickers for him. On the catch-up to Harry's ride, I pray a Holy Wounds Rosary for a quick tribulation period, meditating on Harry's words. It's true. I haven't been going to my quiet place to pray. My dad's chaplet room is probably collecting dust because we both have been super busy and ignoring a major part of our spirituality.

"I could be better," Harry tells me when Buck comes to a lilting stop beside Honey. I nod along to Harry's words, waiting for him to continue as I look out at the beautiful meadow. The grass is dark green from frosting over, some are already brown. The birds I see are grabbing fallen leaves to thicken their nests come winter. The wind was chilly on the ground but Buck's heat wafts up, keeping me warm. "Look at you Daisy, all the shit you do. You're always learning, always bettering yourself but not even for yourself, to help other people. If I better myself I can help others too. I can get Cam and Jim out of their addictions, hopefully out of prison. We've all been to juvie for stupid shit."

"We can learn together," I smile at Harry, tears in my eyes. God is speaking to him and he is listening! That makes this day that much more majestic!

"I have another girlfriend," Harry takes his half-man bun out and waves his hair around. Then he puts all of his hair into a low ponytail. I don't blame him. With the wind, it was whipping into his face.

"Good for you Harry, I pray for you both."

"I want to treat her better than I treated my exes." Buck spooks at a coyote running along the other side of the tree line. Sugar starts barking in warning before she tries to chase after it. I turn Buck in a circle, humming as I rub his mane, telling him it is okay. Harry sidles Honey up to me. "I wasn't," Harry exhales loudly. "I wasn't a good guy to my exes. Ya know? Fighting Jett made me feel like the biggest hypocrite on the planet. I'm f—king ashamed of what I did to them, how I ruined them because of my messed up childhood. Landon gets drunk every chance he can, he has that release but I can't. I drink a sip of alcohol I die. Tyler's got his drugs 'cause he's our dad's whipping boy. I had girls to keep all those f—ked up memories out of my mind but I ended up ruining them just as I am ruined."

"Harry," my heart melts at his words. He seems the most stable out of the triplets so my prayer has been focused more on his brothers. I regret that now. "You aren't ruined. God made you in His image. You are perfect in His sight."

"I was perfect in my uncle's sight too." Harry coughs out, choking on a strangled laugh. My heart stops at his insinuation. I reach out my hand to hold his.

"I'm proud of you Harry." I squeeze his hand gently. "I'm proud that you live with those memories without hurting yourself to run from them. I'm proud that you fight for a life that we all can't see. I'm proud that you are trying to trust me with a broken heart. I'm proud you are loving and protective and cheesy and honest and caring even with your broken heart. I love you, Harry. I prayed for years when I was young for a brother. It doesn't surprise me that God gave me you when I had given up. Thank you, Harry, for who you are."

"Can you pray for me?" Harry's voice cracks at his words. "Pray for me and her. Pray for our relationship."

"Yes." He releases my hand so I put it on the horn of my saddle.

"And can I come to you when I mess up or when I think I'm gonna mess up? I don't want to hurt her like I hurt those other girls."

"Yes," I state firmly. Without a doubt. *Jesus, Saint Raphael, Saint Dymphna, please heal this boy's broken heart. Show him your unending love and mercy. Our Father...*

→ 27 ←

High Tyler

———⇒>·O·<⇐———

It's not very often I sit behind someone at mass but tonight Phil and I had arrived at the same time, six pm for Stations of the Cross, and Denver had run up to the first pew on the left-hand side and claimed it as his. Most parishes pray the Stations of The Cross during Lent but our parish prays them every Friday. It's a supernatural reminder of just how much Christ suffered for us. I often wonder if the Watson family is so faith-filled because they attend Friday night masses after the hour of following Jesus' painful crucifixion. Focusing on the Blood of Jesus that was shed during His Passion makes how much we sin very real. Jonah didn't come today because Layton's grandparents were visiting. Harry is DD'ing Landon, Louis, Rennie, and Tyler. Lee decided to stay home with Sally Anne, Win, Micks, Tinsley, Conan, and Kennedy so I was stuck with the babies. I wrapped Philomena in the cloth carrier strapped to my chest and let Tikara crawl around. It's a perk for me really, she'll tire herself out during Stations of the Cross, sort of following us as we stop at each station, so when it's time to be quiet for mass she will be content in my arms.

Phil brought Vienna as well and holds her tightly into his chest, cherishing their moments together. She recognizes his scent now but she's a wily girl, always wanting to go, go, go. It doesn't help that she wants to chase after Denver who knows that he can walk around his pew but has to keep quiet about it. Vienna hasn't mastered the art of quiet just yet at two years old.

Dickie is the next to arrive with Pierre, BJ, Sadie, and Bianca. They all must have come from the soup kitchen and it makes me happy to know that BJ, Sadie, and Bianca have stepped up to fill my spot there.

Peter arrives soon after, Reece in his arms. He slides into his dad's pew and in mere seconds Reece is in her grandfather's arms. Percy is with Peter, along with Audrina and their five children. Axel's face falls when he doesn't see Windsor and Makayla with me. Percy barely catches Paisley's arm before she runs off to play with Denver. Audrina holds Pamela, and Arlo is asleep in the car seat. As the oldest children, Abel and Axel know to be quiet and still even at their young ages. They don't get the good fortune of sitting with grandpa.

BJ and Pierre carry the candles beside the priest. Axel practically leaps for joy when the priest asks him to carry the cross and his parents are happy with his reaction. It's fun watching him race to the sanctuary to put his altar dress on and double back to bow before the tabernacle. Paul slips into my pew as Axel is carrying the cross to the first station, a serious expression on his face. Axel has been an altar boy for a year now, mostly for Latin mass but Percy takes him and Abel to Friday night Stations of the Cross so they can understand the importance of mass by seeing Jesus' great sacrifice. Paul gently pulls Poppy between us and secures Polly to his right, Aiden is in his arms struggling to sit up and take in his surroundings. I smile at the little family, checking on a sleeping Philomena before I leave the pew to find Tikara. I've learned when the children are quiet they are getting in trouble and I can't hear her crawling around. The priest begins the preparatory prayer as I walk, finding Tikara chewing on a piece of paper that hadn't made it to the garbage can. I bring her to the pews and close the doors. She shouldn't be able to get into any other trouble with them closed so I head back to my pew and stand for the short excerpt of the First Station. Jesus is condemned to death. We say the short responsory before kneeling for the prayers. Tikara crawls around, finding her voice to babel. I pray that she is praying with us as we reflect on Jesus' condemnation to death. I try to put myself in the Passion, where the women following Jesus would have been. I'd probably be worried, noticing his pale, drawn face at what He knew was about to happen.

Second Station - Jesus Carries the Cross. *We adore you O Christ and we praise you.* Would I be with Mama Mary as she cleans her son's Holy Blood spilled upon the stone? Would I be unable to see because of the tears that cloud my eyes as I kneel in His blood?

Third Station - Jesus Falls the First Time. *Because by Your holy Cross You have redeemed the world.* Maybe I was breathless, chasing after You when the word first came back to me that You had fallen under the weight of that heavy Cross, the Cross that bore our sins. Maybe I was pushing through the hateful crowd of people You were *saving* by Your Passion. I just want to check on You, help You, and ease that burden.

Fourth Station - Jesus Meets His Mother. *Jesus Christ crucified, have mercy on us!* The tears aren't only blurring my vision, they are marring my clothes. How could I not weep at Your most loving mother meeting You so broken and bloody, so scorned by the people You desired to save with Your painful Passion.

Fifth Station - Simon of Cyrene Helps Jesus to Carry His Cross. *Holy Mother, in our heart, let us feel, let us mourn, that in it we had a part.* Why couldn't I see that it was my sins that crucified You? Every bad thing I did was a weight added onto the Cross, a whip slashing across Your most Precious Skin. It was me spitting on You as You passed by me, weak and dehydrated, dying for my sins. My only wish now is to help You carry that Cross, no matter how painful it is.

Sixth Station - Veronica. *Lord, let it be me that faces persecution to find a way to comfort You.* Veronica was frightened at the vile soldiers guarding You and yet she slipped past, God cleared the way for her to caress Your face. It's a memory she must have held dear to her heart. I want to hold You close to my heart, imprint Your face onto my heart, O Lord.

Seventh Station - Jesus Falls the Second Time. *You fell, O Lord, to show us we can get up again every time we fall into sin.* I fall, I sin, I do bad, I can commit evil. But You give me hope, hope that I can set those sins behind, accept Your mercy and become a better version of myself. If I was with You, watching You carry my sins, I hope at least that I tried to reach You.

Eighth Station - Jesus Comforts the Women of Jerusalem. *Comfort me as well, I beseech You, Lord, as You comforted them.* Those women were mothers, aunts, and grandmothers; just as Rachel wailed over the slaughter of the Holy Innocents, they were wailing over You. They recognized You as the prophesied Messiah when the Scribes and Pharisees did not.

Ninth Station - Jesus Falls the Third Time. *How great Your Mercy, Christ crucified.* Wouldn't two falls have been enough? No, three falls were sufficient for You to show us that we can relapse, we can fall into sin but You are right there with us, encouraging us to get up, fight Satan and remain free. Just as Peter couldn't believe he had to forgive his brethren seventy-seven times, so we cannot believe Your unfathomable mercy.

Tenth Station - Jesus is Stripped of His Garments. *Every sin You came to undo, even sins of the flesh.* To bare Yourself open to all sins, You, Sinless One, became the worst of us all. Help us to rid ourselves of all attachments to this world, of our bodies, and focus on our freedom, so we are no longer slaves to sin.

Eleventh Station - Jesus is Nailed to the Cross. *What fearful stretching of Your body did You endure, a pain we never can know.* We are weak, Lord, we fall constantly. We are afraid of pain, afraid of what slaves to sin think of us and so we hide. And when we hide, we hide from You, and the blood You lovingly, selflessly shed for us.

Twelfth Station - Jesus Dies on The Cross. *Grant that I may die before I fall into sin again!* You died, Lord, something incomprehensible to us fallen mortal human beings, so that we may be free from sin. That we may run to You, Jesus, who know Godforsaken-ness, even as we run from Your Father.

Thirteenth Station - Jesus is Taken Down From the Cross. *What sorrow to Your mother, O Lord, to see You dead as she cradled You in her arms.* What heartbreak. Parents expect to die before their children and Your mother saw You crucified, the most painful death a human can experience. We mourned even as we hoped in Your prophetic resurrection.

Fourteenth Station - Jesus is Laid in the Sepulchre. *I wish to appear dead to the world.* I know that Satan thinks he rules the earth with sin running rampant, running rampant through me. Give me Your Grace, God, through Christ Your Son, to change my ways. I can do great things through You.

BJ and Pierre put the candles back on the altar as the priest changes into his mass dress. Axel stands by the altar, holding the cross and waiting patiently. Tikara has tuckered herself out so I gently push Philomena to one side of the carrier and hold Tikara on the opposite side. Aiden had fallen asleep so Paul lays him in his car seat and picks up Poppy. She curls her head against his shoulder. It's such a sweet, loving gesture. It must break his heart to leave her and her siblings with Amy and her mother, to walk away from them.

It's a delightful surprise when Jonah squeezes into the pew beside me, Harry, Art, and Tyler behind him. They came to mass without me asking them to, how beautiful! God is great!

"God suffered physically," Tyler points to Jesus hanging on the Cross behind the altar. His head rests against Harry's shoulder when I look back in surprise. "All that blood and shit, the whips and his skin in chunks. You could see bones right? People hating on Him, spitting, throwing shit. Trying to hit Him. We could all go on and on and on about how much He suffered physically..., but what about mentally?"

"He suffered mentally," I turn in the pew to look at Tyler. His eyes are red and watery, his guitar fingers tapping a rhythm on his knees. When he isn't talking he's bopping his head.

"Yeah, how?" Tyler snorts. When Peter, Percy, Dickie, and their families turn to shush him he smirks and throws middle fingers at them. *Lord have mercy.*

"The Garden of Gethsemane, First Sorrowful Mystery: the Agony in the Garden. If Jesus died-," Tyler flippantly rolls his eyes at my explanation. It angers me, and the amount of my anger scares me. I pray that it is zealous anger and the Holy Spirit speaking through me. "Yes Tyler," I snap. Tikara jolts in my arms. Even with all the tantrums her sister and cousins have thrown I've never used such a harsh tone of voice. "If Jesus carried the weight of our sins on that Cross He definitely carried the guilt of our minds. His sweat turned into blood because He fought His human will to do the Divine Will of His Father. Jesus Himself asked His Father if it was possible for the chalice to pass Him but accepted His destiny wholeheartedly to the point where He *desired* to die that we may live!"

"Ok-ayyyy, nice girl," Tyler shrugs my answer off. I turn around, taking a deep breath to let my anger go from the attitude Tyler is showing me. BJ shoots me a thumbs up, and Percy nods. Dickie is showing us all what we should be doing by looking at the tabernacle, nothing taking his attention off our Saviour.

"Why'd they kill Jesus?!" Denver wails, pointing at Jesus hanging on the Cross. Tears erupt in his eyes as his lips tremble.

"Yeah, Daisy," Tyler viciously adds. Harry slaps his head, I know from the loud thunk sound. Harry's always hitting or kicking Landon when he's not being too nice.

"Jesus loved them!" Denver wails again, curling into his dad. Phil is trying to calm him down and tell him how it was God's plan so that we could love Him.

"Jesus sure doesn't show it," Tyler mutters, picking at the threads of his ripped jeans.

"Here Jonah," I pass Tikara to him. With how many younger siblings Jonah knows how to hold her. Paul shoots me a small smile, his hands full with three children under five. I scoot into the pew behind me where Harry, Tyler, and Art sit and push between Tyler and Art.

"What?" Tyler huffs, scowling at me as he crosses his arms over his chest, the epitome of pout. "Dumb perfect ass nice girl."

"I love you Tyler," I sigh, pulling his head into my shoulders. He resists at first, unaccustomed to someone loving him with his negative attitude towards them. I wrap my arms over his bony body and pat his shoulder as mass starts. Tyler is fine at first, silent amidst everyone rising. Soon his shoulders shake as he tries to hold in the sobs that wretch out. The brokenness in his cries breaks my heart. I kiss his forehead and rub his arm as he finally lets his walls down around me, around God. I follow along with mass even when I can't follow the physical emotions, praying this mass, especially for the triplets who have so much hurt.

✦ 28 ✦

Landon's Anger

⟫–◈–⟪

"Is he okay?" I stand beside Harry who is sitting on the kitchen counter. My voice is low as I look at Landon angrily walking the short space from the front door to the end of the hallway. When he trips on Tinsley's doll he cusses it out before throwing it against the wall.

"He just needs to cool off." Harry shrugs, munching on the tomato cake I had made right after school had finished. The walls are all up on the mansion now, and the roof is being added as well. Dad left a room above the kitchen to use as our chaplet slash storage room. He has his bedroom he will share with Aria, and the bathroom in there while the rest of us will have to fight for the other three bedrooms. Two are the same size but one is bigger, with a door leading outside. I'd assumed that room was for Landon, Louis, and Rennie, so in turn Lee, Harry, and Tyler. Windsor and Conan can get a small room and I'll share with Makayla, Tinsley, Sally Anne, Kennedy, and the babies. Harry snickers when Landon trips over that same doll. Again he cusses the poor toy out. The kids all glance at me, worried and scared at his behavior. Of course, their dads are out drinking somewhere, leaving Lee and me to deal with them and Landon's mood.

"Quiet time!" I clap my hands. The bunk bed with the double bottom was taken apart, put upstairs, and reassembled. Sally Anne claimed the top bunk so we put Kennedy, Tinsley, and Makayla on the bottom. The bottom is a little crowded but the little girls don't seem to mind. While we were at that, we also put a bunk bed in my room so I can send Conan and Windsor there while Landon throws his fit. That leaves two bunk beds, the couch, and my bed in the living room. It's a little less crowded now. The children all know what I mean so Sally Anne is the only one who grumbles as they head to their respective rooms. Lee watches Landon carefully from his spot on the top bunk. Tyler is sitting on a kitchen chair, Teddy, the Shih Tzu soaking up pats on his lap. Since I saw Tyler high he barely even looks at me. When the kids are all in their rooms Landon spins to me, eyes blazing.

"If God is so good why does he let bad shit happen?" Landon punches the wall. My eyes widen in surprise but his brothers aren't fazed as he starts pacing the little cabin again. With our log-walled cabin, Landon didn't do considerable damage and probably hurt his hand in the process.

"God gave us the freedom to choose good or bad. Some people choose to do badly. That's why bad things happen." I answer, nervously touching my miraculous medal. It must be time to deal with Landon's mood swings since I already dealt with Harry and Tyler's hurt and anger. I thank the Lord I was never subject to the abuse they went through.

"All the people I know choose badly." Landon stomps to me. A squeak escapes me when he stops a centimeter away from my face. He's scaring me, his anger is directed at me. When he threw that fit in the classroom at least he wasn't angry at me!

"Back off," Harry growls, pushing his brother back. Tyler's eyes observe us warily from his ducked head. Since our talk, Harry has been my constant companion except when he is with his girlfriend, who we still don't know and haven't met. Everyone is guessing in this small town.

"It's so - easy to - choose bad-," Landon hits the cupboards by my head with every second word. My heart stutters in my chest. For the first time, I wish my dad didn't overwork himself with twelve hours minimum. He wouldn't let Landon do this to me. *Jesus, keep me safe.*

"I said back off!" Harry pushes Landon back. I squirrel between them before Landon can react, he'd already moved his arm to punch his brother. Landon is always spoiling for a fight, sometimes his brothers are the only ones around. Has he ever beaten Tyler as their dad does?

"Answer me, Rose," Landon shoves his brother to the side. It's their nickname for me when they think I'm looking through the world with naïve lenses.

"Let's go for a walk," I place my palm on Landon's chest. He karate chops my arm away. Tears well in my eyes from the pain but the only acknowledgment I give it is to offer it up to God. "Cool down a bit."

"Not a good idea," Harry hisses. Tyler shakes his head, fearful wide eyes finally meeting mine. Teddy scurries under one of the beds. Louis and Rennie have fought around him before, he can tell when a fight might break out.

"I'm not Huntley!" Landon yells, veins throbbing on his forehead and neck. What set him off? Why is he so angry? What bad thing happened?

"Stop acting like him!" Harry retorts, holding me back as Landon pulls me forward. It's a tug of war, the cost being my shoulders as they stretch out. I'm reminded of Jesus, nailed to the Cross, His arms wide open to show us that He will welcome us back into His fold and I accept the pain for the triplets to recognize His love and mercy and to accept it.

"It's okay," I tug my arm out of Harry's grip. His face falls when I choose Landon. "We'll be okay."

"I'm not worried about him." Harry and Landon have an angry telepathic conversation with each other. Hand gestures are involved but they aren't universal ones that I understand. Harry sighs loudly. "Don't say I didn't warn you."

"Am I a bad person if I return what a bad person gave me?" Landon kicks at the footpath. He is leading the way to the barnyard. Subconsciously I know he is talking about his father even without naming him.

"Jesus didn't give back what He got in the Passion," I state simply. Landon mulls on my words and the more time I give him to cool down the hotter he gets. Instead of kicking the ground, he's punching trees as we pass them, uncaring if he hurts himself in the process. My stomach rolls when he takes a flask out of his back pocket and chugs some alcohol down.

"Do bad people go to heaven?" Landon stumbles when he kicks at the ground and trips over tree roots. Sweetie meows sharply in the night but runs away when I spot her.

"Depends," I answer honestly. "I know the difference between right and wrong so if I chose wrong I get more judgment than mercy. You on the other hand haven't been taught the ways of God so you'll receive more mercy than me. It also depends on how sincerely we repent and try to stop the bad we do."

"So good people could go to hell?" Landon snorts to himself, muttering about how twisted life is under his breath.

"Yes but no. If a good person goes to hell they weren't very good. They were only acting like they were good."

"So abusive people could spend eternity happy even though they made life hell on earth?"

"I can't tell you where your dad is going to end up, Landon."

"Don't mention my dad!" Landon roughly shoves me. My ankle twists painfully in a hole and I crash to the ground, stunned. After his reaction when Jett hit me I did not expect this. Landon kneels on the ground beside me and lifts me up by the collar of my shirt, his pointer finger jabbing my cheek. My heartbeat quickens and fear causes me to doubt myself. I force my lungs to breathe deeply, in and out. *Jesus, Your will be done. Jesus, I trust in You.* "You don't know what the f—k you're talking about!"

We sit in silence, the night creatures and our breathing the only sounds of the night. Time slows down as I stare into his ice-blue eyes, glinting hard at mine. His fingers are white-knuckling my clothes, the bib of my overalls, and a plain black T-shirt that says 'do small things with great love', a quote from Mother Teresa. She's one of my favorite saints. I aspire to be like her if that is what my future holds, what God has planned for me. If not, I will align my dreams with God's destiny for me. I take Landon's pause in his anger to pray a Memorare before focusing on healing and deliverance prayers for the demons I see battling in his stark pupils.

"How do you know heaven is real? Huh? How do you know this isn't some stupid test and when we die we realize nothing happens? We don't have souls, we're just bodies! How the hell do we know God is real when every time we need Him all there is is SILENCE!" Landon shakes me during his rant. My teeth chatter from the force and my eyes hurt from seeing everything at once in such a crooked order. Harry was right, I shouldn't have come out here with Landon. He knows his brother better than I do. I'm not helping Landon if I'm letting his demons control his actions.

"We wouldn't know joy if we didn't know pain." *Lord, I don't know what to do. I give this up to You. Our lives are in Your hands, this moment needs Your Presence. Show us the way back to Your light from our fall into sin.*

"Stop giving me hope!" Landon shoves me one last time. It's his hardest shove yet and digs my back into a tree's root system. I cry out from the pain, both physical and spiritual, he's so hurt and I don't know how to help, especially when he puts me in such an awful position.

God is really testing my depth of mercy and self-respect. The answer to stopping Landon's madness comes to me suddenly, a light bulb going off. The answer is so simple.

"You are Huntley, I am Jilly right now." Fear thunders in my chest. It was the wrong thing to say. Landon heaves me up and pushes me backward. My shoulder knocks into a poplar, branches scrape my exposed skin, the tree roots unbalance me and I stumble because my twisted ankle can't support my weight.

"If I'm Huntley," Landon shoves me again. His hands don't leave my forearms and they cut off circulation, especially with the jolt from my back ramming into the panel fence.

"Then you are-," Landon shoves me again. I can't catch myself this time and sprawl on the hard-packed earth of the barn. A whimper emits from my throat. I hadn't expected this. Landon promised, he said he wouldn't hurt me again, that he'd retain self-control!

"Jilly who can't f—king defend herself because she doesn't-," Landon throws his flask at me. It bounces off my outer thigh, heavy as a baseball-sized rock. I scream from the unexpected pain. Landon drops down beside me, knees on either side of my stomach.

"Have any f—king self-worth!" He hits the ground by my eyes with hardened fists. I close my eyes, scared to even *breathe.* Where did this come from? How could Landon do this to me? *Jesus, keep me safe. Your will be done. Jesus, I'm scared, send the Holy Spirit to comfort me and keep me zealous for You in this trial.*

"If I'm Huntley-," Landon leans down so our noses are touching. I put my hands on his chest to try to push him off of me. I hate hurting another human being, hate defending myself because Jesus always turned the other cheek and I should do the same but I'm too scared to not try to struggle out of Landon's grasp. Maybe my faith has never really been tested before. St. Marie fought back to preserve her purity. I can do the same.

"Then I'd be f—king raping you right now." I stop struggling against Landon at his words. This has been what was bothering him, probably since the fight with Jett, why he was so shaken up. Why he held me close. Terrible memories were haunting him. I never even assumed that when Huntley beat Jilly that he'd rape her too, or that he does it in front of his sons.

"I'm so sorry Landon," I tug him into a hug. He collapses on top of me, breathing raggedly. I pat his back and hold him tight. "I love you, Landon. My love isn't a free pass for you to hurt me though. I know you have stuff in your brain messing you up but getting physical with another person is not the answer. You broke your promise to me. That hurts worse than you physically hurting me. A broken promise makes trust lack."

"I'm sorry Daisy girl," Landon rolls off of me, chest heaving as he stares at the roof of the barn. Tears leak out of his eyes. His lips wobble. "I'm so f—king sorry Daisy."

"Every time you get angry say the name of Jesus. Say His name with love and reverence and keep saying it. Okay? Can you do that? If not for yourself, for me?" I ask, jumping on the opportunity to convert him. While he debates my idea in his mind I offer the pain he inflicted on me up to the Father, that all those who survive abuse do not become the abuser.

"I'll try," Landon concedes, his Adam's apple bobbing. "But how am I supposed to live with hope? This safe space you and Duncan have given me could be taken at a moment's notice. We aren't emancipated. Huntley could literally show up and drag us back. And just because we aren't there doesn't mean he isn't hurting her. It just means we aren't his scapegoats anymore which means she's getting the brunt of it all."

"We just have to pray." I feel along his thigh until my fingers wrap around his. I hold on tightly, tethering him to the present moment.

"How am I supposed to hope that I can live a life without suffering like this?" Landon's voice cracks. I curl my head to rest on his shoulder, giving him the physical love he craves from his mother.

"Because it's true," I state simply. My dad isn't abusive. He rarely ever raises his voice, although when I tell him about Landon's hissy fit he'll probably have an outside 'talk' with the oldest triplet.

"You're too fricken good, Shawty." Landon sighs. It's followed by a choke-filled laugh. "I'm sorry."

"It's okay," I say, not knowing if I'm lying. My heart is still beating faster than normal. I'm concerned about the children now, will his anger hurt them? Landon is a risk to the children now. Is it time to kick him out until he can control it better? "I think we should talk to my dad." After a beat of silence where it looks like Landon won't answer, I keep speaking, my tongue loose from fear. "You can't keep going like this, brother, you hurt me. You can hurt the children. We aren't just going to take it. Whatever dad decides, you have to live with."

More silence waits for me. I use Landon's quietness to pray. *Our Father...* My connection with God sends relief strumming through my body. *Hail Mary...* This was bad, but I am okay. *Glory Be...* Landon needs help. *O my Jesus...* There is a counselor at school he can talk to. *Hail Holy Queen...* Thank God for His consolation.

"Let's pray," I shake Landon's arm a little. "Let's all go pray as a family, for you, for Tyler, for Harry, for my cousins and nieces and nephews. You all need help from the Big Guy up there." Landon jumps up, rolls his shoulders around, and brushes off straw and dirt from his back. I'm half kneeling when he offers me a hand up. I flinch back, a reaction I didn't even think I would have from his hand jamming forth so quickly.

"I f—king traumatized you," Landon growls, banging his head on the panels as he laughs. It's a strangled sound, breaking my heart all over again.

"It's okay," I repeat, hopping up. Maybe I'm not okay. My twisted ankle is swollen but that is all, barely any pain or heat anymore. I thank God for that. Even as I mumble those words quietly I wonder if they are true. I'm shaken, straight to my core. God gave me a battle I wasn't prepared for and now my faith is *shaken*. I hate that more than what actually happened, hate that it affects me so much.

"You were right." Landon sighs, silent tears streaming down his closed-off face. In the dusk of evening, his face looks like it has edges and points carved of stone. I reach my hand out for his to hold onto. Landon still needs a tether so his mind won't take him out of this world. His reliance on alcohol makes this situation worse. Landon stares dubiously at my outreached hand, guilt exposing itself in his eyes and so much *pain* in those tears. But he takes my hand and allows himself that comfort rather than his drinking. *Thank you, Lord.* "I am my father."

"But you can change," I take a step, tugging Landon forward. "If you trust in God all things are possible." Landon trails behind me, shuffling his feet. My hand is not holding his tremors so I stuff it in my pocket to caress all my rosaries. *Jesus, thank You for protecting me.*

"Shorty?" Landon asks, his voice wobbly and hoarse when we reach the little deck of the cabin. He sits on a step and pulls me close to him.

"Yeah?" I ask, my heart melting when he envelopes me in a hug. Landon's arms wrap around my body, his head rests on mine. It's such a loving action while valiantly trying to hold himself together but *I'm still scared.*

"I'm sorry, it's not enough, I know but I'm so damn sorry." He pulls me into his lap, and nuzzles his nose into the crook of my shoulder and neck. It tickles when he exhales and my little laugh sounds absurd with what all transpired. Landon chuckles softly, squeezing me even tighter. "I just want to help her." So I let him hold me because I know he wishes it was his mother that he was saving from his father.

"You all good?" Harry's gravelly voice asks, light shining on us from the open door. Landon releases me so I stand up, nodding at Harry. "He didn't hit you?"

"Um, no, actually." I laugh softly. Landon hadn't actually punched me, he only hit the ground beside my head.

"Surprising," Harry sniffs before turning on his heel and walking away. All eyes are on me when Landon and I step into the little cabin. My face flushes and I walk slowly to conceal the limp, hating myself for doing so. I don't believe in secrets or protecting bad people.

"You f—king hurt her, you piece of shit!" It's not Harry who shouts. It's Tyler and there isn't enough time to blink before he hurdles across the room and flies into Landon's thicker body. He looks like a twig compared to his brother but his rage is ferocious. Tinsley screams, all the children in the living room or kitchen since Landon had left to cool down. Windsor chants *fight* but a nasty glare from Sally Anne shuts him up. Lee hops off the top bunk, stalking toward the two boys.

"What the hell is going on?!" Dad hollers. The children all duck onto bottom bunks. While I haven't raised my voice, my dad sure has. He must have just got home. Usually, I hear him pull up but tonight I'd been too distracted.

"Landon hurt Daisy," Tyler huffs, kicking Landon's knees. His brother buckles but doesn't fall. It's surprising Landon doesn't retaliate, showcasing the guilt he is feeling.

"On purpose," Lee adds, spitting at Landon's feet.

"That true, my girl?" Dad asks, ushering us all inside. His face is pale and drawn. He's been so overworked and sometimes he comes home to children arguing and the house a mess because it's been that hectic of a day, but nothing as bad as this. Dad's shoulders are slouched, fatigue is the coat he is wearing. His eyes blaze in anger when he sees the dirt and leaves in my clothes, how I'm still shaken while trying to stay strong in front of the children.

"We're going for a talk, outside," Dad states, his voice deathly quiet as he straightens up. He's shorter than Landon but thicker and even though he has a beer belly I know he can lift more than Landon. I know he can hit harder and take a hard hit because of his lifestyle. "You hurt my little girl!"

"Dad!" I yell, scared of the dark look on his face to the acceptance Landon seems to have for a dad. "Please don't hurt him."

"This is why we should pray to Mother Mary," dad pulls me in for a hug and squeezes me tightly. I relax in his embrace, secure and at home in his arms. "Because you just saved Landon from a damn good ass whooping." With that, the door slams shut. I'm so lost, confused, and afraid and I don't know what to do until I realize what I *used* to do in hard situations. Pray.

"Grab the rosaries guys." I clap my hands together. The children all race to the rosaries we keep hanging on the walls as I grab a votive candle and light it with a match. Harry peers out the windows and when he can't see anything, paces just like Landon did.

"I want that one!" Kennedy wails, trying to rip a rosary out of Windsor's hands.

"Me want!" Conan rams his head into Makayla's stomach. I stare at the fighting children in disbelief, they're fighting over *rosaries*. We don't have enough rosaries for them all, they know this, they know that if they don't get the rosaries tonight they'll get them tomorrow. My patience is overrun.

"In the name of the Father and the Son and the Holy Spirit," I speak loudly, tears falling out of my eyes. My heart is empty and drained but so full of everything it shouldn't be. The devil seems to have won tonight. But I know he didn't because we are together, and we are praying.

Screw you, Satan, in the name of Jesus Christ.

Home Sweet Home

———➤·◦·◂———

Rennie, whoa cuz, not cool," I mutter. It's late at night, and the children all asleep. I can hear Windsor snore through the walls and Sally Anne toss and turn upstairs. She barely has room to and I hear a curse word when she bumps into the roof. Stuttered murmurs are Rennie's only defense before he collapses on the couch, dead to the world. I exhale loudly. Everything seems to be happening all at once. The boys joke about me and Sally Anne having mood swings but I never go out and get drunk and start fights and argue until I'm blue in the face. Landon stumbles into the cabin next, swaying heavily but able to walk on his own. He misses the kitchen chair a few times before managing to sit down.

"Looking good Shawty," he grins at me. I look at my dad's room. His snores are louder than Windsor's, indicating he's not waking up anytime soon. Per their 'talk' Landon isn't allowed in the cabin anymore. If he wants a place to stay he can head to the barn loft-like Louis and Rennie are supposed to when they are drunk. Landon starts talking to Riley whoever he or she is as Lee and Harry, talking and laughing like old buddies enter the house. They'd bonded over the Landon-went-berserk-on-me experience.

"Can you help me get them to the barn?" I ask the two sober boys. Lee is a teetotaler by choice, Harry by his allergies. Both boys stop to study me, Landon and Rennie. It would be easier to get Landon to the loft since he isn't passed out but they want to get him in trouble so they pick up Rennie. They also make a racket of noise but through it all, I can hear my dad's snores. He's deep asleep from his hard-working labor job. I don't want my cousins and Landon's drunkenness to wake him. A perk to my dad working so hard and taking in all the children is that he never has time to drink anymore.

"Can you bake me that chocolate cake again, Shorty?" Landon asks, his eyesight crooked as he tries the puppy dog look. His drunkenness sets me off, I'm okay with people drinking but not until they don't have complete function of their limbs.

"You need to get to the barn loft," I sigh, silently praying the St. Michael Chaplet. I might be scared of his reaction. Landon stares at me while he processes my words, his smile falling.

"Oh, yeah," he mutters, all the fun whisking out of him. He looks like a mopey-deflated ball now. I follow him outside, letting him use me as a stabilizer, his arm around my shoulders.

"You never want to do anything that your dad says you can't," Tyler sneers. He has a joint smoking on the steps, watching the dark night. He's high again. Tyler is a lot meaner than Landon when he has drugs in his system unless he is crashing.

"I respect my father," I calmly reply, shutting the front door. Landon stumbles down the steps and crashes into a poplar tree to the left of the driveway. He curses as he stumbles, exaggerated because of his intoxication. How is this my life? Watching children during the daytime hours and drunks during the nighttime hours. I'm exhausted. Taking care of people is taxing, but it makes me thank God for His personal love for us all over again.

"Or you just don't have the balls to live freely," Tyler caustically laughs. Harry and Lee make it to the barn, the light bulb indicates their arrival. I shake my head when they drop Rennie on a pile of straw, not very gently. "You and your rules and laws and obedience to God."

"Routine helps everyone, not just me." My patience with Tyler is thin. I don't like who he is with drugs in his system. *Please, Lord, give me patience.*

"Spontaneity makes life worthwhile," Tyler stares at me, smoke curling into his nostrils. I want to defend myself and show him there is spontaneous stuff in my life but he'd only see them as excuses with his tunnel vision.

"That's fair," I concede, reflecting on all the gifts God has given me that were unexpected. Friends in the triplets, Jonah, Art, and Danae. Having a bigger family instead of us two Ridels against the world. The Watson clan accepted me as their own. Pete randomly gives me a dollar when he manages to save his pennies. The list could go on and makes me grateful for everyone who has been in my life, even peripherally. It helps calm me down. Tyler still wants to egg me on. He's very stubborn. Tyler smirks at me, a gloating look on his face. He's cocky now that he thinks he won the argument, I'm just too tired to fight him on it. We sit in tense solitude. Louis is cursing out Lee and Harry for shoving him up into the loft, trying to fight them with bad coordination that the sober guys easily dodge and deflect. Landon is wandering around the little front yard, talking to himself and following Sugar around. "You ever think about stopping the drugs?"

"All the damn time," Tyler laughs obnoxiously.

"What stops you from acting on it?" I ask genuinely. Tyler balks at my words, considering what exactly I mean.

"I have no f—king self-control I guess," Tyler mumbles. He puffs one more time before squishing it out with his fingers and tossing it in the trees.

"How can I help you stop?" Tyler coughs in surprise, something silver glinting from the moonlight. It's four am, and the night sky is clearing. The cold night air has a bite to it, indicating the snow that is coming any day now.

"You can't! Not unless you can stop the torment in my f—king head!" Tyler shouts, rage flowing through him as he viciously pounds his skull with a fisted hand. I shrink in fear, remembering what happened with Landon when I tried to step in. Tyler's not in the mood for a hug to call him down, or show him maternal love. "You got lucky! You got a good father! A loving home! People treat you like their own, the Watsons! My own damn cousins treat you more like family than they do me! It's f—ing messed up! You get all the love!" My heart seems to slow, and my eyebrows furrow. Is this how all the Trips think of my life? As if I'm some golden girl that has never struggled? How can I break it to them that even with all the horrible stuff their dad put them through they had a mom to talk to, and receive comfort from. Where's my mom? I love her and don't even remember her, I don't know her name or how she looks! And just because my dad doesn't physically hurt me doesn't mean it didn't hurt cleaning up after his drunkenness, mopping up puke, dumping bottles of whiskey, and hiding full ones. Staying up late worrying if he would make it home *at all*. Landon had somehow stumbled into the barn, Lee and Harry glanced over at me after hearing Tyler›s loud, angry voice. Together the boys somewhat shove Landon into the loft.

"Tyler, did anyone ever tell you that God gives us sufferings as gifts to open the door to more beautiful things?" I gently ask, my left hand trying to fruitlessly tuck my curls behind my ear. The curls pop back out immediately, much to my vexation. Can one *thing* go right tonight?

"You and your f—ing God! Where is He? Huh, where was He when my dad was beating the shit out of me? Where was your 'Most Holy and righteous Father', your Jesus, when my own biological piece-of-shit father stuck me with a needle while I was asleep to get me hooked on heroin? Where was the Almighty and ever-good Father when my shitty father raped my mother in front of me!" Tyler rages on, his voice thunderous for being such a tiny human. I can feel the heat reeking off of him from how worked up he is. The drugs really make him angry. My heart cracks, pain seeping into it, a sword of sorrow like my Mama felt when she lost her child Jesus for those three days. Love. God's Divine love. I need to show Tyler God's merciful, unfathomable, deeply personal, and sacrificial love. *Mother Mary, hold me, give me your strength, the strength you had to watch Your Son slowly bleeding out in front of you. Hold Tyler, show him your infinite motherly love.*

"Tyler." My voice is barely a whisper, my throat closing up. "You are courage." Tyler stands up, jumping up so fast it jerks me back in shock. I trip on the bottom step, my body careening to the right. My head is going to have a bump from where it hits the railing, and my breath comes in short pants. I'm still scared of fast movements from when Landon hurt me but I don't want to be. My heart wants to trust that the Trips won't hurt me but my mind isn't capable of wrapping them and safe together. Terror seizes me, I had never seen Tyler this angry. How deep is the pit where he buries his anger and how can I dig through the muck with him? *Jesus, guide me.*

"I am a coward! I use drugs to hide my pain!" Tyler screams, his voice is hoarse. His lips wobble as his overheated face turns a darker shade of red. He's holding his breath now, trying to bottle his emotions back up again. *Jesus, I offer my suffering for this triplet.* A teardrop, one single, lonely tear lands on my face before Tyler is suddenly thrown back by the force of Harry who'd jumped over me, slamming his brother into the thick cabin wall.

"You are courageous! You came here, you listened to me speak of hope and you quit drinking! That is courage! To fight for the good you've never known! Knowing full well that if you quit drinking your dad would beat you! But you did anyway. Courage isn't being brave or strong, courage is being scared and doing it anyway! That is you! You are the embodiment of courage! I've never been as courageous as you have, nor have I been as scared of something." I'm shouting at the beginning, shocking myself and the boys. My patience is gone, the limitless depths I thought I had not very deep at all. My voice cracks at the end and trails off. Tyler is stronger than he realizes. He is beautiful, in this moment of sadness, in this moment of giving it all up into the open air, and he got up and *persevered*. We could all learn a lesson from Tyler. I just hope in some way this leads him closer to God, to our Saviour. Tyler is the embodiment of courage, of that I am certain.

"She is literally trying to help you!" Harry's voice is low, deathly calm, his arm against Tyler's throat. In the glinting light, I can see bitter heartbroken tears flowing down Tyler's face. The youngest triplet is by far more emotional than his brothers. *Lord Jesus Christ have mercy on us sinners.* "Just quit getting high already Tyler. We have a home. A home that has given us hope. We have a chance at a better tomorrow, because of her." Harry's voice breaks as he points to me. "Because of her God, because of her Father. And yeah, we've been struggling. And we will. But we have hope now, a beacon of light in our darkness. We have a guiding light. We have three of us, and ya know, maybe dad separated us because we're too strong together. But no more. We are family. We have a family. We have hope and now a home, a true home. Tyler, we are *home*." Harry's voice is thick with emotion as he drops his arm away from Tyler's throat. As those angry, pain-filled tears stream down Tyler's face, I thank God. *Thank you, Jesus, thank you, Mama Mary, thank you God for sending your Holy Spirit down upon us this night.*

"Damn rights we do!" Landon appears out of nowhere, grasping both his brothers in his arms for a group hug, his eyes glinting in the faint light offered in the darkness. All three boys hold onto each other, chests heaving up and down with heated emotional outlets exhausting them. Landon seems sobered up at the seriousness of this. Lee is watching from the side of the step, not at the boys, but at me. He is also crying, shaking his head at me. I think Lee is seeing that he doesn't have to be like his older brothers. That he can be more like the Watsons. That what he has seen, what he has been through, and how he has stepped up for his nieces and nephews can end here. That they can all start to be better, break through generational trauma. That God heals. That God works through His servants to show love, hope, and faith to those sheep that have been lost. That Jesus will indeed leave the ninety-nine for the one. That He is waiting for us with open arms, running toward the speck He sees on the horizon. That Jesus saves. *Thank you, Jesus.*

We all shuffle inside, even Landon. I don't have it in my heart to kick him out again. The triplets troop to the couch, falling asleep almost immediately. Lee clambers into his bed, dazed-looking at the drama that had been unfolding but had not erupted. I start baking Landon his chocolate cake with cream cheese icing. Oh Landon, ever the loud one, obnoxious, angrily asking for a cake. Probably because he didn't get home-baked cakes growing up, and never had anyone willing to make him one. *Lord, let me make this cake with all Your love, give this Love to your children here who need it.* Children I have seen grow through all the turmoil being thrown at them.

It's dawn now and I can hear my dad slowly rustling around in his room. He'll get dressed, and pray for a little bit before coming out. I put the chocolate cake in the oven and the dirty baking dishes by the sink and find some clean ones to make the icing.

Dad's eyebrows rise as he walks into the kitchen, seeing all three Trips somewhat sleeping on top of each other on the couch. Landon is sitting, Harry laying down and Tyler is squished beside him. "I thought I said Landon had to sleep in the loft?" Dad softly asks. I shrug my shoulders, grabbing a block of cream cheese from the fridge, and trying to think of an answer.

"Oh, dad I didn't have the heart to separate the Trips after this night." I hiccup out, grasping my father. Right now I just need to feel his loving embrace. Tears are free-flowing out of my eyes. I'm a crier, and not too pretty or quiet of one. Dad's arms wrap around me, give a tight squeeze that picks me off my feet, and a soft kiss is placed on the top of my head. "I love you, my girl." He holds on a little longer, before gently letting me go. I relax being held tightly.

"I don't want to know," dad chuckles softly. He's been drunk and knows how some drunk nights never seem to end. I appreciate his response to privacy. I watch him walk back to his room, excited to call Aria. It's time change today, giving everyone less sleep than normal. While it may have seemed like Tyler and I talked for hours it wasn't very long at all. It just felt like it because of how deep the conversation flowed and the raw emotions involved.

Lee wakes up first, routinely waking up early to prepare for his basic training. Win and Conan walk to the kitchen, all yawning and goofy smiles. I'm thankful when Conan walks right up to me and wraps his arms around my legs. As distant as he can be mentally he shows how much he loves us physically. Slowly Sally Anne and the little girls follow rosaries in hand.

"I want a rosary!" Makayla's shrill voice cries out. She had one yesterday, she knows she's supposed to use her fingers today.

"Daisy we need more rosaries!" Win grumbles, wiping eye gunk away and handing Makayla the rosary he was going to use. I let out a little laugh. It's beautiful to see Win give up a rosary. He sometimes acts like a bully with his bossy attitude but he also acts like any dad would, giving up what he wants most for his younger siblings. Maybe Micks was just tired, but being selfless is a virtue and she just helped Win master it. They're both learning good habits young, I think, when I notice her share the rosary with Win. They are giving as St. Martin tore his soldier's mantle for the beggar Christ.

"In the name of the Father and of the Son and of the Holy Spirit..."

⇢ **30** ⇠

A Bag of Rosaries

———⇒▸◦◂⇐———

Nooooo," I drag out the words. Conan grins at me before hopping away from the chocolate bar rack.

"Yessssss," He dances to the next aisle. I don't mind if he runs around, our small town's grocery store is small. I can hear him skipping down the aisle. I roll my eyes, grabbing the chocolate bar and throwing it in the cart I'm pushing. Yes, I did say no but his reaction was just too cute.

"He's playing you," Col chuckles, throwing an arm around my shoulders.

"Worth it," I laugh, turning down an aisle. Kennedy was napping so Lee stayed home with her and the babies while everyone else is at school. Col and I have a flex period and he wanted out of the stale school building and jumped at the excuse to take me shopping for food my family desperately needed. I'd felt like a thief stealing the money Rennie and Louis left laying around but I'm *completely* broke and we are out of food basics.

"Flour?" Col asks, lifting a bag of flour into the cart without an answer from me.

"Grab two more please," I shoot him a big smile. Col rolls his eyes as he grabs the next two bags and puts them in the cart. I used to grind wheat to make my own flour but I don't have enough time in my days to make everything from scratch. While Col grabs the flour I grab two big bags of white sugar. I'm buying in bulk because I bake every evening otherwise we wouldn't have enough snacks for everyone.

"That's a lot," Col whistles. He pushes the cart further down the aisle while I toss in some cans of cocoa, cornstarch, yeast, baking powder, baking soda, and brown sugar. All the basics.

"Big family," I retort, adding a bottle of vanilla extract when I pass it by. Col laughs at me. "Can we still buy eggs and milk from you guys?"

"Yup," Col replies, pushing the cart for me. What a gentleman. "Annabelle is having a calf. Duncan can buy it if it is a female. And the chicks are starting to lay, we can build a coop and give them to you."

"That's very generous," I shoot him a polite smile. My dad probably wouldn't want to accept. It'd mean more work, and a set schedule but we would have fresh milk and eggs. I could step up, milk the cow before school and get Windsor and Makayla to check for eggs.

"Gotcha!" Col catches Conan and throws him in the air. Conan squeals, a big smile on his face. When he lands in Col's arms he erupts into laughter. Col sets him on his shoulders. I take over pushing the cart, going over what we need in my head. We have vegetables from the garden canned and preserved, and herbs growing in pots by the windows. I just need fruit and lettuce. Even with scrounging up Louis and Rennie's leftover tax money and adding it to mine, I'm afraid I won't have enough. With the triplets and my cousins stressing me out I want to fall on the ground and sob my heart out. Col catches my anxious look as I try to steady my breathing and unite myself to Jesus's Most Sacred Heart.

"We'll pay for this," I steer Col and Conan to the till. "Then see if we have enough for fruit."

"I can get it this time," Col offers, his rich brown eyes softening in sadness. "You and Duncan have helped me a lot, all for free."

"Let me use Rennie and Louis's money first," I smirk. Col gently smiles, his face still drawn.

"You've lost weight Daisy," Col sighs. I frown, looking down at my body. My overalls are slightly baggy now, and my shirts loose where they are tucked in. I hadn't noticed my weight loss but it makes sense. As much as I cook and bake I don't eat, the children come first and the triplets and my older cousins don't notice when I don't make a plate because the food is all gone. With the lack of sleep, especially as of late, I'm pale, with big purple bags under my eyes. It could also be the stress of trying to make everyone's lives easier while adding strain to mine. Jesus did all this, so I can too.

"I didn't notice," I shrug Col's concern off. He lifts Conan off his shoulders to lift the big bags of flour and sugar onto the till.

"I'm worried about you," Col states stiffly. I beam at him, deciding to come clean with my thoughts to him.

"Thank you," my smile doesn't falter when I speak. "I was reflecting the other day that you have been my friend for a long time and I never counted it. I took you for granted but you have always been there for me. I appreciate our friendship, a lot."

"You're too cheesy," Col rolls his eyes, focusing on buttoning his long-sleeved shirt back up. He's hard to get emotional with. He doesn't speak again as Conan nabs the chocolate bar with a happy squeal and I count the cash for the cashier. My heart drops, and I don't have any money left over. "Here, I got this." Col races off, I laugh at his tall, lanky body running through the store with a blue plaid shirt, Levi jeans, cowboy boots, and a big belt buckle. He's a cowboy, no doubt about it, the only thing missing is his hat sitting on the dash of his truck.

Cam and Jim walk into the store, cursing and telling each other dirty jokes and at the same time shoving each other. They must be skipping school. I shoot them a polite smile as I load up the bags of flour and sugar and grocery bags full of the other baking ingredients I chose.

If it is possible my heart drops even further. I didn't pick up a pack of oatmeal. Bread isn't as filling, especially with children and I know Col doesn't have too much money to spare. He lives paycheque to paycheque with his rodeo career just taking off.

"Whoa! Conan stay inside please!" I raise my voice slightly for Conan to hear it. He'd found out that the sliding doors open when he walks in front of them and thought it a good idea to go explore there. Per usual, Conan doesn't answer but he does stop in the porch area.

"Hope the kids like this," Col smiles as he drops bags of apples, oranges, grapes, and kiwis on the counter.

"All treats," I assure him.

"Hello!" An unknown voice catches our attention. I look to the end of the till where a young man was standing in frayed clothing, worn-out shoes, and a very tanned face.

"Hi," I wave, sending him a welcoming smile. He returns it, his eyes clear and bright.

"Can you spare an apple?" he asks. I catch myself nodding before pointing to Col.

"You'll have to ask my friend," I wince, noticing the bag tied to the buckle loops on his jeans. It's filled with rosaries of all different colors.

"Yeah," Col answers, tapping his credit card to pay for the fruit. I take an apple out of the bag and give it to the man.

"Thank you kindly," he smiles in relief, fatigue showing in the way he carries himself. Cam and Jim make some harsh jokes about the 'homeless' man.

"Are those rosaries?" I ask. Col wraps an arm around my shoulders, Conan sitting in his other arm.

"Sure are," the man replies, holding the bag out. "Take as many as you want."

"Thank you!" I enfold him in a hug, my heart brimming over with joy. God is so good! Just when we need more rosaries he sends a man selling rosaries to me! "My dad just adopted around ten children and the little ones are sad when they don't get to hold a rosary! Thank you so much, sir! This is a miracle for sure!"

"I'm glad for that," he smiles, opening the bag for me. I grab a random handful and pull, hoping it is enough.

"Col grab one!" I urge, stuffing the rosaries in my overall bib pocket. "Are they blessed?"

"Yes," the man answers, a shine on his face. It looks like a little halo. "Don't be afraid to bless them for your use though."

"Of course not," I agree, spotting Cam and Jim behind the friendly stranger. "He's giving away rosaries!"

"I guess," Col drawls. The rosary he picks out is a knotted brown one, instead of a miraculous medal holding the decades together it is a saint with what looks to be a cowboy hat on his head. Of course, Col would pick a saint with a cowboy hat.

"Who's that saint?" I ask the man. We both lean closer to inspect the medal. Col awkwardly clears his throat. Conan whines to get down so I hand him one of the rosaries I had grabbed.

"That looks to be St. Nicholas Owen," the man smiles. The honest expression lights up his whole face. "Patron saint of illusionists and es-capologists." A guilty look flashes across Col's face, and Adam's apple bobs in his throat. He looks like he is being forewarned of something terrible, something bad that was already hinted at to him.

"I'll going to load the groceries in my truck," Col states stiffly before sauntering off in his long strides. Conan follows him, chocolate covering his face and some stuck on the rosary I gave him. I make a mental reminder to pray for Col, who seems to be struggling with a moral dilemma.

"How can I pay you?" I ask, fruitlessly digging in my pockets for spare change. I have absolutely nothing.

"Nothing, friend," the man waves my objections away. At this, I study him to remember him when I pray. Tall and skinny, with lean muscles as if he was raised on a farm, a sharp jawline, riverbed brown eyes slightly hazel with metallic blue. Button-up shirt but it isn't plaid, whitewashed jeans, at least they are from time spent in the sun. Running shoes that barely have any bottoms. "I'm trying to trust in the Lord. Be a walking disciple."

"Congratulations!" I beam at him. "I'll definitely be praying for you!"

"It's hard," he smiles at me, fatigue etched into his face and drowsiness drawn on his eyes. "You would expect kinder people in this world."

"I can buy you a bag of food!" I speak up, looking in the tip jar. Only a few cents, not even enough for a bottle of water. "Know what? Come to my house, you can have a plate of food and we can pack you some water and snacks for the road! I greatly appreciate what you are doing! I don't have the courage!"

"We are all called to different paths to walk," he sets a palm on my shoulder. "It's okay, friend. I have my bible, my bag of rosaries, and a water bottle. I'm good. Thank you for your hospitality."

"Oh, but I didn't do anything!" I frown, looking over his frail body again. He's not as skinny as Tyler but if he keeps on this way he will be. "Just stay for a meal, one meal! Come to mass with me tonight! Meet a bunch of people to who you can sell rosaries to!"

"I only give them away." The man chuckles, sucking on his bottom lip and tapping his toes. "But I can stay for mass."

"You're faith is amazing!"

"Hey!" The cashier shouts. She must be new, I haven't worked with her yet. Cam takes off, laughter trailing after him while Jim curses him out. He throws a five-dollar bill on the counter. Then he grabs a drink from the coolers and chases after his brother. The five dollars won't be enough to cover the bill. Usually, I would step in but I have no money to my name until the end of the week.

"Get inside," Col's voice is hard. He'd caught Cam and was dragging the boy by the collar of his shirt. Cam cusses him out well before lifting his shirt up and dropping a bunch of items on the counter. Jim trails back in, sniggering at his brother. Cam throws him some vulgar hand gestures.

"Want a rosary?" I ask the twins, holding out two rosaries to them. Cam scoffs at me but does a double take when Jim reaches forward haltingly.

"Ya gon' have teach me to pray," Jim scowls, nabbing a green rosary. Cam takes the blue one.

"I can definitely do that," I beam once again. They were just caught shoplifting but at least they want to learn how to pray! It's a gift that will last them the rest of their lives!

→ 31 ←

Family History

❖

"I certainly hope you enjoy it," I shake Harvey Watson's hand. It wasn't in my plans to sell my moped but he'd seen it parked in the lean-to and wanted to know gas mileage and whatnot and I ended up saying he could buy it so we could have extra cash for emergencies.

"Amelia and Chloe will love it," he grins, pumping my hand enthusiastically. He's a big truck driver, rarely home but he has some vacation days he has to use because they won't switch to the next year so he's been helping Peter's crews build Ridel House, as my dad's mansion has been labeled. The roof is on, the walls insulated, and the wood stoves put in. One crew is working on the kitchen cabinets while the other is working on the stairs leading above the kitchen and steps outside.

"Hey Daisy, Harvey," dad stops beside us. The perk of dad working for Peter is dad never leaves the premises. The last week dad was needed elsewhere but now he's back. The children behave better knowing he is just a holler away. Harry, Landon, and Lee help out with the house when they can, leaving Tyler and me to watch the children which means Tyler lazes around inside with the babies while I watch the older, rambunctious children and cook supper.

"Howdy there Duncan," Harvey smiles, putting the moped keys in his pocket. Dad frowns.

"You sold the moped?" He asks, his shoulders hunched in before he pushes his chest out to stretch his back.

"Yeah," I reply. My dad looks at the moped sullenly, his fingers clenched together. He's angry. I hope it's about the sale of the moped, not that I sold it.

"I better get home to the wife," Harvey shakes my dad's hand. "I'll pick up the moped at the end of the week. See you tomorrow, Duncan."

"Have a good night Harvey," Dad says, unclenching his fingers. I lean into his shoulder as Harvey walks away. Dad exhales deeply, content in the evening dusk. Lee and Harry are putting the children to bed, and Landon and Tyler are out somewhere with Louis and Rennie even with the words of wisdom their brother offered on my behalf. "Let's go pray, my girl."

"You know I can't say no to that," I grin, striding forward with dad. He walks toward the swing, where he had recently put a bench at the base of the tree because he noticed Sally Anne likes to sit and read there. I nab the swing, he sits on the bench and we make the Sign of the Cross.

"O Blood and Water which gushed forth from the heart of Jesus as a fount of mercy for us, have mercy on us. O Blood and Water which gushed forth from the heart of Jesus as a fount of mercy for us, have mercy on us. O Blood and Water which gushed forth from the heart of Jesus as a fount of mercy for us, have mercy on us." I swing slightly as we pray the beginning prayers to the Chaplet of Divine Mercy. *Our Father... Hail Mary... I believe in God....* Lee exits the house when the lights shut off. He waved before taking off for his nighttime run, unafraid of the dark or the wildlife. He'll run to the meadow, trying to sprint the way back. Sometimes Harry goes with him so he isn't alone but I spot Harry in the chaplet room, kneeling in front of our statue of Mama Mary. "Eternal Father, I offer You the Body, Blood, soul, and divinity of Your dearly Beloved Son, Our Lord Jesus Christ in atonement for our sins and those of the whole world. For the sake of His sorrowful Passion, have mercy on us and the whole world...." At the end of the Chaplet of Divine Mercy, we sit in silence, meditating on Christ's love for us with that powerful prayer. The dusk light had darkened considerably and my heart beats in happiness when I feel the gentle cold of a snowflake falling upon my forehead. How elaborately snowflakes are made, each one different. If He put that much care into something that melts how much more care does He put into us? As scripture tells us: even the hair on our heads is counted.

"I guess it's time for me to explain more of your family, huh, Bambi?" My dad sighs deeply again. I nod silently, waiting for him to tell his story. The nickname he called me triggers a faint memory but I can't remember who called me Bambi or why they did.

"Why'd you call me Bambi?" I ask, confused at what my dad called me. Dad has never given me another nickname, it's always been, Daisy or my girl.

"Your mom." Dad runs his hands through his hair. He needs a haircut. He flips it out of his eyes to put his hat on. "She wanted to, awugh, she wanted to name you Bambi."

"Really?" My eyebrows rise in surprise. I thought Daisy was out there as a name but Bambi is really pushing it.

"Yeah, I persuaded her to keep Daisy. She was upset that I didn't agree with Bambi but I'm glad we didn't name you that because she walked off anyway."

"She probably had some good traits," I speak up, defending the woman who didn't love me enough to stay. It twists my gut. I've always considered Mama Mary my mother because I didn't have one here on earth but sometimes the gap is too big for my faith to cross. She is my mother, a woman who nurtured me in her womb. What happened for her to simply walk away? Give me up?

"She did," my dad smiles softly, sadly. "I love Aria, don't get me wrong but I was head over boots with your mother instantly. She wasn't taught a lot by her parents and didn't even know who her dad was but she had a fierce passion for her siblings. I'll never forget how united they were with all the bad stuff their mom put them through. It was a very broken love, but they had each other's backs and tried to take care of each other. Taught me a lot about the world, just like the Smith boys are teaching you. Taking you out of the bubble I raised you in. You were sheltered growing up and I won't take that back at all. It's made you into the beautiful young woman you are."

"Thanks, dad," I tuck my insanely curly hair behind my ear. Its gravity-defying springiness doesn't let it stay back for long, making me miss the corn rows Alex and Bobbi gave me. "How many siblings did my mom have?"

"Five, one sister, four brothers. One was adopted, she was the oldest girl and a twin actually. Her twin brother and the adopted boy were older than her. They grew up tight-knit. Then about a decade later your grandma had her three younger siblings in four years but she was still unbelievably close to them." There are twins in my family, I have an uncle and aunt from my dad and four uncles and an aunt from my mom that I have never met. It's the first time I've doubted my dad sequestering and hiding me from my biological family. This is so *surreal.* I could have cousins my age running around, maybe I wouldn't have been so lonely and struggled so badly to make friends. Maybe I wouldn't have been as socially awkward because I would have socialized with them. I take a deep breath and banish the thoughts from my mind. It's not worth it to think of the what-ifs. My past is my life already lived, something I cannot change. The only thing to do now is move forward, and accept what my dad tells me even if it isn't what I want to hear. *Holy Spirit, send your seven gifts upon me, to learn, to teach as an example. Make me a modern gospel reflection, Your Will alone be done, God.*

"What is my mom's name?" I ask, my fingers wrapped tightly around the swing ropes. It's a question I've been dying to ask for years but my dad's best-kept secret. Dad clears his throat and looks at me guiltily.

"Was," he says gently. I open my mouth to correct him, to tell him that he had lied to me about her death before but the serious look on his face shuts me up. Tears well in my eyes as my heart breaks, a giant tear ripping me in half. She's dead. My mom is dead and I never got to see her, speak to her, or tell her how much I love her even for abandoning me! *Mama Mary, I need you! Jesus, I need you!*

"Why didn't you let me meet her?" I cry out, my breath catching in my throat. That had been my hope for years.

"I'm sorry, my girl."

"What about the children?" I jerk my head up, my little pity party already over. "Where are their moms? Why haven't I heard anything about them? It hurt me so much not knowing anything about my mom, what about them? There are so many of them, their hurt will be amplified!"

"Rennie wants to go back to his children's mom. Her name is Jessica. She's with Taylor, Rennie's mom. The only reason he doesn't leave is that he doesn't have a ride. Louis doesn't want anything to do with the people in his past life so Tinsley and Tikara might not know their mother." I sharply inhale at what my dad says, a replica of what happened to me. Tinsley is such a sweet girl, to go without her mom would traumatize her.

"We have to make that right dad. Even if their mom isn't good they should still be able to see her."

"You are young yet Daisy, and I appreciate your innocence in the ways of the world but if we bring Jessica up here there is going to be another Ridel on the way and we can't possibly take on another child. Lee is being shipped off soon so that means we'll have to find a babysitter for the babies."

"Okay, dad. We'll stop at that part there so I can process it all." I state, wiping salty tears from my eyes. I miss my mom. Even though I never met her my heart aches at the thought of what our relationship *could* have been. Dad thought he was protecting me but how bad could she really have been? I'm repeating my what-ifs from earlier so I exhale again, and inhale. Dad doesn't rush me, just nods to indicate I can ask another question if I wish. He's giving me the information I should have grown up knowing. *Lord, I'm being impatient and hardhearted. Please help me to accept this cross and never stop praying for love and mercy.* "So there is Rennie, Louis, Lee, and Sally Anne, right? But did Uncle Joseph or Taylor have any other children?"

"Remember I told you Joe married Kaitlyn? They never had children but he inherited two stepdaughters. Your step-cousins Amanda and Jade. Taylor was cheating on Joe that whole time and this is the part that gets sort of confusing. Rennie is the oldest and Louis isn't far behind him but Taylor had four back-to-back pregnancies. Rennie with Joe, Stephan with Duke Bouchard, now her husband, Louis with Joe, and Victoria with Duke. Now that she is married she also has a stepdaughter from Duke, Caroline. She's a grandma from Caroline recently, a little baby girl."

"That's wild, dad," I mutter, for lack of anything more thoughtful to say.

"Yeah, that just about sums up the Ridel family." Dad slaps his knees before jumping up. I watch him sadly as he stretches his back and rubs his lower back muscles. He probably misses Aria because she would scold him for working so hard and give him massages at night, helping his body recover.

"I have a whole passel of family out there." It stumps me and blows my mind. I am not alone, not that I was before, having the Holy Spirit with me and all, but I have a physical, real-life, blood-related family to call my own. Even with the tears itching my cheeks at the death of my mother a smile can't stop gracing my face.

"They aren't very good," dad adds, noticing the hopeful look on my face.

"But we can try to make them good," I softly retort. "Show them the love of God."

"I can't right now, my girl." Dad sighs, pacing in a circle at the base of the tree. "I don't have the energy although I admire your resolve. Maybe once we are more settled in I'll think about it but children don't take care of themselves."

"I know, dad," I sigh heavily. He'd given me so much to think about, to talk to God about, and meditate on. It seems impossible to wrap my brain around all this and that's not even including my mother's side of the family! I have five uncles and two aunts, one of whom I'll meet in heaven. It blows my mind. "Are you sure my mom is gone?"

"Yeah," dad replies. His eyes dart to the house where Harry had turned off the chaplet room light and turned on some battery-operated candles on window ledges. My dad's cabin is pretty cute for having mostly just basic necessities. "I called around to all her old friends. She OD'd a year ago."

"Can we go visit her sometime, pray for her, and light a candle?"

"Yeah, she was actually baptized Catholic," Dad answers, his lips pressed in a firm line to compress the wobble that won't stop. She was his first love, the one he never really got over. I shouldn't have expected this talk to be easy for him.

"Thank you for telling me all this, dad," I stop swinging and stand up. I'm a little dizzy being on the stable ground but I shake it off and walk to my dad, wrapping him up in a big hug, holding him tight, and showing him the love he showed me as a child. He doesn't cry in my arms, always the strong one around me; but I feel his ragged breathing as he bottles his emotions up. I pray while he stabilizes himself, praying from my heart all my unspoken prayers filled with passion, compassion, hope, and love for God to send His graces upon my whole, entire, broken family, blood-related or not.

"I'm thinking of asking Aria to marry me," dad drops another truth bomb on me. "What do you think of that?"

"Yes!" I squeal, jumping up and down excitedly a few times. Dad marrying Aria means he won't be living in sin, why would I mind? Besides, I love Aria, I love her whole family!

"I appreciate that," dad smiles at me. "Let's pray about this, for guidance from God on what I should do."

32

Relapse

———⇒⊱•⊰⇐———

O ne week, Daisy," Tyler beams at me, his eyes clear as he bounces on the balls of his feet excitedly. He holds up seven fingers. "I've been clean for seven whole days!"

"Awe!" I go in for a hug, pleasantly surprised when he wraps his skinny arms around me and squeezes too tightly. It takes my breath away, but not my hope. It's been a long, drawn-out, emotional, sort of hectic week because Tyler has been fighting his urge to stick a needle in his arms or at least inhale a joint. "I'm so proud of you!"

"Thanks!" Tyler spins me around, his face looking flushed and so, so, happy. Louis and Rennie look at the smallest triplet, impressed at his words.

"Can't do that," Louis laughs. I've noticed that he doesn't think very well but has pretty sharp humor.

"You one strong motherf—ker!" Rennie adds. They're sober today and exhausted. Rory Watson remained true to his word and had them out working twelve-hour days for his wife's brother. Per Rory and my dad's agreement, Rory will pay half of their earnings to them and give the other half to my dad for bills and groceries. I hate the sneaking behind their back, especially seeing the light in their eyes and the joy on their faces from finding worth in the work they do, but we all know as soon as they get the money they're going to spend it on booze. It's a very delicate matter, one I pray about a lot because my moral attitude doesn't agree with what seems like immoral actions.

"Good for you, man," Col nods at Tyler from his spot at the kitchen table. He came over asking for dad and is content to wait for him. I assume he needs help with something rodeo related. He also brought BJ, Pierre, Jonah, and Art with him. Tyler had been pacing the short floor of the cabin while Landon, Harry, BJ, and Pierre were playing the Watson family's favorite card game of Keyzer. Jonah and Art were playing crib, Col too antsy to join. We'd all been watching Tyler pace faster as the minutes dragged by. Sally Anne is sitting on the counter, flipping her hair out of her eyes as she tries to entertain the boys in conversation with a blush on her face. She likes one of them but most of them aren't paying her any attention. Windsor is whooping and hollering outside, the little girls and Conan chasing after him and fighting with homemade weapons made from branches. Win is a leader, and it makes me so happy to hear about his progress from living in our stable home. He's also parentified at his young age as the oldest child for stepping into the role of his drunk and drug-addicted parents. "Why can't I just go to the mansion?" Col huffs, anxiously checking his watch.

"If it's important I'm sure you can," I speak up, Tyler still holding me in his arms as he walks closer to the table.

"Just gotta make sure the kids don't follow you into the construction zone," Jonah adds, moving his peg up sixteen holes. He cuts a look to Tyler's arm still wrapped around my waist before throwing his handful of cards on the pile Art is shuffling.

"And they will," Landon snorts, then lets out a nice whistle when he wins the hand with the five of hearts.

"Unless you can sneak there," Harry laughs, slapping the deck down at Landon, who appears to be winning with BJ.

"You think you'll drop by the soup kitchen anytime soon?" Pierre asks, picking up some crumbs from the apple crisp I made, effectively using up the last of our oatmeal.

"Sorry Pierre, I won't be for a while." I grimace with a sad shake of my head. All the boys snap their heads in my direction, listening to every word I speak. It's a little disconcerting that they look to me as the leader of the group, being the youngest and all that. "I realize how much I was neglecting here at home just to volunteer. I can't hurt the children like that again."

"I don't do squat shit here," Landon speaks up.

"Except get drunk," Harry pettily throws his brother under the bus. Landon rolls his eyes when BJ and Col laugh. We thought Landon might partner with Tyler in staying clean but that has not been the case. His reliance on alcohol seems stronger than Tyler's reliance on drugs.

"So I guess I can take your spot volunteering for you," Landon finishes calmly. Harry and Tyler stare at their brother, confused and amazed. Landon doesn't clean, or cook. In fact, every time I ask him to help chop vegetables he runs away.

"That's so sweet, thanks Talltree," I smirk at Landon, waiting for his reaction.

"Where the hell did Talltree come from?" Landon retorts gruffly, his Adam's apple bobbing.

"Landon got a nickname," Pierre nods contemplatively. Tyler whistles.

"Damn," BJ laughs. "Finally."

"At least it isn't dumb ass or asshole, f—k up, little b—-h," Harry snorts, slapping Landon's shoulder.

"Shut up little lady," Landon retorts, kicking his brother's leg.

"Don't f—king call me that!" Harry shoves his brother, harder than the teasing atmosphere Landon was projecting called for. His strangled breathing shows us all that Landon's jesting triggered him but I'm the only one who knows why.

"Harry isn't little," I quip, breaking the tense silence. A few of the boys chuckle, Landon stares at Harry but Harry stares at the floor, chest heaving to control the rage brimming through him.

"I'm going for a ride," Harry snaps, standing up so hard his chair falls back. Landon gets up to follow him but I block him.

"He needs to go to the mountains to pray," I say softly. It's the advice Harry gave me, seeming so wise then. Harry often disappears to spend time in nature with God. If he didn't have a girlfriend I think he'd make a good monk. *Lord, help Harry. I don't know how. Show him Your amazing love. Holy Spirit, console his wounded heart.*

"Sure, yeah," Landon licks his lips and throws an arm over my shoulders, tugging me into his chest. Lately, the triplets have really been opening themselves up for loving physical contact, which is great but I'm drained from it all, especially with the children. Conan always wants hugs, they never stop pulling on my clothes or trying to wrestle and dance with me. Tinsley loves to dance, maybe even more than she loves riding Honey with Harry.

"I should get started on the dishes," I state with a sigh. With so many people here the dishes pile up quickly. There is also no leftovers even with doubling the already huge casserole recipes. Apparently my supper today was a big success.

"I'll help," Pierre offers.

"Sally Anne can too," Landon says. "Instead of hiding in the corner hoping to be noticed."

"Yeah, curled your hair, girl," Tyler laughs, throwing the twelve-year-old under the bus. Her face heats up to bright red and I feel bad for her.

"Leave her alone!" I casually slap Tyler's shoulder. He doesn't flinch but it takes him a minute to realize it was playful. Philomena starts crying, and Tyler, Landon, and I turn to check on the baby, forgetting her dad is here, and sober. We all pause in disbelief as he lies on the couch, staring at his phone, oblivious to her cries.

"Hey, dipshit!" Landon shouts. "Do something!" Rennie ignores Landon's demand until Landon stalks toward him and then he scrambles up, scared of the younger man, still a teenager. My cousins are on the smaller side and only like to fight people smaller than them when they are drunk, proving their 'toughness'.

"Any leftovers, Daisy?" My dad asks, kicking his work boots off at the front door. He blinks when he sees Col and the rest of the pack of boys all at the table.

"Saved you a plate," I pull the plate out of the broiler, covered with a steel lid my dad made for this exact purpose.

"Thanks," dad glances at the table. It's suddenly a cluster of emotion as Tyler and Landon leap to random tidying and BJ picks up Harry's knocked-over chair. Col is the only one still at the table when my dad sits down and they both chuckle at the boys' reaction. I pour my dad a cup of water as he stares Jonah down with an evil eye I know isn't that bad. Not taking his eyes off Jonah as he chugs the water down, he holds it up for me to fill again. Tyler and Landon flop on the bottom bunks, quietly visiting. Louis and Rennie curiously glance at my dad, aware that he's hard on them. This week he hasn't strong-armed them too much because they've been exhausted when they come home.

"I need to talk to you privately, Duncan," Col states seriously, his fingers drumming on the table. Jonah hooks his thumb over his shoulder and murmurs something about seeing the horses. Art and BJ follow him. Sally Anne busies herself with drying the dishes Pierre is washing.

"Girls need some fresh air," Rennie slaps Louis's shoulder. Louis grumbles under his breath, laughing at whatever he says. Landon groans as he gets up.

"Sure," he mutters playfully. "Kick me out of my damn house."

"My house," dad's voice is loud and the look he cuts to Landon is sharp. He's still upset with the way Landon treated me, long gone is the 'Jesus saves' high-five' dad I knew.

"I'm glad it feels like home," I beam at Landon, joy filling my heart at the words he didn't plan. Pierre is drying his hands, Sally Anne rubber necking out the kitchen window. I see the guy she has a crush on walking to the outhouse. BJ Leon, Watson cousin.

"What kind of advice?" Dad asks, shoveling tuna rice casserole into his mouth. It being a Friday, I'd made a fish casserole so the whole family could fast from meat.

"Religious, moral, I guess," Col answers, his fingers now drumming on his thigh. It's quieter that way, and less annoying to my dad.

"Let's go outside," I steer Sally Anne to the front door. Something has been bugging Col and now he's asking my dad for advice, I pray he is alright. Sally Anne runs to the swing, where BJ had been sitting on the bench at the base of the tree. A truck is driving up our pothole-filled driveway, rusted out frame and lights smashed in.

"F—k," Landon hisses under his breath, glancing at Tyler who hasn't noticed the truck pulling up. "I'm not ready to deal with his shit today."

"Your dad?" I ask softly, my nose wrinkling at the dirty smell wafting from the unrolled windows even with the brisk air. Jonah and Art appear on either side of me, scowling at the beat-up-looking Ford.

"Hey son," Huntley casually glances over all of us before staring at his son. It's my first time seeing the triplets father, maybe ever, and I balk at the comparison I'd made in my mind. Jilly is white and Huntley is treaty First Nation, their children are a mix. While the Trips have varying shades of brown hair their dad's head is stock full of black hair starting to grey. It's long like Harry's and in a braid down his back. Tyler got his beautiful green eyes from somewhere up the generations, and Harry and Landon's blue eyes from the Watsons. Huntley's seem almost pitch black and they glint with a dangerous tinge. The lines on his tanned, brown face make it look as if he's never smiled although he shoots a fake one my way, his mean brown eyes raking slowly over my body.

"What do you want?" Landon growls. With Huntley's attention quickly off me, I make the Sign of the Cross, thanking God for His protection, and ask Him to send His warrior angels to defend me.

"Oh shit," Tyler flinches before drawing into himself. Fear causes his body to tremble before he controls his reaction. *Lord, please protect Tyler. Show him Your love and mercy and give Him the courage to face his adversity, his Cross, and his father.*

"Just came to see when my boys are coming home," Huntley says. Even his voice is cold, some sort of detachment from the emotions present on his face. I understand vividly why Tyler is terrified of his father. He scares me standing there and I have never met the man before, maybe it's because I see Satan lurking in his eyes. *Run devil, run, in the name of Christ our Saviour. Amen. Run because Mama Mary has her mantle covering us and God the Father is with us.* "It's been two months. Thought your little tantrums would be done by now."

"We're comfortable here," Landon states firmly, arms crossed over his chest. His jaw ticks. Art cocks his head, nervously shifting from foot to foot. Jonah's face has gone blank as he studies Huntley, his hands fisted tightly. It's a very angry look for someone who isn't really friends with the triplets.

"You're living in a two-bedroom," Huntley waves his hands flippantly at my dad's cabin as he jumps out of his truck. Tyler warily walks closer to Landon, prepared to have his brother's back although he wants to run the other way. "Shack."

"It's home," Landon retorts, his jaw clicking with the pressure he is clenching his teeth together with. The front door opens and my dad steps on the porch, studying the scene in his front yard.

"Huntley," he nods, leaning against the railing. His back is bugging him but I'm the only one who can see that, it causes him to walk with a slight limp. My dad hasn't mastered turning the other cheek. He calls the triplets his boys now, three of his fifteen children and he'll fight for them if he has to. He's done it before and he'll do it again.

"Prick," Col adds, spitting on the ground. Huntley laughs, obnoxiously fake as his cunning eyes hone in on Tyler.

"Got you a present," Huntley grins. We all watch as he walks to Tyler, and bumps into his chest to push him back before holding out a baggie of green stuff and another baggie of needles. I've never really seen them before but with a sickening heart, I know what they are. Huntley found out that Tyler stopped his drinking and drugs. Tyler doesn't say anything, just shoves the baggies in his pockets, his head ducked down, and his eyes not staying still. He's terrified, Huntley terrifies him when he's safe here at my dad's house, on my dad's land.

"Get inside," dad waves the children away. They'd noticed the drama unfolding and were staring nosily. Dad cleans his teeth with a fingernail and clicks his tongue. "Sally Anne, take them inside."

"Whatever," Sally Anne snaps back, her go-to answer when she knows she won't win the argument. Windsor decides it's best if he goes inside and the children follow him, still chatting and playing.

"The boys have made their decision Huntley," dad speaks up, trotting down the steps. Col is to his right. I'd never noticed before how muscled and tall Col is until I'm seeing him beside two grown men. He looks fierce, like an adult, a man, a warrior. It makes me realize I've never thought of him as grown up but with our age gap he is grown up.

"But they're only boys," Huntley doesn't take my dad's words seriously. He hops back into the rusty grey Ford seemingly uncaringly. "They don't know how to make decisions for themselves."

"We've been making our own damn decisions since we were ten years old!" Landon hotly retorts. Tyler shakes at the wicked glare Huntley shoots his brother's way.

"I'm gonna have to show you some respect when you finally decide to come home."

"This is home!" It's Harry who yells, cantering Honey into the yard. He doesn't slow her down until she takes on a mind of her own and skids to a stop, her nose reaching in the unrolled window. Landon laughs caustically when his dad curses and backs away. Harry jumps down, livid as he pushes Honey back and shoves his face in Huntley's truck. "Get the f—k outta here. I ain't ever going back. Tell mama I love her but I'll see her when I f—king throw the dirt in your piss ass grave."

"Watch your tone, boy," Huntley lowly growls out. "I can still give you a damn good ass whooping. Teach you to respect me."

"F—king try it," Harry taunts, Landon sidling up to him. Huntley slams open his door, violently pushing the two boys back. Harry stumbles over Landon's feet, losing balance but it's what saves him from Huntley's thrown fist. I clutch onto Jonah's hand, holding tightly at the thumps and curse words and taunts thrown around. *Lord Jesus Christ, Son of God, have mercy on us sinners!* Then I start the Memorare ten times for immediate intercession from our mama in heaven. Tyler has joined in the fray, terrified but not letting his brothers go down without him. Huntley doesn't have much of a chance with all three boys. It's why he's always picked on them one on one. I drop to my knees, close my eyes and lift my arms out how Jesus had them on the Cross. The words that come out of my mouth are foreign, I don't know what they mean as I pray the most earnestly I ever have in my whole *entire* life. *Please, Lord Jesus, keep everyone safe. Send Your Holy Spirit to open their hearts to love and mercy, forgiveness, and friendship. Help them to be strong, o Jesus, as You are strong in Your deep, abounding mercy.* Pierre and BJ join me, knees hitting the dirt and hands holding mine as the Our Father becomes our chant.

"F—king crazies," Huntley spits on the ground when Dad, Art, and Col break the fight up. Art is holding Landon back, Col struggling against Harry who won't stop trying to attack his father and Dad is standing between Huntley and Harry, trying to keep the peace. Tyler is lying on the ground, breathing hard. His frail body is swollen at his midsection, the fight could easily have re-injured his ribs. *Jesus, help and heal him, please. Saint Raphael stay with Tyler through his suffering.* I've never begged God like this before, depended so strongly on His intercession.

"Shut up," Jonah scowls scornfully. It's such an odd look on his usually peaceful countenance. Jonah's aura screams calm and gentle, it's who he is. It's weird seeing a new side to him.

"You need to leave," Dad says threateningly. "Before I call Abe and Annakin again. I know you got two more boys at home you treat like these three. I'll take them in, too."

"I did what I came here to do," Huntley shrugs, rubbing a red, swelling spot on his face. "Your mama's gonna learn your lesson for letting these bad habits grow out of control."

"F—k you!" Harry jumps at his dad. Col is knocked back a few steps from the force, an elbow landing in his face.

"I'm gonna f—king kill you one day," Landon vows, slapping Art's hands off of him.

"No, you aren't." Art shoots back. The look on his face is scared but relieved. "Your siblings will hate you even though they won't have to worry about being hurt by him again. They'll want his good side, his happy side, his playful side. It isn't worth it to kill him."

"Bye, my sons," Huntley waves as he backs out of the driveway. Landon gives him the bird. Tyler fiddles with a needle that he just took out of the bag.

"Is it worth it?" He mumbles to himself, staring lustfully at the needle. I'm too caught up in Art's statement. It sounded so truthful, spoken from experience. Art is very private about his family, all we know is that his dad is overseas and his mom died giving birth to Dekka. I'd just assumed his dad gave them a hefty allowance to run the family and farm themselves but is it too far out of reach to think Art-, no I won't go there. That is judging Art way too much.

"Get your shit together bro," Landon softly kicks Tyler's feet. BJ pulls me up, Pierre sitting down to rub his knees where loose gravel dug into our skin.

"You guys ready to go?" Col asks his friends.

"Go untack Honey, brush and rub her down," dad points to the barnyard, stepping in front of Harry to block his view of their dad driving away. Harry scowls and slaps my dad's hand down. Dad reciprocates before the blink of an eye. He's tough, I know my dad, and his hands are super strong. When I got spankings as a kid, which rarely ever happened, his hands felt like steel. It's what shocks Harry now as he stares at my dad, jaw dropped. He hadn't expected my dad to shove him. "I didn't deserve that." My dad speaks up, his voice hard. Harry gulps, stuffing his hands in his pockets.

"I'm sorry," he whispers before walking away, shoulders hunched in. Pierre trails after him, offering words of kindness and mercy.

"That feels so damn good," Tyler sighs.

"What the f—k is wrong with you?!" Landon shouts, kicking Tyler's legs. He drops to his knees to dig in Tyler's pockets for the drugs Huntley gave him. Tyler smirks, his eyes glazing over. It's not a happy look, especially when I see the needle sticking out of his elbow. "You were clean for how f—king long! Where's your pride?"

"It feels good," Tyler laughs at whatever thoughts are in his head.

"Have some f—king self-control," Landon punches Tyler's leg. Tyler curses Landon out, rubbing his leg.

"Cut it out, boys," my dad orders, stretching his back. He breathes in relief when we all hear the loud, satisfying crunch.

"He's being selfish!" Landon hisses out, stomping down on the needles he'd retrieved from Tyler's pocket. He hasn't found the weed yet but at least that isn't as bad as the needle drugs.

"Says the one drinking all f—king week," Tyler coughs out.

"Get off my property if all you guys are gonna do is bitch at each other," Dad snaps, rubbing his back. I balk at his words, he must really be in pain. Landon curses under his breath but trails off, understanding my dad's threat. BJ raises his eyebrow in a 'shit just went down' kind of way. Art nods in agreement, scanning Landon for the hate that was clear in his emotions toward his father.

"Okay," Tyler states coldly, hiding the emotions he was feeling. I'm scared at how lost he seems without showing what he is feeling, but how hard and mean he looks. That expression is a lot like his father's. "Let's go party, Rennie, Louis."

"I'm down," Louis smiles and laughs. Rennie shrugs, looking pleased.

"Not saying no to that." He's more the pothead while Louis likes his alcohol. Rennie is probably going to steal some of Tyler's weed once he's slightly out of it.

"Can we get a ride outta here, Col?" Tyler asks, finally sitting up.

"Yeah," Landon hisses. "Go f—king run away."

"F—k you," Tyler retorts.

"Boys, that's enough," Dad grinds out. Screams erupt from the house and he sighs deeply.

"I'll go check on the children," I offer, sprinting to the house. The wails had gotten louder in those few seconds. My feet stomp on the steps, loud because I'm more concerned about the children than running properly. When I open the door the screams are cut off. The children stare at me, scared. Tears dry on Tinsley's face, the wailer of the group today.

"It wasn't me," she declares when my eyes hone in on her.

"It was her!" Windsor throws his little cousin under the bus.

"Kennedy took her pencil," Makayla adds, chewing on her nails. It's a bad habit she has taught her younger siblings.

"We don't scream, okay Tinsley?" I kneel down to her level and pull her close to me. "We thought you were hurt. Next time take a big breath and ask Kennedy to give you your pencil back, sound good?"

"Uh huh," Tinsley murmurs, drying her tears.

"Thank you," I kiss her head. "Why don't you all get ready for bed? And remember, do everything with love."

"Whatever," Sally Anne still says but not with her usual bite. Then a smile springs forth before she can turn it into a frown. "At least you didn't yell at us like Uncle Duncan."

"Go to bed before he does." I shoo the children away. Conan throws himself on me for a hug as Makayla runs up the stairs, Sally Anne keeping an eye on Kennedy behind her.

"You need to do laundry again, Aunty." Windsor grins at me.

"I'll have to tomorrow," I shoot him a mock glare. When it was just me and my dad I used the old-fashioned hand washing board for cleaning our clothes but with all the children's clothes, and because some of them still wet themselves, I take garbage bags of clothes to the laundromat in town. And since I don't have a debit card or MasterCard and my dad doesn't have change on him and Rennie and Louis spend all their money I end up asking Percy, Peter, or Paul for money. They never let me down or ask for it back even though dad told Peter he could take it out of his paycheck. God bless the Watsons. "Please go to bed now Windsor."

"But Aunty I'm-," Windsor doesn't finish his sentence when my dad walks in.

"The house better be quiet!" My dad threatens in a loud tone for the girls upstairs to hear him. "I'm going to sleep!" Then he shoots me a wink and gives me a hug before squirreling away into his room for the night.

"I can pray with them," Pierre gently closes the door behind himself, Art and Jonah. "You could probably use a break. Go to the mountains if you want."

"Thanks, Pierre," I smile at him, slumping into a kitchen chair. When my eyes follow him to the boy's room I spot the dishes still needing washing and sigh deeply. The work never ends. I'm always so tired. The teachers at school know my situation but that doesn't mean they appreciate when I can't think in class because of my fatigue or when I fall asleep. Lately, I've been worse because of Landon, Harry, and Tyler's mood swings. It seems to be Tyler's turn tonight, not that I blame him. He saw his dad, the man that abused him his whole life and he's still so traumatized that he can't handle the eruption of emotions flowing from the encounter.

"We'll do the dishes," Art elbows Jonah into an agreement.

"But this is your mountain time," I yawn, resting my head against the table. Art shrugs at me care-freely.

"May and Junie have really stepped up this year." He says. "Besides, you've helped me out a lot over the years."

"Thanks," I yawn again, my eyes fluttering shut. It'll be so *nice* to sleep through the night, especially falling asleep this early in the evening. Sleep is something I desperately need. Lee watches the children during the day but he refuses to get up when they cry even when he wakes up to their cries. Landon, Louis, and Rennie are usually passed out and now usually sleep the night in the barn. Tyler takes his medication at night and that knocks him out until morning. Harry is the only one that gets up at night but he won't clean up Conan or Kennedy when they wet themselves or the bed. I wonder what my family would do if I started saying no to them. Besides my dad's income, I seem to be the rock holding us together.

A scream wakes me up, a pain-filled wail. When I come to my sense I realize it is me screaming. I'm on the floor, my arm bent at an awkward angle. The kitchen chair I fell asleep on is half lying on me, and half on the floor.

"Shut up!" Landon scowls at me, kicking another chair. I listen to him, scared at what I'm waking up to. Jonah rushes to my side and helps me up, carefully bending my arm to a correct angle. It's a painful movement and when he feels my arm, it hurts my elbow.

"What happened?" I ask, leaning heavily on Jonah. Pierre picks up my chair. *Jesus, I offer this pain to those who endure chronic pain.*

"Tyler's still out there," Harry glares at me, arms crossed over his chest from his perch on the table. Then he turns his glare to Jonah, who urged his wrath by helping me stand up.

"How long was I asleep?" I ask Landon, who is cursing some more. My neck is sore, with a crick in it from where I had it leaning against the table. With a sheepish look Jonah catches, I wipe off the puddle of drool with my sweater sleeve. He rolls his eyes at me.

"I don't know but it's midnight," Art smiles at me while putting cards into a pack. Pierre is putting the crib pegs into the board. Apparently, I slept through them shuffling cards near my head.

"We try to put the children to bed around eight." I yawn, wiping eye guck out of the corners of my eyes. If I fell asleep at eight I got four hours of sleep, my usual for nights lately.

"Col's coming," Art stands up with a stretch. Well, it looks like four hours of sleep is all I'm getting. We'll have to go out looking for Tyler and take care of him when he gets here, watching to make sure he doesn't drown in his puke or overdose on drugs. I worry about him but not my cousins. Rennie and Louis drink and do drugs until they are severely intoxicated but they never get to the point where they might kill themselves from it, at least not suddenly in OD. Their hard life is killing them slowly.

"Not fast enough," Landon huffs. Harry slaps his back and they have one of their triplet telepathic conversations where the rest of us watch in silence. Barely any emotions flash across their faces but they read the other's little lip twitches and blinks and winks and eyebrow lifts in a secret language we don't understand.

"BJ should be watching out for him," Pierre speaks up as he pushes into a kitchen chair. I stand up, pushing mine in as well. BJ is a Watson but he isn't a faith-filled one, he's known to get buzzed, sometimes drunk, and find his way home like that, usually after a fight or making some kind of mess with the jocks of the school. He stands by his cousins, something the jocks don't like.

"Tyler doesn't listen to anybody when he's high," Landon hisses out, pounding on the door when he doesn't see Col's truck lights appearing in the driveway. I stare at his fists, scared at how hard he hits the logs. At least he's hitting the wall, not a person.

"We should pray," I state. Landon scoffs bitterly, Pierre nods in agreement and Harry stares at me contemplatively. "While we're waiting," I add, my stomach flopping in my body. I'm scared for Tyler, worried about him using the drugs his dad gave him. How much can someone take before they overdose?

"Won't hurt, eh?" Art shrugs. Pierre hands him a rosary from his pocket. It warms my heart when Jonah pulls one out from under his shirt and lifts it over his head. It's a white, metal rosary that contrasts deeply with the black shirt and hoodie he is wearing.

"Well shit," Landon sighs, releasing some pent-up anger with a few stomps of his feet. Harry grabs two rosaries from the wall and shares one with his brother. One has holy water from Lourdes and the other one was touched by St. Mother Teresa. They are very powerful rosaries. We are lucky to have them.

"Pierre, would you like to lead us?" I ask, sitting on the floor with my back against the fridge. He's the baby of his family, probably was led in prayer unless he went up to the mountain so I want to give him the opportunity to lead us, his friends and cousins, in prayer.

"Precious Blood?" He looks around to see what everyone else thinks. Only I nod at him, the others don't know how to pray the Precious Blood rosary. "In nomine, et Patre, et Filiae, et Spiritui Sancti. Amen." Pierre makes the Sign of the Cross in Latin, confusing the boys but he prays the rosary in English. *First Mystery: The Nailing of the Right Hand of our Lord Jesus.* "O most Precious Blood of Jesus Christ heal the wounds in the most Sacred Heart of Jesus..."

"Amen!" I finish making the Sign of the Cross. Landon sniffs before stomping out of the house. Harry nods at me and Pierre before following his brother.

"That was powerful," Jonah laughs, especially when his voice cracks. We all pause when we hear Conan whimpering in his sleep, headlights filtering down the driveway. Col is arriving.

"I'll go make sure he's okay," I stifle a yawn.

"I got it," Lee jumps off the top bunk. My eyes widen in surprise. He didn't join us in prayer, I hadn't even known he got home.

"Thank you," I reply as Jonah drags me out of the house when Landon and Harry holler for us to hurry up. I guess I'm going to a party. I did just get the boys to pray with me so when I am pushed into the middle front seat of Col's truck, oddly absent of Danae, I stay quiet while they converse. It's a short drive to town but we aren't sure where Tyler is. The boys all look out the windows while I pray, first the Holy Wounds rosary, then the Chaplet of Divine Providence for Tyler's safety and healing. The longer it takes to find him, the more ornery Landon gets. It frustrates Col so I elbow him when we drive close to a street light, showing him the rosary moving between my fingertips. Col shakes his head with a smile, lifting up the Cross from his. It's the knotted rosary and he has it lopped on a belt buckle to dangle from his jeans. We grin at each other like we are sharing a secret: trust in God.

"Of course," Landon huffs, pointing at the party house. People are milling about outside as music blasts from the inside. "He chose to party at the Martel mansion."

"Dumbass," Harry mutters scornfully. "Who knows what shit they'd do to him."

"We'll split up." Col decides, shutting his truck off after he parks on the edge of the street. I look at the huge house, multiple big windows, large front lawn, and one of the biggest lots in town. Cars are parked double-breasted along the loop driveway. With the darkness of fall, the house looks like a carved pumpkin with a candle lit in it. "Jonah and Art, Harry and Landon, and I'll take Pierre and Daisy."

"Sounds good," Landon mutters.

"Keep an eye on the goody two shoes." Harry waves at me and Pierre before taking off. He's not making fun of us, just pointing out our naiveness from our sheltered lives. We don't party.

"Don't take any drinks, cups, or baked food from anyone," Col helps me hop out of the driver's door after him as he speaks. He closes the door while casually wrapping an arm around my shoulders. "People will be friendly for the most part, smile and nod along even if you never talk to them. Our parents can handle the booze better than these young kids."

"Yeah, okay," I reply, my heart skipping a beat in concern about his words. Drunkenness sets me off. I devote myself to internal prayer as I scan teenagers stumbling around, multiple couples making out, and people dancing provocatively in the living room, everyone visiting, practically yelling over the raucous noise level from the bass-shattering music. It makes me shrink into myself as Col steers me into the kitchen, checking over his shoulder for Pierre. People smile as we pass by, asking about Leo and Danae and commenting on our outfits which hadn't changed from when they saw us earlier today. I feel safe in Col's arms, the protector that he is; so when he hears the scuffle coming from the kitchen and takes off, my nerves become more apparent.

"You think we should follow?" I ask Pierre. He shrugs at me, shoulders hunched in and his hands in his jean pockets. He doesn't like it here and seeing him with his hood on makes me wish I brought a hood to lessen the sound of music blasting in my ears. I shrug back, stumbling from someone knocking on me. She turns to me, a drunken apologetic smile on her face before bursting into giggles. I shoot her a thumbs up before walking through a cleared space. *Lord, I don't know what to do and I want to start judging them. Help me to interact with everyone mercifully.* When we get to the kitchen Sadie is sitting on the floor crying against the island, Betty and April doing their best to comfort the sobbing girl. My heart melts into compassion so I kneel on the floor, bringing her in for a hug and making the sign of the cross over her. Bad things happen at parties and it looks like something bad happened to her.

"Back the f—k up!" Col shouts, barely heard over the music as he jumps between Harry and Landon and a drunk guy holding onto the counter for support. Harry punches Col, fists flying through his fury. Col does his best to defend himself without retaliating but with Landon helping his brother it's not the best idea. Col starts throwing hands too when the guy falls to the floor and Landon stomps on his face.

"F—king - touch - my cousin - again," Harry threatens with every kick to the man's stomach while Landon has Col distracted. It's a wonder no one else has joined in to stop them but then I remember everyone is afraid of the Smith Triplets. I look to the horrible fight scene that makes my stomach queasy and to Sadie crying in my arms. *O Jesus, I surrender myself to You. You take care of it.* Seemingly out of the blue

BJ jumps into the fray, pushing Harry back. *Thank You, Lord, for Your Divine intervention.* The music is cut off suddenly, leaving the sounds in the room awkwardly. Sadie looks around in despair, trying to hide her face with her hair.

"Let's take you home," Betty inserts herself between us, wrapping her arms around Sadie. I nod at her to thank her. She nods back, rubbing circles on Sadie's back and humming soft little words to her. I don't want to ask Sadie, or anyone, what happened. It doesn't look good.

"We'll take her home," April shoots me a polite smile, taking Sadie's other side.

"I'm going to f—king kill you if I ever hear or see you trying to take advantage of another girl," Landon stomps on the guy's face. With a saddened heart I recognize him. It's one of the guys in that truck that wanted me to pick up garbage. Of course, I know him, this is a small town. With the certainty laced through Landon's words, I believe him.

"You just about did," BJ snaps, slapping Harry's shoulder before running to the front door. He's probably going to stay with Sadie, and offer her a male presence to feel protected.

"Let's go find Tyler," Landon huffs, wiping blood from his knuckles onto his white shirt. It's a horrible contrast. "F—king pedophile."

"Jonah, go get a vehicle from your house," Col commands. Teenagers standing around the kitchen see that the excitement is over and start to leave, gossiping about what went down in their slurred tongues. When Jonah stands frozen, staring at the body, Col snaps. "Run!"

"Holy shit," Art's face pales when he pushes through the receding crowd. He drops to his knees to look for a pulse. Col leans on the counter, staring at everyone and evaluating what to do.

"Art, Pierre, you take this guy to the hospital when Jonah gets back. He's heavy and out cold so you guys might have to carry him. Grab a blanket if you need to. Try to wake him up, sit him up or lay him sideways." Col lists off, reaching for my hand. I let him grab it numbly.

I've sort of seen this side of Col but never so clearly before. He's cool and collected but most of all calm even with his heavy breathing and the red swellings on his face. His left hand absently rubs against one of his pecs where I see a hole in his shirt. Col was the only one brave enough to go against the triplets, knowing how vicious they get. "We'll find Tyler and get the hell out of here."

"Heavens yes," I manage a grin but my stomach is in knots. Sadie might have been sexually assaulted, Landon and Harry already got into a fight, and Tyler is hopped up on drugs. Col shoves past people, dragging me along. He searches the living room, a den, a library, a pantry, and two bathrooms before we trot upstairs. The music doesn't lessen and a headache forms in my head so I offer the pain up for everyone here to be safe. Col barges into a bathroom throw open a shower curtain and opens cupboards before dragging me down the hallway. I make the sign of the cross, praying the Precious Blood rosary. It calms me down immensely and I add on nine Memorare's for Tyler, Sadie, and the guy that Landon and Harry beat up. Col stalks into the master bedroom of the mansion, I'm amazed at its size. We can easily fit two of my dad's cabins in here, that's not including their him and her walk-in closets. The richness of people in this small town astonishes me, we have so many poor and hungry here that they could be helping. Jesus asked us to feed the hungry, clothe the naked, visit the imprisoned, and care for the sick. They have so much space to do so! I take a deep breath, worrying I am getting into judging territory as Col slams open the bathroom door.

"F—k!" Col hisses out, dropping to his knees by the oversized bathtub. Tyler is wrapped in somebody's blankets, passed out to the world. His skin is pale, his bright blue veins sticking out more than normal, thick cords against his white skin. "Here," Col hands me his keys and his phone before scooping Tyler into his arms. "We'll drive him to the hospital, I have a Naloxone kit in my truck. You drive."

"Okay," I squeak out. I manage to make the sign of the cross over Tyler's limp body when Col passes me. People scurry out of his way when they see him carrying Tyler. The music is loud but I can hear Harry and Landon hollering for their brother, the sound is a distant thrum in my head. My fingers caress my rosary beads in both pants pockets, one with Holy Water from Lourdes, the other a relic from St. Carlo, a new saint. Dickie had given it to me, having been given it by one of his cousins. *St. Carlo Acutis, pray for us. St. Bernadette, pray for us. Our Lady of Lourdes, pray for us. Queen of Peace, pray for us. Holy Mother of God, pray for us. Virgin Most Powerful, pray for us.* One of the Martel's stares at us, a smirk on his face before he pulls over a mask of concern.

"You want me to come?" he asks.

"F—k no," Landon hisses, walking out of a bedroom.

"You take him," Col thrusts Tyler into his brother's arms. "I'll move my garbage, get the meds. Daisy's driving."

"Harry's in the backyard," Landon states, grunting at Tyler's weight.

"Okay," Col concedes. "I'll take Daisy to the truck then go get him." With that, he grabs my arm and drags me behind him again. I run after him, glad to see my running days kept me fast. In my concern my thoughts and prayers are muddled, not making sense to human standards but God knows what is in my heart. *Holy God, Holy Mighty One, Holy Immortal One, have mercy on us and on the whole world...*

33

Scaffolding Failure

"Col!" I grin at Col, way too strongly for a greeting.

"What do you want?" He deadpans, setting his cowboy hat on the rack by the door. He holds a chair out for Danae and pushes her in when she sits down. Louis and Rennie took off drinking after work today, Lee is out for a run, and Sally Anne is actually putting the babies to bed. Windsor and the children are playing outside while they can, winter boots and mitts in the darkening light even though the snow has melted and frozen mud into little ruts.

"A ride to town," I laugh sheepishly. "Sold the moped and I can't legally drive yet but I wanted to bring this chocolate cake to Landon and Harry for their first day at work."

"You're so sweet," Dani laughs, pulling the cake closer to her. She inhales deeply, nodding at the aroma greeting her nostrils.

"Nah uh uh," I pull my cake back. It's a recipe ingrained in my head. "They deserve some gratitude and love for this decision they made. One of the clauses was that they won't drink or do drugs. We have to support them in their journey!"

"I gotta drop Danae back home so I don't mind," Col shrugs, pulling the deck of cards to him from the windowsill. It fit widthways between two potted herbs.

"Great," I chirp, "let's go."

"Who's gonna watch the kids?" Col raises an eyebrow, taking the cards out of the pack to shuffle. It's a loud noise in the quiet room. Sally Anne glares at him to be quiet, gesturing to the sleeping babies. I don't speak up, knowing from experience the babies can sleep through yelling and fighting. Sally Anne is trying to help out so I'm going to respect her decision. Col chuckles and dramatizes putting the cards away.

"Tyler," I say simply.

"They let him out?" Col asks, leaning over the table to inspect the cake. "Damn Rosie, you got cream cheese icing too!"

"They deserve a treat," I shrug my jean jacket over my sweater and button it up. The doctor had Tyler stay overnight twice to keep an eye on him and to check on all his bruises and swellings, even x-raying him. "They had a rough couple of days."

"We all did," Col snorts. The guy Landon and Harry beat up tried pressing charges on them, quoting BJ and Col in it as well. Col got into a fight with Chris and Karl because they found out about his and Danae's relationship. Sadie hasn't been in school since the incident. The Watsons all know but don't really know because Sadie told Harvey and his wife not to tell anyone but we're all praying for her.

"I heard my name," Tyler mumbles, sitting up in bed with a groan. He's not been feeling the greatest since his relapse, and guilt is making him even sicker.

"Col's driving me to town to pick up Harry and Landon. You are in charge until Lee or my dad get back." I say firmly, squinting at him. I've left Landon and Harry in charge but never Tyler, first, he was too injured, then sick from withdrawals, then we noticed his uncomfortableness around the children. I'm done having no work pity him. We worked so hard to keep him clean, and to have mercy and he took our hard work for granted. He has to be better this time for the same kind of mercy. I'm tired. Tired of the drunkenness and drugs, the late nights and lack of sleep, the too many voices melding into each other, and having to take care of everyone with no one taking care of me. Pierre, Col, Jonah, and Art step up around me but they don't live with me. School and work are what are mandatory for me to complete. I'm sad to say I only get to daily mass twice a week now, usually on Mondays and Saturdays. My personal relationship with God has become impersonal, I no longer feel like His cherished daughter. With Rennie, Louis, Harry, and Landon all working now I can't go to the mountain to pray because Tyler doesn't pay any attention and I give Lee a break from watching the youngest three or four children during the day. It isn't fair to saddle the children on him. Phil, Percy, Peter, Paul, Shawn, and Julia have offered to babysit the children but my nieces, nephews, and cousin aren't their problem. Corinne can't handle the children unless Dickie and Peter are with her and that is never during the day because Dickie has to run Big Patrick and Big Peter's farm and Little Peter has to run his construction business. He needs another week for some parts for the house to come in and then my family can move into the mansion. Paul is still going through his divorce, something he really doesn't want but can't move around. No papers are signed because Amy is asking for alimony, child tax, and everything under the sun which is not fair. Paul will be the one watching their three children while running his hotels. He's super tired, overworked, and emotionally drained. In my fatigued state, I have pity for him. Shawn has two under three and another one on the way, and Julia has three under five and another one on the way. Phil can't take on additional children while trying to fit back into his family after six months away and night terrors that keep him up at night. Percy is in the off-season for fire fighting but spends early mornings training with Phil, Francis, and Louis and helps Dickie, Big Peter and Big Patrick on the farm in the mornings, then helps Audrina homeschool their children, along with Julia's oldest son and Phil's children.

"I can!" Sally Anne puts pillows around Philomena and Tikara so they don't roll over and fall off the bed. Then she bounces over to me with a brilliant smile beaming on her face. "You can trust me."

"Can you partner with Tyler?" I ask, not wanting to put a damper on her ambition today, more so this evening. Something in the smile was a little too... eager. If I'm out, then she has the run of the house with all the adults gone. Tyler won't put up a fight if she decides to party. Apparently, she has before, according to her older brothers.

"That works," she mutters. She spins on her heel and strides to the living room, flopping on the couch. She's dying for a phone, begging my dad for at least an iPod. It's an expense we cannot afford.

"Landon and Harry work weekends too, then?" Col asks, throwing an arm around Danae. She leans into his body, smiling somewhat secretively. I stare at Col, worried for him. He's tempting bad things with his relationship with the younger girl and he doesn't seem to care. Everyone around the school has seen them together. It's only a matter of time before Drake finds out. They're hiding because they don't have their parents' blessings but that means they should wait and pray long and hard about it.

"Saturdays," I reply, realizing I have to cut the cake now so the boys can eat it there. I pull it to the end of the table and take the lid off, sighing deeply at the aroma wafting up. I'm a wonderful baker.

"Good for them," Col says. Dani whispers something to make him shake his head with a chuckle. I quickly grab a butter knife from the drawer to cut the cake. When I turn to the table Danae has it sitting in front of her.

"Don't you dare!" I pull the cake back.

"I can have a piece there though, can't I?" Dani sends a sucking-up grin my way. The naive maturity in her eyes makes me blink. She used to never have this known-it-all way about her bossy attitude.

"Once I give it to the boys it's not mine to give away," I answer, cutting the cake pretty crookedly for my standards. The boys won't mind, as long as they get a piece. Landon swears he's gained weight since living here and eating cake or some sweet dessert baked good every night, usually baked fresh with Makayla helping me. Snacks are super expensive to buy, time savers but expensive and not as holistic as making them.

"I'm dropping you off first, Princess." Col kisses Danae's head, close to her ear. They're spending more and more time together. It's worrying me. *Lord Jesus, take this worry. Give me peace to rest in your Will.* "Looks better if Daisy is with me."

"Huh?" I gasp, mostly exaggerated for effect. "Are you using me?"

"Drake already threatened me about dating Dani." Col shrugs, fingers drumming on the table. I don't think Danae sees the anxious look that flashes across Col's face before he schools his features. "At that time I wasn't interested in her but that's changed and he made it very clear what he would do if I ever did start up with her." Col frowns, picking something out of his teeth as he glances at his girlfriend. The question is simmering in his eyes: is she worth whatever will come?

"You can leave anytime now," Sally Anne deadpans, sitting up on the couch. She brushes crumbs off her clothes. Conan had escaped the kitchen with his snack last night and I'd asked Rennie to clean it up. It's apparent he hadn't.

"Okay," I put the lid on the cake, offering the knife to Danae to lick off. She takes it with a happy smile. "The children have to go to bed soon, and you stay up half an hour later to make sure they're in bed but you have to go to bed right after that."

"I know, Daisy." Sally Anne rolls her eyes at me. I kick on my work boots. They are waterproof and slightly thicker than my running shoes on the frozen ground.

"I should be home in an hour. Uncle Duncan or any of the boys can be home whenever so we'll know if you didn't listen." I warn, pulling a toque Marie Watson knitted for me over my head. With my poofy hair it barely stays on but it's better than nothing. Then I slip on matching mitts. The pan is metal and will get cold pretty fast.

"Yeah, yeah, bye," Sally Anne waves sassily. Danae sticks her tongue out at the tween.

"I'll hold down the fort," Tyler groans as he sits up. Then he rubs his stomach as he stares at the cake pan in my hands. "Maybe save a piece for me?"

"Depends on how helpful Sally Anne says you are," I shoot my cousin a wink before stepping out the front door.

"Thought you can't give it away once you give it away," Danae retorts, flipping her hood over her head to protect herself from the wind chill.

"He doesn't know that," I grin widely.

"Did Daisy Ridel tell a half-truth?" Dani gasps dramatically.

"A half-truth is a full lie," Col intones ever so wisely.

"I'm sorry guys!" I wail, my eyes widening in panic. I hadn't meant to lie, I'd forgotten I was giving the cake away, still thinking it was mine. Besides what I said to Dani was a joke! "I made a mistake!"

"We're just bugging," Col laughs at me. Danae slaps my back.

"You're not the only one who can tease," she hops into the passenger seat.

"You're giving the cake away, Aunty?" Windsor runs up to me, Tinsley and Makayla behind him. Conan and Kennedy are busy trying to ride Sugar, who gives me a very unimpressed look.

"Yes Windsor," I pull him in for a hug while I have the chance. "I made it as a gift."

"Can you make me one, as a gift?" He asks, grinning cheekily at me. A laugh bursts out of me. Way to bend the rules so he doesn't need to share.

"I can't promise that but I will think about it." I open the back seat door and slide the cake towards the middle.

"Oh, me too!" Micks and Tin-tin chime in. I pull them in for hugs as well, surprised at the heat wafting off of them. They've been playing hard. It means they'll sleep well tonight.

"I'll think about it," I laugh, gently pushing them away. "You guys listen to Sally Anne and Tyler."

"We will," Windsor grins at me. It's such a Sally Anne expression with the sucking up and slightly sneaky wink.

"Sit up front with us," Dani grins at me as she pats the seat. "We need to play some hand games."

"I don't know if I remember any," I smile sheepishly, running to the passenger seat. I haven't played them in so long that I forgot how. Col starts the drive to town as Danae teaches me the song and hand motions to Miss Mary Mac. Either Dani or I lose concentration and mess up, bursting into giggles before trying again. We never make it to the end, one of us accidentally slapping the other. My cheeks hurt from smiling, the first time in a while, maybe since the triplets moved in with us.

"Bye, Col." Dani quickly kisses the corner of his lip before her dad's house comes into view. I grunt when she crawls over me and pushes me into the middle seat. My elbow stings when she smacks it into the seat belt buckle.

"Bye, Princess," Col smiles when he pulls into Drake's driveway but his eyes glaze over in worry when we both spot Drake and Karl peeking out the living room window. "Shit," Col hisses under his breath. His window is unrolled even with the cold air floating in.

"Bye Daisy!" Danae turns back to the truck with an exaggerated wave. She must have seen her dad too.

"Bye Dani!" I holler out the passenger window, clicking my seatbelt on. With Danae's actions, I feel used, as if she wanted me here just to prove her point of singleness to her father, which is the truth. Col dropped her off first so her dad could see me with them. Drake wouldn't think bad things about me, no one does.

"It was nice seeing you be a kid again," Col reverses out of Drake's driveway. "Laughing and giggling and relaxing. Not trying to take care of everyone else."

"It was nice," I say wistfully, fixing my toque on my head. My thick hair was pushing it off. Giggling about little things, making carefree mistakes that won't have horrible consequences. The lack of responsibility in our relationship, it's refreshing. Maybe I should listen to the Watsons and lift some chores from my shoulders. I'll run myself into the ground before I graduate and start a family of my own if that is God's plan for me. It's my cross to carry, I just have to figure out how to carry it without straining my back.

"We could ditch dropping the cake off," Col grins mischievously, rubbing his hands together. My heart jumps in my chest, not seeing his hands firmly on the steering wheel. "Keep it for ourselves. Kick back this evening."

"Rude," I scoff, sticking my tongue out at him. My heart slows down when he grabs the steering wheel with his hands and turns into the business side of town. "And super duper, absolutely, totally selfish."

"Jeez, make me feel cheap," Col pretends to pout.

"Not my fault my baking is delicious," I shrug, a wide smile staying on my face. C'mon Col, admit it was the Creator that gave me the gift!

"Uh, kinda is," Col chuckles, turning into Peter's construction lot. I throw my head back with a groan.

"You were supposed to say God did it for me," I laugh while flapping my arms around in a dramatic outraged motion.

"Don't go getting religious on me now," Col shoots back playfully but there is a biting edge to his words. *Lord, help me to talk to Col, comfort him, and counsel him as Your Holy Spirit and angels do for me.* I stare at Col, contemplating my next words to him. They could backfire and completely upset him or he could get some help for whatever his problem is. I'm pretty sure I know what his problem is now: his rising feelings for Danae. Adults are telling him to back off, his dad, her dad, his brother, my dad, and teachers who are sticking their necks out by getting involved in Col and Danae's personal life. I want to be one of those people, tell him they can wait but that's probably not what he wants to hear.

"Four years is the blink of an eye compared to an eternity," I say softly.

"I know," Col sighs, gearing his truck down into the park. "I know but I don't want to." He lifts his cowboy hat off his head and runs his hands through his hair with a frustrated sigh. "I haven't even slept with her. Don't plan on it but I don't want to lose her to time."

"It's her choice, too," I say ever so wisely. *Holy Spirit send your wisdom down on Col. Amen.*

"If she had her way we'd be living together already," Col huffs. It's followed by a sad little laugh and a bittersweet smile.

"Pray about it," I offer, frowning at Harry and Landon arguing with their cousins Avery and Shawn. Why is there already tension on their first day of work? They only came after school so it's been less than five hours.

"Yeah, maybe," Col states, blocking his emotions.

"It doesn't look like I should bring cake over there," I point to Landon holding Harry back from shoving Shawn. Col nods, his fingers drumming on his thighs.

"Let's go interrupt," I jump out of Col's lifted Dodge, glancing at the back seat where my cake is sitting. It might be a good peace offering. I shrug and bring it along, hoping for the best.

"Oh my God, Daisy, what are you doing here?" Harry groans, glaring at me. I take offense, not knowing what I did now to upset him.

"He's not mad at you," Landon quickly informs me before slapping his brother. "Don't take it out on Daisy!"

"Oh, so only you can?" Harry shoves Landon. The oldest triplet doesn't respond, his jaw ticking as he stares his brother down.

"Low f—king blow."

"What's wrong?" I ask, standing in the little circle that was formed. Avery shakes his head at me.

"Heyyy, kid," Shawn throws an arm over my shoulder, his eyes lighting up at the cake pan in my hands. "What's that?" His words are loud as he tries peeking at the dessert. I realize it is to get Harry and Landon's attention off each other.

"Chocolate cake with cream cheese icing," I say, offering a bright smile the two triplets way. Tears well up in Harry's eyes as he scoffs at me.

"Thanks but not now, Rosie," Landon says curtly before turning back to his brother and whispering heatedly to him. Col and I share confused glances before looking to Avery and Shawn for clarification.

"What happened?" I whisper, not as quietly as I'd hoped when Harry blows up at me.

"I f—ked up Daisy!" He screams at me, stomping forward. "All I was thinking about was the mess Tyler made and Landon beating you up and the talk we had on that ride and how I told you some stupid shit you shouldn't believe and I wasn't watching what I was doing and I f—king killed someone!"

I gulp, backstepping when he shoves forward, Landon trying to hold him back. Harry kicks my shin before a hand slips through, knocking my cake to the ground.

"Stop the hissy fit," Col laughs angrily, stepping between us. "F—k, you guys need to learn to control yourselves. Grow up!"

"Screw you," Harry turns his wrath to Col. I see now that it was Col's plan. My hands are shaking so I can't pick up my cake, it fell lid first on the ground and now all the icing is stuck to the lid and dirt got on the cream cheese when I lift the pan up, the cake falling out.

"Hey, I got it, Daisy," Shawn says softly, placing a hand on mine to stop them from shaking as he picks up my cake with his other one. Landon joins Harry in trying to fight Col. They always stick together. My whole body trembles, remembering the way Harry held my wrist and Landon shoved me around. Tears slip down my cheeks.

"C'mon guys," Avery jumps between the three boys. "Uncle Dickie already has a prayer vigil set up. We'll go to church, pray it all out."

"Pray to the God that let this happen?" Harry scoffs bitterly. "F—k that."

Pray. Right. I grew up praying. Why didn't I think to start praying when I got scared? I make the Sign of the Cross over myself and devote myself to the Chaplet of Divine Mercy. The prayer and God's love give me the strength to stand up with Shawn's help.

"He's not dead," Shawn speaks up. "Just injured. We should all pray for God's Divine Providence before he does die."

"He's probably dead!" Harry hisses, pulling his hair out of the man bun he always keeps it in.

"No!" I shout. The boys all turn to me. "Where is your hope? Huh, Harry? Surrender to God. Hope in His Will. God can change his mind! Where is your hope?" I chastise him, quite angry myself. More tears stream down my face as my throat aches. "What happened to 'this is home'? Have I not taught you anything? My mom was dead for a year before I found out but I still *hoped* I could meet her! I still *hope* I will see her in the afterlife, preferably in heaven!"

"Stop yelling at me!" Harry retorts, slightly as a reaction but mostly in shock that I yelled at him.

"Why?" I stomp toward him. "This is how you treat me!" Harry's Adam's apple bobs before his ice blue eyes stare at the ground, guilt filling them. His fingers flex. Col casually steps beside me, ready to defend. Landon kicks the ground before walking in a circle around us. Shawn sets my cake on the hood of his truck, watching us carefully with Avery. *I'm sorry Lord, for getting fed up with everything, for not having patience and not loving mercifully.* "I just want to *love* you!" I whisper, my voice is hoarse as I launch myself into Harry's body. He grunts when I hit him, his arms reflexively wrapping around me. My tears wet his shirt as I squeeze him tight. "Let me love you, Harry. Let us and God all love you."

"I didn't put a pin in properly. All the scaffolding fell. Guy broke his back." Harry huffs out. I hold on tight, tethering us together.

"Hope Harry, believe. Trust in God." My voice is muffled against his sweater. "And pray with us."

"I guess we're going to church." Landon slaps Harry's back with a forced grin. I grab his hand and squeeze it. Once, twice, three times. *I love you, brother.* And again, once, twice, thrice, four times. *God loves you, brother.*

"I'll drive them," Col offers. Shawn hands him the cake.

"I'll get to church. I have to check up on the fam first. Roxy only got a vague text and is probably worrying." Shawn joins my and Harry's hug. With another forced grin, Landon joins as well.

"C'mon, Col," I smile cheekily.

"Join up," Avery chimes, wrapping his arms around Landon and Shawn. Harry and I are stuck in the middle, especially after Col completes the hug. My shoulders start to hurt, sore from being squished between the men.

"Peace be with you all," Shawn releases us from his bear hug. Avery waves goodbye as we all repeat Shawn's words back to him. I love his St. Francis greeting, and storing it for further use by myself.

"We don't need to talk," I say, holding onto Harry's hand and pulling him behind me. I want to offer him a safe place to be emotional, and get himself together after exhausting himself of feelings. "That's up to you."

"Nah," he opens the back seat door. Even when he is emotionally wrecked he still puts Landon before him. It's a selfless, brotherly bond that makes my eyes water. The boys can be as good as they are bad. "Let's just pray. What's that one you always wake up saying?"

"The rosary?" I beam at him as I climb into the backseat. He sits in the middle seat and lays his head on my shoulder.

"Yeah that one," Harry replies, shutting his eyes. "Let's pray that one. I want my mama. I miss my mama."

"Me too," I sigh, leaning my head on his as I pull out two rosaries. One for me and one for him. Col has two up front if Landon hasn't started carrying one around from living with me and my dad. "But we have a mama just waiting for us to ask for her love." Without further ado, we begin praying. *I believe in God... Our Father... Hail Mary... Hail Mary... Hail Mary... Glory Be... O my Jesus...* We only get to the first decade by the time we arrive in the church parking lot. My heart opens in gratitude for God's people coming together for Harry and the injured man. Dickie, Peter, Paul, Percy, Phil, and about five other vehicles are in the parking lot.

We walk up the steps silently, Landon throwing an arm over Harry's shoulder. I'm standing on his other side, holding Harry's hand but really Harry is clamping onto mine. He's relying on me, trying to trust someone human. I'm praying he will trust in our Father up in heaven. Col trails behind, slightly nervous about entering the church building he hasn't been in in years. The Watsons and a handful of other people are praying the rosary as we make our way to the front, sitting behind the rest of the Watsons in the first three pews. Harry cries when we kneel, full-out bawling soon after. I pray the rosary, urging Mama Mary to cover him with her mantle, as I rub circles on his back. It's my turn now to catch his tears and I do so without complaint. Around me, I can hear a few other people sniffle and sigh. We pray the Chaplet of Divine Mercy, the Precious Blood rosary, the Chaplet of Faith, the St. Bernadette rosary, and both Franciscan Crown rosaries. Both Phil and Percy have to leave to put their children to bed and Dickie and Pierre have to close up the soup kitchen but Shawn and Avery replace them, along with Danae's family, Jonah and Larry. Harry kneels through the full two hours of prayer while the rest of us give up and sit down or stand up to bring relief to our sore knees. I don't think I've ever seen a more guilt-ridden man. Harry desperately wants his coworker to live. My knees are sore and aching because my juvenile arthritis is acting up but I kneel down and offer up my pain and discomfort for Harry and the injured man when Fr. John brings out the Blessed Sacrament into the monstrance. If the visionaries kneel for Mama Mary when she appears to them I can kneel for Jesus when He is in front of me. Another hour passes by while we all pray silently and separately, worshiping, thanking, praising, and asking. My heart is so full and joyous at all the support Harry is receiving. I pray hard, full of heart, and very earnestly. Jesus gives us the time of day when we call on Him so I can do my best to be present with Him. The goal is to focus on prayer when we get distracted. Distraction is Satan's tool and we don't want him to win. We end adoration of the Blessed Sacrament off with singing Holy God, We Praise Thy Name. A phone rings right when we finish when Jonah is leaving to take Larry home and some elderly couples want to get home before it gets too dark. In the midst I see my old boss exiting the doors.

All the people in the church are related or are pretty close friends with the Watsons. I wonder silently where she fits in.

"Hello?" Peter answers the phone at the back of the church. While everyone else shut off their phones and left them in jacket pockets or in the back or in their vehicles he had put his ringer to full blast because the hospital was going to be calling him about workers' compensation. Peter closes his eyes and jams his fist in the air with a brilliant smile. "Okay, thank you."

"What is it?" Harry asks, licking his lips. He's still kneeling. "Tell me!"

"Doctors can't figure it out," Peter beams with a laugh, hugging Pierre, who is the closest person to him. "They were trying to do surgery, all the scans said he was paralyzed but he can wiggle his toes! Praise God!"

"God is good!" Landon shouts, slumping into a pew and wiping his face with his hands.

"All the time!" Jonah, Pierre, BJ, and I shout back, smiles erupting on all the drawn-out, exhausted faces. Earnest prayer is hard work.

"God is good!" Landon shouts again.

"All the time!" Paul, Peter, and Percy join in our chant this time. The elders stare at us, probably never having seen this done in church.

"God is good!" Landon elbows Harry to respond.

"All the time!" Dickie, Rory, Phil, and Harvey chime in this time as well, accepting the belief of the next generation.

"God is good!" Landon and Pierre both elbow Harry this time, who kneels in the gloom.

"All the time!" Everyone else shouts, even Fr. John. I clasp my hands to my chest, tears welling up in my eyes. This is such a beautiful moment!

"God is good!" Landon shouts again, everyone seems to be staring at Harry, waiting for him to shout the response. I look at everyone else, judging their backgrounds, and their belief from the years I've worshipped God and celebrated mass with them. I'm looking for the saint in our midst, the saint who healed Tyler's leg, and now, the saint who healed a paralyzed man. My faith is strong, I know that, but even I find it hard to believe I have seen, maybe touched, and even talked to a living saint. *Praise God!*

"All the time!"

34

Pastor McGregor

———⟫◦⟪———

A h," I sigh deeply, staring at the large Crucifix hanging upon the altar. My heart seems to sigh in peace as well. "Home sweet home."

"This is church." Makayla looks quizzically at me before running down the aisle, chasing after Windsor, who is a stomper when he runs. Tinsley leans into my thigh, arms wrapped around my upper leg. When I twist to dip my hand in the holy water she bumps into the stand. She flinches but stays quiet, careening around my leg to look at all the people already in the church. Per usual, we missed the rosary because someone always sleeps in or decides to have a bad morning. This time it was Tikara crying, we think she is getting sick.

"Sign of the Cross with holy water," I softly order Tinsley, showing her what I mean as I cross myself. She follows, getting her shoulders mixed up. I cross Philomena, my right arm is sore from carrying her car seat with her in it. I'm not used to the weight. Usually, we take her out to bring her to church but now it's too cold to do so. It doesn't help that Conan had jumped on my back when he was climbing out of the truck. Landon took the opportunity to set him on my shoulders. I didn't complain because this is the first time in a while Landon hasn't been on a drunk Sunday morning. I bend down so Conan can dip his hand into the holy water font, jumping back when he splashes it on my face.

"That's enough," Dad grasps Conan's hand. "Make the Sign of the Cross and go sit down." Then he shoots me a look to get to our pew. I follow Tyler, Landon, and Lee carrying Tikara in her car seat. Harry is behind me, Kennedy attached to his hip. I like genuflecting for three seconds, one second to thank each member of the Holy Trinity but it's hard with three children surrounding me. I slide down the pew until I get to the middle, Tyler, Landon, Lee, Tikara, Sally Anne, and Windsor to my left. Micks nabs the spot right next to me, squishing tightly against me. Tinsley does the same to my other side while Conan dances on the kneeler. I kneel down, setting Philomena's car seat on the pew before us and dedicating myself to St. Thomas Aquinas's preparatory prayer for mass. It's a short prayer, and very distractedly said when I have to stop Conan from running around and comfort Philomena because she hates car seats. The altar boys usually carry the cross and the candles up by themselves so it warms my heart when Axel Watson and David Barnes ask Windsor to carry the cross and Sally Anne and Makayla to carry the candles. Makayla and Windsor are excited but Sally Anne drags her feet. She doesn't drag her feet for long when she sees the older altar boys walking to the back. Jeremiah Crisp and Bradley are fourteen, used to being altar boys, and here to train the younger ones. I feel like I breathe better, and relax when the girls aren't scrunched up against me. That is until I have to pull Conan in my lap to stop him from moving. His ADHD is bad in the church because he can't walk around or move or be loud. Then I take Philomena out of her car seat because she started crying again. Pierre is in the choir, along with two other Watsons and a couple of other parishioners. The pianist starts up while Paul walks up to the pew.

"Can you read today, Daisy?" he asks, looking back at his dad when Aiden starts to fuss. I love how big the Watson family is, and how Paul can leave his children with the family so he can volunteer in church. I nod at him, curling Philomena in my arms. Lee has Tikara, Harry has Kennedy and my dad somehow ended up with Poppy Watson. Landon and Tyler won't hold the babies so I'm taking Philomena with me. Tinsley tries to walk with me but Landon holds her back, allowing Conan the time to roll under the pew in front of ours and run after me. It's not worth the fight to take him back, besides, some of the Watsons have brought their children to the ambo before. We all huddle in the back room, four altar boys, two readers, and an additional four children. It's slightly cramped but I love it. That means there are plenty of people worshipping the Lord today!

"Let's pray," Fr. John says when he walks past the doors. Conan runs to hug him, causing the priest to smile. The rest of the children line up, shorter ones in front so we can read the prayer hanging on the bulletin board. Paul swings Conan into his arms and stands beside me, also slightly behind me. Philomena fusses in my arms, trying to sit up. I rearrange her in my arms so she can look around. Axel and David wave at her, Makayla follows so she isn't outdone. I cut her a look to pray with the rest of us and when she doesn't listen, I focus on the prayer, hoping she will follow by my example.

"Amen," I make the Sign of the Cross and do so for Philomena as well. It seems to help her stop whining. Paul sets Conan down and grabs the liturgical book of readings, then we all line up at the entrance. Jeremiah goes first with the thurible, Bradley following with the incense and spoon. Windsor is next with the cross, Makayla and Sally Anne slightly behind him. David and Axel are last, hands folded in a similar prayer position. Paul is next, holding the book above his head. I line up behind him, holding onto Conan's hand. If Poppy left my dad he can grab him. As we walk up the aisle we join in singing the gospel song: I Was Full of Joy. We all bow, those of us not holding anything genuflecting as well to follow Fr. John. Paul lets me take the first seat. Windsor, Makayla, and Sally Anne walk back to my dad's pew as Conan nabs a seat with the altar boys. I give him a stink eye to behave himself. Fr.

John starts mass with the Sign of the Cross, a short reflection on the readings, and a prayer. The choir leads Lord have mercy... reciting Glory to God as well. Paul reads the first reading, from the Old Testament. Then I go up to read. The reading is from the first Letter of St. Peter and is about tending the flock of God in our midst. I sit back down, mulling over the reading. We all rise for the Gospel acclamation and remain standing while Fr. John reads. The excerpt is from the gospel of Luke, about Jesus telling His disciples that the greatest amongst them is the least and the leader is the servant. I glance at the pews, my eyebrows rising at who I see. In the middle of the church is the man who gave me the rosaries but it isn't him. He's not tanned enough, there is more muscle mass on him and he's dressed in a suit. We sit for the homily and I try to listen intently to Fr. John while comforting Philomena, who doesn't want to be held right now. Paul takes her from me, curling her tightly into his chest and swaddling her in her blanket. Almost immediately she is content again. Paul has the magic touch, I swear. With Philomena resting peacefully with Paul I can concentrate on the homily, only catching the last part of it: feed the hungry, clothe the naked, care for the sick, visit the imprisoned, don't just believe, act in faith because faith alone will not save us. Then Fr. John lists all the spiritual and corporal works of mercy and tells us to get to work and do it all with a loving heart, quoting Mother Teresa. Fr. John allows a moment of silence before continuing with the liturgy of the Eucharist. I meditate on his words, wondering how I can help people. Keep giving Pete a place to clean up, eat, and new clothes. Keep showing the triplets a different way of life from their old one, filled with hope and love. We stand for the profession of faith, the prayers of the faithful, the Hail Mary, and end with an amen. Then Paul and I walk to our pews, him still with Philomena sleeping in his arms. I guess that means my dad and I really are part of the Watson family if we're trading children at mass. Conan runs to catch up to me, not wanting to be without his family close to the altar. I lock him between my arms as we follow along with the liturgy of the Eucharist. The rest of mass seems to fly by as I hold Conan so he won't fidget loudly while staring lovingly, longingly, at the heart of Jesus hoisted in the air as the Eucharist. Windsor grabs the cross, Sally Anne and Makayla the candles, and I the book of readings to process down the aisle. It's in the same order as before, lacking the incense equipment.

Almost immediately, without waiting for the exit song to be sung, the newcomer in church beelines straight for Fr. John. Paul bounces Philomena in his arms, waving me over. "She needs to be changed."

"Diaper bag is up front," I shrug, tickling her chin. She smiles at me, still contentedly snuggled up in Paul's arms.

"Daisy, c'mere," Fr. John waves me to him and the stranger. Stranger sounds weird, he's more a brother in Christ.

"Hi," the man sticks his hand out for me to shake. "Pastor McGregor, how do you do?"

"Good, thanks," I shake his hand. He has a strong grip, warm brown eyes that look familiar, and a suit. The button-up shirt looks familiar as well.

"I was just telling Mr. McGregor about that friend you invited to mass a while back." Fr. John leaves us to chat as he greets parishioners leaving mass.

"The one with the bag of rosaries," Pastor McGregor adds.

"What a lovely man!" I beam, catching Conan in my arms. He'd launched himself at me. "He taught me a lot in the little span I saw him."

"That's good," the man says briskly. "Did he tell you where he was going next?"

"Sorry, no," I reply, setting Conan down. He chases after some other children running outside, Ridels, Watsons, and others. I motion for Sally Anne to keep an eye on them. She does so with one of her huffs.

"Here's my card," he holds a business card out to me. "Please call immediately if you see him. I'm worried about him. It's going to be winter soon, he can't keep sleeping on the road."

"I think it's very courageous," I speak up, defending the rosary man.

"He's my younger brother," the sharply dressed man returns quickly. "And he's doing this to piss us off. We all know he should come back to his Protestant roots."

"I disagree," I say smoothly, catching the diaper bag Landon throws at me. Guess that means everyone else dibsed out changing Philomena. "Catholicism is the best religion to know and understand God."

"I'm not arguing semantics with you," Pastor McGregor shoots back. He places his hands on his hips, his eyes flashing angrily.

"Can I challenge you to do something? To try and understand your brother's faith?" I ask. Watson and other parishioners circle around us, noticing his angry stance. No one wants to argue with a stranger.

"Doesn't mean I'll do it," he shrugs flippantly.

"If you understand him you might know where he will be or is going," I say firmly yet gently. I need to open his eyes to Catholicism without pushing him away. It's too deep to talk priest, prophet, and king with him but what about visiting God in the tabernacle?

"Get on with it," McGregor motions with his hands. I take a deep breath, asking God to sanctify my impatience. His attitude is really pushing my buttons.

"Is there a Catholic Church where you live?"

"Yes."

"Then I challenge you to spend ten minutes a day in front of the Blessed Sacrament," I state clearly. McGregor raises his eyebrow at me.

"You want me to sit in a church ten minutes a day?" He sighs impatiently. "I can do that at my church."

"No," I retort politely. "I want you to spend ten minutes a day kneeling in front of the tabernacle, thanking God for His blessings, asking Him for His help, wanting to discern *His* will for your life. I want you to form a personal relationship with Jesus who is right in front of your arms, within reach of you to touch. I want you to feel His presence in such a holy place!"

"If I do that, will you let me go?" McGregor asks, motioning around the building. The rest of the congregation is outside, vehicles pulling away as everyone leaves for whatever plans they have for the day. We get together one Sunday a month for pancake breakfast, one Sunday a month for a potluck, and in the summer, another Sunday for hot dog roasts.

"I'm not forcing you to be here," I say softly, a little hurt at his interpretation of my words. He swiftly turns on his heel and walks out. "God bless you!" I call after him.

"Huh," I deadpan when I step outside. Only Paul's truck remains in the parking lot. Did my dad forget me amongst the hustle and bustle of all the children?

"Daisy!" Paul hollers at me with a big wave of both hands. "Your dad took the triplets and Lee somewhere. Something about Rennie and Louis causing a disturbance. Jonah took Sally Anne, Win, and Micks to his house, Peter took Kennedy and Conan and my dad took Tin-tin."

"Oh," I mumble, trotting down the steps. It's a warm afternoon for being this late in the fall. The sun is beating down nicely, a warm blanket covering my skin. "Okay. Can I change Philomena before we leave?"

"Sure," Paul opens the back door behind the driver's side. I peek in to see Philomena's car seat there, Aiden's in the middle, and Tikara's on the far side. Three babies. That's a lot but it's not a long drive to my dad's house, or Big Patrick's, where the Watsons meet up after church.

"Where's Polly and Poppy?" I ask, taking Philomena out of her car seat. The two girls are always together, happily the best of friends.

"With Grandpa," Paul rolls his eyes. "Apparently he's better than me."

"At least they get that opportunity." I shrug, setting Philomena where we place our feet. It's lower for me, and easier for me to see how badly she needs to be cleaned because she sure stinks. "Can you move your seat up?"

"Actually, uh, Daisy, can you change her from the front seat?" Paul asks, picking up the diaper bag and setting it on the driver's seat.

"Oh, yeah, sure," I reply, wrapping Philomena in her blanket and tucking her into my chest. Paul closes the door and walks me to the passenger side as I hear a car pull into the parking lot. I peek out the driver's window when Paul closes the passenger door, depressing the lock button so I'm locked in his truck with the babies. He's taking serious safety precautions for whoever drove up. I gulp when I see Amy Leigh, his wife, saunter up to him. A cop truck pulls in next. Fear thumps in my heart so I cross myself and devote myself to prayer, offering to change Philomena's smelly surprise for peaceful interaction between them. I can't hear words as Amy yells at Paul, with cranky hand motions, pointing into the truck and then smiling coldly and cuddling up with the police officer. It's when I climb over the center console to buckle Philomena into her car seat I remember Paul's words from Dickie's Watson reunion. *She has a boyfriend already, some dirty cop Andrea can't stand.* The cop is tall, taller than everyone I know, and thick, built like a tree.

"C'mon Daisy!" Amy lunges for the truck. Paul steps in her way, hands clasped together behind his back. "Tell me the truth! Who has Paul been seeing!"

I gulp, glancing at the babies in the backseat. Aiden and Tikara are asleep, and Philomena just getting there. The two Ridel babies are used to yelling and fighting, but is Aiden? Can he recognize the sound of his mother's voice? Will that upset him? *Lord Jesus, keep these babies safe as your Father kept you safe in the manger. Mama Mary, cover these babies with your protective, motherly mantle. Amen.* Amy pushes passed Paul and slams her fists on the window by my head. I jump, my eyes widening. I never knew she was crazy, she was always so quiet!

"Amy, please," Paul steps between the truck and his wife. "Leave her alone. She has nothing to do with our problems."

"Your problems," Amy hisses. The cop, a black one who Landon, Harry, and Tyler cannot stand, leans on the grill of his truck, hands on his work belt. "I know you can't lie Daisy!" Amy punches Paul, it knocks his head sideways but he doesn't move out of the way, even when she starts slapping him. "Tell me what you know about Paul! He probably hasn't told you how he's hurt me!"

I shake my head, tears welling up in my eyes when she slaps Paul hard. She put her whole body into that motion, it sounded like it hurt with how loud it was but Paul doesn't move away from the door.

"I need you to back away, Amy," Paul states firmly, his jaw clenching. I can barely hear the rest of his sentence because as soon as he starts talking Amy starts screaming. "I have Aiden in the backseat, along with two other babies. We can discuss this further later."

"Back away from the truck, Paul," the officer steps forward. He has a hard face with a smirk constantly on it. Landon had told me to stay the hell away from him because he'd murdered people before, claiming it was self-defense. All his witnesses seem to disappear. "You can't stop a mother from seeing her son."

Paul steps away, his hand reaching into his jeans pocket as he does so. Amy runs up to the window, slamming her palm into it. "Paul has hit me, Daisy! Don't protect an abuser! Not even if he's in church every day, rich and good-looking! Don't let him get away from the justice that is waiting for him!"

I gulp, diverting my eyes from her red, angry face. She hits the window again but I look at Paul, at the reaction on his face to her accusatory words. He's not happy anymore, his lips are in a straight line, sometimes wobbling. He's hurting badly, in mental anguish, heartbroken, and probably confused at what she is saying. He shakes his head quickly at me, imperceptible unless you were looking for it. His divorce proceedings must be *ugly.*

"Give me the keys, Paul!" Amy stalks to him. He doesn't have time to brace himself when she sucker punches him. Her cop boyfriend laughs when Paul doubles over, his face turning red. He backs away from her, his hand digging into his pants pockets before he turns and throws his keys into the tall grass in the lot next to the church. He has a new truck, recently command started so the babies can stay warm for now. "Daevon!" Amy whines, stomping her foot. "See what he did!"

"Yeah, babe," the cop steps up. He pulls Amy back, and whispers in her ear. She smirks at him and pecks him on the cheek, then spits at Paul's feet. She saunters back to her car, both the men watching her leave. Daevon's isn't a nice one look and Paul's is heartbroken. Paul is too busy watching Amy walk away from him again to see the fist Daevon throws at him. It twirls him around like a rag doll and he careens into the back bumper of his truck, his head bouncing on the edge before he flops on the ground. I scream, tears dripping out of my eyes when he lies on the ground, still as a rock. Then the officer walks to me, pulling his gun out. He uses it to motion me to roll down the window. I only open it a crack, just to hear his voice better. My body trembles, my tongue is thick, and I couldn't talk even if I wanted to. He points his gun at me and I can't *breathe.* "Don't think I don't know who you are or what you do." Then he walks away, holstering his weapon. I curl into a ball, sobbing my eyes out as he turns around in the church parking lot and spits rocks to drive away. I only feel safe to leave the truck when he's a mile away, then I climb out, falling to the rocky ground in the process. I crawl the rest of the way to Paul.

"Wake up," I beg, turning him onto his side and gently slapping his face. I don't want to see Amy's slap marks on one side and Daevon's bruise on the other cheek. Tears stream down my face as I try to catch my breath, my breathing ragged. "Paul, wake up. Please. God, please help me! Help us!"

I don't have a phone. Paul doesn't use his phone on Sundays, wanting to focus on God. I can't call anyone. I can't drive anywhere because he threw the keys in the long grass. I have to leave him and look for the keys. If it takes forever, are the keys close enough to start it? It's a new truck! I don't know how to use new vehicles!

"Paul!" I yell, my voice is hoarse and wobbly. The shout is more like a whisper. "Please wake up! Please! Aiden needs you! Polly needs you! Poppy needs you! Your family needs you! Wake up! Paul! Wake up!" Nothing seems to work so I lay him on his side in the recovery position. Then I scan the road for oncoming traffic. Nothing. The after-church crowd has already dispersed. I run to the other lot, diving into the grass. *Please Lord, let me find his keys. Don't let him die when I know I could have saved him. St. Anthony help me find his keys. St. Raphael, watch over Paul. Amen.* My fingers shake, my arms tremble, and my legs are weak as I crawl in the grass looking for anything silver, shiny and small. Absolutely nothing. *God, please!* Clarity hits me and I sit crossed-legged in the long grass, staring into the parking lot, at the truck, and Paul lying on the gravel. *I surrender to you, Lord. Let Your will be done. I trust You. I trust Your plan. I love You no matter what happens.* Bam. Right in front of my face is a black key fob. I grab it and run to the truck, sticking the keys in a cup holder because it is a button start. I start the truck, check on the babies, thankfully still sleeping, and run out to Paul. He hasn't moved. I roll him onto his back and squat, pulling him to his truck. It terrifies me to see the path his limp feet create. I'm just behind his truck when a vehicle pulls in, turning toward us. I lay Paul down and run to the stranger, waving my arms like a maniac. "Help!" I squeak, my voice is hoarse as my lips wobble. "He won't wake up. I don't have a phone. He's not awake. Nothing is waking him up! Help please!" I sputter out frantically, pulling on the guy's shoulder to convince him to come. "The hospital is just up the road!"

"Okay! I'll help!" My eyes blink in surprise when it's the cranky Pastor McGregor.

"Thank you!" I sigh in relief. "Thank God!" I run back to Paul, who is groaning on the ground, trying to sit up. "Oh thank God! Paul, are you okay?"

"Don't tell," he mumbles, his eyes rolling around in his sockets. All I see is white. "Don't tell the fam. Don't tell... dad... not yet..." he fades out again, spiking alarm through my mind. Isn't falling back asleep worse? Pastor McGregor and I lift Paul into the passenger seat, the man doing more work than me.

"Are you okay to drive?" McGregor asks.

"Yes!" I don't give him time to respond as I run around and jump in the driver's seat. Aiden is fussing in his sleep. *Lord Jesus Christ, son of God, have mercy on us sinners!*

→ 35 ←

What Would Jesus Do?

I'm glad you are feeling better," I squeeze Paul's hand. The doctors kept him in the hospital for two nights, making sure the tests they ran on him were still clear. Part of his head is shaved bald where they had to stitch his scalp closed from falling on the bumper. For now, he is staying at Big Patrick's house with Phil to take care of him as well. I think Phil is staying at Big Patrick's house as well so his night terrors won't wake up his children or he won't hurt them in his sleep.

"Thanks for getting me to the hospital," Paul smiles at me, sitting back in the kitchen chair. Dickie and Kaitlyn are watching his children. Amy hasn't been heard of and Paul isn't pressing charges. Everyone knows Daevon is a bad cop but being a police officer is a brotherhood they don't want to break. Only Watsons are brave enough to turn on them but Paul won't let them.

"I have to go," I smile apologetically. "Tutoring the triplets and Col today."

"Have fun with that," Paul chuckles, trying to stand up. He gets dizzy and has to stop, sighing in dissatisfaction.

"They're ready to beat someone," I shake my head sadly. Landon and Harry especially are moody, shoving kids in the hallways just for the hell of it. Everyone has been walking on eggshells around them. "Antsy to 'talk' to Daevon." I shivered involuntarily at the name.

"What did Daevon do to you?" Paul asks, wincing at some pain or other. His hands clutch onto the edge of Marie's table, his fingers white with the amount of force he is using.

"He, um, he pointed his gun at me." My fingers tremble so I stuff them under my thighs. Paul inhales sharply.

"Besides babies and children, you're the most non-threatening person in the world." My eyes tear up and I swallow saliva, my throat super dry. Phil clears his throat, crossing his arms over his chest. His reaction was similar to that of his Uncle Rory: beat the shit out of Daevon.

"He, uh, he, um, he said that, that I, that he knows who I am and uh, that he knows, um, knows what I do." I stutter out, ducking my head to hide the tears streaming down my face. I breathe out loudly, snot plugging my nose. "I'm not a bad person! I only do good things! Everyone calls me Rosie because I'm so naive!" I jerk my head up. Paul nods along to what I say, agreeing with me. Phil clears his throat.

"Paul might not remember because it was sixteen years ago," he speaks up, looking directly at me with his serious blue eyes. "But you need to talk to your dad about your mother."

"He won't talk about her," I state, shaking my head. My dad is obstinate about not releasing my mom's identity to me. I hate not knowing her name! But maybe he is doing it to protect me, she still has family alive, maybe even around here.

"He will," Phil says confidently. "Once he knows why Daevon pulled his firearm on you."

"I better go," I stand up and pat Paul's shoulder. "Just wanted to come to check on you but now I gotta go tutor the boys."

"You must be calm under pressure," Paul smiles ruefully, taking a sip of tea from a blue coffee cup.

"No," I laugh, my face warming in embarrassment. I reach up to tuck my hair behind my ear but leave it be, deciding it could stay in my face to cover my humiliation. "I was screaming and crying like you wouldn't believe."

"I'm sorry to have scared you like that," Paul sighs, his left hand reaching up to scratch the stitches before he thinks better of it.

"Paul," I laugh in surprise. "It wasn't your fault."

"I should have-," Paul begins to speak.

"-no," I cut him off, walking to the head of the table and placing my trembling fingers on the top of a kitchen chair. "It wasn't your fault. No could have, should have, or would haves. You are a good person, close to God so Satan is attacking you. Keep praying, keep loving, and keep believing. Don't let him win just because he's found a way to attack you and question your understanding of the world. This world doesn't matter, heaven matters, so fight for it."

"Nice pep talk," Phil grins, stretching in his chair. Despite the grin he broadcasts, there is sadness in his eyes. What did he go through overseas to wake up terrified every night?

"God bless you guys!" I wave at them, and Big Pat and Peter, who are napping on their respective couches. While they are down for the count Marie is spending her time puttering outside, petting the kittens and the horses.

"God bless you, Daisy!" I trot down the steps, feeling better now that I know Paul will be alright. Schoolwork was incomplete the last few days because I had been very distracted, worrying about Paul. Col is parked at the end of Big Patrick's driveway, a fifteen-minute drive out of town. I haven't run in a while, for fun or training, so I take off running, pushing myself as hard as possible.

"Woo! Go, Daisy!" Landon hollers, sitting on the window ledge and slapping the roof. He has a wide grin on his face, making me smile because he was scowling all day. I fist pump to show him I appreciate the cheering. "Better run, better run, outrun my gun with those pumped-up kicks!" Harry and Tyler boo him down, Harry going as far as pushing Landon so he wobbles on the ledge.

"Why don't we sing a gospel song?" I huff out, walking in a little circle to cool myself down. The boys all groan and complain.

"Are you serious?" Danae deadpans, uncurling herself from Col's shoulder.

"Absolutely," I confirm. Harry opens the passenger backseat door and I climb in, skimming over his thighs because he won't move to the middle seat. I lean forward, head between Col and Danae. "Sing with me."

"Please don't," Landon groans, sliding lower in his seat. Col and Harry grin at me, ready to join in.

"Peace is flowing like a river, flowing out of you and me, flowing out into the desert, setting all the captives free." I lead the song, and Harry, Tyler, and Col sing along with me. We smile at each other, Danae covering her ears and Landon shouting at us to shut up. We sing the next two verses much to Danae and Landon's regret while Col starts the drive to school. During the last verse, Danae joins in, off-tune and louder than the rest. It throws us all off track and Tyler is the first to start giggling, the rest of us joining in right after.

"Princess," Col huffs in laughter. "You suck."

"But you like me so you like it," Dani retorts, sticking her tongue out. Col grabs it with his fingers so Danae starts gagging. She slaps his hand away with a laugh. "Not cool!"

"Do you guys want to pray?" I ask, patting my pockets for my rosaries. We have enough time to pray the Chaplet of Divine Mercy or Faith before we reach school.

"Naw, Shawty," Landon shakes his head. Harry hums in agreement, cracking his knuckles.

"We prayed with you at lunch," Dani says as Tyler leans against the window, pretending to be asleep. What a juvenile. They prayed with me at lunch but it was the quick blessing meal prayer and half of them didn't even make the sign of the cross because they were too embarrassed to make it in the middle of the cafeteria.

"My truck, my rules," Col grins at me through the rearview mirror. I grin back although I don't see him reaching for his knotted rosary looped through his belt. He's teasing our friends, he doesn't actually want to pray.

"Let me walk," Landon groans, placing his hand on the door latch. My heart is saddened at their negative reactions, as goofy as they tried to make them.

"Do you guys ever think that I ask you to pray for me? That I need people praying with me to support me in prayer, keep me praying?" I ask softly. Soon I feel bad when Danae and Col share a guilty look. "It's okay guys. God's grace carries me. I just have to focus on that."

"So are you saying the more you pray, the better you are?" Tyler asks, chewing on his nails. It seems like Micks taught him that bad habit as well.

"Sort of." I agree, sitting back to focus on him since he was the only one who spoke up, and showed any interest. "Praying is a virtue. I don't know but it's a good thing, right? Brings us closer to God. The closer we are to God the less likely to sin or the more fight we put into stop sinning."

"And you, goody two shoes, need help?" Harry says, crossing his arms over his chest.

"Yes," I laugh lightly. "I'm not as good as everything thinks I am. You all place me on that pedestal but I sin just like the next person."

"But like you said," Dani points out. "It's because you try to fight sin, we don't."

"That's why I need people to remind me to pray, to hold me up in prayer," I add on, pushing my hair out of my face. Maybe I'll ask Alex to put corn rows in again, they really helped me see better without my brown halo puffing out around me.

"Well then," Harry huffs with a roll of his eyes. "Let's pray."

"Too late," Landon sighs gratefully. "We're at school."

"Another time," I wave off Col and Harry's concern. Landon jumps out of the truck, scowling when he sees Jett Hendrix getting in his black, lifted, tinted, decked-out Toyota Tundra. Then he throws him two middle fingers. I open my mouth to ask him to stop but I don't want to nag him too much.

"You all go," Dani waves the triplets and me off, her eyes twinkling mischievously. "We'll be a minute." I glance at Col to see his reaction. He shrugs his shoulders in his 'I'm hiding that I care' way of his.

"There's the brats!" Landon elbows Harry roughly with a grin.

"Let's go say hi," Harry laughs and they both begin running to their younger twin brothers. Cam and Jim are surrounded by the junior jocks of the football team, which really means all the grade seven, eight, nines and some sixes are all trying to fight them. Cam and Jim have had to fight hard to remain enigmas like their three older brothers. There are twenty boys surrounding the Smith boys.

"I better go help them," Tyler sighs, shaking his head before running after his four brothers. I flinch when Landon throws the first punch at an unsuspecting seventh grader. The fight is on, the sixth graders running away, the seventh graders cheering and the eighth and ninth graders fighting the Smiths. I make the Sign of the Cross, meditating prayerfully on Jesus's scourging as I dive into the fray, dragging a small eighth grader out. Everyone is cursing and hollering, hitting and tackling. I'm elbowed and knocked into, racking up my anxiety. My anxiousness makes me angry. I never used to be anxious about breaking up a fight until Landon beat me and that cop pointed his gun at me.

"Stop!" I screech, jumping on Landon's back. "Stop!"

"Really, Shawty?" Landon laughs, tucking his hands under my thighs to hold onto me. I'm happy to see he looks more relaxed now but throwing hands never resolves anything!

"Go home!" I point at the junior football team.

"We have practice," one boy retorts snottily. Cam slams his fist into his face, knocking him into his friends.

"Harry!" I holler, "stop your brother! No fighting! Please, guys! Stop the violence!"

"Shut up," Harry glares at me but he pulls his brother back. Insults and curse words are thrown around as the football team jogs off to the practice field. Landon uses my leg to kick Jim.

"Wasn't me!" I say quickly. Jim rolls his eyes and kicks Landon's shin.

"Nice of you to join us." He wraps Tyler in a headlock, giving him a noogie. It must burn when I see Tyler's scalp turn red from the force but he doesn't complain.

"My pleasure," Landon grins, using my leg to kick Jim again.

"Was not me!" I enunciate, holding onto Landon's neck with one hand and pointing at him with the other.

"Was too!" Landon replies, forcing my leg to kick Jim again.

"I would never hit anyone!" I inform Jim seriously, pointing at Landon's hand on my knee.

"You sure?" Landon asks cheekily, spinning me in a circle. I squeal, unprepared for the fast movement as I lose my grip on his neck. My back and head fly out, connecting with Jim's chest. He grunts and curses me and Landon out but pushes me up. I get a better hold of Landon because he doesn't stop spinning, making me dizzy.

"I'm-gonna-puke," I groan, tucking my chin in Landon's shoulder. He continues spinning around, laughing in glee. I jam my lips shut, my stomach queasy. Then we crash, Landon stumbles on the ground and we roll in the grass. My head won't stop spinning even when he scrambles up, walking like a drunk dude. "I don't feel good," I whine, rolling on my side and swallowing whatever was trying to come up my throat. I close my eyes, feeling the grass around me to find support for help.

"Here," Tyler says. I'm assuming it is him who grabs my hand. He helps me up, my legs wobbly before I careen to the left, my balance still off from my dizziness. Tyler laughs, wrapping his arms around my waist and tugging me into his body. "I got ya."

"Thanks," I groan, opening my eyes to the bright sun. Landon is hunched over, laughing at me.

"You'd be a lightweight if you drank," he slaps his knee, his eyes watery from laughter. "Too f—king funny!"

"What the hell were you guys thinking?" Harry slaps the back of Cam and Jim's heads. They scowl and step away from him but don't retaliate. "Fighting twenty guys. You damn idiots!"

"We're sick of their uppity, better-than-thou attitude!" The twins huff, mimicking someone from the football team with fake smiles and dancing stupidly.

"Can't join them, beat them," Landon says before bursting into more laughter. I deadpan stare at him. Getting dizzy easily is not that funny.

"Don't beat them!" I cry out, jerking my head up. The top of my head rams into Tyler's chin and we both groan and dance around to overcome the pain. "What would Jesus do?"

"Hell if I know," Cam shrugs, glaring at me.

"I'm not turning the other f—king cheek," Jim growls, kicking at the ground.

"Yeah," Harry adds, spitting on the cement sidewalk. "Look what it did to Paul."

"No!" I sigh, standing beside Tyler. "But yes! Don't hate the boys because they sin, hate the sin not the sinner! Jesus died so we could live! Why not die so you can live?"

"Whatever, Rosie," Cam snaps, slapping Jim's back.

"We out, losers." Jim slaps Harry's back.

"Wait!" Harry grabs his wrist. Only I notice the way Jim's eyes widen in fear before he masks it with a scowl directed at his brother. "How's mama?"

"Come see for yourself," Jim retorts, jerking his hand away.

"He has less people to beat on now that you all left." Cam glowers at his brothers. I'm concerned at the rage I see bursting through his body.

"You said you weren't gonna pull a Simon," Jim bites out. "F—king cowards."

"I'm sorry," I say softly, curling into Tyler's side. I'd been so concerned with helping the triplets get out of the trauma I forgot about their younger brothers still in the abusive environment.

"Come live with us, too," Harry offers, his fingers clenching. Landon's jaw clicks.

"And leave mama?" Jim laughs caustically.

"F—k that," Cam scoffs.

"Thank you," I whisper, tears filling my eyes. "Thank you for taking care of her. Thank you for that love in your heart." They run away at my words, unaccustomed to someone thanking them or seeing the good that they do. I've condemned them in my mind and for that I am sorry.

"F—k!" Landon screams, throwing himself on the brick wall. He punches the bricks, bloodying his knuckles but he doesn't stop until he falls to the ground, sobbing. Harry stands frozen, his eyes glazed over. I've seen that look before when Landon triggered him. He's dissociating. Tyler pats his pocket, then takes a clear baggy with weed in it out. I snatch it from him and stuff it in my bra. Then I put my forehead on his and fold my hands on his neck.

"Tyler," I whisper firmly. "Harry needs you. Go help Harry." Tyler gulps and then nods when he sees Harry standing frozen. I drop to the ground beside Landon and curl him into my arms, holding him tight. "I love you, Landon." I kiss his forehead. "Your mom loves you. God loves you. Your mom loves that you were able to get away from your dad. She loves you and she's happy you don't have to live through that abuse anymore, okay, Landon? Your mom loves you and is happy with where you are. She doesn't blame you." I fold his hair out of his face, whispering kind words to him, hum and rock him and do the same for Tyler and Harry when they join us, all the while praying. Praying for healing, for hope, for love, for understanding, for Landon, for Harry, for Tyler, for Cam, for Jim, for Jilly, for Simon, for Huntley.

⇴ 36 ⇷

Drunk Lady

⇴———⦿———⇷

B rr," I shiver as I put my seatbelt on.
"Cold out, hey?" Jonah asks with a laugh, turning the fan up a notch. I slump into the seat when I feel hot air wash over me.

"Yes!" I wave out the front windshield. Tin-tin, Conan and Kennedy are standing in the front door, waving at me and shouting something I cannot hear. Jonah waves at them, careful not to back over Teddy or Karen, my cousins' dogs who love chasing vehicles. Sugar is lying in her doghouse, nose peeking out and Teddy is leaping at the children, trying to play with them.

"You going to the mountain?" Jonah smiles, signalling out of the driveway.

"Yeah," I reply, blowing on my hands that feel like icicles. It's cold out. Winter is coming which means Halloween is just around the corner. Windsor and Makayla have already been talking about candy and trick or treating but I didn't have the heart to tell them we don't do that. Instead we go to the graveyard to pray for all the lost souls. "Thanks for driving me."

"No problem," Jonah turns his wipers on. I side eye him to see how he is doing. Usually he is better at making conversation, or am I just over thinking that this is awkward because we agreed to just be friends? "Why do you need mountain time?"

"Just everything lately," I sigh, brushing my hair out of my face. "I've never been this scared or stressed before. Like I have had guns pointed at me before but that was hunting and stuff, just making sure the gun was clean. I've never seen a handgun before and it was a cop pointing it at me for something I did, but I don't do anything bad. The whole thing is making me second guess every decision I make or have ever made and the children are so distracting that I can't breathe and focus on surrendering to Jesus. The Trip's all have problems of their own and I don't know how to help them and they don't know how to help me. My cousins are big time drunks, I can't rely on them. Dad has been sober for a while, I'm afraid he'll break and go on a week long bender. Aria hasn't been able to check in on him because she's away most of the time and I haven't had a good night's sleep since the children arrived. Lee takes care of the babies all day and he needs the reprieve of night to keep him well rested but no one else gets up for them like I do. I'm so tired! It's like when I close my eyes they only have a second's rest before someone starts crying or Conan's wet the bed and having a nightmare. Then there's the whole thing with Paul and Amy. What if they try to use me as a material witness for what went down that day in court? Obviously they can't because most of what Amy did was illegal and Paul isn't going to make her look bad. But what if he did? I hate to say that but what if Paul made Amy look bad so she can't get custody of the kids? Children need their mothers but is a bad mother better than no mother, but can I even say that? She could be a good mom for all I know? My goodness, what if what she said was right? Paul is abusive? I've never seen that from him so I don't want to believe it but people hide themselves." Tears had sprung to my eyes at my thoughts and I duck my head to wipe them away. "I just want to be a little girl again and have my dad hold me and take care of everything."

"Isn't that what God is for?" Jonah's asks nervously. One hand taps his hands on the steering wheel and the other pats my shoulder awkwardly. "I think if I said all that to you you would tell me to go jump in Jesus's lap or something." He laughs awkwardly.

"You're right," I sigh, curling my arms over the middle console and laying my head there. "I just need a good dose of Jesus. I need to open my heart to Him, show him my worries and let Him carry it like He carried my sins on that Cross."

"Couldn't have said it better myself," Jonah grins at me. His face isn't as drawn, he looks somewhat relieved. While he is focused on the road I take a good, long look at him. His blue eyes still shine with determination, a sort of perseverance that will never go away. His drivenness is what makes him who he is. The bags under his eyes show that something has been keeping him up at night, and I feel horrible because it might be me. We agreed on friends but what if he can't handle it? I think I'd be okay losing a friend because I'd only just made friends recently but he was sort of the first one to befriend me. That would be a bitter pill for me to swallow. Jonah looks skinnier too, as if he hasn't been eating as healthily as he should be. He's still running and had started hitting the gym with Chris and Karl. The Laytons do have a maid, paid generously, but Annakin and Vanessa prefer if their older children clean their own rooms and wash their own clothes. Is that why Jonah's clothes look a little worse for wear? Has he had more sad days than good days? I mentally kick myself in the butt because I'd been so focused on helping the triplets I forgot about Jonah and his mental state. It must hurt to be rejected although he took it well.

"How are you?" I ask genuinely, realizing we haven't hung out with just the two of us since the half marathon. He looks good, recently got his hair cut again, same healthy, happy face, but his eyes look a little tired though.

"I'm alright," Jonah shrugs, smiling sadly at me but bravely trying to mask it. I make a mental reminder to pray for him. When I get home I'll put his name in my prayer jar.

"That's good, I guess," I shrug as well, scanning the side of the road. The leaves are brown on the dead grass, the trees bare and the sunlight grey today. The forecast called for rain but it feels like it might snow. I know so because my wrists and knees are more painful today, and have been the past few days.

"How about you?" Jonah asks, checking me out carefully. I sigh, thinking back on my life the past few weeks. Jonah let me decompress and now wants me to validate whatever hurt feelings I have left. Landon shoving me around, breaking up fights, the cop hurting Paul and pointing his gun at me. Those circumstances were all very unexpected, and hurtful, and I'm still not sure I'm through processing them. "Heard some stuff."

"Yeah," I sigh again. "I never expected any of it but I have to keep going forward, right? Trust in the Lord and put one foot in front of the other." I phrase my statement as a question, repeating what Jonah reminded me to do earlier.

"And Louis and Rennie?" Jonah takes his foot off the gas pedal when we reach town limits. I look at the streetlights making the grey sky orange, the grey clouds deepening in colour, the rays of white sunlight that break through, and sigh a third time.

"I guess they're in jail." I murmur. It's a kick to the gut. How am I out and about helping strangers and acquaintances when I can't even stop my own cousins from sinning, from drinking and drug use and fighting? They're very lucky the guy they beat up woke up otherwise they'd have been charged with manslaughter. Since both of them have records they have to stay in lock up all weekend. At least that gives them two days of sobriety.

"We should plan another little get together," Jonah diverts the conversation. I'm thankful for that. It makes me so sad to see what my dad's family was like when he was a boy but also how happy I am he left all of it to raise me even while going out on his occasional drunk. "You, me, Betty, Angie, Jesus, Col, the Watsons, Karl and Chris, the Trips."

"Maybe Harry's girlfriend," I add, grinning at Jonah. He forgot about Danae. Lately her name has been behind Col's in everything. Col and her wanted to keep the relationship quiet but with all the sweets he put in her locker and all the girly details about the relationship Danae is sharing with the girl group I've been introduced to, the rumours have spread like wildfire. Col seems like he's just waiting for the relationship to blow up in his face. I pray they wait for their relationship. It doesn't fit society's standards and I don't want either of them hurt.

"Harry has a girlfriend?" Jonah coughs as he pulls into the church parking lot. He raises an eyebrow and shrugs it off. "He hasn't had one since he dumped Selena." That is true. From what Harry has entrusted to me, he was a horrible boyfriend and this time he is trying to be better. Better than his history with his dad and mom, climbing his way out of the stigma that surrounds him.

"Hey, Jonah?" I peer out the windshield. It's cloudy and grey and windy but I'm certain the church steps aren't that rounded. "Is someone sleeping on the steps?"

"I think so," he replies, reaching for his keys.

"Leave them in," I shake my head. A black lump is curled up next to the church doors, too big to be a dog. "We might need to take them to the hospital."

"Let me check it out," Jonah asserts, climbing out of his truck. He paid for the expensive repairs out of his own pocket and explained the situation to his parents. They didn't like it but they didn't discipline him, understanding why he did it and who they were. I follow Jonah, staying behind him just in case it's Pete on one of his drunks. I've never found him on the church steps before. I spot Fr. John walking to the church from the rectory and wait for him at the bottom of the stairs.

"Good morning, Daisy," Fr. John greets, a rosary in between his thumb and pointer finger. I smile at the picture. It looks like Fr. John follows Jesus' advice to pray constantly.

"Morning, Father," I reply, shoving my fingers into my pockets for warmth. Guess who didn't wear her gloves this morning? "Jonah's just checking on that person up there."

"Oh, dear," Fr. John smiles sadly before striding up the steps. I shrug and follow him, taking the lead from the two men. The wind whips through my winter coat and stings ice into my eyes. I shiver and duck my head, feeling for the poorly dressed woman heaving up.

"Oh, hi," she mumbles, wiping snow and ice from clothes. "It's super, uh, like cold."

"It is," I say warmly, kneeling down to her level. Jonah and I pause at the scars on her face from previous bug bites and the bugs crawling through her toque-less head. Not nits, actual bugs are crawling in her greasy black hair. She's been on this drunk for a while, it's honestly disgusting to look at and I understand the look Jonah sends to me perfectly. He doesn't want to spread the lice to his siblings, once one starts, it is an epidemic. Is helping this poor, drunk lady worth the risk? Yes, without a doubt. This lady is Jesus hung up on that cross, a leper in our times so I do what Jesus would have done for her. I help her up, bugs, grease, urine, vomit and all. "Let's get you home, ma'am."

"This has got to be the coldest day so far," Jonah shivers as he carries the weight of the lady on her other side. I smile at him to show my appreciation, the disgust is still visible in his wrinkled nose and his covered head leaning away from hers. And the disgust is still felt in my roiling stomach. It's not so much as I fear bugs but I despise the creepy crawly critters digging into my skin, burrowing into my bloodstream, planting eggs and eating me from the inside out. Okay, so maybe most bugs don't do that but that's what I think whenever I see any bug.

"God bless you both!" Fr. John beams at us. "I'll wait for you to start mass and will be praying in the wait!"

"Appreciate it," Jonah responds. I don't like praise for me, it's Jesus working through me, so I don't respond. It's not humility, it's comprehension of the poor sinner that I am.

"So cold," the lady mumbles, her head falling on my shoulder when she misses a step and careens into me.

"I got you," I confirm when she desperately grapples for my arm to hold onto. Her fingers are icicles, blue and purple in the whiteout of the morning from the harsh wind and small, hard, snow flakes. My ears ring in pain but I offer it up for this lady, and for any other drunks making their way home and all who are under dressed for their weather conditions, no matter the circumstances.

"Where do you live, miss?" Jonah asks, holding her up with one arm while he opens the back passenger door.

"On the Rez," she mumbles, more so falling onto the seat when she climbs up, being pushed up by me and Jonah. I cut a look at Jonah, concerned for our welfare. I have some Indigenous in me, enough brown that they accept me, but Jonah is as white as they come. He's also never been on the Rez, and depending on which Rez, I haven't either.

"We can't drive that far," Jonah speaks up. I close the door so he can run around the back of the vehicle. When I climb into the passenger seat she is mumbling about the cold and us being angels sent by God, too holy for her to associate with. When I try to deny her assumption she raises her voice, swinging her arms wildly to prove her point. "Thanks for thinking of us that way," Jonah intervenes, shaking his head at me to pipe down.

"My auntie lives up the hill," she mumbles, gagging deep in her throat. She covers her mouth with her hands, hunching over the bench seat. Jonah winces, expecting vomit to spray onto the fabric.

"Which house?" He asks instead of berating her for the saliva dripping on the black mats. I'm carefully watching her to see to her needs while praying internally for her, and any other not so lucky people or drunks caught in this horrible weather unprepared.

"Blue, blue trailer," she answers, falling deeper into the seat. Jonah cuts me another look, impatience and irritability showing on his face. I shrug with a little laugh.

"Take a deep breath, Jonah, God'll work things out."

"It's not that easy for a convert," he retorts, his fingers tightening on the steering wheel. "I wasn't raised to believe in something I can't see."

"You believe in the wind although you can't see it," I refute quietly, respectfully.

"Wind makes noise, it moves things." Jonah replies. He signals and shoulder checks before turning left on top the hill, to the low income housing instead of Big Shot Lane, as the locals call the row of town plots opposite the business sector.

"How do you hear the wind?" Jonah cuts me another look at my question. This one isn't as annoyed, he's thinking now. The woman groans in the back seat as he pulls up next to a blue trailer.

"I don't know," Jonah sighs in frustration. "You just hear it, feel it, know it's there."

"Yeah, okay, that's good, but-," he groans at my but and parks his truck. The buttons locking the doors depress, unlocking the doors. "-if the wind isn't howling, if it's just a soft breeze, how do you know it's there? You sort of have to stop, right? Stop and?"

"You listen?" He finally asks, his fingers tapping on the steering wheel.

"Yeah, we have to listen to the wind when it's a soft breeze." I agree wholeheartedly. "So with God we have to stop what we are doing, clear our minds and focus on what He's trying to say to us. I think it was Elijah in the wilderness when he heard God speaking to him *after* the storm."

"I get the point," Jonah sends me a square smile. I let the defiant attitude in his words drift away, aware that I was trying to convert him pretty hard from my standards. "You go wake whoever's home. I'll help the woman out."

"Sounds good," I reply, reverting back to my inner prayer for the woman. Now I'm praying we got the right trailer and that they'll help her out. I feel horrible thinking this because I still help Pete out when he's in a bind, but I don't want all the children getting whatever she has. I'm human, just like the rest of us. I hop out of Jonah's truck, wind whipping into my face and through my clothes as my feet clomp on the frozen earth. My fingers feel like breaking when I knock them on the front door so I shrug them in my pockets, shivering to stay warm. Besides the wind whistling in my ears and throwing snow around my eyesight, it is quiet. The house is quiet too, so I brace my hand and knock again, louder and longer. I look back to the truck to see Jonah holding the woman up. She's leaning heavily against him, arms wrapped around his hips while bending over, gagging. I knock on the door again, finally hearing someone stumble to the entrance. It's dark in the house and the man only opens the door ajar, squinting at me against the cloudy, windy sunlight.

"What do ya want?" He asks with a yawn. I step back to point at the woman Jonah is walking to the door.

"She said we should drop her off here," I shrug, tucking my arms into my sides and shivering from the cold. It feels like the middle of winter already.

"Oh," the guy mutters, adding obscenities under his breath but he opens the door fully. "I'll take her."

"Thank you," the woman beams at me and hugs Jonah. "You two are too holy, thank you!" She stubs her toe in the doorframe and curses before cursing some more after realizing she swore in front of two 'angels'. I tell her I'll pray for her before the door is slammed somewhat unkindly in my face.

"Thank you," I smile at Jonah after we've rushed into the warm truck. "That was super nice of you. Thanks for taking her home."

"It was your idea," Jonah rolls his eyes, breathing on his fingers to warm them up. "All those bugs were gross. I've never seen that big of lice before. And the welts on her arms, they gotta be bed bugs. If you weren't there I would have left her."

"Oh, thank you for helping," I add, clicking my seatbelt in place. Jonah turns the heat on full blast.

"I'm not gonna argue with you about who did it better. Your idea, I agreed. We both helped her. Let's leave it at that, okay?" I laugh at his brisk tone, humbled by his answer. He shivers now, sort of like a dog shaking his coat free from water. "I need a shower."

"The bugs were kind of gross," I agree, rubbing my hands on my knees to warm them and my thighs up. "But Jesus-,"

"Yeah, yeah, Jesus went to the lepers." Jonah sighs deeply. His fingers are tapping on the steering wheel, indicating his anger. "But Jesus was God and could heal them and probably not get the bugs and shit. We aren't God, Daisy."

A hundred little scenarios run through my mind, ways to explain that the disciples healed people and sometimes even raised them from the dead. But Jonah is right, I don't know if Jesus ever got bed bugs or lice. Jesus was human as well as divine, he was raised by human standards. They had lepers in those times, whatever those ill people suffered from, and were contagious. The Gospels don't say if he ever got sick or suffered from something but they barely touch on His childhood. I finally settle on one that is sensitive to me, one that always brings tears to my eyes because it reminds me of me. "You heard of St. Francis of Assisi?"

"I think so," Jonah answers. His shoulders are hunched as he drives, leaning forward to squint through the window into the billowing mess of snow. He isn't paying as much attention to our conversation as I wish he was but it's the best I can expect in these circumstances so I continue.

"I for one, despise bugs. Even spiders. Sometimes I even think about killing them when I see them." I shiver at the thought of bugs crawling on me at night when I lie sleeping. Jonah looks at me incredulously, then bursts out laughing.

"You, Daisy Ridel, are scared of bugs?" He manages to chuckle out.

"We don't need to dwell on that," I roll my eyes, shivering at imaginary insects crawling over my skin. "So St. Francis of Assisi was born rich, very rich and so he had servants growing up. And he fought in the army wanting glory for himself and prestige and all that but one day he left everything behind because he felt God calling him to. So God put a leper in his path, someone diseased that Francis was disgusted by as some sort of test I guess and Francis swallowed his disgust and helped him, cared for him, bathed him and fed him. So yeah, when I saw the lice bugs crawling through that lady's hair and wanted to run the other way, I didn't, because St. Francis of Assisi didn't and Jesus sure didn't."

"I get that," Jonah agrees. "What's the word to be made into saints? It's God trying to make us grow in virtue through sufferings?"

"Sanctification?" I probe, receiving a nod in response.

"Let's pray that we were sanctified through that," Jonah sniffs and glances into the backseat. "'Cause I'm gonna spend all day cleaning up my truck."

"I can help if you want," I offer. Jonah shrugs and that seems to be the end of our conversation. The rest of the quick drive to church is silent. I think Jonah is processing what I said but I'm praying my litany of pray for them. Anyone I know, any name I've heard in passing or every face I've ever met, I ask the saints to pray for them. The frozen, drunk lady made me realize I haven't been praying for people as often as I should. My prayer life has drastically changed since dad took in the children. I miss my days of prayer, hours and hours spent in the Chaplet or outdoors but now God must be calling me to a different form of prayer. Physical prayer, where I pray while washing dishes or folding clothes or changing diapers or cooking food or actually interacting with the children instead of just mothering them to the best of my abilities. Playing with them when they get too energetic, talking with them when they seem too quiet or in a bad mood, helping them with homework or giving Sally Anne some teenage girl time. My dad's mansion is a blessing. The price of it broke him but we won't be over cramped in the cabin and driving each other nuts.

"I'm gonna leave her running," Jonah informs me when he parks in the church parking lot. I nod, with the wind and the snow and the low temperature it is a fantastic idea. Mass in the morning is amazing, it makes me feel like I start my day off right. Of course, God doesn't need to give us consolations but I'm peaceful and grateful when he does. Usually I weather spiritual dryness in good spirits as well, knowing even in the blindness that God loves me and that I love Him.

→ 37 ←

Psychology

━━━━━◦◦◦━━━━━

I flip the page, awed at what I am reading. Venerable Solanus Casey met in person Saint Brother Andre and they blessed each other! Tears spring to my eyes at the thought of the two men, both thought of as saints with different upbringings and languages seeing God's Holy Spirit in each other and blessing each other. When I speak about little acts of great love causing me to weep tears of joy, this is what I mean. Catholicism is so beautiful, with such a rich background. I wish the world could know about the church and her teachings and history and traditions and sacredness. I want to shout it on rooftops but alas, most people would think I am crazy. So I'm content to try and find ways to whisper it on the breeze to those who need to hear it most. Most people misinterpret the church and bible and I want to rectify that, which is why I try to spend as much time as possible reading church history books even if they bore me. I wipe my tears with a joyful smile and close the book to blow my nose, jumping when I spot someone sitting in the chair opposite me in the library. I'd finished my assignments for class early and my teacher had allowed me to visit the library, which was thankfully empty. If there was a lower grade of students here I would have felt compelled to read them the few Catholic children's books I keep in my locker. With no space at home, I badly need my mountain time, as Harry so gracefully coined the term.

"Hi," I greet the student opposite me with a wave and a smile. I hate judging, absolutely hate it but this is one of the students I rarely see because I sort of avoid them, not knowing how to interact with them peacefully without causing a scene. Even though I should know most of the townspeople I don't, so I don't know if he is a she at birth or a he but she is definitely trying to be a he with the boy's clothing and haircut but curvy woman's body. It's not the average tomboy situation. Usually I keep quiet because I don't want them to feel like I'm attacking them as a person, I'm simply attacking the sin they clearly let into their lives.

"Hey," she replies, closing a book of her own.

"How are you?" I ask, setting my book aside to focus my attention solely on her. She smiles at me, eyes watering before she ducks her head with a shrug. "You finish all your class work?" I ask casually, continuing to talk to make her feel comfortable around me. "I finished mine so my teacher let me out."

"Uh, no," she replies, wiping her eyes and sniffling. I send her a small, caring smile to show her I don't mind the display of emotions. "I have a flex period."

"Oh, cool," I smile easily, setting my elbows on the table and holding my chin up that way. "I can't wait to get one of those."

"A lot of the time it is kind of boring," she shrugs. While she is talking she moves the plastic cover of the book onto the page she was on and closes the hardcover copy. I look at her quickly, scanning the honest and open expression on her face and decide to take the leap of faith.

"I wouldn't think so, not to disagree with you," I speak up. Everyone knows me. She must know that I'm religious and take my religion very seriously. "I'd love that free time just to decompress and visit God."

"God," she huffs, sliding her boyish haircut out of her eyes with a leather band bracelet filled wrist.

"I'm Daisy," I hold my hand out. She stares at it before giving me a limp handshake.

"Daniel," she replies, confirming my thoughts. She is a transgender. I have to tread carefully so I won't disturb her too much but I also refuse to let her lead me into sin by lying.

"Is that your preferred name?" I ask gently. She understands the hint I'm throwing. Surprise shows on her face at the slightly discreet tone I use. I don't want her to get defensive and hate me right off the bat, broaching this subject with uninformed minds is a delicate task.

"Yeah," she says.

"What name did you discard?" She knows I'm asking her the name her parents gave her, the name on her birth certificate. She's either going to continue our conversation at this point, or leave.

"Danielle."

"That's pretty," I respond. My nerves are a little tight, making me want to fidget so I breathe deeply, allowing room for the Holy Spirit to fill me. "Was it a family name?"

"Yeah, sort of of." She smiles, chewing on her fingernails. "My uncle's name was Daniel. He passed away the year I was born."

"Such a rich history." I smile softly, giving her time to add more if she wants. I really don't want it to seem as if I'm trying to indoctrinate her into the Catholic Church. Faith comes at its own times, by the grace of God.

"Yeah," she says, still chewing her nails. "I never met him obviously but all the stories I hear about him are amazing." She laughs lightly. "Kinda makes it hard to live up to his name."

"I wouldn't mind hearing some stories," I encourage her gently. It'll be nice to get to know her as a person, not just some statistic I'm trying to change. I love people, love them but I don't like their sin. Maybe when this conversation is done we will be friends, who knows?

"You know how people say there is always a good twin and a bad twin?" She asks, curling her hand through her short hair to move it to the side.

"I've heard that vaguely. But there are multiple twin saints. For example, St. Benedict of Nursia and his twin sister, St. Scholastica. Both twins can be good." I pipe up, apparently full of facts. I purse my lips when I remember that I'm trying to get her to open up to me.

"That's actually cool," her eyes light up. "Kinda like twin super-hero's."

"That's an awesome way to look at it," I agree. "I haven't thought about it like that but I guess it's true. Saints are heroes of sanctification."

"Whatever that means," she waves her hand before sticking it back in her mouth to pull on a hangnail. "Anywho, my uncle was the good twin and my mom the bad twin. So I'm trying everything I can to live up to who he was, not who my mom is."

"That's beautiful." It truly is a beautiful story. She also gave me the answer to why she wants to be a he. Her mother isn't a very good person, or mother, so she wants to distance herself from her bad maternal figure and strive to be as close as possible to her deceased, wonderful uncle.

"So, like, he never really drank, ya know?" Tears spring to her eyes at the memories so I reach for her hand and squeeze it. "My family is a bunch of drunks, I swear this whole damn town is. But he was different. He didn't drink. He wasn't caught up in everyday drama. He was better than all that without seeming better than everyone. All the stories everyone has told me is like he was some hero because he didn't break under the pressure to drink, to stop being the good person he was."

"He sounds like a saint," I smile. My throat aches when her eyes brighten at my words. Danielle really seems to be thinking about what being a saint means.

"Do you think he was a saint?" she asks, wiping her eyes.

"I couldn't tell you," I shrug. "We'll find out one day."

"What exactly is a saint?" She clears her throat and slides her book away from between us.

"I don't know what the dictionary says," I laugh lightly. "But to me a saint is someone who carries their daily cross."

"Sometimes Daisy, you sound like you speak a different language." Danielle laughs at me. She once again fixes her black hair to the side. "What the heck is a daily cross?"

"Just living your life with a smile." I shift in my seat, wincing a little. I haven't been doing the best of carrying my cross. "My cross is schoolwork, watching my cousins, cooking for my family and cleaning up after them. It's so exhausting. Two months ago it was just me and my dad and now there are two babies, two toddlers, three children, a preteen, four teens and two adults that are basically children."

"Tell me about it," Danielle sighs loudly in annoyance. "I have four younger sisters and two younger brothers, three of them already trying to outdrink each other."

"It seems like a contest between them!" I agree wholeheartedly. "Rennie tries to outdrink Louis, which he usually doesn't do because he's outdid him on the weed!"

"It's a whole cycle that just keeps on repeating! I feel like I'm stuck in the rut!"

"Is that why you want to change genders?" I ask bluntly, waiting for a lash back. Danielle stares at me, stunned.

"That's none of your business." She says sharply, backing away from me defensively.

"I love you Danielle, as a sister in Christ," I say firmly, pressing on because she hasn't jumped up and walked away or started yelling at me. "And I want to see you in heaven. But to get to heaven you have to sanctify yourself and what that means is denying sin. Trying to change your gender is sinning. God made you for a reason and God made you perfectly."

"Like you don't sin," she scoffs, biting on her fingernails. One of them starts bleeding but she doesn't notice.

"I do sin," I admit bravely. Tears well up in my eyes at all the times I hurt God, whipped Jesus in the scourging because of my sins. All I want to do is love God but I am human and I fall and I hurt Him. "And I'd love it if you could tell me when I'm sinning so I can break that bad habit."

"Really?" Danielle squints at me in disbelief. "You're not gonna pretend you're holier than everyone else because you go to church on Sundays?"

"Nope," I say cheerfully. "I'm a sinner. I make bad decisions and have to learn from those mistakes. And just because someone goes to church Sunday morning doesn't mean they're religious. That's getting into a whole different argument so I'll leave it at that."

"What's wrong with me wanting to switch genders?" she asks, ripping off a part of her pointer finger nail so low it must hurt.

"It isn't physically possible-," I begin.

"-Doctors perform the surgeries," she interrupts me. I take a deep breathe to control my rising anger. If there is anything that angers me more than people denying what God gave them, it is doctors acting like God.

"Only some doctors and those doctors are most likely the ones that murder babies in their mother's wombs." My voice is hard so I clear it, hoping whatever retaliating words I use next won't be as harsh. Danielle had stopped looking at me when I mentioned abortion.

"You're pretty opinionated," she murmurs after a moment of silence.

"Let me ask you this before I continue to change your mind about what you think is right for your body," I say, sighing loudly. No one has called me opinionated before. I don't quite know how to take it so I decide to let it go. "Does God make mistakes?"

"Is that a trick question?" She furrows her eyebrows, clearly agitated. Her fingers interlock, some tapping her knuckles with her thumbs squeezing too tightly onto her skin.

"No," I reply, "it's a yes or no answer."

"Well, yes," she says with a flippant shrug of her shoulders. "Why would he put me in a female body if he knew I want to be male?"

"That's not God tempting you," I state gently yet firmly. "That's His greatest adversary trying to win your soul. Satan wants you to think you are male and act on your thoughts because God would lose your soul to him."

"What if I have doubts?" Danielle's voice is shaky as she asks this, wiping tears from her eyes. I offer her a tissue when snot threatens to drop from her nose. I can't imagine the struggle of this emotional battle. God has never made me fight through body dysmorphia.

"If you have doubts that means God is speaking to you. You don't hear words. For me, most of the time I feel this strong emotion in my gut. I call it the Holy Spirit. When I follow Him I always make better decisions." I reach out to hold her hand again. She smiles valiantly before tucking her head into her arms. "If you are having doubts, Danielle, that means Satan is losing. Instead of feeling sad and lost, praise God because He is fighting that internal, spiritual battle for you."

"Just keep talking," she manages to speak through sobs, hands waving in the air. "You're making so much sense right now. Everyone else doesn't fight me, they just agree to whatever I say."

"Oh," I purse my lips. "Okay. Um, I'm sorry if it seemed like I was attacking you. I just really wanted to get this out in the open so maybe you can understand where I'm coming from. Thank you so much for listening with an open mind." I realize I'm starting to rant so I take a deep breath and lick my lips, giving myself time to form my thoughts. "God made man first, than woman. That's right at the beginning of the bible, in the book of Genesis and repeated throughout the bible. God created Adam and spent time making him companions until finally he made Eve out of the ribs of Adam's body. God didn't create Adam and Steve, he created Adam and Eve because the two were meant to be the best of companions and to procreate. Men and women can make babies, men with men and women with women can't make babies. Women don't have the biological ingredients needed to have a woman on woman relationship that allows procreation. Farther on in the bible that is why Lot offered his daughters to the men from Sodom. The sin of adultery to him wasn't as bad as the sin of sodomy. Also, we know that men and women's genitalia is different for the specific reason of procreation. A good example showing why men can't become women and women can't become men or have same sex relationships is using a kitchen chair to chop wood. That kitchen chair is meant for sitting, it's probably sanded and painted so when you set a block of wood on it and chop it will hurt your mind, your heart, and your soul to chip it with each stroke of the axe. All that work spent on it from cutting down the tree, measuring and sanding, nailing it together and painting it, that was a lot of work. Probably made you proud of your work. We are the chairs in this scenario and God is the craftsman. He works on us lovingly, counts every single hair on our head, loves us imperfect beings perfectly; and when we let Satan screw with our minds and lead us into sin, that is Satan chopping wood on us kitchen chairs. That is Satan destroying what God made because he is jealous of God's love for us."

"I still don't know what to think," Danielle breathes heavily, blowing her nose. "But thanks for being honest with me. You did seem a little pushy but if you are right it was worth it."

"Thank you," I smile at her and pat her hand. "Is it okay if I call you Danielle?"

"Oh my goodness," her head hits the table with a thump. My eyes rise in surprise at the unexpected reaction from whatever she is thinking. Her brown skin is darkening with red. "I'm so embarrassed. I've been trying to be a boy for three years."

"Oh, really?" I ask, surprised. "I only noticed this year."

"You're funny," Danielle bursts into giggles. It's gut wrenching with the tears contrasting the happy sound. I shrug it off. I wasn't joking around, I'd only noticed her female body in men's clothes and attitude this year but especially because I saw her using the boys' change rooms and bathrooms. She clears her throat, letting the few straggling giggles out. "Just call me Dani. Most people do."

"Can I tell you what helps me make good decisions? Where I can relax and rest in God's embrace? It might help you with your future decisions. There is no reason to be embarrassed about searching for good in your life and sticking to it." I curl my hair behind my ear, amused when it pops back out faster than normal. It's more staticky now that snow found its home here.

"You will anyways, won't you?" Danielle laughs with a watery grin. "I feel like I've just been mentally whiplashed."

"I want you to spend ten minutes a day with the Blessed Sacrament." I begin giving her the spiritual homework I use for myself.

"-Hold up," she interrupts me. "What is the Blessed Sacrament?"

"Short answer: Jesus." I answer speedily. "When you get more comfortable with God and religion I'd be happy to go more in depth. But for now just go to St. Bernadette's every day you can make it and stay for ten minutes. Try visiting with God as if He is your best friend. Just vent to Him, pray however you know how to, I want you to form a very personal, loving relationship with God. Just so I'm not confusing you, God is everywhere. You can talk to Him anywhere but it's nice to reach out to Him, to go to Him and make that space for Him."

"No promises," Danielle responds with a small albeit hopeful smile. "But I'll try."

"Thank you!" I beam at her. "That's all me and God are asking!" Our conversation has come to an end and we sit in a slightly awkward silence until the bell rings and the library doors open for us to greet the students coming in.

"Kinda looks serious," Betty says easily. Esther juts her thumb over her shoulder. "We can come back later."

"Nah, we could use some conversation starters." I share a warm smile with Danielle, my newfound friend. God bless her!

"Hey Daniel," Betty sits beside Danielle. I look at the interaction, aware of the flush in Danielle's cheeks because her thought process about her gender and sexuality is changing. "Daisy wasn't trying to convert you, was she?" Betty leans close to Danielle and whispers conspiratorially. "She has a tendency to do that."

"I think she did," Danielle beams at me, reaching her hand out for me to hold. I grasp onto it, giving her the courage to say her true name, given to her by her parents. "'Cause I know my name now. It is Danielle, sister in Christ."

"Whoa, not cool Daisy." Betty glares at me, Esther backing her up. "Daniel had such a hard time coming out and now you probably bullied him back into the closet."

"No way," Bianca and Sadie speak up, defending me. "The Holy Spirit just opened Danielle's eyes and gave her one of His gifts."

"'Kay, girls," Danielle rolls her eyes. "I can fight for myself."

"Let's go get lunch," Sadie intervenes. I smile at her, and the other four girls around me. My friend group is growing every day, for that I thank God but I'm always going to rely on Him before them. I sigh in relief, Betty and Esther dragging Danielle to the cafeteria with them as Bianca and Sadie wait for me. A weight seems to be lifted from my shoulders. Danielle and I worked together by God's grace alone, of that I am certain. Who else would have let that difficult conversation go that smoothly. Praise God!

38

Move In

———⟫-◦-⟪———

Today's the day!" Kennedy screams in my ear, spit flying on my face. I groan from her germs drying on my face and roll off the bottom bunk, rubbing my tired eyes. Louis and Rennie tried fighting each other last night and woke up nearly everyone and dad booted them outside and for the first time since I was a baby, the front door was locked shut. Because his dad and uncle got into a fight Conan had extra rough nightmares and refused to sleep without me by his side, but that meant I had to wake him up every two hours so he could pee because I didn't want to be peed on at night, since we conveniently ran out of pull-ups for him the night before. Kennedy and Tinsley didn't fall asleep for a few hours after the fight, having been refreshed enough from their sleep in the beginning of the night. Landon and Tyler were also out on drunks with Harry and Col driving them around which meant that I had to stay up with the girls when Dad went back to bed. Lee didn't even get out of bed when Louis and Rennie were fighting.

"We get to move into the mansion!" Makayla squeals, jumping on my back. I pat her head with a yawn, my eyes bleary.

"You remember the plan?" I ask, shaking my head when I yawn again. My eyes catch the time on the clock and I sigh deeply, greatly irritated. It's six in the morning. The children were supposed to let me and dad sleep until eight. I look around the living room. Windsor is tickling Tikara into a fit of giggles. Conan is playing by the wood stove, ignoring everyone around him and playing with imaginary friends with only underwear on. Tinsley is the only one still in bed but that's because she is holding Philomena close to her.

"Yeah," Makayla laughs loudly in my ear when I shake her off, helping her land carefully on the double bottom bunk bed. "Me and Tinsley gotta fill our drawers with our clothes."

"Then get to it," I stand up to stretch. Kennedy lifts her arms up for me to hold her so I scoop her up.

"Pannycakes!" She giggles in her loud voice. My heart melts. This little girl is going to be a heartbreaker, it's so hard to say no to her.

"Pancakes sound good with you guys?" I ask the rest of the children. Lee's bunk is empty, he must be out on his daily five mile run.

"Gross!" Windsor hollers with his goofy smile and a wrinkled nose. I put a finger to my lips so he stage whispers his disagreement.

"Yeah!" Makayla shoots her older brother a dirty look.

"No berries," Tinsley says in her quiet voice, barely audible with Conan's muttering to himself, Kennedy's whooshing and whistling in my ear, Tikara's heavy breathing and giggles and Windsor and Makayla's speedy argument.

"I know," I smile gently at Tinsley. She is the only one allergic to anything and she has a bunch of allergies. Strawberries, apples, bananas, all nuts, penicillin, bees.... We're just waiting to see what else the poor girl might be allergic to.

"Pannycakes!" Kennedy shouts in my ear. My eyes widen at the loud voice next to my ear but when I freeze the children all freeze too, hearing what I heard. My dad is waking up. I laugh at the children's reactions. Windsor rushes to put a shirt on. Kennedy scrambles from my arms to play on a bed. Makayla and Tinsley rush to do their chores. Apparently my dad is a scary person. I do have to admit the children listen to him more than me because they have a fear respect for him while mine is a gentle respect. The two attitudes prove just how much children need mothers and fathers.

In the five minutes it takes the children to realize my dad is not waking up I have the pancake batter mixed and the stove warming up. Makayla sneakily stirs the batter as I wait to flip the pancakes. "I wanna help," she announces, chewing on her fingernails. I gently pry her fingers from her mouth.

"You have to wash your hands if you want to help." I say firmly. "And you can't bite your nails after you wash your hands." She looks at the sink, the stove, the bowl of batter and me before making her decision.

"Never mind," she says loftily before walking away. I chuckle at her antics but the little happiness doesn't last for long. I didn't do the dishes last night and no one else got around to them. Lee refuses to wash dishes, the closest he gets is rinsing the babies' bottles out to fill with more milk. The Trip's hadn't made it home last night. They may even have stayed the night with their parents because Huntley has been exceptionally nice the past few days. Harry is convinced he just wants something from them but Landon thinks Huntley turned over a new leaf and Tyler is just following whatever his brothers do. I check on my pancakes in the pan. They aren't ready to flip so I start running water, filling the children's cups up to use the cold water and when it is hot I plug the sink, stacking dishes in it. Lately I've been so tired I haven't wanted to carry my daily cross and I procrastinate which leads me to crankiness. Big plates go in first, then little plates and bowls on top of them. Utensils in the front and cups wherever there is room. They'll soak while I flip the pancakes and put fresh batter on, it makes for easier washing. I have a stack of pancakes cooked and the right hand sink filled with clean dishes when we all hear the clatter of something moving around outside.

"Aunty, there's someone out there!" Windsor exclaims, crouching near the window to peek out.

"Windsor Wilde!" I hiss, "get away from there!" The girls all scramble to the beds with the babies on them as he peeks his head up again. I tug him back.

"But Aunty-," his grin is even wider than normal. Even in my worried state it makes my lips twitch into a little smile.

"Go to the beds!"

"Why aren't you?" he retorts, ever the manly one. I've found them all to be super bossy kids because they have been raising themselves for the majority of their lives. With me and my dad caring for them they have found time to actually be children but the bossiness has remained.

"I'm making sure it's not Lee or the Trips or your dads first!" I retort, giving him an answer whereas my dad wouldn't. With some more cluttering and curse words, I peek again, spotting Landon crashing into my dad's rocking chair. I grit my teeth while I quickly switch over pancakes and batter, the children peppering me with questions. Then I make my way to the little deck of my dad's cabin and gently close the door even with the anger billowing through me. I'm sick of the bad example the Trips and my cousins show the children. I've never really had the urge to drink but I see them drinking and getting drunk after a particularly tough day and I want to put a bottle to my lips. I hate the thought especially when I don't care for the drink!

"Hey Shawty," Landon grins at me. His arms rise for a hug, one hand with a beer bottle in it. He must have fought last night because his face has some fresh bruises and cuts and his knuckles are scabbed and swollen.

"Landon," I sigh deeply, pinching the bridge of my nose. *Jesus, I'm angry. Help me to surrender this anger to You and use it for my sanctification. Amen.* "Are you drunk?"

"Nah Shawty," he grins at me stupidly, followed by a wink. Then he pinches his pointer finger and thumb together. "Okay, maybe just a little buzzed. Or a little more than buzzed."

"I'm making pancakes," I sigh, leaning on a post. My hands make their way to my ears to tuck my gravity defying hair in but it doesn't help, adding another annoyance to my day. To think I thought today would be a terrific day. I shake my bitterness off, throwing away my anger and bad mood like an apple. Today we are moving into Ridel House. Today is a good day because my dad had decided that the Trips and Louis and Rennie can stay in the cabin if they are going to continue drinking and partying. Today is a good day because Windsor and Conan finally get their all boy room and Sally Anne, Makayla and Tinsley get their all girl room. Today is a good day because I won't be sharing a living room as a bedroom with my three older cousins and the trips and babies. The only ones I'll have in my bedroom are the babies, Kennedy and Lee. "I'll make you a plate."

"Noooooooooo," Landon drags the word out. It's still only six thirty in the morning but we hear a vehicle pulling into the driveway. "Daisy don't go!" With whatever Landon is thinking he starts laughing out loud.

"I have to flip the pancakes." I state firmly, seeing Phil's Expedition parking behind my dad's truck. Why is he here so early?

"Nooooooo," Landon grasps my wrist with his free hand and tugs me into his body. I lose my balance when my knees knock into his and end up falling in his lap. The chilly fall morning isn't as cold with his overheated body burning against mine. I look over his shoulder to the barn, where Col's truck is parked. Landon must have escaped Col and Harry's sight, they usually put him up in the barn if he's still drinking.

"Landon," I state firmly, with a harder edge in my tone. "I don't want the pancakes burning."

"Aye, Phil!" Landon waves at Phil and Percy exiting Phil's SUV. Then he takes a big slurp of his beer. Towards the barn we hear yelling and cursing and some crashing. Phil and Percy make the quick decision to split off and Phil hops up onto the deck while Percy jogs to the barn. "Go flip the pancakes," Landon orders his older cousin, chugging down some more beer. I sigh in relief when the bottle is just about empty.

"You okay, Daisy?" Phil asks, crossing his arms over his chest. He knows it's a delicate situation right now, calling me by my first name. He must see that Landon's arm hasn't let my wrist go. Am I the only one who has noticed just how clingy Landon can be sometimes?

"Yeah, can you please go check on the pancakes? If Sally Anne is up you can tell her to do it." I say, subtlety trying to tug my arm out of Landon's grasp. It isn't going anywhere.

"Sure," Phil replies easily, his eyes telling Landon to let me go. The oldest triplet laughs and tugs me closer, letting his chin rest on my shoulder.

"Landon," I place my hand on his chin and force him to look at me. He rests his forehead against mine. "You need to let me go. Okay? I don't mind hugging you but I don't want to be sitting on top of you. That isn't right. You know so."

"But Daisy," he whines, holding me even closer. "My dad's a f—king piece of shit."

"Awe," I wrap my arms around him. Harry was right. His dad just wanted them back for something. "I'm sorry you had to go through that."

"Me too," Landon grins. He holds the beer bottle out to me. "Want some?"

"Not really," I reply but my stomach lurches because I actually want to put the bottle to my lips. I see my dad do it, the Trips, my cousins, and I want to taste what the big fuss is. Landon makes airplane sounds and brings the bottle close to my lips before zooming away, giggling as he does so. I roll my eyes. Landon can be such a child sometimes.

"Open up," he coos, bringing the bottle back to my lips. I do open my mouth because he'd started tipping the bottle up and I don't want to stink of beer all day. The drink burns down my throat and sits heavily in my stomach, flushing my cheeks. In three big swallows the drink is finished and that distracts Landon enough for me to stand up. Everything is warm and fuzzy and that seems to take the edge off of the emotions that were building up inside me.

"Landon," I put my hands on my hips. "I'm gonna go cook the pancakes. Come inside and warm up."

"Nah Shawty," Landon grins at me while struggling to stand up. "I needa find some more beer."

"Landon, what the f—k are you doing?" My dad storms out of the house. He's still in his long johns which makes me laugh but the anger in his expression startles me. He starts manhandling Landon, shouting at him. "I don't let you live here rent free to get away from your dad so you could force my daughter to drink! What the f—k is wrong with you?"

"Sorry," Landon says sombrely before bursting into giggles. Phil steps out onto the deck, closing the door behind him. Windsor and the girls were looking through it behind him. I shoot Phil a dirty look, he ratted Landon out.

"Dad, it's okay," I intervene, stepping slightly between them.

"I knew this was a bad idea, Daisy," Dad huffs, shaking Landon roughly. "They have to leave."

"But dad we're going to the mansion. They'll be at the cabin," I quickly retort. Percy, Col and Harry are walking to the cabin. Tyler must be in the barn loft with Louis and Rennie.

"You are my daughter, Daisy. It's my job to protect you. You come first, not them," Dad snaps, leaning Landon over the railing. Landon's face is green and he is unusually quiet. If someone is laying hands on him he is usually fighting them back.

"What are you doing?" Harry cries, trotting up the steps. Phil blocks him.

"Why don't you ask your brother?" My dad hisses, turning Landon around in time for him to vomit on the grass. I gag at the sounds and run to the edge of the deck where I too spit up what little I have in my stomach. Some of the edge wears off but I still look at my dad, the angriest I've ever been.

"You're blaming Landon, really?" I accuse, wiping spit from my chin. "All my life, every time something gets hard, you reach for the bottle. Since Louis and Rennie got here they drink whenever they can. The Trip's drink to hide from the demons in their minds. If there is anyone to blame for me drinking just a minute ago, it's all of you! It's all I see. Oh no, I had a bad day. Take a drink, get the edge off. I could have told Landon no but I wanted to see what you guys think is so special about drinking! There's nothing to it! Drinking makes you feel emptier than when you weren't drinking. Just go to Jesus dammit!" My dad lets Landon go and stares at me in shock. I don't think I have ever raised my voice to him before. Col snickers in the background. Percy elbows him to shut up.

"Don't you ever use that tone of voice with me again, Daisy." Dad orders sternly before pulling me into a hug. Tears well up in my eyes because his arms around me is such a familiar thing. It's home, it's comfort, it's protection, it's love. Since the children came here we don't spend nearly as much time together as we used to. I think we need some father daughter bonding time.

"I'm sorry, daddy."

"Me too, my girl, me too." He kisses the top of my head. "I've been doing better," he says quietly for only me to hear. "There's been so much more stress but I haven't drank in two months."

"I'm so proud of you," I sob, squeezing tightly.

"I don't know why these Watsons are here so damn early," dad huffs teasingly while letting me go. I stand beside him, his arm looped around my waist as I lean my head on his shoulder. "Since I told them eight o'clock!"

"Heard something about pancakes," Peter retorts with a grin. I feel an embarrassed flush go through my body. Peter and Paul must have arrived when I was yelling at my dad. I want to fall on my knees and cry because of the disrespect I showed my dad, especially in front of people but I bottle my emotions up for now. Fr. John is going to hear one heck of a confession from me tomorrow.

"You guys might as well come in," dad ushers the Watsons inside. "I need to get dressed for the day." He slaps Phil's shoulder on the way in the door. "Thanks for telling me."

"I hope you'd do the same if it was my daughters," Phil shrugs. He glances back at me. I shoot him a square smile. Percy slaps my back with a goofy grin.

"Didn't know you could talk like that." I blush brightly, wanting to die on the spot. Apparently I have a bad side, and now they won't ever let that go. Percy hoots in laughter before Peter shoves him inside.

"Pancakes, delicious!" Peter grins, rubbing his stomach. "I'm hungry!"

"I guess I'm not the only one going through some stuff, huh," Paul says quietly beside me. The sadness in his eyes washes away my embarrassment. Paul is this town's saint, I just know it. "I'm here if you want someone to talk to." Paul invites, giving me a quick hug. It's a stiff hug, too. He probably doesn't hug many people because of Amy's irrational jealousy so I'm not taking his hug for granted. It must have meant a lot for him to do.

"Thank you," I send him a small smile. He closes the door behind him, allowing us teenagers to regroup. Col lifts me up in a hug and spins me around.

"I'm sorry Daisy." He says seriously. His lips are in a firm line, making his scar protrude. "I was your only real friend throughout childhood and it must have hurt to see me turn to booze the same as our parents. I'm not gonna stop drinking but I am sorry I left you alone."

"It's okay." I lean my forehead on his pec, relaxing in his embrace. Col doesn't judge, he's not going to care that I was arguing with my dad. All he's going to do is hold a safe space for me, let me be me and get all the bad stuff out.

"No," Col responds. "It isn't. I was under the same pressure as you seeing everyone drink, and drink, and drink but the difference between me and you was that I fell, you stayed strong. And sober."

"It's a f—king disease." Harry adds, spitting on the grass. "Be happy you don't have it." Without planning it we all turn to Landon, expecting him to say something next but he's passed out on the deck. "We'll take him to the loft." Harry sighs.

"Sorry we let him out of our sight the first time," Col hugs me again and kisses the top of my head. "What a dumbass."

I stand on the deck looking at the scenery in front of me. Sugar lying in her dog house, she'd known it was just Landon and hadn't barked or growled in a warning. That's why I assumed the clattering outside was someone that lived here. Karen is yipping at Sweetie near the barn, and she's hissing in return. The trees are barren from leaves and a light dusting of snow covers the ground. I succumbed to Satan's temptation. It infuriates me more than anything else, the fact that I let Satan win for a moment in my life. I want to grab my dad's sledgehammer and whack him upside the head but I'll leave that for Mama Mary to do. But I'll help her do it by praying. So I regroup myself by quietly praying nine Memorare's.

When I enter the cabin dad is at the stove with Peter, making a pot of coffee. Peter is flipping pancakes. Phil is chasing Kennedy around the living room and Percy is throwing Conan in the air. Paul is sitting at the table with a red faced Philomena. She must have been crying while I was engrossed in prayer. As usual, he has the magic touch and she is quickly calming down. Upstairs, Sally Anne is yelling at Windsor and Makayla to leave her alone. Tikara is crawling around, chasing after Teddy, the dirty Shih Tzu. He badly needs a bath.

I quickly wash the children's plates. We only have enough for them to use once and then wash them to use for supper. We don't have the cupboard space for more plates, another perk about the mansion I will enjoy because I won't have to use dishes just to dirty them again. More cupboard space means more room for dishes. Sally Anne is twelve, old enough to wash and dry the dishes by herself. Makayla has complained to me often enough about having to do all the dishes when they lived with my uncle Joseph so I never make her wash dishes. Peter dries the dishes when waiting for the pancakes to cook and Percy makes the children's plates with each new clean dish, cutting up the littles' pancakes. I want to melt in gratitude for their help. It makes the tedious process so much faster. Phil rounds up the children, making sure they have clean clothes on before sitting them at the table to eat. My dad leans his tailbone on the counter between the fridge and the stove, taking a sip of steaming black coffee. When Aria is here she buys cream and sugar but he doesn't make a fuss when she is gone. He sets his coffee cup down and licks his lips, noticing the full table and impatiently waiting children.

"Let's pray," he speaks up loudly. Kennedy smiles widely, dropping a piece of pancake on her plate. She was the only one who tried eating before praying, the rest know to wait after the time they've spent together with us. Dad leads us in the sign of the cross and the blessing of the meal. As soon as he is done, the Watsons and I get back to work and the children visit and eat, all trying to speak over each other. Phil's head ticks and his knuckles clench into fists. Paul speaks quietly to him before leading him outside. The noise must bother him, maybe it's a reminder of something that happened overseas wherever he was. "You kids, quiet down!" My dad orders with pancake stuffed in his mouth. They're quiet for about five seconds before getting louder again. I laugh about it with Peter, washing the dishes dirtied this morning.

"Sounds like home," Peter grins at me, tapping the top of my head with a plate before putting it in its proper cupboard.

"How's Corinne?" I ask, rinsing the batter bowl.

"Getting bigger and moving less," Peter's smile is so happy and huge it makes me smile. His smile slowly falters, showing his worry. "She has to go the hospital every three days for all the extra amniotic fluid to be drained."

"What are the doctors saying?"

"They want to induce, it's safer that way. They're also suggesting we get her tubes tied." Peter leans on the counter, rubbing his hands over his hair. "It wasn't this bad with Reece but with every baby it'll get worse. The next pregnancy could threaten her life."

"I am so sorry, Peter," I say, my heart going out to him. Out of all Dickie's sons, he was the one most like his father, wanting the super big, close knit family. Phil was good with his first four children but Arlette was raised Catholic, they are Catholic high school sweethearts and she wants as many children as God will give her. Phil hasn't been able to say no although he did get her to agree to space them all roughly two years apart.

"Whatever God wills," Peter shakes his gloom off. "It's gonna hurt but carrying that Cross hurt, too."

"Amen."

"Makayla and Tinsley!" My dad booms. The two girls drop the toys they are playing with and look at him. "Take your drawers over to the mansion. Windsor, you too."

"Yay!" The children all shout and shriek in joy.

"Stack everything in the living room for now!" Dad's raised voice is barely heard above their clamour. Even Sally Anne is rushing to bring her things to the big house.

"I'm watch the littles in the living room," Peter offers. Dad nods.

"Phil and I will set up everything in the mansion," dad says. His coffee is now in a coffee mug.

"I'll help the children carry everything over," Percy adds. My dad had brought a few big cardboard boxes to load up the cupboard and storage items.

"Thanks," dad hollers over his shoulder. He begins walking, visiting with Phil while carrying his nightstand to the mansion. Phil is carrying my dad's rocking chair. Paul loads the boxes with kitchen dishes, emptying cupboards. Percy takes a box when it is full. Windsor, Tinsley and Makayla take all their clothes in the dresser drawers and when they are done that, they curl the blankets and pillows into balls and race them to the mansion. When I'm done the dishes I grab a box and empty out cleaning supplies from under the bathroom sink. Harry has joined Percy so he doesn't get too far behind, his face very pale with deep purple bags under his eyes. If I'm exhausted he must be doubly exhausted. Harry follows his drunk and drugged up brothers around all night, making sure they get home safe. If anyone should be having a mental breakdown of some sort, it is him. When the box is full I put it by the door. There is only one box left and Paul and I reach it at the same time.

"Kitchen's done," he says with a soft smile, taking the box so I won't have to.

"You work fast," I raise my eyebrows and blow some stray strands of hair out of my face.

"Not hard," Paul laughs lightly, "considering you only have ten cupboards."

"That's fair," I roll my eyes and point upstairs. "I guess we can pack up the Chaplet."

"You know," Paul sighs, looking at the very steep stairs that are basically a ladder. "I've never actually seen Duncan's Chaplet."

"It's beautiful," I reply, motioning for him to go up the stairs first.

"Ladies first," he replies. The front door opens and Percy enters with an empty box. Paul passes me the empty box he was holding to get Percy's. "Still need me up there?"

"We need another ten boxes," I joke, climbing up. Any religious papers Fr. John and other priests have handed out dad has stored in his bookshelf. That doesn't include the monthly missals I store to read when I've finished all my spiritual books. It's nice to go back and reflect on them. All my spiritual books are stored up here as well, that makes three separate bookshelves.

"Wow," Paul breathes out, reverently touching the feet on our statue of Jesus's Divine Mercy. Then he kisses the toes of Jesus on our large crucifix. "My Lord and my God."

"It's peaceful, hey?" I laugh serenely as I pack up my books in the box.

"I can feel His presence." Paul's eyes are watery as he falls to his knees. I leave him alone, allowing him this prayer time. The box is heavy but Harry is at the bottom of the stairs when I drag it to the top. He throws up his empty box and climbs up the first few steps. I push the box into his arms and he grunts from the weight. Harry doesn't expect the heavy weight and I'm still holding onto the box so when he drops the box I fall through the rectangle, my heart in my throat. "Daisy!" Paul exclaims, jumping on me. Harry curses me and the box when he falls down the stairs, his ankle hooked in between two steps and a thick, hardcover book lands on his hand. My upper body hangs in the space, Paul holding me up by sitting on my legs.

"You all good?" Peter asks, looking up the stairs with Tikara in his arms.

"Yeah. I think my hands can reach the stairs," I mumble, closing my eyes at the blood rushing to my head. I reach my hands out, unable to reach the stairs. I'm in the perfect spot of missing the steps and not being able to reach the walls. "Never mind." Paul laughs.

"I'm going to get off your legs Daisy," he talks me through his movements. "I'm still going to put pressure on your legs with my hand to keep you there but I'm also going to wrap an arm around your waist and pull you up. Got it?"

"Are you even that strong?" I ask, not quite finished the question when he heaves me up.

"Are you insinuating something Daisy?" Paul narrows his eyes at me. "Maybe that I'm not as thick as my brothers?"

"No!" My eyes widen. I only thought that he couldn't lift me because, well, because he doesn't have as much muscle definition as his brothers. "Maybe," I wince. "But I am heavy."

"You look so scared," Paul laughs, slapping my back. "I was just teasing you, kid. I've always been the scrawny boy. Can only blame my momma."

"You're always so serious," I grumble, grabbing the empty box and following him into the Chaplet room. "And then pop goes the weasel you have some sort of humour and it's always unexpected."

"Thank you," Paul smiles with a laugh. I load up another box with books with Paul and walk it down the stairs. Harry is back again and he glares at me before walking around me to load up another box.

"Take it yourself," he mutters grumpily. I let it slide, noticing the limp in his steps. Even after a night of fighting he doesn't limp like that so now I feel bad. I throw my coat over my shoulders and slip my winter boots on. I walk to the mansion, breathing hard from the fast pace and the heavy box. Percy is visiting with my dad and Phil when I enter the mansion. It still amazes me how big it is, how new everything seems even though the sinks and toilets and floorboards were donated by Paul.

"Oh great," I chirp, "coffee break."

"Not for you," dad retorts, taking the box out of my arms. He just about drops it, not expecting the weight. I dance back, laughing at him.

"You heard the boss," I slap Percy's back. "We don't get a break."

"Sheesh," he responds cheekily. "He's a slave driver, ain't he?"

"You said it," I laugh when my dad sends me a halfhearted glare. Percy loops his arm around my elbow with a laugh and drags me with him as he races to the cabin. "What are you doing?" I ask incredulously, just about tripping in the snow. At the rate he's going he'd be dragging me behind him if I did trip.

"You can feel it in the air!" Percy shouts to the open sky. "Doesn't it make you just wanna fly?"

"The air? Fly? Are you talking about the breathtaking brisk, fresh, fall air?" Percy nods, not picking up on my slight sarcasm as I tease him.

"It's beautiful! God's earth is beautiful!" he shouts. Windsor and Makayla are running passed us, dresser drawers in their arms and they look at him weirdly.

"Did you fight a fire recently?" I ask with a chuckle as Percy pulls me into the cabin. Besides being a firefighter in the summer he volunteers in the winter at our small town's very small, four man firefighting team.

"Yeah, MVA last night." Percy answers with a wrinkled nose. "Awful smell, horrible oxygen. This brisk farm air is so beautiful!"

"Is he ranting about the air again?" Peter tuts, rocking Philomena in his arms. I make an internal reminder to pray for whoever was involved into the vehicular accident. "Just ignore him."

"At least I'm not talking about my wife." Percy retorts in good nature. "That's all you do. Corinne this, Corinne that, Corinne is amazing."

"'Corinne has me whipped'!" Paul shouts from upstairs. I laugh at the brotherly bond they share, the banter that passes so easily through them.

"So the Trip's are getting the cabin?" Percy asks. "Did they fight over the rooms yet?"

"Not really," I reply with a shrug, picking Tikara up because she is trying to crawl out the open door. "Tyler's getting my room." All three Watson boys whistle at my words. I roll my eyes at their antics. They're worse than high school girls. "Landon is getting the storage room up there and Harry the Chaplet. Louis and Rennie are gonna share my dad's room." Percy drags the next box of books down the stairs, eyebrows raised at how hefty it is.

"We should carry this together," he decides on a whim. Harry passes down the large crucifix. I set Tikara down, grab crucifix and tuck it into my left side, looping my elbow around it. My other hand holds onto the box as Percy trudges forward, still just about running. We trot down the steps, Percy still teasing Peter about Corinne when we run smack into Fr. John. Percy catches the weight of the box when I slip in the snow and fall on my back, clutching Jesus crucified close to me. Fr. John steps back from the force, his back hitting the grill of my dad's truck. "Whoops," Percy grins his cheeky smile. "My bad, Father."

"No problem," Fr. John smiles, holding a hand up for me to grab. I use it to pull myself up and shake to get rid of the snow coating my clothes. "It's nice to see your enthusiasm for work and your charity to your neighbours."

"Awe," Percy's grin widens. "Stop buttering me up." He adds in a girly voice. I snort, unable to stop my laughter and point to him.

"I think he's high on air."

"I see," Fr John takes one side of the box of books. "He's high on the Holy Spirit."

"Oh, amen Father," Percy agrees heartily. "Don't you know it!" I roll my eyes, trailing behind them. Thankfully Percy walks at a decent pace with Fr John helping him. My dad greets the priest, Percy visiting with them when we enter the house. Phil seems a little off, his body has tension reeking off of him and his jaw is clenched tightly. Today must be a bad day for him.

"Hey Phil," I say, sidling up to him. "Can I talk to you?"

"Yeah," Phil blinks. It seems to shake off his tension. Does Phil dissociate like Harry does? Is that a sign of PTSD? "Sure, kid."

"I'm sorry for glaring at you," I speak up, wiping my hands on my pants. Rarely do I have to apologize to someone. I'm not used to making mistakes. It's a punch in the gut to my pride in my self-inflated humility. "And being mad at you for getting my dad. That was fair."

"It's okay, kid," Phil tucks his hands in his pockets and hunches his shoulders in as we step outside. "Payback for you saving Jasper." He adds with a little grin. "You walked away so fast I didn't get to give you proper thanks."

"Thanks be to God for allowing me to do that," I respond, sitting on a bench that Peter had made for my dad as a housewarming gift. Phil sits beside me. "Thanks for intervening there, with Landon," I nod my head to the cabin. "I'm kind of scared of him," I admit, tucking my hands under my thighs so Phil can't see them shake. "He's thrown stuff at me and shoved me around but he hasn't hit me yet. I'm scared he will. I think Landon is the one that is going to have to fight the hardest not to be like Huntley."

"I understand your fear," Phil says slowly, catching my eye to understand his seriousness. "But don't let it control you."

"I didn't know I could ever be this scared of him. He's still my friend, still sort of like a brother; but I think about how he hurt me too much. It's always on my mind. Like that cop holding his gun at me. Those scenes are stuck in my mind. I can't let them go. I want to, I want to surrender to Jesus and let Him carry me but opening my vulnerability to anyone, even God, is hard. How do I trust when it's so tender, so close to my heart?"

"God is calling you to a deeper trust within Him," Phil licks his lips and runs his hands over his hair. His blue eyes look pained but full of love, like Jesus' in the scourging and carrying of the Cross. "He's using this internal struggle, these mind baffling emotions to ask you for the one thing He wants: to rely solely on Him. Trust in Him and love Him because only He understands what you are going through."

"Thank you," I say softly. I'd asked Phil to help me but I'm hoping he'll reflect on his words when he is having a difficult time with his memories. We both jump when Percy sticks his head out the door, hollering for everyone to run to the mansion. Fr John is ready to bless the house and needs all of us to pray together.

39

Family Time

Hey Win," I whisper, tip toeing to his bed. It's a little chilly in his room because he and Conan slept with their door closed.

"What, huh?" He mutters quickly, surprisingly alert sounding for just waking up.

"Wanna go for a ride?" I ask, bending down to check on a fitfully sleeping Conan on bottom bunk. He threw a tantrum last night wanting to sleep on top bunk with Windsor. When he wouldn't stop crying dad finally called it quits and shut the door on him and Windsor, letting him cry it out.

"Yeah," Windsor jumps out of bed. He's shirtless and rummages around for a shirt before following me out of his bedroom, stumbling and mumbling because the floor isn't as crooked as he remembers or as short of a walk. We enter the kitchen and I have to open three cupboards before I get to the right one, with bowls in it for a quick bite of cereal. It takes two more cupboards for me to find the box of Cheerios while Win sits at the table in the kitchen, our old kitchen table from the cabin. Peter is building a custom dinner table that seats twenty for us that is shrinkable. I open all six drawers before finding the utensil drawer, digging out two small spoons for me and Windsor. Thankfully everyone else is quiet. Lee is up because he always gets up at five am but today he agreed to take a rest day so I can spend the morning with Windsor. Since the children came I haven't focused on them one on one and I want to change that, to create a space to know each one of them personally.

"I'll let you ride Honey," I inform Windsor as I set our full bowls and spoons on the table. Our mismatched chairs are still mismatched but when Peter drops off the new table we'll keep the four matching chairs and give the other three to the residents of the cabin.

"Sweet," Windsor grins, chowing down on dry Cheerios. I roll my eyes as I get the milk out and pour some in his bowl, then mine. "Where we going?"

"Not far," I respond. "It's a little cold out there and your first ride without me leading you, so just on the road."

"Sweet," Windsor mumbles around a mouthful of food. I shake my head at him before bowing my head, making the sign of the cross and praying the blessing meal prayer and the Angelus. He chows down, oblivious to the prayerful example I'm showcasing.

"I'm gonna teach you how to tack her up and groom her first." I say between bites of cereal. "If you want to ride a horse you have to be able to take care of them."

"Feed and water, that's all you gotta do." Windsor smiles cheekily, gulping down milk.

"Do I just feed and water you?" I retort, slurping up the last of my cereal to match his speed.

"Yeah," Win sassily says as he all but throws his bowl in the sink.

"Bathe and school and take care of you and all that," I raise an eyebrow, stacking the dishes we dirtied nicely in the sink.

"Okay, okay," my nephew relents. He quickly hops into his snowsuit that he secretly loves but pretends to despise because he isn't a child and should be allowed ski pants and a jacket. "Whatever, you win."

"Just for that you can try catch Honey on your own," I shake my head at him, jumping into a snowsuit of my own. It's easier than pulling on my nice pair of ski pants and Sunday jacket. I don't want to get my nice, clean, Sunday clothes filled with horse hair and slobber.

"Awe man!" Windsor groans with a loud bellow at the soft flurry of snow caressing the ground. "How we supposed to ride when it's snowing?"

"Exactly how we ride when it's sunny," I retort, gently closing the door.

"But we can't see!" Windsor exclaims, turning in circles to catch snowflakes on his tongue. I jab at him, laughing when he jumps back.

"Thought you can't see!" I tease him, patting my pockets. I still have some grains of oats I can use to lure Buck to the hitching post. The darn old gelding is allergic to any type of work because my dad has pastured him lately, too busy at work to ride him.

"You know what I meant!" Win laughs, slapping my shoulder. Karen runs up to us, sniffing a fresh track trail of rabbits. Sugar walks by my side, old enough to know not to get caught in my heels as I walk, unlike Karen, who was never taught.

"Grab the halters from the barn," I gently order Windsor. He takes off running, tripping over his feet or tree roots and flies face first into the snow. I double over in laughter when his brown face looks at me, covered in a layer of snow melting on his skin.

"Aunty!" he exclaims, jumping up. "How did that happen?"

"Were you looking where you were walking?" I ask, brushing snow off his back. I'm also checking for any pain he might have because he's much too manly to admit any aches and pains to me. That's why I didn't ask if he was okay, he would have told me to stop babying him.

"Who doesn't?" He shoots back, brushing powdery snow off his chest and legs.

"You!" I stick my tongue out at him, hook my foot around his ankles and pull him back. He falls to the ground in a fit of giggles, vowing revenge. I run to the barn, glad that I'm a runner and for the few feet headstart as he shouts at me, telling me I'm going to get a face full of snow just like him but worse because he's going to rub it in. When I reach the barn I take Buck and Honey's halters off the nail hammered into the wall, considering the barn door off limits. Windsor doesn't and barrels into me, shoving me back into the wooden panel fence. I grunt at the unexpected pain and push him off of me, holding him back by my hand on his head an arm's length away.

"Aunty!"

"I'm gonna tell your dad!" I threaten with a laugh, dancing back when he swipes out with his arms.

"Yeah?" Windsor retorts. "He ain't gonna do nothing!"

"I'll tell my dad!" I chuckle when he suddenly backs up and I stumble forward. My curly hair is icy from the cold air and my warm breath. It's really chilly for early November. "Truce?" I ask, wiggling out of his grasp. He'd tried pulling me into the snow but it didn't work out too well for him.

"Fine!" He huffs with his goofy grin. "But only 'cause you're showing me how to ride. Then I'll have something to brag about to all my girlfriends!"

"Girlfriends!" I exclaim, opening the gate to the horse pen. We go through and I lock the gate securely. "Girlfriends! You're too young for a girlfriend!"

"Aunty, I'm ten! I'm a man!" Win giggles when he dodges my hands that were trying to push him, in a friendly way. Windsor is too small to wrestle with his dad and uncles and the Trips and too big to wrestle with Conan, who is less than half his size.

"You are a child!" I retort, clicking my tongue and whistling for Honey and Buck. My mare listens well, eagerly trotting up for the treats she knows I keep in my pocket but Buck pins his ears back and turns his hind end toward me.

"Tell that to my fifteen girlfriends!" Windsor chuckles at my shocked expression, jaw slung open in disbelief. How does his class have fifteen girls, let alone fifteen classmates? There must have been a baby boom that year!

"That's so disrespectful!" I hold a treat out to him. He grabs it and lays it in his palm, making sure his palm is flat. Honey gently takes the little treat bale and crunches on it, shaking her mane. I pat her neck and throw the lead rope around her neck, holding it in a circle. Honey won't run away but I'm teaching Windsor how to catch horses.

"I only really like one anyway," Windsor shrugs, scratching Honey's soft nose.

"So break up with all the rest," I tut, pulling the halter up through Honey's nose and flinging the strap around her ears, tying it tightly but with enough wiggle room it won't be uncomfortable. "You see what I did there?"

"Yeah," Windsor replies. "Weird knot thing."

"You don't need a girlfriend," I advise him, pulling him to my right so I can show him how to check and clean horse hooves. Using the button method, I tap three points on Honey's body and tug at her fetlock. She lifts her leg up and I curve it to point her hoof upwards, taking my pick out and cleaning out her hooves. Windsor watches intensely as I show him which direction and how deep to go while being careful of the frog.

"Everybody I know has a girlfriend," Windsor smiles cheekily at his argument, staying well behind me when I clean Honey's next hoof at her back end.

"Tyler doesn't," I say as I move to the next one. Honey's ears are facing me, telling me she is listening as I pat her rump and lift her leg up.

"Tyler isn't normal," it takes Windsor a moment to laugh and he only does so after I shoot him a look to be nice. "Just kidding Aunty, I'm just kidding."

"Landon doesn't," I quickly shoot back as I lead Honey into the round pen. Harry is usually up this early in the morning, either just getting to bed or just waking up after a couple hours of sleep. Since today is Saturday morning, I figure on the first. He only has to be at Peter's construction site at ten a.m. so he'll sleep until nine.

"But Landon's a player," Windsor whistles, walking by my side. I turn Honey around to close the round pen gate, studying the ground. It's not too unleveled because we didn't keep the horses in here during the summer. It's a work pen, where we run them in circles until they are ready to listen to us. "A darn good one."

"No!" I cry, tying the lead rope together as a set of reins over Honey's neck. "Landon doesn't respect his body or the girls' bodies that he uses."

"I'm kidding Aunty, I'm kidding," Windsor laughs. It's deep in his throat, bubbles out from his stomach. Even with his horrible, toxic, neglectful upbringing he is still superbly happy. It must be a blessing from God.

"You better be," I side eye him for a minute. "We're going to focus on Honey now."

"She's huge!" Win whistles, stepping on my feet to back up when Honey steps closer, investigating my pockets for another treat.

"Yeah," I agree, slapping her back end. Honey starts walking, knowing the drill. "She's beautiful."

"Is my dad gonna get another job?" Windsor asks, walking with me to the middle of the round pen.

"There isn't many jobs around here," I click my tongue and wave my arms. Honey picks up her speed, ears flicking at us. "So hopefully he can."

"He was happier when he was working," Windsor sighs. I step back, letting him work with Honey and control the speed and direction. He runs to the side to reverse her direction and walks back to me, clicking his tongue. "How you do that Aunty? My tongue is so sore!"

"Been doing it all my life," I shrug. Honey notices he isn't paying attention and slows her trot to a walk. I raise my arm. She snorts but picks up speed again.

"That's what she said," Windsor guffaws.

"I don't appreciate that type of humour," I state seriously. "And you are much too young to be thinking that way."

"Awe Aunty, it was just a joke." Windsor mumbles, his grin fading when I don't laugh or even smile. I start walking away.

"Keep working Honey, I have to catch Buck." I call over my shoulder. Windsor clicks at Honey and turns in the circle with her, trying to get her to a lope.

"It didn't mean nothing!" Windsor hollers at me. "I'm sorry Aunty!"

"Pay attention to your horse! Knowing her makes it easier to understand her!" I peek back to see him turning Honey in the opposite direction again. That's good, it'll keep her mind focused on him. Buck, on the other hand, is a tough old guy. He's lazy, which means he isn't running away from me when I walk towards him with the lead rope although he does walk away. And he refuses to budge when I have his halter on and tug him forward. I brush him there, clearing the snow off his coat and digging hay out of his mane and tail before working on his feet. His hooves are in worse shape than Honey's because he hasn't been used as much but all in all he is healthy and in perfectly good shape to ride. When Buck first denies my cues I feel the frustration. I'm trying to teach my nephew how to ride, how to properly take care of a horse and respect the animals God gave us and the stubborn horse is making my job that much harder. Instead of getting cranky from my annoyance

I take a deep breath and tie him up. Honey is warmed up, breathing slightly elevated and Windsor is getting bored.

"I wanna ride her now," he says when he notices me opening the gate.

"Grooming comes next," I respond, grabbing Honey's lead rope and leading her to the barn. Windsor runs passed us to the barn, digging in the little chest I've had since a child for the brushes and combs. He starts on the right side, close to her ears and slowly works his way down as I tie Honey up and give her another treat.

"This is actually kind of fun," Windsor says. I watch him interact with my horse for a while, impressed at how at ease he seems to be.

"Don't forget her belly," I remind him, noticing how he doesn't brush underneath her. He still has a pretty big fear of getting too close to the thousand pound animal. I pull my bareback saddle out and set it on Honey's back.

"Aunty!" Windsor exclaims incredulously as he points at the Navajo saddle my dad's friend Earle gifted me. "That's not a real saddle!"

"You don't get a saddle until you can ride bareback." I inform him, cinching the latigo tightly but making sure there is enough space for three of my fingers to squeeze in.

"How is that fair?" Windsor groans with his never failing smile.

"This way you can feel Honey move," I reply patiently. "Any good rider listens to his mount."

"Okay," Windsor's grin widens, especially when he throws the brush and it lands in the open chest. "I'm ready."

"So get up," I motion for him to get up. Honey pays attention to him and me as I untie her and loop the rope around her neck, making reins. Honey doesn't need a bridle to turn her, she listens to words or a slight nudge on the reins and neck reins relatively well. Windsor sticks his tongue out in concentration as he grabs a fistful of Honey's mane and sticks his left foot in the stirrup. The only tricky part for him is throwing his leg over her side. Honey is carrying winter weight, making her thicker than normal. "Good job," I pat Honey's neck and fist bump my nephew. He sits back, scrambling as he just about falls off when Honey rests one hind leg.

"What she do?" Win exclaims with laughter bubbling out of him as he holds onto her mane tightly.

"She's just relaxing," I chuckle. "I'm going to mime balance exercises and you follow along on top of Honey."

"I have good balance," Windsor retorts. Honey shifts again and he leans down to hug her so he won't fall off.

"But you don't have horse balance," I refute patiently as I mime the first exercise. My right hand reaches behind me, twisting my midsection until I was looking behind me. We hold the movement for eight seconds before switching to the other side. Then we reach to the opposite sides frontward, as well as reaching down to our toes and lying back to back.

"Those are hard!" Windsor declares, looking at my body with a newfound respect.

"See what I mean now?" I ask and he nods energetically. I tap his toes. "Heels down."

"When can I ride?" Windsor whines a little, looking at the driveway. Aria's Jeep is pulling up. It's nice to see her here. She's been working a lot of shifts lately while some of her coworkers take vacation time.

"I'll lead you around for now," Windsor groans at my words. I keep talking until he gets it through his head that once I know he hears my explanation he can ride freely. "Toes up, back straight, look forward, chin up, hands loose and low, let them move with her head motion. Good job!"

"I'm free!" Windsor giggles, throwing his arms up in an airplane and leaning back. It's bad timing. I'd just clicked my tongue for Honey to speed up into her trot and she does so, Windsor falling off her right side. He lands with a loud thump and a scream.

"Are you okay?" I drop the lead rope and rush to him. My nephew is spitting snow and dirt out of his mouth, eyes wide with adrenaline.

"That was fun!" He spits some dirt out. I don't mention the frozen shards of horse poop in them.

"You know what you do when you fall off a horse?" I ask, pulling him up.

"No, what?" He quickly answers, brushing snow and dirt off his snowsuit.

"Get right back on," I whistle through my teeth. Honey walks up to me and nudges my shoulder. I grab her lead rope, pat her neck and boost Windsor up. "I'm gonna let her trot. When she speeds up you sort of want to count the bumps and when you have that down, you're gonna start posting. That's standing in the stirrups when her outward front leg and her inside back leg are moving forward."

I watch in silence, observing how Windsor is riding and Honey is trotting. At first they are not in sync and my nephew is jostled quite a bit. He sticks his tongue out in concentration, watching her front outside leg. It takes a few mistakes and early or late rises and three circles for Honey before he understands the movement and can keep up to it. "Aunty!" Windsor cries, his laugh bubbling out right after. "My legs hurt! I don't like this!"

"Walk Honey," I speak up, "just walk." She slows to a walk, nickering for Buck, her buddy. Windsor exhales loudly and lies down, hugging Honey's neck.

"Let's just go for a walk ride," he laughs, breathing in Honey's hay and fresh air smelling coat.

"Honey should be fine here," I say. "She might move around a little but won't move. I'll go get Buck and we can ride."

"Hurry!" I jog to the pen and untie Buck. He nudges me with his nose so I hand him a treat, hoping that will encourage him to work nicely with me. I grab a fistful of his black mane and swing my leg up, a hard feat with my snowsuit but I manage it on the first jump. Then I click my tongue and dig my heels in. Like a truck rumbling to life Buck slowly steps forward, one foot after the other.

"Step up, Buck," I command. His next four steps are faster before he gives up and swishes his tail at me. Windsor's feet are hanging because his ankles are sore so I decide that the pace Buck set can work for us. Any faster and Windsor would have to sit more alertly.

"How come you didn't take me riding before?" Windsor asks, dropping the lead rope. I urge Buck closer to Honey and untie the loop, holding onto the rope myself just to have a human in charge of my horse.

"Didn't know you were interested," I reply honestly.

"And you were too busy," Windsor throws me under the bus. It's a good dose of humility for my pride. "Always cooking and cleaning and everything. Doesn't give you much time to actually do stuff with us."

"That's why I'm making the time." I state firmly. My throat aches at his words. My nieces and nephews were neglected, and although me and my dad are better caregivers we'd still neglected their emotional needs.

"Better late than never, right?" Windsor smiles at me. "That's what I think about my mom. Maybe she'll show up one day. Maybe she'll stop drinking. Maybe she'll be able to love me like I'm the child."

"That's what I thought." I state honestly, baring my soul to my young nephew. It takes a lot of courage to be vulnerable to him. I feel like I shouldn't act so lost and confused and hurt and sad, I'm supposed to be setting a good example for him but I figure an honest example is better than a bad one. "When I was your age. My mom left when I was a baby. Until you guys and the Trip's showed up it's just been me and my dad."

"I thought your mom died," Windsor says bluntly. I cough, clearing the ache in my throat.

"She did." For a moment they are the only words I can mutter, the only words my mind can grasp. *My mother is dead.* I clear my throat. "She died two years ago. I can't remember her so I don't really think I met her. And my dad doesn't talk about her."

"My dad doesn't talk about my mom either," Windsor smiles sadly at me. My eyes water so I wipe the tears away before they can freeze my cheeks. This is why I wanted to pull him aside, visit him by himself and get to know him personally. We are connecting here, where he doesn't have to try to be a dad to his siblings. I point out prairie chicken tracks to him, the different sounds between birdsong and squirrel chirps. Sugar isn't far behind us, never one to stay at home if she could help it. Windsor asks about the different types of trees so I do my best to explain their uses and history along with the clouds in the sky. It's a science lessen he won't forgot because it's never been taught to him outside of a classroom.

"We should get back," I sigh, patting Buck's neck. He'd been surprisingly well behaved. "I have to make bread for the next couple of days and Micks wants to help."

"Okay," Windsor says cheerily. "This was fun. Thanks Aunty."

"Don't tell me you're a cowboy now?" I joke, holding Buck back from trotting because we are going home.

"Just getting started," my nephew grins. I bellow in laughter. Windsor is good for the soul, that's for sure. When we get to the barn I show him how to tie the lead rope to a tree or fence railing, groom his ride and give her a treat. The way Win walks makes me double over in laughter, he's already bowlegged like a cowboy!

I shake off in the large mud room of my dad's mansion. With his "fifteen children" he made it large. The washer and dryer are standing side by side with a counter to the right of them and a sink attached to the wall while on the left side is a little closet sized room hosting a toilet. Coat hooks hang along the wall from the entrance door to the toilet room door, already filled with winter ski pants and jackets and snowsuits, while boots line the floor.

"Good ride?" My dad asks from the kitchen table, Aria seated to his right.

"Win's a little sore," I laugh, giving them both a hug.

"It's good to see you, kid," Aria hugs me tight. When she lets me go and steps back, it's with a frown. "You've lost weight, Daisy."

"It's nothing really," I wave her concern off as I reach into the fridge to pull out the big pot of overnight oats I'd made last night for breakfast. The big bowl is filled with milk, oats and the last bites of our yogurt. With Aria here my dad will no doubt be sent on a shopping spree but we haven't been keeping up with all the groceries.

"It's the stress of the kids on her, Duncan," Aria frowns, massaging my dad's shoulders. He leans back in relief. "She's used to a quiet house and now there is twenty of you. Who gets up with the children at night?"

"I'm gonna get the children up and at her," I jut my thumb over my shoulder to walk away.

"Not so fast, young lady!" Aria snaps. Her dark blonde hair is pulled into a high, tight ponytail that makes her seem that much more serious. Dad looks away, his fingers flexing. "Someone answer my question!"

"Daisy," dad answers. He takes a sip of his coffee and sets his cup on the table. "She's been taking care of the kids because I got Louis and Rennie temporary jobs with Rory Watson's brother-in-law and they aren't allowed in the house when they are drinking, which is every night. Lee needs a break from the kids so we don't make him get up and I'm lucky if I only work twelve hours a day, if not more."

"She's a fifteen year old girl!" Aria cries, pointing at me. I gape at her, surprised at her emotions. My dad is shocked, too.

"I'm totally fine with it," I speak up, defending my dad. I know how hard he works, how draining his job is and how nice it is for him to come home to a clean house and fed children.

"Go get the kids ready for the day," my dad gently orders. I nod and slip away, very conscious of the glare Aria is sending my dad.

"You're running yourself into the ground and you're making your daughter mom and wife!" I have never heard Aria's voice this loud, or upset.

"We are doing the best we can," my dad hisses, his voice low. "And when Daisy gets back with the children we will be a united front. We can talk about this later."

"You know what they need?" Landon grins at me from the couch, an all knowing look upon his face. Then he thrusts his hips upward with a twinkle in his eye.

"Landon!" I hiss, my face flushing, "that's my dad! Don't do that! Chastity is a thing you know!"

"Chastity is only a thing for you," Landon rolls his eyes, lying back on the couch. He didn't party as late as he usually does but his eyes are still lined with red and his face looks flushed.

"Aren't you supposed to be at work?" I shoot him a mild stink eye.

"I called in sick," Landon groans, holding his stomach. He looks so sad and desolate so I have pity on him and kneel down, placing my hand on his forehead. I thought he was hungover but his skin is burning, indicating his fever.

"Does your stomach hurt?" I ask, poking his stomach with my fingers. It isn't hard and bulging so constipation is out.

"It's worse than a hangover, Rosie," Landon blows his hair out of his eyes. He shoots me a suck up look, folding his hands in a prayer position. "Can you get me a pail or something just in case I don't make it to the bathroom?"

"Sure," I fold his hair back because it had fallen in his eyes again. The Trip's have been here for a while but with their recent stay at Huntley's again Landon was triggered. He'd flinched when I'd reached out to touch him. I don't mention it as I grab him an ice cream pail, ignoring my dad and Aria in the kitchen. They're still sort of arguing about something.

"Thanks Shawty," Landon curls the bucket in the crook of his arm and smiles at me. I give him a thumbs up before walking to the girls' room.

"Morning Tinsley," I shake her lightly. She is curled on one side of the bed with the quilted blanket and Micks is on the other side with the crocheted blanket. Tinsley mumbles something and curls in deeper. "C'mon Tinsley, it's time to get up. You better go use the bathroom before I wake everyone else up."

"Okay, Aunty," she mumbles, yawning right after. Tinsley is the child that has to pee right when she wakes up. We learned that when they first got here and someone else was in the bathroom so we made her go to the outhouse. She only got halfway through the yard before she had to drop her pants.

"Hey Micks, you still wanna bake today?" I ask. She was already up, shivering in her blanket.

"Yeah," she whispers, pointing to the top bunk Sally Anne is asleep on. Then she makes some crying faces and pretends to wipe her eyes.

"Okay, go brush your hair," I pat her leg, deciding to leave Sally Anne alone. Her dad, as bad as he was, recently passed away. Maybe I've been taking it too hard on her, not letting her mourn the way she needs to. Tinsley and Makayla roll out of bed around the same time so I enter the boys' room. Conan has his blankets thrown off of him but is sweating, his face flushed.

"Mama," he whimpers, reaching out to hold me. I crawl on his bed and hold his hand, feeling his forehead with the other. Conan has whatever bug Landon has. It could be what kept him up crying last night.

"You not feeling too good, tough guy?" I ask, wrapping his baby blanket around him and snuggling him into my chest. He whimpers, burrowing into my body. I kiss his forehead and hold him tight, giving him the comfort he craves. While I am holding him and smoothing his hair and patting his back I mumble healing prayers and Ave Maria's, asking the saints of healing to intercede for him to Jesus.

"Aunty!" Tinsley pops her head in the boys' room. "I'm really really hungry."

"Okay, I'll be there soon." I say, sighing deeply. This must be what breaks mothers' hearts at the same time it builds them up. Leaving a sickly child to tend for her older children. It also leaves me grateful because God is with us personally everywhere and anytime. He doesn't go between us like we have to as humans. "I'm gonna get them breakfast and come back, okay Conan? I'll bring some water and medicine and Holy Water and we'll all pray you get better." I gently climb out of his bed, shooting one last worried look at him. Conan is tucking his blankets around him now, probably getting a chill. I want to rush my chores, sloppily fill their bowls and ignore my promise to Mick of baking bread with her but that wouldn't be carrying my cross diligently. Of course I can care for Conan extra sweetly today but I can't let my other chores lax.

"Conan's not getting up?" Dad asks, taking a sip of his coffee.

"He has whatever Landon has," I dig in a cupboard for bowls and a drawer for a big spoon. Tinsley, Makayla and Kennedy are sitting at the table with my dad, waiting patiently for their food.

"Tylenol's above my bathroom sink," dad says, swishing what is left of his coffee before downing it. Aria busies herself getting the girls cups for water as I spoon the overnight oats into their bowls, less for Tinsley because she eats the least amount. "Aria and I are going shopping. We'll take Philomena and Tikara so you don't have to worry about them."

"Thank you, dad," I smile at him.

"Pray first," he tuts at the girls. They always forget to pray in the morning. I excuse myself and grab the medicine and Holy Water for

Conan. Aria is bringing him a cup of water. When I spot the adult Tylenol I grab a couple for Landon. He swallows them dry and rolls on the couch to get more comfortable.

"Come sit up," I softly urge Conan, pulling him. He leans heavily against me as I help him sip some water. "You just chew these," I hold the pills up to his mouth. Conan slowly chews and swallows them, quite often sipping the water. It takes him a while and I have to hold his head up towards the end because he is so weak. When his throat is clear I lay him down and make the sign of the cross on his forehead, praying God will heal him and that Conan can suffer sanctification through this. He is cold again, probably because of the water flowing through his body so I tuck him in, patting his flushed cheeks. It looks like my plans for the day have changed. I can't take care of Conan and Landon while spending individual time with the rest of my family.

40

Family Dinner

I set the oven gloves on the counter and close the oven door with my hip. The two chickens were roasting for a good part of the afternoon, potatoes, carrots and celery soaking in the water as well. It's a recipe Aria used from her grandmother who it got from Mary Watson, Big Patrick's grandmother.

"Can you dry the lettuce?" Aria asks, pulling on an oven glove to lift the lid of the roast pan and check on the chicken.

"Sure," I reply, diverting to the sink where the romaine lettuce are drying in a bundle. Sally Anne sits at the table, smacking on gum and watching us work. I dry the lettuce with a dish towel, looking out the window to the darkening fall light. Windsor is playing cowboys and Indians with Makayla and Tinsley while Kennedy is trying to catch Sweetie which ends up being a game of hide and seek the cat is winning. Conan is trying to ride Sugar but she won't stop rolling on him.

"Can you grab me a plate?" Aria asks Sally Anne. Her hands are full with a fork, knife and sliced chicken. "Since Duncan doesn't have serving platters."

"We never needed them," I defend my dad in the jolly, teasing tone she had used. My hands are freezing from the brisk water and cold lettuce. "And my mom took anything of value when she left. We haven't replaced it."

"I'm gonna change that," Aria laughs as she sets the pieces of chicken on the plate Sally Anne sets on the counter near her. "Can't have no serving dishes when we'll be eating at my parents' every week."

"What?" I deadpan with a surprised cough. Sally Anne stares at Aria in disbelief, as if socializing with a devout, religious family is the last thing she wants to do.

"Brunch at my grandparents every Sunday," Aria laughs, scooping more chicken onto the plate. "It's a Watson family tradition."

"I see," I say softly, not wanting to disrespect her with my response. "But we have our own Ridel traditions."

"The cinnamon buns before church on Sundays," Aria nods with a smile. "I love it."

"And going to the river in the summer," I add, throwing the towel around my shoulder to rip up the somewhat dried lettuce because there is a stack.

"I love swimming," Sally Anne sticks her nose up at Aria as she throws her legs up on another chair.

"Wouldn't we be able to do that after brunch?" Aria asks, her eyebrows furrowing slightly. She peeks over her left shoulder to check on my dad and Paul visiting in the living room and watching the babies with Louis, Rennie, Landon, Harry and Tyler. Since Aria's been back she's had one of her brothers or cousins over at our house to help us with the children. It's amazing help but I don't appreciate taking them out of their own lives. It makes me feel like me and my dad can't handle what we took on ourselves.

"Need any help?" Paul asks as he walks into the kitchen, hands in his pockets. "Duncan, Rennie and Harry have started this competition about how much they love their girls and I just had to leave."

"Awe," Aria empathizes with her brother, quickly giving him a hug. "Maybe Sally Anne wants your help setting the table."

"That means going back in there," Paul points both thumbs over his shoulder. He surveys the kitchen: Sally Anne grumbling about the stacks of dishes she has to carry to the dining room, Aria filling the plate with chicken and me drying the lettuce. "I'll rip the lettuce for Daisy."

"Suit yourself," Aria shrugs.

"How's she going?" Paul asks amiably, digging in cupboards for a salad bowl.

"Better," I admit, blowing my gravity defying hair away from my face. "You Watson's have a been a lot of help."

"We're family," Paul smiles at me as he sets the biggest bowl we have on the counter by the sink. I want to reply that my father's family is no where to be seen, nor my mother's but I leave the semantics alone. I need to let my self pride go and accept the help they are giving me. Jesus accepted Simon of Cyrene's help when He was carrying the Cross.

"How about you?"

"I'm good," Paul says immediately, making me frown. He's going through a tough ordeal, it's okay for him to be not okay. "When I think optimistically." He adds with a laugh, noticing my frown.

"Oh," I say, handing him a leaf of lettuce. The brisk snapping sound is soothing.

"Just trying to focus on what God wants me to do, breathe deeply and take it all in, and ultimately close my eyes to let Jesus take care of everything." Paul states, closing his eyes and breathing deeply, showing me what his words say.

"Easier said than done," I finish drying the last leaf of lettuce and throw the tea towel over my shoulder. Paul shifts away from me so I can help rip the lettuce into pieces.

"O Jesus, I surrender myself to you. Take care of everything." Paul quotes, swishing the ripped pieces of lettuce around the bowl, making sure he didn't forget any.

"The Surrender novena," I nod in approval. "I try say that everyday."

"What are you two nerds talking about?" Aria butts in, hands on our shoulders as she looks at us snapping lettuce. My fingers are red from the cold.

"Praying," we answer at the same time. It causes Paul to chuckle, making me smile. It's nice to see a smile on his face.

"Sorry to break you up but only one of you needs to rip apart lettuce," she says, pulling on Paul's shoulders to drag him away. "You can crunch up the bacon I cooked earlier. They need to be just that much smaller," Aria pinches her fingers together to make the estimate. Paul rolls his eyes at me. Sally Anne came back to sit on her chosen chair but Aria is making her set out the utensils, all the forks, spoons and butter knives my dad owns.

"Your hair has grown back," I make a circle around my head to point at the scar on Paul's head.

"Yeah," he replies a little sullenly, probably remembering how he got the scar. "Stitches all came out nice."

"That's good to hear!" I beam, whatever else I was going to say cut off by Aria.

"Shred cheese when you're done with the lettuce, Daisy, finely shredded, super small!" I shrug it off, offering the tedious tasks I'm completing for jobs for people in need of an income.

"She's just nervous because it's the first supper she made for you all in the new house." Paul says, looking back at Aria digging through the fridge for condiments she thinks should be on the table.

"It'll be delicious," I confirm, laughing when Sally Anne gets stuck with hauling the condiments Aria chose to the dining room.

"Landon, go get the kids!" Aria hollers, wiping her hands on her pants. Then she starts scooping potatoes into the biggest pot we have. Supper is done for the most part, Paul and I just have to hurry up the salad. I root through cupboards until I find the cheese grater, still not accustomed to the changes of everything's place in the new house. "Tyler! Come get the candles for the table! Sally Anne, each plate setting gets one of these linen napkins." Aria holds a pile of napkins out to Sally Anne, who frowns and glares at Aria.

"Fancy," Landon comments with a smirk, stealing by me to pop some shredded cheese into his mouth.

"It's our first dinner as a family in the new house with the new table," Aria squints at him and makes the 'I'm watching you' gesture. "You better be on your best behaviour, son."

"Only the best for you, dad," Landon retorts, getting the last word as he closes the door.

"He better not do anything embarrassing," Harry huffs, peering anxiously out the window. He sighs deeply and cracks his knuckles when he doesn't see who or what he's looking for. "Kira should be here any minute."

"You're introducing us to your girlfriend?" I gasp, wrapping my arms around him. "That's wonderful!"

"Yeah, whatever," Harry gruffly pushes me away. He pushes out of habit, there is a happy sparkle in his eye. Lights shine in the driveway and Harry disappears from the kitchen in a flash. The house is noisy now, the children all stomping in and yelling because they're used to using their outside voices. I lean against the counter to watch them get out of their winter clothes, chuckling at how Landon helps Kennedy take her snowsuit off, basically throwing her in the air.

"Shred that cheese!" Aria thunders, snapping her fingers at me. "We're waiting on you."

"Yes ma'am," I laugh when Aria rolls her eyes at me. I turn back to the counter to shred the last of my block of cheese. Paul is dumping the crushed bacon into the salad bowl, adding the homemade bottle of dressing. Aria loves spices and sauces and dressings, spending hours making her own. Sometimes she lets us taste test them, which is pretty fun. "Huh," I laugh, looking at the bowl filled with dried bread corners from the homemade bread I made. We save the crusts for this purpose.

"What's that?" Paul asks, his head ticking. I quickly analyze the situation, at the way he holds his hand to the ear where his scar is, from Kennedy shouting at Conan to wait for her and Windsor teasing Sally Anne and Makayla in his loud voice, they in turn raising their voices to get their points across. He has a head wound. Did Phil, too then, if the noise bothers him?

"You okay?" I ask. Landon grins out the window, at Harry holding his girlfriend's hand while walking her to the door.

"I have some embarrassing to do," he rubs his hands together gleefully.

"You be nice!" Aria catches Landon's ear, turning him to the living room. "Go make sure the children all wash their hands."

"You're no fun," Landon pouts, laughing when Aria pushes him away. Paul places his hands palm down on the counter, hunches his shoulders in and closes his eyes.

"Louis, Rennie! Come make the kids' plates!" Aria blatantly ignores Landon. She is a powerhouse in the kitchen, now scooping out the celery and carrots into a pot. And boy, is she fast! She peers into the living room, around the fridge and notices something she disagrees with. "Light those candles Tyler!"

"Paul," I whisper, not wanting everyone else to worry just yet. Paul is pretty private compared to his siblings. "Are you okay?"

"My ear is just ringing," he answers, standing up. He makes the Sign of the Cross over his injury and begins stirring the salad. "What was that 'huh' for?" he asks, his eyes blinking as he tries to overcome the pain.

"Nothing really," I laugh, dumping the shredded Parmesan cheese in. "I just realized that a salad is basically a dry soup."

"It doesn't have to be perfect." My dad pecks Aria on the cheek. She gives him a stink eye. "You didn't let me finish," he laughs, totally sucking up now. "It's perfect with you."

"Suck up," she coughs but returns the kiss. "Out of the kitchen, Daisy and Paul just have to finish the salad." She walks out of the kitchen with her pot of vegetables. Dad shrugs at me with a smile on his face before following her. I clean up the few dirty dishes left in the kitchen so there are less for later, letting Paul take his time with the salad because the noise in the living room is reaching the highest crescendo. The children calling spots and running to them from the bathroom, Windsor and Sally Anne fighting for the seat they wanted, Rennie telling Conan to just sit down and stop pouting, Landon teasing Harry about some childhood things so Kira can laugh at him while Tyler is trying to stop Landon.

"You have Holy Water?" Paul asks, sitting at the little table in the kitchen. The salad is ready to go but when I peek around the fridge into the living room, no one is prepared for it just yet so I reach to the top of the fridge and pull out the plastic pop bottle of Holy Water for him.

"Your ear and your scar?" I ask, dipping my thumb in the bottle. Paul nods, tilting his head for a better angle to the injuries. I make the sign of the cross with holy water over his injuries, whispering prayers for St. Blase, St. Raphael, St. Liduina of Schiedam, and Blessed Giovanni Liccio intercession for Paul's healing, adding in the Holy Innocents. Paul leads us in three quick Hail Mary's to end off the prayer.

"Pain's gone," Paul laughs. It's a strangled sound and he holds his hands in front of his mouth to hide the quiver from his lips. I twist the cap on the bottle and put the Holy Water away. "Thank you, Daisy."

"You really thought that was me?" I laugh and shake my head as I grab the bowl of salad. I'm a horrible sinner, God couldn't work that fast and easy through me. "That was you," I stop by his shoulder. "I think *you* are the saint." I pat his back and enter the living room, feeling conviction in my gut. Paul healed himself, Tyler, and Harry's coworker. How can he not see it?

"More food!" Landon cheers, his plate already heaping with food. A big pile of potatoes, around ten pieces of chicken, a quarter of his plate is filled with carrots, celery, creamed corn, dill pickles and carrot pickles. Gravy covers everything. He grabs my hand and pulls me close to him. "Dish out, Rosie!"

"Patience, child!" I roll my eyes but comply. Louis motions for salad as well so I make my way around the table, giving a scoop or two of salad to whoever wants it. A few of my family are visiting but most are looking to my dad, waiting for him to lead the blessing meal prayer so they can dig in. Only Micks doesn't want any so I split the remaining salad between me and Paul's empty plates and take the big bowl to the kitchen so it won't take up space on the table. I set the bowl on the counter by the sink, spotting someone outside. My heart skips a beat in excitement. Only one person I know wears parkas with fur hoods and cuffs and tanned leather boots with rubbers to keep the snow out. "Oh my goodness, dad! It's Earle!"

"What?" Dad asks, jumping up with a smile on his face. I run out the house, slamming into Earle's burly chest.

"Hi!" I laugh, tears coming to my eyes when Earle hugs me back. "It's been too long!"

"Yes, it has, North Star," Earle says in his soft, slow speech. He pats my back after releasing me. I loop my elbow through his and we walk to the house together. He surveys the mansion, shocked at its size. "You and your dad have changed."

"The family has grown way more than you'd know," I throw my head back with a laugh. "We just moved in a week ago."

"Earle Bulldog!" Dad smiles radiantly. "It's been way too long!" He holds his hand out for a handshake and they shake before enveloping each other in a bear hug. Aria, Landon and a few of the children are peeking out the kitchen window. "Come in, take a seat, stay a while!"

"Brr," I shake the cold off of me when I step into the mud room. Earle's eyes take in the extra winter outfits and children's boots without the surprise I expected him to have. Inside the house Earle's smell becomes more prominent. Burnt sage, fresh air, pine trees, tanned leather, and cold snow. Smelling it again, I've realized just how much I've missed him. Growing up, Earle was the uncle I never had. Four years is much too long.

"Let's go pray," dad wraps his arm around my shoulders and leads me to the dining room. I wipe my eyes, hoping I won't start bawling at the dinner table. Everyone on the opposite side of the table shuffled around, making room for Earle near the head of the table to sit next to my dad. My side of the table is two long benches while that side has eight chairs. The head and the foot of the table each have two chairs so Aria and Dad sit side by side and Rennie and Louis took over the foot, Tikara in a high chair with Rennie holding Philomena. "In the name of the Father, the Son, and the Holy Spirit," my dad begins and we all follow, making the Sign of the Cross before holding each other's hands. My right hand holds my dad's while my left holds Conan's. We all bow our heads and pray together. The children all rush to make the Sign of the Cross and are surprised when Earle adds more in Beaver.

"Dig in!" Aria laughs when the hungry children all shovel food into their mouths, unbeaten by Landon. Already his cheeks are full. I look around the table, the big smile on my face hurting my cheeks. Aria is being introduced to Earle, Paul is helping Tinsley scoop up a crouton, Windsor is trying to put his carrot pickles, which he's decided he doesn't like, onto Landon's pile of food. Tyler has his head ducked, his fingers twirling his fork more so than eating anything. Sally Anne is arguing with Lee about celery being better than carrots. Louis and Rennie are teasing each other about something I didn't catch, sitting so far away from them and all. Makayla is eyeing Kira, not knowing what to think of her. Conan and Kennedy are pointing at each other's plates, giggling at whatever they see.

"Man, he real native looking," Landon points with his chin to Earle. Tyler slaps him to shut up. Lee and Harry hide snickers.

"He's traditional," I defend Earle. His long hair is braided into two braids, the claw necklace around his neck, the leather vest, even the shape of his face, how tanned it is for this early in winter. It's such a contrast from how the triplets look.

"He's the one that taught you how to hunt?" Harry leans over Conan and Kennedy to whisper in my ear. I swallow a delicious bite of soft, spiced and roasted potatoes before nodding at him.

"Yeah, that's Earle." My smile is hurting my cheeks. Having my family together is a wonderful blessing, add in Paul and Kira and I feel like standing on my chair and singing Alleluia to praise God. I never really felt alone before my family came to me but my heart has never been this full so I thank the good Lord for His consolations.

"Can you teach me how to hunt, Earle?" Harry speaks over the chatter of the children and Earle's conversation with my dad. Earle sets his fork down and looks around, trying to find the face of the voice that spoke to him. Harry raises his arm that wasn't wrapped around Kira's shoulders.

"No," Earle replies bluntly before continuing his conversation with my dad. I cover a laugh with a cough and my hand when Harry glares at me, very unimpressed with Earle's reaction.

"You have to follow Protocol," I snort in my laughter, cringing when chewed food lands on my not chewed food. I'll have to eat what I already ate and offer my sacrifice for myself, so I won't be disgusted by the gifts God gives me just because they change shape.

"Protocol?" Harry hisses, "I'm Métis!"

"Earle's Treaty," I remind him, stirring my somewhat mashed potatoes around so I won't see the spit up food in my plate. Out of sight, easier to chow down. "But Métis follow Protocol, too."

"Well, thanks for telling me," Harry snaps.

"You could have asked me," Kira speaks up, hurt seeping into her tone of voice. "My dad is Treaty and he loves hunting. He takes my brothers and cousins out whenever we need more food."

"You want me to meet your family?" Harry deadpans in shock. He points his thumb to his body and taps harder than necessary. "You want *me* to meet *your* family?" he repeats, looking stumped at her words. "But I'm Harry Smith. I'm, well, I'm... me."

"You're letting me meet your family," Kira waves to all of us sitting around the large table Peter built by hand. It really is a beautiful table, solid too and we can make it smaller if needed.

"This isn't my family," Harry immediately says, quite defensively.

"You're not my uncle?" Micks gasps. She looks around the table, at her dad and uncles visiting with Tyler and Landon and to her siblings and cousins. "How does that make sense?" The poor girl looks heartbroken but I'm at a loss of words. Harry technically isn't her uncle but since they call me Aunty and I've considered out loud that the Triplets are my brothers, they've taken to calling them their uncles. It's a delicate topic with their lack of family surrounding them, mothers and grandparents and Tinsley and Tikara's half siblings and aunts and uncles and cousins.

"Nonsense," Kira waves Micks concern off. She even holds Micks' hand to get her point across. "Harry is your family. He's your chosen family. Just like how my parents aren't my parents, they're my uncle and aunty but they're my parents because they've raised me since I was six."

"Where's your real parents?" Micks asks genuinely. She leans her head into Kira's side for a hug, her fingers making her way to her mouth. I motion for her to take them out but she's too involved in her conversation.

"My bio parents. My real parents are my aunt and uncle." Kira reaffirms Micks expression. "My bio dad passed away when I was six and my mom, she just broke, she couldn't take proper care of me so my dad's cousin stepped up."

"I had no clue," Harry murmurs. While Kira was telling her story he hadn't taken a bite of food. Now he twirls the fork in his fingers, dwelling on Kira's backstory. "Now my family doesn't seem as broken as yours."

"You don't know the half of it," Kira laughs, waving his concern away. "We'll talk about it another time. I'm just thankful my parents showed me how good Creator is."

"I love you," I state simply, a huge, happy sigh following it. Kira sounds like she is good for Harry, she'll help him become who God destined him to be!

"She's my girlfriend," Harry mutters jealously. I roll my eyes.

"I don't like her like that," I laugh, wiping my greasy lips with the linen napkin Aria insisted on. I do admit, they are coming in handy. "I just like her as my newest sister and best friend."

"I'm good with that," Kira agrees with a laugh. We fist bump over Harry's head, many voices carrying on conversations around us. My eyes water as I start a litany in my mind, a litany of all the thanks I give God because of all his gifts. All glory to God, nothing more needs to be said. Paul catches my eye with a smile, a real smile, and his eyes shine, something they haven't done since Aiden's birth. He'd seen my lips praising God and adds his two cents.

Deo gratias.

To order more copies of this book, find books by other Canadian authors, or make inquiries about publishing your own book, contact PageMaster at:

PageMaster Publication Services Inc.
11340-120 Street, Edmonton, AB T5G 0W5
books@pagemaster.ca
780-425-9303

catalogue and e-commerce store
PageMasterPublishing.ca/Shop